SMOKE AND MIRRORS

By Nicole Edwards

Standalone Novels

Unhinged Trilogy

A Million Tiny Pieces

Inked on Paper

Bad Reputation

Bad Business

Filthy Hot Billionaire

RULE

The Walkers Of Coyote Ridge

Kaleb

Zane

Travis

Holidays with The Walker Brothers

Ethan

Braydon

Sawyer

Brendon

Curtis

Jared

Hard to Hold

Hard to Handle

Beau

Rex

A Coyote Ridge Christmas

Mack

Kaden & Keegan

Trey

Rafe

Violet

Brantley Walker: Off The Books

All In

Without A Trace

Hide & Seek

Deadly Coincidence

Alibi

Secrets

Confessions

Bounty

Off Course

Chain Reaction

To Have and To Hold

Missing Pieces

Smoke and Mirrors

The Jamesons Of Coyote Ridge

Hot Chocolate Wishes

Rough & Dirty

Club Destiny

Conviction

Temptation

Addicted

Seduction

Infatuation

Captivated

Devotion

Perception

Entrusted

Adored

Distraction

Forevermore

PIER 70

Reckless

Fearless

Speechless

Harmless

Clueless

PRIMAL INSTINCTS

Chase (Volume 1-3)

Capture (Volume 4-6)

Claim (Volume 7-9)

HEROES & HAVOC
(Sniper 1 Security, Devil's Playground, Southern Boy Mafia)

Wait for Morning

Beautifully Brutal

Without Regret

Never Say Never

Beautifully Loyal

Without Restraint

Tomorrow's Too Late

NAUGHTY HOLIDAY EDITIONS

2015

2016

2021

Smoke and Mirrors

Brantley Walker: Off the Books, 13

NICOLE EDWARDS

SMOKE and MIRRORS
Brantley Walker: Off the Books, 13

COVER DETAILS:
Image: © vectorwin (233026855) | 123RF.com | *Design:* © Nicole Edwards Limited
INTERIOR DETAILS:
Formatting: Nicole Edwards Limited

ISBN: (ebook) 9781644181096 | (paperback) 9781644181102 | (audio) 9781644181119

Check out these five-star reviews for *Brantley Walker: Off the Books* series:

⭐⭐⭐⭐⭐

"This book had me turning pages as fast as I could, and anytime I had to put it down, I was hurrying to get back to the story." ~Goodreads reviewer

⭐⭐⭐⭐⭐

"The tension and vulnerability of these characters just work for me. Add in some mystery, snark, family drama, and hot sex.. and BAM! You've got a Nicole Edwards book." ~Goodreads reviewer

⭐⭐⭐⭐⭐

"Can you say HOT!! Brantley and Reese … my God! Help me! This is the 2nd book for these two and I'm on the edge of my seat waiting for the next book!" ~Goodreads reviewer

⭐⭐⭐⭐⭐

"This book was amazing!! And it's not just because I love Brantley and Reese, because I do! It's the growing love and passion between these two that jumps off the pages and smacks you upside your head." ~Goodreads reviewer

⭐⭐⭐⭐⭐

"This series keeps getting more complex and interesting with each new installment. I am so happy to finally have Reese and Brantley in a place where they feel rock steady. SO rock steady that Brantley is counting down the days until the wedding and I CANNOT with how much I love the way they love each other." ~BookBub reviewer

Armed with revelations that could flip their world upside down, the Off the Books Task Force is diving into a case that's as unpredictable as a coin toss. This time, they've assembled a full house, and it's not a poker game.

Brantley Walker and Reese Tavoularis are still at the helm, but they're taking a backseat, letting their two newest team members take the wheel. At Brantley's behest, Atticus James and Archer Halligan are stepping up to the plate as team leaders, ready to swing for the fences.

With a to-do list that includes interrogating a mob boss and searching a former team member's childhood residence, the task force is chasing leads across the great state of Texas. While new information keeps them moving, relationships are being put through the wringer, while new, unexpected ones are forming.

Can the team find more than smoke and mirrors to pin their hopes on, or will they end up in a tangled web of intrigue and unexpected alliances?

This book is dedicated to second chances.

When you're offered one,
grab on with both hands and hold on for the ride.

CHAPTER ONE

Saturday, October 1, 2022

IT TOOK ONLY A FEW MINUTES TO get from his house to the diner. With each passing minute, Brantley Walker's guts twisted more and more.

Maybe he jumped the gun on this.

Maybe he should sit on the information for a little while. Process it before passing it along.

Or rather, before he altered a man's entire existence.

"No," he said aloud, refusing to back out. Travis deserved to know. Hell, he *needed* to know, and, as Travis's cousin and friend, it was Brantley's responsibility to deliver it.

Consequences be damned.

By the time he pulled into the diner's parking lot, his heart was racing. Funny that. He'd walked into battle, faced off with the enemy on numerous occasions, without the amount of anxiety that was coursing through his system right now. Hell, most of the time those guys were armed with AKs, some with rocket launchers, yet he wasn't sure he'd sweated them as much as he was sweating this meeting with his cousin.

Here he was, hovering on the brink of a panic attack simply because he was having a sit-down with Travis.

His former SEAL team would have a field day with the jokes if they could see him now.

The frantic heartbeat didn't let up from the parking lot to the door, or during the brief trek through the minimally occupied restaurant that smelled of bacon, maple syrup, and coffee. It was still early on a Saturday, and he assumed most people were sleeping in.

He probably should've done that.

Brantley spotted Travis sitting at the back, his steel-blue gaze locked on him as he approached. He imagined he could see the questions simmering in Travis's brain, and every one of them was reflected in the man's hard stare.

"Hey," he managed, although he was pretty sure the single word came out as a croak. "Thanks for meeting me."

"You said it was important."

Travis was just as curt and unfriendly as ever. At one point, Brantley was positive his cousin hadn't been quite so surly. Perhaps he was never the bubbly sort, but he hadn't always shot daggers from his eyeballs the way he was now.

Which didn't make this any easier, even if Brantley understood the man's never-ending bad mood.

Sliding into the booth, Brantley exhaled heavily.

"Where's Reese?" Travis asked.

"At home. I told him I needed to do this alone."

That was something else he'd second-guessed during the drive in. Probably should've brought backup. For some dumbass reason, he thought this would be easier. For the record, it wasn't.

Travis frowned, his gaze shifting to the aisle.

Brantley felt the waitress approach, but he held up a hand to wave her off before she could dive into pleasantries. He wanted to get this over with, not drag it out with unnecessary chit-chat and food.

Trying to hold it together until they were alone again, Brantley used the silence to put his thoughts in order. He stared at the table, envisioning the best way to say this. Unfortunately, it felt like a waste of time and energy. Even if he pondered it for a year, it wouldn't matter. There was no good way.

"What did you need to tell me?" Travis asked, his tone as disinterested as his countenance. "I've got things to do today."

Don't we all.

Brantley lifted his gaze, meeting Travis's. "As you know, we're lookin' into the circumstances of Meredith's disappearance. I've assigned Archer and Atticus to lead the investigation."

Thinking Travis might have something to say about that, he paused, gave him a minute.

Clearly he was wrong. Travis's expression remained impassive, his eyes hard and cold, and yeah, there was a hint of impatience glimmering in there, too.

When Travis only continued to stare at him like he was a pain in his backside, Brantley continued. "They worked all night to put together a timeline that'll allow us to start pursuing leads."

Travis continued to stare at him, eyes cold.

"When they were going through Holt's notes, they found something. Something that … well, it sounds insane. So insane that I confronted Holt and Simon about it this morning. They assure me it's real."

Frowning, Travis leaned in. "What the hell are you tellin' me this for?"

Taking a deep breath in, Brantley willed the words to come out and sound reasonably sane. "I know you're not gonna believe this any more than I do, but…"

He swallowed past the desert that had taken up residence in his throat.

"Goddammit, Brant—"

"They've uncovered evidence—" Brantley tried to dislodge the glitch by shaking his head, still holding Travis's stare. "I honestly don't know how to say it."

"Just spit it out so we can move on with our lives."

"That's the thing. I don't think we can."

Travis's glare turned arctic. "Tell. Me."

It would have been easier to walk away, to tell Travis he was wrong, that there was nothing to tell him. He wanted to. In fact, he wanted to race back home, jump into bed, pull the covers over his head as his inner seven-year-old was telling him to do, and pretend this never happened.

But before he could come up with reasons for bowing out, the words tumbled right out, spilling into the space between them. "They've uncovered evidence that leads them to believe Kylie's alive."

He held his breath and waited for Travis's reaction.

It didn't come.

And it still didn't come.

Jesus Christ. Maybe he hadn't said the words aloud.

"Travis?"

3

The man's eyes remained glued to his face. His mouth twitched, but no words came out.

Brantley was waiting for him to throw a punch, to land one right to his jaw. He would've deserved it.

But that wasn't what Travis did.

Oh, no. What happened next was much worse.

Travis's eyes narrowed, his initial reaction disappearing as though the words hadn't just struck a nerve. "I want to see the evidence."

Brantley nodded. What else could he do?

Fifteen minutes later, Brantley was typing in his code to unlock the barn while Travis stood directly behind him. They'd driven separately, but Travis had ridden his bumper like the two vehicles were insects getting ready to mate. At one point, he thought about throwing the truck in *neutral* to see if Travis would push him home.

Opening the door, Brantley tried to brace for the difficult part. His shoulders tensed, his stomach cramped, but at least his brain was no longer on the fritz. His gaze instantly sought his husband. He found Reese perched on the corner of a desk, his expression concerned. Just seeing the man gave him some semblance of relief, which allowed him to shore up his nerves.

Once Travis was inside, Brantley led with introductions. "I'm not sure who you've met and who you haven't," he told Travis as they moved closer to the group. "This is Archer Halligan and Atticus James. I'm pretty sure you know Simon and Holt."

Travis nodded at all four men, not bothering with greetings or handshakes. "I want to see this evidence."

Holt's eyes snapped to Brantley, and he mouthed, *You told him?*

"Hey, you're the one who came up with it. It's only fair to bring him in."

"You should've told me about this already," Travis grumbled, glaring at Holt.

For a brief moment, Holt looked like a deer trapped in the headlights of an oncoming semi. He stood there, teeth grinding, likely trying to come up with an excuse or ten.

Simon nudged Holt, who glanced over as though realizing where he was.

"Right." Holt stepped toward the desk. "To be fair, I didn't know about this when I talked to you." He turned the computer screen so Travis could see it. "Trust me, if I had, I would've led with it."

Everyone waited while Travis skimmed the document. When he was finished, he stood tall and gestured toward the computer screen. "This?"

"It looks legit, don't you think?" Reese prompted.

Several heads nodded in response.

But not Travis's. He shook his head, glancing back at the screen. "This is convoluted conspiracy bullshit. I don't buy this for a second."

Brantley had feared he would say that.

He'd also hoped that'd be the case, as it would make proving one way or the other that Kylie was alive a challenge his team could take on without Travis looking over their shoulder. Sure, he loved Travis—the guy was family, after all—but he would be the first to admit he wasn't the easiest to deal with.

"Next time you come up with some asinine bullshit to feed me, at least make sure it's got substance," Travis growled softly as he made a beeline toward the door.

Brantley half expected Travis to summon him to follow. When he didn't, he let out a relieved breath. As he continued to stare at the door, he felt Reese's presence when his husband moved up beside him. They stared together, watching as Travis made his exit.

"Well, that went well," Atticus quipped.

Brantley took another deep breath, let it out. "It changes nothing."

He had every intention of seeing this through to the end. A thorough examination of this so-called conspiracy was warranted. If for no other reason than to take down some corrupt feds.

Figuring there was no time like the present to do this, he turned to look at Holt. "Now you can go into detail on what prompted you to come to this conclusion."

"You didn't think that would've been something you'd want to hear *before* you dragged him into it?" Simon asked, gesturing toward the door.

"When it comes to my cousin, I've found that transparency is the best option. If he found out I knew and kept it to myself…"

He let the sentence hang because they could fill in the blanks with pretty much anything that resulted in severe bodily harm. And while he wasn't scared of Travis, loyalty was something he prided himself on. When it came to family, no one or nothing would interfere with that.

Not to mention, the man deserved to know that his wife could be alive.

At least that was what he told himself. In truth, Brantley wasn't buying it any more than Travis was. But now he felt vindicated in his reaction. With that, he could proceed without bias.

"Speaking of your cousin," Atticus drawled when there was a knock on the door.

"I'm not lookin' forward to this," Reese muttered, looking over Brantley's shoulder at the monitor.

Brantley wasn't either.

Archer got to the door first, opening it and stepping back out of the way.

Travis stormed in, his expression harder than Brantley'd ever seen it.

Brantley held his ground when his cousin marched up to him, all but getting right in his face. A lesser man might've taken a step back, perhaps gotten offended by the fury in his demeanor, but Brantley wasn't the sort to back down from a fight. Not even when it was with family.

That and he had an inch on Travis and probably a good thirty pounds of muscle. No, Travis wasn't a lightweight, nor did he look like a man who sat behind a desk all day, but Brantley was seven years younger and still in his prime.

"Do you honestly believe my wife is alive?"

He heard the threat, but in it was something else. Optimism? A twinge of hope, maybe?

Brantley's fight-or-flight instinct fizzled, transforming into sympathy for a man who'd lost so much. "I don't know," he admitted, holding Travis's stare. "But I can assure you, we won't stop until we know for sure."

Silence settled heavily over the room as Travis continued to stare at him. Brantley wasn't sure what Travis was looking for, but he suspected he found it a moment later when he took a step back, his shoulders relaxing.

"As much as I want to believe it, I can't," Travis said, his words spoken softly. "Not until you give me real, definitive proof."

"Understood."

Travis took another step back, his gaze swinging to every person in the room. "I expect that you'll be discreet. I do not want this gettin' out."

"Only those who absolutely need to know will have the information," Reese told him. "And it'll remain that way."

Travis nodded, then glanced at Brantley once more. "Keep me updated."

"Of course."

Everyone remained silent as Travis made another hasty exit.

When they were Travis-free once again, Reese looked over. "You really think he's gonna let this go?"

Absolutely not. "One can only hope." Brantley turned to Holt. "Your turn."

"What would you like me to say?"

"Maybe start at the beginning. Tell me how you came to the conclusion that Kylie's alive when I was at the funeral. I saw her when they lowered her into the ground."

A knot formed in his throat just thinking about that day.

"You saw her?" Holt sounded genuinely curious. "You actually saw Kylie in that casket?"

Brantley frowned as he thought back to the events that followed that horrific day when Juliet Prince plowed into Kylie in downtown Coyote Ridge. The hospital, the devastating news, the numbness that followed. The family had insisted on a closed casket because Gage feared their children would never get over seeing their mother like that. At the time, it made sense. Then again, Brantley had selfishly been grateful for the reprieve. Seeing her would've caused the guilt to weigh heavier on his shoulders.

"No," he admitted. "I didn't. But I'm sure Travis and Gage did."

"What about at the viewing?" Simon prompted.

Shaking his head, Brantley said, "No. They had a photo beside the casket."

Brantley recalled that perfectly because he'd thought the point of a viewing was to see the deceased one last time.

Holt looked at Simon.

"Why?" Reese asked. "If you're sayin' what I think you're sayin'..."

"Which is?" Brantley insisted, not interested in the cryptic bullshit.

"That Kylie wasn't in that casket," Reese said, still staring at Holt. "Why would they do it?"

"And how would they know they'd keep the casket closed?" Atticus tacked on.

"It was a risk they had to take," Holt explained.

"So, what? They filled the casket with a hundred and twenty pounds of sand so no one would notice?" Archer sounded dubious.

7

"And just hoped they'd keep the casket closed," Atticus repeated. "Faking her death with so many people around would've been quite a gamble, don't you think?"

"Faked her death?" Brantley swiped a hand over his hair. Hearing it out loud sounded so much worse. "For fuck's sake. Why?"

"I don't think it was intentional," Holt explained. "Simply convenient."

Brantley felt a cold chill race down his spine. The same one that washed over him the first time Holt used that word to describe Kylie's death.

"Not her death," Holt said defensively. "The events of the day. The car accident, her going to the hospital. Yes, it was a tragic turn of events, but for those with an agenda, it was convenient. They took advantage of the opportunity. Manipulated the situation because it aligned with their needs."

"There was no *accident*," Brantley seethed, breathing through his nose as anger flooded his bloodstream.

"I—"

"Juliet Prince hit Kylie with her car," Reese said calmly. "It wasn't an accident, but it wasn't premeditated. Not that we can tell, anyway. Kylie was in the wrong place at the wrong time."

"I know." Holt shook his head. "I know this sounds insane. Maybe it is. But based on the information I ascertained, it was the perfect situation to take advantage of. Kylie's injured, and if someone were hoping to lure her mother out of hiding, what better way to do that than to fake her death?"

"Jesus Christ." Brantley took a step back. "That sounds like fictional bullshit. Yeah. I can understand an agenda, but that's goin' too far. How the hell does one woman hold so much power over the Adorites? Even if Meredith witnessed a hit, there's nothin' to say it would take down the whole family."

"But she didn't," Atticus contributed. "Which makes it even more questionable."

"You're right," Holt continued. "It's a stretch, I'll give you that. But something makes me think everything that happened that day happened because it needed to." He turned to Atticus. "And you're right, too. According to Decker, she didn't witness a hit. But I think Martin Calloway's convinced himself it's the key to takin' down the Adorites."

"Why's this guy got a hard-on for these people?" Atticus asked. "Because they're doin' illegal shit? That seems like overkill, no?"

Simon chimed in with, "Yes, it does. My guess is, Calloway's not after Max because he's a criminal."

Atticus frowned. "Then why?"

"More than likely," Archer spoke up, "something happened in the course of the original investigation that made it personal."

Brantley frowned. "You're sayin' he's out for revenge, and creating a fake witness is gonna take him down?"

"I doubt Meredith's the only weapon in his arsenal," Simon stated. "But until he finds her, she's a loose end."

Brantley hated to admit that it made sense. Some of it, anyway. As for the possibility that someone could fake Kylie's death ... he didn't see that it was feasible. He remembered that day. The family had descended on the hospital, everyone waiting for news. The doctor came out and delivered the devastating blow directly to Travis and Gage.

"I want someone to look into the doctor who signed her death certificate," Brantley told Atticus. "I want everything there is to know about him."

"Got it," Atticus said, typing something on his computer.

No wonder Travis was spiraling. Brantley could only imagine what the man thought when Holt told him this fucked up fiction. And now Brantley had dragged him into it. Although Travis had walked out, Brantley knew deep down the man would not be able to brush this off. Not without a flame of hope burning until they knew for sure.

Holt looked his way. "I can already tell you think I'm nuts."

Yeah, well. If the straitjacket fits...

Brantley shook his head, but it wasn't to deny the accusation. "I don't believe for one second—"

The words ended abruptly. He couldn't finish that sentence. No, he didn't think it was true—that Kylie was still alive and breathing—but he couldn't deny there was a twinge of hope, a tiny flame sparked from the need for it to be true.

What if?

He didn't necessarily believe in questioning things he couldn't see, but in this case, it was difficult not to.

"Say there's some merit to it," Archer prompted. "And we already have mention of FBI agents lingering in town. We haven't identified them, but they could be around."

9

"They are," Holt confirmed.

"And what?" Reese prompted, looking at Holt. "You think they're hangin' out, hopin' Kylie's mother will pop up again because she's heartbroken and wants to mourn her daughter's death?"

"Nearly two years later?" Brantley tacked on.

"I don't believe in coincidence, so yeah." Holt nodded. "I think they're waiting for something."

"Yeah? And what?" Atticus chimed in. "They've got Kylie locked up somewhere? Holding her hostage?"

Holt shrugged. "Possibly. Or it's possible she's willing. Depends on what they've told her."

Brantley took a step forward, intent on arguing, but Simon stepped between him and Holt.

"Think about it. A mother of five, Brantley. They could manipulate her simply by telling her that her kids aren't safe."

Reese's hand landed on his arm. "If they're persuasive enough, I can see it. Kylie would want to protect them all."

Brantley glanced from one person to the next until his gaze finally landed on Reese. "As ridiculous as it sounds, there's only one thing we can do at this point."

Reese nodded. "I agree."

Looking back at Atticus and Archer, Brantley said, "Keep movin' forward. But I want this little detail"—he pointed at the computer—"kept on the DL. For now."

"And the objective?" Atticus prompted.

Brantley looked at Reese momentarily, then addressed the two investigators directly. "I want to prove without a doubt whether Kylie's alive. And if she is, where the fuck is she?"

"Why don't we just exhume the body?" Atticus asked.

Brantley canted his head. "If you can convince my cousin to disturb what might just be his wife's final resting place, you go ahead and try. But when he beats you bloody and leaves you for dead, that's on you."

"Very vivid picture you paint, boss. No exhumation. Got it." Atticus stepped forward. "I'd like to ask that we bring Evan into the fold. Where that's concerned, I mean."

"Why?" Reese asked.

"Because Baz is out and Evan can be discreet. We can pursue different leads, and he can assist with that."

Brantley felt Reese's gaze on him, waiting for an answer. He had one, but he wasn't sure his husband would be happy with it.

Without hesitation, he said, "No."

Atticus looked pained by the response.

Gesturing to Atticus and Archer, Brantley said, "The four of us—" He stopped, looked at Simon. "Make that five. We'll pursue that lead. You can assign all other aspects of the conspiracy to the team. For the moment, no one outside this room needs to know about Kylie."

Atticus looked appeased by the response. "Understood. And JJ?"

That was a good question. Brantley knew he couldn't keep the information from her. She deserved to know. "Reese and I'll go by the hospital and fill her and Baz in. I'll see if they have time to help out when they aren't with the twins."

"What about RT and Z?" Reese asked.

"No." Brantley knew it didn't make sense, but he wanted to keep this close to the vest. For now.

He looked at his husband, expecting an argument.

"Okay."

He tried to hide his surprise at Reese's acquiescence.

"I get it," Reese said quietly. "The fewer who know…"

Exactly.

Looking at Holt and Simon, Brantley said, "I want you both to keep this to yourself."

Holt nodded.

Taking another cleansing breath, grateful that the panic had subsided and his focus had returned, Brantley started toward the kitchen.

"Let me make coffee, then we'll get started."

CHAPTER TWO

Travis sat in his truck, staring out the windshield.

The landscape surrounding Brantley's property was dotted with maple trees and dogwoods, some of them starting to change colors as fall settled in. Others, like the live oaks, were still lush and green, daring the season to change.

That was Texas for you.

He saw none of it. Not even the reds and oranges that his wife had loved. Had Kylie been alive, their house would've been decorated for fall already. Signs and wagons on the front porch, arrangements of fake flowers, seasonal throw pillows and blankets scattered in the living room. There would be figurines in the kitchen and colorful pictures that the kids had drawn on the refrigerator.

But his house wasn't decorated for fall because his wife wasn't alive. Kylie was dead, a piece of his heart right along with her.

Travis glanced down at his wedding ring. It wasn't the one he'd worn when she was alive. No, that one had been melted down and used in the new set he and Gage wore at her request, the diamonds used to create necklaces for Kate and Avery. All because Kylie had the forethought to leave them a letter in the event of her death. Something Travis had never even considered. Then again, Kylie had been the planner, the one who thought of everyone but herself.

As he did almost daily, Travis pulled out his wallet and retrieved the letter. The paper was beginning to thin, threatening to tear along the creases, so he unfolded it gently and started to read.

Dear Travis and Gage,

If you're reading this, it means I'm no longer of this earth, and I have to hope it's after we've lived a long, happy life together. After my babies have grown up, graduated high school, college, gotten married. But if for some reason it's not, then you should know that every second I had with the two of you and the five of them made for a life more complete than I ever thought possible.

If there was some unfortunate event that took me from this world, then there are some things I need you to do for me. Things that might be difficult because, if nothing else, I know exactly who my men are. I know how you both think; I know how you both love. And I know without a doubt that the two of you will retreat because you think it will benefit the other in some way.

First of all, that's complete nonsense and you should move forward remembering that every single day. While I have never doubted for a single second how much I am loved by both of you, I also know how much you love each other. If I have a say in the matter, Travis, you won't be stubborn, and Gage, you won't let him be. You will both suck it up and move forward, hand in hand, where you belong.

Provided these still make sense, here are the things I need you to do for me:

> ~ Take my wedding band and my engagement band and have them melted down, along with both of yours. But don't worry, I don't want you to be without them for long. From those, have new bands made, one for each of you. That way, you will both have a part of me with you forever. After all, the three of us are stronger together, even if we aren't all there.

His throat tightened, a familiar reaction to his life these days. They had done as Kylie requested, melting down her wedding rings and using them to create new ones that they now wore. Travis couldn't say that he felt closer to her because of it, but every time he saw the ring, it was a reminder of what was missing.

> ⁓ Now for the diamonds. They don't melt, so I would like you to take the diamonds in my rings and make them into necklaces for our daughters. One for Kate, one for Avery. I want them to have a little part of me with them always. You can give them to them whenever you feel is the right time.

They had done that part, too. The diamonds from her band were now in new settings, which dangled from gold chains that Kate and Avery wore for special occasions. They'd allowed the girls to pick out jewelry boxes to keep their necklaces in, to keep them safe. Kate would sneak hers from its box and tuck it under her pillow at night, though she didn't think they knew.

> ⁓ For Kade, Haden, and Maddox, I've set aside some things that belonged to my father, things he has given me over the years. There's an old compass that belonged to his grandfather. One of them might like that. There's also the toolbox my dad gave me when I first moved out on my own. Nothing fancy, but I know Kade has enjoyed helping me with projects. Also, the miniature airplane collection. I'll let them or you decide who gets what. Hopefully, there won't be any fighting.

They hadn't yet completed that task because they were waiting until the boys were older. Kade was six, so Travis figured they still had some time yet.

> ⁓ As a family, I would like y'all to plant a tree for me. More than one, preferably. Yes, even now, I want to help the environment. Hopefully, if this time ever comes, the kids'll be old enough to select one they know I would've liked. I leave it to both of you to decide where. But if you're having a hard time, I think a magnolia tree would look lovely in Curtis and Lorrie's front yard.

They'd completed that almost immediately after her death. There were now magnolia trees in his parents' yard, as well as in Jessie's and their own. There were times when Travis would catch Gage sitting on the porch, staring at the tree, oblivious to everything around him. It was in those times his heart broke even more, knowing he couldn't heal the man he loved any more than he could heal himself.

In an attempt to clear the tears forming, Travis diverted his attention to his surroundings. His gaze darted to the barn where his cousin remained. He wanted to tell Brantley and his team that they were on a fool's errand. That there was no way his wife was alive. He'd seen her body the day she died. Broken and battered and so very still after the doctors failed to save her life.

Was that the last time he saw her? Had to be. Gage had convinced him that a closed casket was necessary because the kids wouldn't be able to handle seeing their mother in an unanimated state. The funeral home director had chimed in, earnestly advising that it would be much easier on the children. Travis had agreed because it made sense at the time.

A tear trickled down his cheek. He didn't bother wiping it away. They still fell on a daily basis, but he did his best not to let Gage or the kids know that he hadn't stopped mourning. They would've understood because they still did, but he didn't want to burden them with it.

He turned his attention back to the letter, resumed reading.

> ~ And last but not least, I want the two of you to get married. It's what I've always wanted, although it was never an option. We did things our way, the three of us, but now it's time for the two of you to move forward. Together.

And yes, they could check that one off the list, too. Travis had married Gage in front of the magnolia tree in his parents' front yard. That day had been bittersweet.

I hope you both know that I love you with my whole heart. I am truly blessed to call you both husband. Sure, it might mean that I've had to complain about two pairs of socks on the floor or ask twice before someone agrees to take the trash out, but in return, I've received twice as much love as most women get. I wouldn't trade our life for the world, and no matter what happens or when, you should both know that I've had the best life anyone could be lucky enough to have.

Love always and forever,

Kylie

Taking a deep breath, he resigned himself to going home. After carefully returning the letter to his wallet, Travis backed out of Brantley's driveway, keeping his foot steady on the accelerator rather than slamming it to the floor the way he wanted. He needed to remain calm, to think this through.

Should he tell Gage? Would Gage benefit from having this information? Doubtful. It would only hurt him because every time they dredged up the past, they both experienced a setback. To the point Travis had to wonder whether they would ever move on.

He could pretend the conversation with Brantley never happened. Not until there was some definitive proof. Because, *come on* ... Kylie alive? Yeah, it would be an answer to his prayers, but Travis knew that it wasn't possible. It was Holt's fiction wreaking havoc with reality. The man was clearly off his rocker if he thought for one second that some rogue group of corrupt government officials kidnapped his wife and was holding her captive somewhere in an effort to take down Max Adorite.

Max fucking Adorite. The head of the Adorite Crime Family. Or the Southern Boy Mafia, as the media preferred to call them.

Travis knew Max. He wouldn't say they were friends, but they were probably more than acquaintances. After all, Max had done Travis a solid by tracking down the woman who killed Kylie and taking her out of this world for good. Travis owed Max for that, and he knew he would one day be called upon to pay that debt.

Not that he minded. He didn't lose a minute of sleep over the fact that Juliet Prince was dead.

But Travis wasn't supposed to know that Brantley was running on the assumption that some crooked FBI agents were holding Kylie captive somewhere. That wasn't the information Brantley had given him to justify his crazy assumption. No, that was the information Travis had gleaned from the electronic board in the conference room. The one they probably didn't want him to see.

But he'd seen it.

Now that he had, Travis couldn't deny he had the urge to call Max, find out what the fuck the man knew.

He headed back toward the town proper, windows down so the cool breeze could clear his cluttered brain. By the time he reached the house, he felt better. Calmer, at least. There was still a burning sensation in his gut, the one that usually led to him going off half-cocked, but he was doing his best to ignore it.

As soon as he pulled into his driveway, he felt some of the stress lift. That was what happened these days when he came home to Gage and the kids.

When he stepped inside a minute later, he heard laughter coming from the kitchen. He followed the sound, eager to see his children, his husband.

"Hi, Daddy!" Avery shouted as soon as he walked into the room.

"Hi, Pop-*tart*!" Kade called, making Maddox laugh as he always did when Kade called him that.

"Hi, Pop-*sicle*," Haden said, grinning from ear to ear.

The kids were experimenting with what to call them, insisting they both couldn't be called Dad or Daddy. Because Travis referred to his own father as Pop, they were keeping along those lines for some reason.

"What's for breakfast?" he asked, his gaze darting to Gage, hoping the man didn't hear the tension in his voice.

Gage, leaning against the counter with a cup of coffee, met his gaze, held it. Yeah, he definitely heard it. The former police officer had damn good instincts.

"I'm havin' cereal," Avery supplied.

"Waffles!" Kade shouted with glee.

"Ceweal," Haden offered.

"Where's Kate?" Travis asked.

"In her woom," Haden answered.

"Room," Avery corrected. "R. *Rrrr*. Ruh-ruh. *Room*."

"Ruh-ruh-*woom*," Haden mimicked.

17

The kids giggled.

"Have you checked on her?" Travis asked, moving closer to Gage.

He could feel his husband's steady gaze as it caressed his face, an attempt to read his mind.

"I was about to." Gage lowered his voice. "You okay?"

Travis shook his head. As much as he wanted to leave Gage out, to pretend not to have this potentially life-altering information, he knew he couldn't. They'd been through too much together, and though neither of them had gotten over losing Kylie, they'd found solace in one another. They worked together as a unit, taking care of the kids and each other. He owed it to Gage to be honest with him.

"You wanna talk about it?"

"Yeah. Let me check on Kate first."

Gage sipped his coffee and nodded.

With the kids continuing to tease each other, Travis headed for the stairs. He heard Kade shout, "See ya later, Pop-*corn*!" causing more giggles. Travis couldn't hide his smile as he ascended the stairs slowly.

When he reached Kate's door, he knocked and waited for her to invite him in. That was one of her new rules. Evidently, when you were almost eight, you'd earned the right to have people knock. Or so she'd told them.

"Who is it?"

"Me," Travis answered.

"Come in."

He opened the door, then leaned a shoulder against the jamb, watching his daughter as she sat in her bed with her journal in her lap.

"Whatcha workin' on?"

She didn't spare him a glance, just kept writing. "I'm writin' down my dream."

That had become her thing for the past few months. She claimed that it was important to write down dreams because they might come true if you did. Travis didn't have the heart to tell her that wasn't possible. Especially not since she continued to dream about her mother. According to his cousin, Piper, the psychiatrist, it was normal for children to hold onto hope, and writing in a journal was a positive way for Kate to process the loss of her mother.

"What'd you dream about?"

"Mommy," she said simply.

"Did she talk to you this time?"

Kate nodded. "Uh-huh."

"What did she say?"

His daughter looked up, her brown eyes serious when she said, "She told me to hang on a little while longer."

"Hang on for what?" he asked.

Kate put her pen on the paper again and shrugged. "I don't know. She didn't say."

Well, that wasn't helpful. The good thing was that Kate had weekly sessions with Piper, so Travis knew she would be getting the help she needed to get through this difficult time.

"You wanna come down for breakfast?"

Still not looking at him, she said, "In a minute."

"All right." Travis turned to leave.

"Shut my door, Daddy-O!"

Smiling, Travis reached back and grabbed the doorknob, pulling the door closed. He headed back down to his first-floor office, mentally preparing to tell Gage that Brantley and Reese thought their wife was alive.

WHILE BRANTLEY GOT COFFEE, REESE HEADED INTO the conference room and reviewed the timeline that Archer and Atticus had put together. He had to admit, there was a lot more information than he had initially anticipated. And not because he thought Archer and Atticus would slack off.

No, he honestly hadn't thought there was that much information in the chaos that Holt had put together. Seeing it now, it told a fairly decent story, starting back when Meredith Prescott and Decker Bromwell crossed paths when he was in the ninth grade. It grew from there. They even had notes on the Adorites, including Samuel Adorite's death.

What they didn't have were Meredith's whereabouts. If he were a betting man, Reese would say she was no longer sitting in that New York brownstone watching someone else's kid. If there were a hint of truth to this theory, Meredith Prescott would've spent the past twenty years on the run, moving frequently to keep off the radar. Now would be no different. While Decker claimed to know where she was, Reese wasn't sure that was the case anymore. Then again, if he did, the chances of him giving up her location were slim to none.

Which meant they needed to get a team on it soon.

"I think we need to go to Dallas and have a sit-down with Max Adorite," Archer stated when Brantley joined them.

Or they could do that.

Reese accepted a cup of coffee when Brantley passed it over and waited for Archer to elaborate.

"We know that an FBI agent was blackmailing Meredith Prescott into testifying to a murder. What we don't know is whether there's any merit to the accusation. Just because she didn't see it happen— according to Decker—doesn't mean it didn't happen."

"And what?" Atticus grinned. "You just wanna walk up to a mob boss and ask him if he offed someone? I see that turnin' out well."

"I think that's exactly what we'll do," Brantley stated.

Reese couldn't help it, he grinned, hiding it behind his coffee cup. He could absolutely see Brantley confronting Max. The man was not the least bit intimidated by the notorious mob boss.

The problem was, perhaps he should be. While Max seemed like a laid-back kind of guy, he had a black heart. His attempt to transition to legal activities after marrying Courtney hadn't quite taken root. Not entirely. From what Reese had heard, Max was actually in the process of solidifying his territory by restructuring his entire organization. The news proclaimed the Southern Boy Mafia was on the verge of a turf war with Sabrina Moroso, and that rivalry had been strengthening ever since she killed her brother to take over as head of her family. Whether it was accurate that they were at odds or merely speculation was anyone's guess. But Reese knew Max well enough to believe it was the former.

"When do we leave?" Simon asked, looking far too eager to sit down with the mob boss.

Brantley looked his way, and Reese knew he wasn't hiding his anxiety well.

"I'll do whatever's necessary to get this closed," Reese told him. And he meant it. He didn't look forward to confronting Max or potentially seeing Madison while he was there, but he would do it in order to get this over with. Hell, he would walk through fire naked if it would get them one step closer to finding Kylie, provided she really was alive.

And no, Reese wasn't sure he was buying all of it, but he had to admit, it didn't sound quite as crazy to him as it probably should.

"It's after eight, now. We'll need a few hours," Brantley told the room. "I'll book the hotel and send you the location. Anyone wanna ride with us?"

Simon raised a hand. "I wouldn't mind."

"I'll catch a ride with Atticus," Archer said, looking at his partner. "If that's cool with you."

"Yup."

"We need to be on the road no later than two," Brantley said before looking at Reese. "You can call Max and get us a sit-down for tonight or first thing tomorrow."

Reese nodded. He wasn't eager to talk to Max, but as he said, he would do whatever was necessary to get through this.

"We're gonna run by the hospital, see JJ and Baz," Brantley told Simon. "We can swing by and pick you up when you're ready."

Simon nodded.

With that, Reese followed Brantley out of the barn, Tesha trotting beside them. He plastered on a neutral expression and pretended his stomach wasn't twisting in knots. It would serve no purpose to let Brantley know he was already dreading this plan.

"I'm gonna shower before we go," Brantley said when they walked into the house. "Join me."

Reese closed the door and turned, expecting to see Brantley standing there, waiting for a response. But he wasn't there. He was strolling across the living room.

Okay then. Clearly that was a command rather than a request.

"Now, Reese!" Brantley called when he turned down the hallway.

Evidently his husband was past the point of saying please. Or asking nicely.

Because he understood the way Brantley's mind worked, knew in his soul what the man needed, Reese followed. When he reached the bathroom, he found Brantley stripping off his shirt. Reese stared, admiring the hard body beneath those clothes.

21

When they met, Brantley had been on the mend, rebuilding his strength after nearly being crushed by a building during one of his SEAL ops. He'd put on some pounds—all muscle—since then. His daily regimen of running, weights, and time spent with the hanging bag had honed that body into a work of art. His arms and shoulders were exquisitely sculpted. His broad shoulders, too. But those abs… The way Brantley's chest tapered downward, his abdomen chiseled as though an artist had designed it, made Reese's mouth water.

And that ass and those thick, tree-trunk thighs… Lord have mercy.

It was safe to say Brantley did it for him in so many ways.

It was Brantley who had taught Reese things about himself. Things that had altered the course of his entire life, given him a chance at real happiness. Before Brantley, Reese had spent his life dating women. He couldn't even recall ever thinking a man was attractive. Not until he met Brantley, and then it was as though someone had given him sight for the first time.

And now that man, that body, it belonged to him because the wedding rings on their fingers said so.

"Naked, Reese," Brantley ordered before stepping into the shower.

Getting with the program, Reese stripped off his clothes, tossing them into the hamper alongside Brantley's.

The moment he walked into the shower, Brantley was on him. He hissed when his back hit the cold tile, smiling a second before Brantley's mouth slammed down on top of his.

And then he was a goner.

The steam formed around them, heating the room as their body temperatures rose from one another's touch. Reese surrendered to Brantley's plundering mouth, accepting what he was giving him. He let his hands roam, soaking up the smooth, hard contours of Brantley's beautiful body while their tongues dueled.

"I'm only gonna say this once," Brantley said when he broke the kiss.

Reese met Brantley's gaze, wondering whether he should be concerned by the frustration in Brantley's tone.

"I hate Max Adorite," Brantley growled softly. "He's the reason you damn near died. I'll never forgive him for that."

He wasn't wrong. Technically, Madison was the one who'd left him for dead, but according to her, she'd done so under duress. Her brother had sent his bodyguard to pick her up and whisk her away. He knew Madison hated Max for that because she'd told him so. But it had been for the best.

Granted, he probably wouldn't think that if he'd died from the bullet he took to the chest.

Unable to speak, Reese held Brantley's stare.

"But I have no problem using him to get what we need to find Kylie."

He noticed Brantley was already talking as though she were alive.

"You belong to me, Reese. That ring on your finger says so."

His heart turned over the same way it did whenever Brantley made such a possessive proclamation. Reese had never belonged to anyone before. Not like this.

"And you'll have to forgive me if I feel the need to prove that in the coming days."

"Prove it? How?"

Brantley's smirk was slow and wicked. "Like this."

The world spun when Brantley grabbed his arm, aggressively tugging him away from the wall before spinning him around. Reese barely got his palms up to brace himself before Brantley was pinning him against the tile. He was rough, proof that he was wrestling with his demons.

Reese didn't mind. He loved when Brantley allowed himself to feel everything. Those moments when he came unhinged were some of the most exciting. Especially when it involved this man proving how much he wanted him.

Reese groaned when Brantley bit his neck, his shoulder. He kicked Reese's feet apart at the same time his hands made their way down his body. One hand reached around, firmly gripping his cock, the other slid between the crack of his ass, fingers teasing roughly.

Overwhelmed by pleasure, Reese tipped his head back, gasping and moaning, accepting everything Brantley was giving him. The sensual assault left him breathless, the aggressive manhandling left him aching for more.

"Brantley…"

"I'm gettin' there, baby," Brantley said, his voice gravel-rough.

Electricity arced across his skin as Brantley stroked his cock and fingered his hole. Reese was on the verge of orgasm when Brantley released him. He had only seconds to catch his breath before Brantley's hands were on his hips, pulling him back, a hard hand landing between his shoulder blades, pushing him forward. Reese leaned over, palms still planted on the wall, and groaned when Brantley's thick cock breached his ass.

He tried to relax, accepting the intrusion. Brantley was rough, but Reese was used to that. Hell, he craved it.

"Mine," Brantley growled when he was lodged deep inside him. "Say it, Reese."

He didn't hesitate. "Yours."

"Damn right." Brantley kept his hand firmly planted on Reese's back as he slowly pulled out, paused.

When he drove back in, his entry was smoother. He did it several more times, and Reese realized he was drizzling lube on his cock each time.

"Goddamn, I love this ass," Brantley grunted, dropping the bottle on the floor before gripping Reese's hips and slamming into him. Again and again, he didn't hold back.

"Oh, fuck," Reese hissed, the pleasure intensifying tenfold. He saw stars as his nerve endings were electrified.

"Mine, Reese," Brantley repeated.

"Yes." Reese clawed at the wall, attempting to remain upright as Brantley plowed into him, fucking him hard.

Brantley shifted again, changing the angle, penetrating him deeper. Reese cried out when Brantley's cock grazed his prostate.

"You wanna come?"

Unable to utter more than rough groans and gasps, Reese nodded.

"Tell me you love me, Reese."

"I love you," he said instantly, moaning around the words.

Brantley slammed into him. "You better."

"Oh, fuck, yes. Brantley ... oh, God. Make me come."

His husband's response was a rough growl as he slammed into him again and again.

Reese reached down, grabbing his cock. He stroked in time with Brantley's rough, punishing thrusts. Within seconds, the electricity pulsed in his spine, rushing up and out through all his extremities. He cried out as he came.

"Mine!" Brantley barked, slamming in deep, his cock pulsing as he emptied himself inside him.

Reese managed to stand up straight and found himself once again pinned to the wall as Brantley rested against him.

"Mine," Brantley growled, pressing a kiss to Reese's shoulder. "Never forget that."

"I love you," Reese whispered in response.

"I love you, too, baby."

They remained like that for a minute, maybe two.

When Brantley stood and cool air washed over Reese's back, he instantly missed his warmth.

At the same time, he was left with a sense of contentment that he'd never felt until this man came into his life.

CHAPTER THREE

Simon left the barn feeling better than he had when he got there.

Not much, but yeah, better.

The story he'd envisioned for the past couple of months was taking shape, and now that Brantley and Reese knew the truth, he got the feeling this one would go down in history. An FBI conspiracy to take down the mob results in the kidnapping and confinement of a mother of five.

Seriously. The headline wrote itself.

Of course, he owed most of the credit to Holt. If his friend had truly stumbled on the information as he claimed, then Holt should probably play the lottery because he was one lucky son of a bitch.

Granted, he prayed they would find Kylie and the story would have a happy ending. His rarely did. Since he tended to work on cold cases, the best he could usually hope for was closure for the loved ones. In this case, he didn't want closure. He wanted to find the woman, bring her home, and take down the corrupt officials. In that order, if possible.

By the time Simon pulled into Violet's driveway, he was feeling pretty good. The sun was up, he had some coffee in him, and now he needed to pack for a trip. He would finally get the chance to sit down with Max Adorite, the notorious head of the Adorite Crime Family.

Telling Violet was the first step in making that happen. He knew she wouldn't be happy, and he couldn't blame her. The Adorites were dangerous, but Simon doubted his life would be in jeopardy. It was a meeting. He was sure mob bosses had meetings all the time.

Using the key she'd given him, Simon let himself into her house, hoping she was still asleep. He'd been living there for a couple of weeks now while they waited to close on the house they were purchasing together. Because they were in limbo, he'd settled in as much as he could, which was hardly at all. Since Violet was slowly but surely packing her things into the many boxes now cluttering the guest bedroom, he had a couple of drawers in the dresser and a sliver of space in the closet.

He wasn't complaining by any means. He loved Violet. He would gladly keep his shit in his car if it meant seeing her every single day.

"Hey, Hermione," he greeted the big feline who hopped up onto the sofa as soon as he closed the door. "Where's Harry?"

At the sound of his name, Harry came prowling into the living room, the enormous Maine Coon moving with purpose.

"There you are. Now, where's your mom?" he asked them.

Hermione meowed, but gave no clue as to where Violet might be. Harry ignored him altogether, moving to his space at the front window so he could observe the neighborhood as it came awake.

Since they were evidently not impressed with his arrival, Simon headed for the bedroom. He heard Violet's voice as soon as he reached the door.

"I know. I will." *Frustrated sigh.* "Okay. I get it."

Frowning at the irritation he heard in her voice, Simon opened the door to find Violet sitting on the edge of the bed, her phone to her ear. Had she not been annoyed, he would've gotten an instant boner from seeing his woman wearing his T-shirt. Which, in his opinion, was just about the sexiest thing he'd ever witnessed.

Violet's eyes lifted slowly, her frown firmly in place.

"I know, Mom. I said I would."

He met her gaze and instantly knew something was wrong.

"Simon's home," she tacked on. "I'll talk to him and let you know." She rolled her eyes. "Yes. I will. Bye."

"What's wrong?" he asked when she tossed her phone on the bed beside her.

"My dad's missing," she said, exasperated. "Or my mom claims he is."

His brain processed the words, but Simon wasn't sure what the appropriate reaction was. "Just out of curiosity, what constitutes missing for a man who doesn't stay in one place for longer than a night?"

27

"She claims he was supposed to come over last night but didn't show."

"And that's unusual, how?"

She smiled. "That's what I said."

Simon figured that went over well.

He'd met Violet's mother. Drama was Daphne Walker's middle name. Especially when it came to her cheating ex-husband, who also happened to be the love of her life. Although they'd divorced long ago and Harold Anderson had never upheld a single promise he'd ever made to his wife or daughters, Daphne still had a soft spot for him. And in an ironic twist, she was now the mistress since Harold was in a relationship with another woman. Simon wasn't sure that was still the case because Harold's relationships seemed to change with the sunrise. Or so Violet told him.

"I assume she tried calling him?"

Violet nodded. "Said it went straight to voicemail."

"Maybe the battery died."

"Or maybe he's off with another woman," Violet huffed. "I mean, he cheats on his girlfriend with his ex-wife. Who's to say he's not screwing a whole harem of 'em?"

Simon hoped for everyone's sake that they practiced safe sex. And yes, that thought made his stomach turn.

Violet shifted closer, rested her cheek on his shoulder. "Where'd you sneak off to so early?"

Thank God for the change in subject.

"Brantley wanted to talk."

She lifted her head, met his gaze. He could see the question tumbling around in her head long before she asked, "You're goin', aren't you? To talk to the mobster."

Since the first time he mentioned Max to Violet, she'd been terrified of him going to talk to the man. No matter how often he tried to reassure her that it was par for the course, she didn't seem to believe him.

"Yes."

"When?"

"Today."

Violet's dark eyebrows angled downward. "Today? Why?"

As much as he wanted to tell her the details of the case, he couldn't. Violet was a Walker. Which made her Brantley's and Travis's cousin. If Simon told her what they suspected, he doubted she would be able to keep the information to herself. It was just too big. So to spare her and everyone else until they had something concrete, he had no choice but to keep it to himself.

"Because he's making time to see me," he lied. He hoped that Max Adorite was making the time, but he didn't know for sure. Not yet.

"Is Archer going?"

"Of course."

"And Brantley and Reese?"

Simon nodded. "And Atticus."

"You promise not to meet with him alone?"

He smiled, cupping her smooth, warm cheek. "I promise."

When Violet leaned in to kiss him, Simon took what she offered. He couldn't resist. Hell, he didn't look forward to the idea of spending even a single night without her in his bed. Their relationship was still relatively new, but it was solid. As much as he hated being away from her, he knew it had to be done.

Simon was sinking deeper into the kiss, his hands beginning to wander, spurred by Violet's husky moans. Unfortunately, it was cut short when her cell phone rang.

Violet flopped back, groaning. She grabbed her phone, stabbed the button to answer. "Hi, Mom."

Figuring she would be otherwise preoccupied with her mother, Simon went to the closet to pack. It took him no time at all to throw some things into the small carry-on he used to travel. He was coming out of the closet when Violet called his name.

"Yeah?"

"He's missing," she said, this time sounding far more concerned.

"Are you sure?"

Violet nodded. "My mom found his truck."

"Where?"

"In a ditch."

Frowning, Simon set the suitcase on the floor. "Did she check local hospitals?"

"She's doin' that now." Her eyes welled with tears. "She's so upset."

Apparently, Daphne wasn't the only one. Violet worked hard to conceal her emotions, especially when it came to her deadbeat father. But deep down, it was clear she loved him.

"She wants me to call Brantley," Violet said, her eyes pleading.

Usually, that would've been the right thing to do. However, Simon knew Brantley wanted to remain solely focused on their current case. He would likely scoff if Simon suggested they drop everything for a possible missing man. One who had a track record of disappearing and showing up again when he was good and damn ready.

"I'll call Archer," Simon offered. "Tell him what's going on. Since he's part of the task force now, he can talk to Brantley."

"Okay."

Digging his phone out of his pocket, Simon made the call.

"Hey, man. What's up?" Archer answered on the first ring.

"Where are you?"

"The B and B. Why?"

Simon relayed what little information he had to Archer, not sure what the man could do, but hoping he would have a plan. As much as Simon wanted to drop everything and help Violet, he knew he would probably not get another chance to talk to Max Adorite anytime soon.

"Let me call Atticus, tell him what's goin' on. He'll know what the team usually does for stuff like this."

"Let me know," Simon told him.

"Will do. Talk to you in a minute."

The call disconnected.

Simon set his phone on the dresser and sat on the bed beside Violet. He put his arms around her, pressed a kiss to her temple when she leaned into him. He wanted to assure her everything would be all right, but he didn't. He'd heard stories about Harold Anderson, not one of them good. Hell, the man had broken into Violet's bookstore and stolen money from his own daughter. The worst part was she'd known he would do it, so she'd set it up so he could only walk away with a few bucks in his pocket.

The man certainly didn't deserve his daughter's help. At the same time, the fact that Violet would go above and beyond for her family—deserving or not—was one of the many things Simon loved about her.

ATTICUS HAD EXPERIENCED A LOT OF FIRSTS recently.

His first place to live as an adult that wasn't a motel.

His first relationship, no matter how ridiculously complex.

His first job that required people to put their faith and trust in him.

His first friend who was a girl. In the short time he'd known her, Becs had become rather important to him.

Today, he was experiencing another: His first time going home and dreading walking through the front door.

And no, he wasn't blameless. While he wanted to shirk the responsibility, he knew any adverse reaction Slade might have was solely his fault. After all, he had spent the night at HQ. With Archer.

Not together, of course. They'd slept on separate couches. Hell, on separate floors even. Regardless, he suspected Slade would have something to say about it.

Fine. Perhaps he could've softened the blow if he'd bothered to text or call last night, but he didn't. On purpose. Which was probably worse. Not to mention, it was petty since he'd done it to punish Slade for how he was acting.

Yep, that was him. Childish *and* petty, a double whammy.

Honestly, he wasn't too keen on listening to Slade's accusations. He'd already faced a confrontation in front of Archer when Slade stopped by HQ to remind Atticus about their plans—dinner with Slade's parents, of all things. Since Slade didn't believe him when he said he completely spaced, Atticus had to reassure him. Lately, it seemed like a lot of that was happening because Slade tended to assume the worst. But Atticus was pretty sure he hadn't given him any real reason to.

Well, not until last night, anyway.

Not that anything had happened, but he seriously doubted Slade would believe him when he said as much.

Slade would just have to suck it up.

When he made his way up the steps to the house, Atticus wasn't surprised to find the door unlocked. Slade tended to get up early, not only on weekdays. More than likely, he'd come outside to see if Atticus's truck was there and just left the door unlocked afterward.

Walking inside, he felt the tension in the air. It could've been his imagination, then again, probably not.

NICOLE EDWARDS

Because he wasn't eager to have an argument, he made a beeline for his side of the house to shower and pack. Without wasting time, he got the shower out of the way, taking a few minutes to shave and brush his teeth. When he was finished, he wrapped a towel around his waist and made the short trek down the hall to his bedroom to find Slade fully dressed, sitting on his bed, propped against the headboard, feet out in front of him, ankles crossed.

Slade's gaze raked over his mostly naked form as he said, "Did you have fun last night?"

Atticus turned away to get clothes from his dresser. "I wouldn't call it fun. More like work."

"Yeah? You and Archer hard at work all night?"

"Actually, yes," he said, turning back to put some of the clothes in the duffel bag.

"What're you doin'?" Slade asked, jumping to his feet like the bed was on fire.

"Packing."

"What the fuck, Atticus? Seriously?"

Frowning, Atticus turned back. "That's kinda how it works."

"You're movin' out?"

Atticus slowly pivoted back around. "I'm goin' to Dallas with Brantley, Reese, Simon, and Archer."

Slade stared at him, eyes wide. "When?"

"Today."

When Slade didn't say anything, Atticus turned back to his task. Not realizing what he was doing, he continued to shove more clothes into his bag. He didn't stop until the drawer was empty.

Realizing he needed something to wear, he dug through the bag, pulled out jeans and a T-shirt. Forgetting underwear, he dug around more for those.

With Slade staring at him, Atticus managed to get dressed. He sat to put on his socks and boots.

"When will you be back?"

Standing up, Atticus grabbed his phone charger from the nightstand. "I guess when they say it's time to come back."

"No."

Slowly, Atticus looked at Slade again. "Excuse me?"

Slade shook his head emphatically. "You can't go to Dallas. Not with… Someone else can go. Evan. He's got more experience."

32

Atticus was dumbfounded. Not to mention, hurt by Slade's lack of faith in him. So much so, he considered going into the closet, grabbing another bag, and filling it with the few items he'd hung in there. That was all it would take to pack up every single thing he owned and walk out of Slade's house and not look back.

Kinda sad that the contents of his life could fit into two duffel bags.

He paused, took a deep breath. He couldn't end things. Not like this.

Instead, he slipped out of the room and into the bathroom, grabbing the toiletries he would need. When he returned, Slade was standing there, mouth agape, staring. Was it his imagination, or was Slade shaking?

Reminding himself he did not want to get into it, he took a deep breath. It took a moment, but he got his wits about him. Atticus zipped his bag, then hefted it onto his shoulder. His backpack with his laptop was at HQ, where he'd left it, but he glanced around the space to ensure there wasn't anything else he needed.

When he turned, he found Slade standing in the doorway.

"Talk to Brantley," Slade said firmly.

"About what?"

"About someone else goin' to Dallas."

Oh, for fuck's sake. "We're not havin' this conversation, Slade."

"Tell him you've got obligations here."

"It doesn't work that way."

He should've expected Slade to stop him, and that was precisely what he did, blocking the doorway, making it impossible for Atticus to pass.

"I don't want you to go."

"I have to." He avoided meeting the man's gaze. "Please move."

"Atticus."

He looked up into Slade's eyes.

Slade's voice was pleading when he said, "If you care about me at all, you won't do this."

Atticus's ire rocketed to a blaze in an instant. "*Won't do this?* Are you fucking serious right now? *This* is my job."

"Your job is here," Slade insisted.

"My job is wherever Brantley and Reese say it is."

"You don't find it weird that Brantley assigned this to you and not someone with—"

Atticus filled in where Slade left off. "Someone with more experience? Someone who's been with the team longer? Someone who knows what they're doing?"

"Well, yeah."

"Move," Atticus insisted, putting his hand on Slade's chest.

Slade didn't budge. "Are you fucking him?"

"Jesus fucking Christ," Atticus said through clenched teeth, barreling past Slade.

"You are, aren't you? Is that where you were last night? In his bed? And now Brantley's sendin' you to Dallas with him so y'all can be together?"

Atticus didn't bother asking him why the fuck he would think Brantley would do something like that. Their boss didn't give a shit about their personal business.

"I knew this was gonna happen," Slade hissed. "I knew you were gonna cheat. They all do."

Atticus ignored him. He continued toward the door. Before he reached it, his cell phone rang. Figuring it was Archer trying to figure out when he'd be back at HQ, he answered.

"Yeah?"

"Hey, man. We've got a situation."

He stopped, setting his bag on the arm of the couch. "What's that?"

"Violet's dad is missing. Simon just called to let me know. He asked me to call Brantley, but I figured I'd call you, see what you thought."

Atticus was pretty sure Violet was the woman who owned the bookstore, and he thought he'd heard something about her dating Simon, but he wasn't positive. From Archer's tone, she sounded important. "I'm headin' back to HQ. I'll give him a call."

"You mind swingin' by and pickin' me up on the way?"

"Sure. The B and B?"

"Yep."

"See you in a few."

Atticus ended the call and shoved his phone in his bag. He started toward the door, intending to walk out without saying goodbye. Unfortunately, the thought of leaving Slade in this state didn't sit well with him. No, maybe things weren't working the way he'd hoped, but that didn't mean he wanted to put a rift between them. Even if their relationship ended, they still had to work together.

Exhaling slowly, Atticus turned around to find Slade standing there, staring. He looked pained. Atticus wanted to feel bad for him, but the man's reactions were outrageous. Slade had no reason not to trust him, yet it appeared that was exactly what was happening.

"I'm gonna head to HQ. I've gotta pick Archer up on the way. We're drivin' up together. I don't know how long we'll be up there. That's not up to me. But I'll text you when I can."

"Is this it?"

Not sure what Slade meant, Atticus frowned. "Is what it?"

Slade gestured between them. "This. Is it over?"

Half an hour ago, he wouldn't have known how to answer that question. But after this, he knew there was only one right answer. Only he couldn't bring himself to say it.

"We'll talk when I get back."

Slade's jaw ticked. "You're fuckin' him, aren't you?"

Atticus exhaled, grinding his teeth, trying to hold onto his patience. They were wearing thin. "Archer's my partner. We work together. You know that. I didn't touch him. I didn't fuck him. And I don't intend to. We. Work. Together. That's all."

"Then why does it feel like it's over?" Slade demanded.

Atticus stared at him for what felt like an eternity. "Isn't it obvious?"

Not waiting for a response, Atticus spun on his heel and walked out of the house.

CHAPTER FOUR

"WHAT'S ON YOUR MIND?" REESE ASKED FROM the passenger seat.

Dragging himself out of his thoughts, Brantley cut his gaze over briefly before looking back at the road. "Oh, you know. A little of everything."

"Holt's theory that Kylie's alive?"

His hand tightened on the steering wheel. "You and I both know that's not even a possibility."

It couldn't be. No matter which way he tried to spin this theory, it never worked out for him. How could anyone fake a woman's death when that woman died surrounded by her family and friends? If they had done it, then it was a complete stroke of luck because it shouldn't have been possible.

When Reese didn't respond, Brantley glanced his way. "It's not possible, Reese. We were at the hospital. We went to her funeral."

"We did. You're right."

He didn't sound convinced.

"You think somehow there was an elaborate ruse right under our noses, and what? Kylie was carted out of that hospital, locked up in some medical facility somewhere—if she was lucky—and cared for until she could get back on her feet? The extent of her injuries..." He trailed off, not wanting to remember how she'd looked after the accident. Someone had caught the crash with their phone and had posted it on the internet for the whole world to see. During those days when they'd been searching for Juliet, Brantley had watched it more times than he wanted to admit, wishing like fuck he could turn back time and change where Kylie had been standing.

"That would mean we buried an empty casket, Reese. Do you think we buried an empty casket?"

Brantley knew he sounded irritated. He was. Immensely.

"I honestly don't know what to think at this point." Reese shifted, facing him. "Trust me, I've thought of little else in the past couple of hours."

Brantley understood that all too well. He'd been tossing around various scenarios in which it could be possible for Kylie to be alive. And every one of them was preposterous. This was the sort of shit you saw on fictional television. It didn't happen in real life. There weren't rogue FBI agents who kidnapped people in order to force an outcome.

And fine. Perhaps that shit did happen. But it was rare. Very.

"It's wishful thinking," he muttered, flipping on the turn signal as they neared the hotel where JJ and Baz were staying until the babies were released from the hospital.

He had a hard time wrapping his head around it. But that didn't mean there wasn't a shit-ton of hope buried beneath all his doubt. It was a stretch to believe any of Holt's nonsense, but that little thing called wishful thinking had Brantley by the throat.

Ever since their initial conversation with Simon and Holt, he hadn't stopped thinking about the duo's contrived theory. Admittedly, he'd been drawn into it because of the conspiracy. The thought of some pompous asshole using people for his gain pissed him off to no end. Thinking that Calloway's manipulations had somehow crossed into Brantley's family made him see red.

But this… thinking Kylie was alive … well, that was just Holt grasping, desperate for there to be a happy ending. The guy was an author. That was what they did.

In this case, he couldn't fathom a happily ever after when there wasn't a lick of proof that agreed with Holt. Not that he'd seen yet.

"Don't you wish there was some truth in it?"

Brantley sighed. "Damn straight I do. But am I gettin' my hopes up?"

He let the question hang because he didn't want to admit to Reese that he was already headed down that road. Despite his best efforts.

Now he needed to figure out how to break this information to JJ. The only thing he knew for sure was that he could not lead with, "There's a chance Kylie Walker's not dead." That seemed like the worst segue ever. Especially since he didn't have anything to back up the claim.

No, his rational side didn't believe it for a second, but there was that tiny thread of optimism that he wanted to pull. Which was why his hackles were raised, but still.

"I think it's worth pursuing," Reese said, his tone calm, as though he were talking to a wounded animal.

"I agree." That much was true. There was enough information to see that something was off. He wasn't sure it substantiated Holt's theory that the FBI faked a woman's death, but yeah, there was something.

As he pulled into the parking lot of JJ and Baz's hotel, he allowed himself to believe for a moment that Kylie was alive. That they would find her and bring her home. That Travis and his family's world would be put back together. It was an absurd notion to even consider. But that was exactly what Brantley was doing. Considering it.

He could still hear Holt's words. *You saw her? You actually saw Kylie in that casket?*

The fact of the matter was, no, he hadn't. Not once. So, of course he was looking for reasons to believe there was a modicum of truth to it. But there wasn't. It was a fucking conspiracy theory.

Brantley pulled into the first empty space he came to and put the truck in *park*.

"How do you plan to tell JJ?"

"That's a damn good question," he told Reese. He honestly didn't know.

"I know you want to keep this on the DL, but I think we should tell them."

Brantley had already decided that he would. Of all people, JJ deserved to be read in. She'd been with them since the very beginning. Hell, they wouldn't even have a task force if not for her.

"She'll insist on helping."

Reese nodded. "She can do that from the hotel room when she's not visiting the babies at the hospital."

They could certainly use her help. JJ had skills no one else had, and when she put her mind to something, there was no stopping her. If they wanted to figure this out sooner rather than later, it made sense to bring her in.

"Okay."

Five minutes later, they were walking into JJ's hotel room. It was a run-of-the-mill kind of place with a king-sized bed, complete with a blue and orange floral-patterned comforter, pillows that looked like bricks, and cheap, laminated-wood nightstands on either side. Across from the bed was a television in an enormous cabinet that also played the role of a dresser. Beside it, a desk and a rolling, black leather, slope-back chair.

And yeah, it was strange that this place looked like a pay-by-the-hour motel compared to the hospital room JJ had spent the last two weeks of her pregnancy. But he wasn't about to bring it up.

Tesha headed right for Baz, seeking attention. After a quick pat on her head, she turned, obviously looking for JJ.

"We were about to go to the hospital," Baz informed them, gesturing toward the closed bathroom door. "JJ's getting ready."

"We won't keep you long." Provided JJ didn't have a million questions once they told her the truth.

"Something wrong?"

"Not sure it's quite right," Brantley admitted as he pulled out the chair from the desk, spun it around, and straddled it.

He could tell Baz wanted to ask more, but he preferred not to go through this twice. Thankfully, the bathroom door opened, and JJ stepped out.

"Hey," she greeted, looking at each of them as she moved closer. "This is a surprise." Tesha was instantly in front of her, causing JJ to bend over to pet her. "Hey, girl. Oh, my goodness, I've missed you so much."

All eyes were on JJ as she showered love on Tesha.

When she finally stopped, Brantley waited until she looked his way. "We've got some information we need to share, and it couldn't be done over the phone."

JJ glanced at Reese. "Is it just me, or does he overwhelm with pleasantries?"

Reese grinned. "It's been that kind of mornin'."

"Oh, really?" She looked worried as she perched on the corner of the bed, so she could continue petting Tesha. "What's goin' on?"

Brantley decided to lay it out for her. "Last night, Atticus and Archer were compiling Holt's data, attempting to outline it."

"I saw their timeline," she admitted. "Quite impressive."

"Yeah." Brantley looked at Reese, then back at JJ. "There was something they found that Holt had left out."

"About?"

Brantley tried to get the words out, but they didn't come.

Reese spoke up. "Kylie."

JJ glanced between them. "What about her?"

This time, Reese was the one to clam up, so Brantley tossed out, "Holt thinks she's alive."

Yeah, so much for not overwhelming her with it.

Brantley watched JJ as she processed the information. Her hand stilled on Tesha's back, and her expression ran the gamut of emotions: surprise, reflection, contemplation, hope, disbelief, and finally resignation.

Before she got a word out, Reese's phone buzzed, signaling a text. He pulled it from his pocket and glanced at the screen. Brantley watched him to ensure it wasn't anything urgent. His husband's quick shake of his head told him it wasn't.

"Alive?" JJ finally asked, looking at Brantley.

Assuming she was seeking confirmation, he nodded.

"And you believe it?"

He shrugged one shoulder at the same time he said, "No."

JJ smiled. It was slow and hesitant, but it was definitely a smile. "So you don't believe it, but you want to."

"Something like that."

"Okay." She chewed on her bottom lip. "Regardless, we have to look into it. It's the right thing to do."

"It is," he agreed.

She started petting Tesha again. "What do you want us to do?"

Well, that was far easier than he'd expected. He thought for sure he'd spend half an hour trying to answer all her questions.

"Look. I know it's just a theory right now," JJ said, clearly picking up on his bemusement. "But something led Holt to believe that. I'm all for digging in until we know the truth. Whatever that may be."

"We don't want to take away from your family time," Reese said.

"Trust me, you won't," JJ said decisively. "I'm at the hospital during visiting hours. When I'm not there, we're either findin' food or we're here. I've got plenty of time to assist."

Brantley looked up at Baz for confirmation.

He nodded. "She's right."

Feeling a little better about dragging them into it, Brantley said, "We're headin' up to Dallas. Simon wants a sit-down with Max Adorite. We need to know what happened that night, if anything. Once we get the team up to speed, I'm hopin' to get some info on this Calloway guy. I'd like to get eyes on him while we're up there. See if we can catch him doin' somethin' dirty."

"You make it sound easy," Baz said with a snort.

"Maybe it will be. Who knows?"

JJ huffed a laugh. "Nothin' we've done so far has been easy, but I like the wishful thinkin'."

"Archer and Atticus are in charge of this investigation, but I'll make sure they know you'll be handlin' anything related to Kylie's death. Until we know more, I don't want the team to know."

JJ nodded.

"The first thing we need you to do is look into the doctor who signed the death certificate." Brantley looked at Baz. "If possible, you can meet with him." He shook his head before Baz could say anything. "I do not want it to take away from your family time. Only if you've got a few minutes. If not, we'll figure it out."

"But we need you to keep this to yourselves," Reese tacked on. "We've told Travis, but we're keepin' this quiet for now."

JJ's eyebrows shot toward her hairline. "You told Travis?"

"Had to," Brantley explained. "If he heard about it elsewhere…"

"Good point." JJ nodded. "Who else knows?"

"Simon, Holt, Atticus, and Archer."

"Not Evan?" Baz asked.

Brantley shook his head. "Not yet. I don't want anyone to get their hopes up. And I damn sure don't want it makin' its way to my family before we have some answers."

JJ looked at Baz. "We'll keep it quiet."

Baz nodded.

"How're the babies?" Reese asked, quickly changing the subject.

JJ smiled. "They're doin' good."

"Better than good," Baz added. "They've said they may go home on Tuesday or Wednesday."

"That's great news," Brantley said, getting to his feet.

"I know." JJ stood, grinning from ear to ear. "I can't wait."

Figuring he'd better contribute to earn some social points, Brantley asked, "You got names for 'em yet?"

JJ looked at Baz and smiled. "Yeah."

"And they would be…?" Good grief. He was pretty sure pulling teeth was easier.

"Naomi and Noah."

"Beautiful names," Reese stated.

Brantley winked at JJ. "What he said. And with that, we'll get outta your hair. Like I said, we're headin' up to Dallas in a bit, but we'll keep you updated."

"And we'll look into the doctor," JJ added. "See what dirt we can find."

"He might not know anything," Reese said.

JJ cocked an eyebrow. "I wouldn't bet on that."

Brantley had to agree with JJ. If there was even a remote possibility that Kylie was alive, someone, somewhere, had manipulated things to make her death appear real. And the first place to look would be at the source.

TRAVIS LOOKED UP FROM HIS COMPUTER WHEN Gage walked into his home office.

"Where are the kids?" Gage asked, his hair still wet from his shower.

"My parents picked them up."

"They goin' somewhere?"

He shook his head. "They're just gonna hang out at the house for a couple of hours. I didn't want them to be here for this conversation."

Gage's eyes narrowed as he eased into the chair across from Travis's desk. "What conversation?"

For the past hour, Travis had been tossing around the idea of telling Gage about Brantley's ludicrous theory. He hadn't come up with any sure-fire ways of delivering the news without pissing the man off. That was generally what happened when Travis opted to go in a direction Gage would disapprove of. This was likely one of those times, and since it was inevitable that Gage would get upset, he figured he should just come out with it.

"Promise me somethin'," he said.

"What?"

"That you won't get mad and you won't overreact."

Gage was silent for a moment before saying calmly, "You know I can't do that."

Leaning back, Travis exhaled. "It was worth a shot."

Gage's eyebrows formed a perfect V. "What is it, Travis?"

Before he choked on the words, Travis said, "Holt's got a theory that Kylie's still alive."

He watched a storm of emotion play across Gage's handsome face. But it was the ice in his gaze that told him that he'd once again succeeded in pissing off his husband.

Well, that and the fact Gage shot to his feet and marched out of his office without saying a word.

"Could've gone better," Travis mumbled, following behind him. "Gage!"

"No." He went for his keys and his wallet. "I'm not gonna listen to this."

"I told you not to get mad."

Gage spun around, stabbing a finger in his chest. "Fuck Holt. And fuck you for even putting that thought in my head."

"I get it." And he truly did. The more he thought about it, the more ridiculous he knew it was. Unfortunately, his heart was involved, which meant he was entertaining the idea of something he knew was impossible.

Gage gritted his teeth. "No. You don't."

Grabbing Gage's wrist, Travis gripped it tightly, pulling his husband toward him. "I do."

"You've done a lot of stupid things in your life, Travis, but this…" Gage swallowed hard, shaking his head, but at least he'd stopped trying to pull away.

"I didn't want to tell you," Travis admitted. "Not until they give me something real to go on."

"Then why did you?" The torment he saw in Gage's eyes mirrored what he'd been feeling ever since the day Kylie died.

"Because I made you a promise."

Gage's eyes skimmed over his face. "You promised to tell me the truth."

"This *is* the truth. As they know it."

"No, the truth is she's dead."

Travis heard the pain in Gage's voice, the grief that still encompassed them both.

"I'm not gettin' my hopes up," Travis whispered, stepping closer, cupping Gage's face. "But I had to tell you."

"She's dead," Gage repeated, his eyes glassy.

Yes, she was. But there was no denying that Travis would trade anything for that not to be true. Hell, he'd give his own life if it meant bringing Kylie back.

"Why does Holt think that?" Gage jerked back. "No. Don't answer that. It doesn't matter. It's not true."

"Probably not, but…" Taking a step back, Travis dropped his hands and exhaled heavily.

"But what?"

At least his husband was now engaged in the conversation.

"They think there's an FBI conspiracy to take down Max Adorite."

Gage frowned but didn't say anything. Travis had expected a snort of derision at the very least.

When he still didn't say anything, Travis elaborated. "A conspiracy that goes back two decades and involves Kylie's mother."

Again, Gage simply stared as though he was processing the information and it was making sense.

"Gage?"

"Hmm?"

"Why aren't you rantin' that this is pure horseshit?"

Gage turned away from him.

"Do you know somethin' I don't?"

"No," Gage answered quickly, honestly. "But it doesn't sound as absurd as it should. Takin' down Max, I mean. Not the part about Kylie. That's…"

Travis frowned. "Wishful thinkin'?"

"Exactly."

Travis could tell there was something Gage wasn't saying, so he waited him out by sitting on the arm of the couch. A minute passed. Two.

When Gage turned back to face him, Travis expected him to speak, but he didn't. He knew better than to rush him when he got like this. Unlike Travis, Gage preferred to think through his thoughts before they shot out of his mouth. And based on the crease in his forehead, he was considering his next words carefully.

His patience was rewarded when Gage met his gaze and said, "Remember back when you found me workin' undercover at Club Destiny?"

Travis didn't have to think too hard on that. He remembered it as if it were yesterday.

"Travis, come over here. I'd like you to meet someone," Logan McCoy said. Without hesitation, Travis joined him.

"Travis, I'd like to introduce you to the newest member of the temporarily disbanded club. Chance Reed, meet Travis Walker. If you like our club, you're going to want to get to know this man personally."

"Chance Reed, huh?" Travis did his best to hide the heat churning in his veins. "Interesting, considering all this time I thought your name was Gage Matthews."

"What about it?" he asked Gage now.

Gage scratched the side of his neck. "Back then, when I was workin' that case, there was a rumor of some rogue FBI agents lookin' to bring down the Southern Boy Mafia. They thought the senator had ties to the mob and asked if I'd look into it."

"Did you?"

"Not officially, no." Gage tucked his hands in his pockets. "I was ordered not to work beyond the scope of my case. Since takin' down the senator was key, I did my best to stay in my lane."

Travis considered that for a moment.

"The group called themselves Censorious," Gage continued.

Travis frowned. He'd heard that name before, but he wasn't sure where. Then again, he met all sorts of people, considering he owned and operated one of the most prestigious fetish resorts in the country.

"Is that who Brantley's goin' after?" Gage prompted.

Travis shrugged. "I honestly don't know. I was able to glimpse a bit of information, but I was too shaken up to stick around."

"I want to talk to Brantley."

Raising his eyebrows, Travis stared at his husband. "About what exactly?"

Gage took a step toward him. "I don't believe for a second that Kylie's alive, Travis. I wish I could, but I saw her."

Travis had, too. He'd seen her lying still and cold on that table. He shook his head to dislodge the memory. Whenever he thought about it, his entire body threatened to shut down.

"But I'd like to see what they've got," Gage continued. "If they're workin' on takin' down Censorious, maybe I can help."

Travis was surprised by the request, although he wasn't sure why. At his very core, Gage was the sort of man who wanted to take down the bad in the world. It was a wonder they'd made it this far together since they both knew Travis walked a very fine line between right and wrong. And there were times when he knowingly stepped over. However, he kept those instances to himself. No sense rocking the boat any more than he did on a regular day.

"I think they were headin' to Dallas at some point."

"Call 'em. If they haven't left, I want to go over there."

Since he couldn't very well tell Gage no, Travis grabbed his cell phone and made the call.

CHAPTER FIVE

Leaving Baz and JJ's room, Reese let Tesha lead the way to the elevator. He pressed the button and stood back, waiting for Brantley to catch up. He was there before the *ding* sounded, signaling the car's arrival.

"You good?" he asked Brantley, making small talk.

"Yep. You?"

Smiling, Reese nodded as he stepped into the elevator. The doors had just closed, sealing them inside, when Reese's phone buzzed with another text. He dug his phone out of his pocket and scanned the incoming message, fearing it was going to be another message from Slade.

Brantley leaned against the wall. "Who's texting you?"

He nearly breathed a sigh of relief when he saw that it wasn't Slade.

"This time it's Atticus," he answered as the doors opened to the lobby.

"This time?"

They walked toward the exit, then stepped out of the hotel into the muggy October morning.

"Slade texted while we were in their room." Twice. But Reese didn't bother to clarify that. The text message was bothersome enough.

"What does he want?"

He purposely misunderstood Brantley's question, answering with, "Atticus says it's important. It has to do with Violet's father."

"We can call him in the truck. What did Slade want?"

Because he didn't think it was worth discussing, he changed the subject. "I need to swing through PetSmart on the way home."

Brantley nodded as he walked around to the driver's side of the truck. Reese helped Tesha in the backseat, then climbed into the passenger seat.

"Don't think I didn't notice you deflecting," Brantley said, starting the truck. "What did Slade want?"

Reese considered lying but knew he couldn't.

Brantley gripped the steering wheel as he looked over at him. "Is it bad?"

"Well, it's certainly not good."

"What does that mean?"

Exhaling heavily, Reese leaned into the seat. "Slade wants us to partner him with Atticus."

Brantley scrunched his nose. "Why?"

Reese looked at him, cocking an eyebrow. Surely Brantley wasn't oblivious to what was going on between Atticus and Slade.

"What?" Brantley glanced his way. "Why're you lookin' at me like that?"

"Slade's jealous."

"Of?"

"Atticus and Archer."

"Oh, for fuck's sake. That's stupid."

Maybe, but it was the only explanation Reese had for the number of texts he'd received from Slade asking him to realign the teams so that Slade could partner with Atticus.

Brantley's gaze remained on the road. "That *is* stupid, right?"

"Yes. Of course it is."

"So there's nothin' goin' on between Atticus and Slade?"

"I didn't say that."

"But there's nothin' goin' on between Atticus and Archer?"

"Not that I know of."

"Are you gonna do it?"

"What? Shift the team? No," he said in a huff.

"Good. I think we've got strength the way it's laid out right now."

Reese didn't disagree. He didn't have too much to go on yet, but what he'd seen of Atticus and Archer, they would play to one another's strengths. And Evan and Slade worked well together.

Plus, that whole mixing business with pleasure didn't work out most of the time. Of course, it wasn't a hard and fast rule he would enforce—after all, that was how he and Brantley got together—but he certainly didn't intend to encourage it.

"You wanna call Atticus?" Brantley prompted when they pulled out of the parking lot.

Since Brantley's phone was connected to the truck's Bluetooth, Reese grabbed it and pulled up Atticus's contact. He tapped the screen to dial the number.

It began to ring. Once. Twice.

"Hey, boss."

"What's up?" Brantley replied, stopping at a red light.

"Is Reese with you?"

"I'm here."

"Okay. Good. It sounds to me like Violet's dad is missing."

"Harold?"

There was a slight pause, followed by, "Is that her dad's name?"

Brantley chuckled. "Yep."

"Does she have more than one dad?"

"Nope."

"Then I guess that'd be the one."

"How long's he been missing?"

"Damn fine question. No one seems to know anything other than they found his truck abandoned in a ditch, his cell phone and wallet were inside."

"Maybe he was drunk. Wrecked the truck. Walked to town."

"Yeah, maybe."

"What do you want me to do about it?"

"Violet would like the team to look into it."

Reese glanced at Brantley, waited for him to lay out a plan. Only he didn't.

"Where're you right now?" Brantley asked.

"Back at HQ with Archer."

"We're headin' that way. We have to make one stop first," Brantley told Atticus. "We'll talk more about it when we get there."

"Sure thing, boss."

The call ended.

"You don't seem surprised that Violet's dad is missing," Reese told Brantley.

"The man's a flight risk. Always has been."

"Meaning?"

"Meanin' one minute he'd be back in Daphne's life, pretendin' to be a doting father to their girls. The next, off on a new adventure with a dozen excuses as to why he couldn't stick around."

"They're divorced, right? Daphne and Harold."

"Oh, yeah. But she has a soft spot for him."

"I guess we should check in with Darius, see who's available to help."

Brantley nodded. "Let's get there first. As much as I wanna help Violet, I need as much focus on this case as I can get."

Reese understood. With the possibility of Kylie being out there, they couldn't put it on the back burner. Then again, that was why they had a team of people. They could easily assign a couple of them to focus on finding Harold.

Nearly forty minutes later, after stopping at PetSmart to pick up what Tesha needed for a road trip, they were parking the truck in front of the house.

"What's Luca doin' here?" Brantley asked as they were getting out of the truck.

That was a good question. Luca worked whenever they needed him to, but rarely did he come to HQ on the weekend. He preferred to work remotely unless it was during regular business hours.

Granted, they didn't really have regular business hours, did they?

Reese took a detour through the house to drop Tesha's stuff off so he could pack it in a bit. Once that was done, he followed Brantley out the back door, across the yard, and right into the barn.

The second they stepped inside, Luca shot to his feet. "I need to talk to y'all."

Reese glanced at Brantley, surprised. Luca was the laid-back sort. Rarely did the man show any emotion whatsoever. Even when things were chaotic, Luca was cool under pressure. Today it looked as though someone was holding their finger on his panic button.

"What's up?" Brantley prompted.

"Honor's dad is missing."

Reese recalled the conversation he'd had with Brantley not too long ago regarding the Anderson sisters. Brantley's family had been groomed to protect their cousins—Whitney, Amanda, Violet, and Honor—mainly from their father, since Harold Anderson was prone to breaking their hearts. The four girls had been raised within a protective bubble, treated as though they were fragile and in need of a knight in shining armor. Reese didn't know the sisters all that well, but from what he'd seen of Violet and Honor, they certainly weren't damsels in distress.

He also remembered how defensive Brantley had been, determined to confront Luca.

Evidently, Brantley had forgotten that he was supposed to be the protective voice of reason because he said, "Do you need our help?"

Luca glanced between them. "I know the team's focused on Simon's case, but…"

"You wanna find Honor's dad," Reese filled in when he let the sentence hang.

"Yeah."

"Okay," Brantley said without hesitation.

Luca seemed surprised by that.

"We don't really have anyone to spare, so you'll have to lead the charge. We're headin' up to Dallas."

"Who's we?" Luca inquired.

"Atticus, Archer, and Simon are goin' with us."

"How long?"

"Quick trip. Don't know when we'll be back," Brantley explained. "If you need someone to help, reach out to Slade."

Nodding, Luca exhaled. "Thanks, boss."

"Let me know how it goes."

"Yeah. Okay."

With that, Luca was out the door, laptop tucked under his arm.

Brantley grinned. "Well that was easy."

Reese turned to look at him. When he did, he caught a glimpse of the monitor showing the parking area near the house.

"This may not be," he muttered, jerking his chin in the direction of the screen.

"Shit," Brantley grunted. "What the hell are they doin' here?"

Brantley wasn't surprised to see Travis. After their conversation earlier, it made sense that he had gone home and grabbed reinforcements—namely, his husband.

Then again, he'd been banking on Travis being Travis and keeping the information to himself. If there was anyone who could shut out the entire world and carry the full weight of whatever burden he was dealing with, it was Travis.

Not this time, apparently.

And of course, they decided to drop in without calling first.

Nope. Not at all surprised.

While Travis likely had a legitimate reason for showing up without warning, Brantley didn't have time to soothe his ruffled feathers or explain why or how they were doing what they were doing. He preferred to get on the road so he could get this conversation with Max out of the way. And since Travis and the mob boss exchanged pleasantries and phone calls often, he didn't care to enlighten his cousin about his plans.

If he thought he could've gotten away with sneaking out the back, he would have. Unfortunately, there was nowhere to go, so he stayed rooted to the floor, waiting for Travis and Gage to come in.

"I can tell 'em you're not here, boss," Atticus joked as he pushed the door open. "I guess we should've catered in breakfast."

Gage walked in first, his gaze sliding throughout the space. He looked as though he was admiring the decor, but Brantley figured he'd already accounted for every single soul in the place. Those he could see, anyway.

"Hey," Gage greeted when his eyes stopped on Brantley. "Sorry to drop in like this."

"Not a problem," Brantley lied. "We were just gettin' ready to head outta town. What's up?"

Gage looked at Travis, then back to Brantley. "Travis told me you're workin' on a case involving Censorious. I'd like to see what information you have."

Brantley narrowed his gaze, stalling so he could come up with an excuse. He did not want to share that information with anyone, least of all Travis and Gage. Not until they could narrow the scope and flesh out the details.

"Look," Gage said, clearly catching onto his tactic. "I know you're workin' this thing like it's hot. Maybe it is. But I might have some information that'll help."

Reese moved up beside him. "What information?"

Gage looked at all the faces staring back at him before settling his attention on Brantley again. "A while back, I was workin' a case in Dallas to take down a corrupt senator. At the time, our focus was only on him, but in the course of the investigation, I came to learn about Censorious."

"How so?" Archer inquired, joining the conversation.

Gage glanced at Archer, a curious gleam in his eyes.

"Gage, Archer," Brantley said quickly. "Archer, Gage. How so?"

"Archer Halligan," Archer said formally, holding out his hand to Gage. "I work with Simon Jennings, and I recently joined the task force."

Brantley huffed. He did not have time for this shit.

"Nice to meet you. Gage Matthews, Travis's better half," Gage said to Archer.

Atticus chuckled from behind them.

Unable to hide his frustration, Brantley interrupted the pleasantries. "That's Atticus. You can be all touchy-feely later. How'd you come to learn about Censorious?"

With a smirk, Gage shifted his attention back to Brantley. "There was a rumor of a corrupt FBI agent lookin' to take down the Southern Boy Mafia. I was restricted from lookin' into it at the time, but I did a little digging of my own."

"And?"

Gage's smirk returned. "You show me yours, I'll show you mine."

"As much as I'd like to do that, we're gettin' ready to go to Dallas," Brantley lied. Well, the first part was a lie.

"For?" Travis asked.

"To meet with Max," Archer informed him.

So much for keeping that on the DL.

"We'll go with you," Travis said, his tone lacking any sort of request.

Gage frowned, his gaze shifting to Travis.

"I don't think that's a good idea," Brantley told him.

"But it's a good idea for *you* to meet with him?" Travis snorted. "If I recall correctly, you were plannin' the man's demise after he left this one"—he jerked his chin at Reese—"for dead."

Brantley's blood heated the same way it did whenever he thought about how Max Adorite had sent in his goon to sweep his sister off to safety while turning a blind eye to the man who'd taken a bullet for her. He had no problem admitting he hated Max with all that he was, but in this case, he would put aside his anger in order to deal with the matter at hand.

"Before I agree to anything," Gage interrupted, "I'd like to see what you've got."

"We've got some time," Reese said beside him. "It might help."

Brantley huffed, then gestured toward the conference room. "Atticus and Archer have it outlined in there." He jerked his chin at Archer. "Show him."

When Gage followed Atticus and Archer into the conference room, Brantley got Travis's attention. "What'd you tell him?"

"What you told me."

"How'd he take it?"

"He doesn't believe it any more than I do," Travis said, eyes cold. "But he thinks the information he has might help to take down the corrupt FBI agent."

"His name's Martin Calloway," Brantley supplied, although he wasn't sure why he did. They didn't need Travis sticking his nose in.

"When are you meetin' with Max?"

"I left a message," Reese answered.

Travis's gaze passed between them a few times before he pulled his phone from his pocket. He tapped a few things on the screen, then it started ringing, the sound coming from the phone's speaker.

"Why're you botherin' me this early?" a familiar voice answered.

Travis smirked. "We need to meet. Today."

"We?"

"Brantley and Reese are here with me."

"I left you a message," Reese added.

"I've been busy this mornin'," Max said. "Haven't gotten around to callin' you back."

"No shit," Travis said. "If you had, he'd have the meeting time and I wouldn't have to call."

"You're just a giant ray of fuckin' sunshine, you know that, Walker?"

"So I've been told. What time can we meet?"

"You comin' here?" Max asked.

"Yep. Take us a few hours to get things in order and get up there. I'd say this evening works best."

"Seven?" Max offered.

Travis's eyebrows lifted in question.

"Seven works," Brantley said, trying to keep his tone cool. He did not like being put on the spot like this. And he damn sure didn't like Travis bulldozing his way over his op.

"You got a place in mind?" Travis asked Max.

"I do. I'll send you the address an hour before. See you then."

The call ended.

Travis cocked an eyebrow. "I guess I'll be taggin' along."

Son of a bitch.

While he generally preferred not to go toe to toe with Travis, Brantley's frustration had skyrocketed to DEFCON 3, which meant he was only two levels away from hitting an imminent nuclear war. He stepped forward, met his cousin's eyes as he invaded his personal space.

"I'm in charge of this. Understand?"

Travis held his own, not backing down. "Did you honestly think I'd slink back home and hide under the covers when you told me someone thinks my wife's alive? You know me better than that."

Actually, Brantley hadn't thought that. He'd *hoped*. And in this case, there was a big difference.

"You told me to keep you apprised. That's my intention."

"Now you don't have to. I'll be right by your side."

"The fuck you will. I don't need you goin' off half-cocked like you usually do."

"Let me tell—"

"Let's play nice," Gage said, talking over Travis as he walked up to stand beside him.

Brantley continued to stare into Travis's eyes, ensuring he knew how serious he was. "I'm in charge of this op."

"Yes, you are," Gage agreed, grabbing Travis's arm and pulling him back. "And now we're askin' if we can be part of it."

"No one's asking," Travis growled softly.

"Yes, we are," Gage insisted, urging Travis back more, taking his place in front of Brantley. "I know you think we'll get in the way, but I know how to play nice in the sandbox."

"He doesn't," Brantley said, his gaze darting to Travis.

"You're right." Gage grinned. "He doesn't. But he will. You have my word on that."

Brantley took a step back, exhaling heavily. He did not want to fight. It wasn't helping matters.

"Technically, Archer and Atticus are runnin' this show," Reese said. "So it's really up to them."

Inside, Brantley was grinning. On the outside, he kept his expression impassive as they all turned their attention to the two men watching them from the sidelines.

"Our objective is to talk to Max." Archer stepped forward. "It's not to piss him off. If you think you can refrain from doing so, I don't have a problem with you comin' along. We need as much information as we can get."

Brantley refrained from chiming in. Reese was right. Archer and Atticus were in charge, and he had already agreed to let them run it how they wanted.

"Appreciate that," Gage said. "We'll—"

"What the hell's your brother doin' here?" Brantley asked Reese when he saw movement on the monitor, showing RT's Cadillac Escalade parking beside Gage's truck.

"Don't know. I didn't call him."

Just what they needed, more overbearing people looking to stick their noses where they didn't belong.

CHAPTER SIX

ALONG WITH EVERYONE ELSE, ARCHER WATCHED THE monitor as four people—three men and one woman—spilled out of the black SUV in the parking lot. As soon as the woman's face became clear, he recognized her from the photos he'd seen numerous times over the past month or so.

"That looks like ... um ... *Eddie*," Atticus said from beside him, his voice low, but probably not low enough.

"Because it is," Brantley confirmed, still watching the screen.

What were the odds that the woman at the center of this conspiracy just showed up at their door? And yeah, okay. That was a stupid question since that was most definitely her.

"Who is she?" Gage asked, looking to Brantley for an answer.

"I guess technically she's your mother-in-law."

Gage's head snapped around, eyes slamming into the monitor. "That's Kylie's mother?"

"It most definitely is," Brantley said, sounding a little too chipper to be sharing that information.

"I thought her name was Meredith."

"Eddie's a nickname."

"Did you know she would be here?" Travis prompted. He didn't look entirely surprised to see her.

Brantley shook his head. "Had no idea. Then again, I didn't know *you* would be here."

"Who's the guy with her?"

Archer figured Gage was referring specifically to the glaring man who had taken her hand and was leading her toward the barn.

"Decker Bromwell. He works for RT and Z," Reese explained.

"How does he fit into this?" Gage asked.

"He had a relationship with her when he was a teenager," Brantley said, his distaste for the subject evident. "She was his teacher, he was her fourteen-year-old student."

"Jesus Christ," Travis muttered. "That's disturbing."

"Understatement," Brantley added.

Archer would've found this situation somewhat comical if it weren't quite so dire. The entire case they were working sat like a house of cards right on that woman's head, and here she was, making an appearance in Coyote Ridge. He wondered how long it would take the feds to figure out she was there. And once they did, what were they intending to do about it?

Which, now that he thought about it, maybe that was how they could draw out Martin Calloway. If they used Meredith as bait, Archer was sure the guy would come running. Then again, he was a Fed, which meant he'd likely pull rank and haul her off, throwing up protections as a federal witness that would keep them from getting to talk to her.

So maybe they needed to keep her presence a secret.

Reese moved to the door, opening it when the group approached.

"Hey," RT said softly, eyes full of apology.

"Inside," Z ordered Decker, looking as though he was ready to kick the guy to get him moving.

Beside Archer, Atticus stared in wonder, looking confused and intrigued in equal measure. Archer understood the feeling all too well.

Welcome to the Big Top, folks. Archer was positive the price of admission to a show like this would be astronomical. And here he was with a front row seat.

Once inside, Z made introductions. "Brantley, Reese, meet Meredith Prescott. Over there, that's Atticus and Archer."

Not sure what to do, Archer lifted a hand and waved. He felt like a fool, but his brain was momentarily on the fritz. Just last night, they'd been deep diving into this woman's existence, and there she was.

No one said anything in response, and somehow the tension managed to ratchet up another notch, which Archer didn't think was even possible. Based on the tension Decker had carried into the building with him, they were moments away from turning into pink mist. As it was, he was fighting the urge to tug on his shirt collar, wondering if anyone else was choking on the suffocating silence.

Finally, Brantley spoke up. "This is my cousin Travis and his husband, Gage."

Meredith's eyes widened as she took in both men. Based on her expression, she recognized them. Their names, at least.

Because no one seemed to know what to do, Archer decided to take the lead. That was his job, after all. He moved closer to the group. "Did you drive here?" he asked Meredith directly. "From New York?"

Her eyebrows tipped downward. "I did, yes."

"Very recently?"

"I got here yesterday."

He noticed the lingering question, so he nodded toward her left arm. "You've got a tan on one arm. That's usually from driving long distances." And since it hadn't faded, he knew she hadn't been in the area long.

Meredith put her right hand on her left arm and rubbed.

"Why's she here?" Brantley asked, his tone lacking civility.

"She showed up at the B and B late last night," RT explained. "We figured it was safer to keep her presence on the DL."

Driving her around Coyote Ridge was this man's version of the DL? Good to know.

Reese stared directly at her. "You realize there are feds lookin' for you."

It wasn't really a question, but Meredith nodded.

"What do you expect us to do with her?" Brantley asked RT.

RT looked at Z, who looked at Reese, who was still staring at Meredith.

"Is there somewhere she can go that won't draw attention to her?" Archer asked when no one else seemed to know what to say. "I think it's in her best interest to stay off the radar. We don't want the FBI swooping her up."

Meredith looked at Decker.

Archer was surprised to see he didn't look directly at her. Although they'd walked in hand-in-hand, Archer got the feeling Decker was trying to put some distance between them. For a man who'd gone on the defensive to protect her honor not too long ago, he didn't seem to be thrilled that she was there.

"She can stay at our house," Gage offered.

"The hell she can," Travis bit out.

"The kids'll be with your parents," Gage said, his tone calm. "We'll be in Dallas. She can stay there until we get back."

"I can't ask you to do that." Meredith's voice was soft, almost meek. Completely unexpected.

"You're right," Travis said, glaring at her. "You can't."

"She can stay at the B and B," Decker said, still not looking at her.

"I'd prefer somewhere that isn't in the heart of town," Archer told them. "What about a hotel in Round Rock? Or maybe Taylor? It's not too far from here, and it'll reduce the risk of anyone seein' her."

"Good idea." Z pointed at Decker. "You can take her and keep an eye on her."

Decker's heated glare could've melted plastic.

Gage opened his mouth to say something, but Travis cut him off with, "I'll spring for the room."

Meredith was watching him closely, probably not sure how to take the gruff, outspoken country boy who clearly did not like her.

"Now that that's settled," Brantley said, "we need to get packed so we can head up to Dallas. We're meetin' with Max," he told RT and Z.

"We're headin' back, too," Z informed them. "Figure people might start talkin' if we stick around."

"Especially if we're not here," Reese noted.

"Where's Simon?" RT asked, his gaze scanning the room.

Shit.

Shit, shit, shit. Archer forgot all about Simon.

"He's with Violet," Brantley answered. "Her dad's MIA, so he's workin' on that. We'll pick him up on our way outta town."

Well, at least the guy was otherwise preoccupied. Perhaps he might even forgive Archer for forgetting him.

"You two get to a hotel," Atticus told Decker and Meredith. "And stay put."

Decker nodded, looking none too happy at being ordered around by anyone. Archer, on the other hand, was impressed by Atticus's desire to take the lead. He might not have a lot of cases under his belt, but he got the feeling the man would come into his own soon enough.

Atticus turned to Brantley and Reese. "If it's cool with you, we're gonna head up in a bit."

Brantley nodded. "We'll send you the hotel info when we have it."

"This one's on me," Travis said, not looking at anyone as he turned toward the door. "I'll get the reservations taken care of and send you the details."

"We'll see you at seven, if not before," Gage said to the room before following Travis out.

ATTICUS SWORE THE ROOM DEFLATED WHEN TRAVIS left. He figured it would ease up even more as soon as Decker sought fresh air. The tension those two brought to a conversation was the equivalent of an atom bomb. Geezus.

Now it was just a matter of grabbing his stuff and urging Archer out into the sunshine. A three-hour drive was just what the doctor ordered to relieve some of the stress that was currently weighing him down.

"Can we have a quick chat before you head out?" Reese asked once most everyone had left the barn.

Oh, boy. A one-on-one with the boss was never a good thing.

"Sure, what's up?"

"I got a text from Slade."

Speaking of shoulder-hunching stress…

Reese didn't continue right away, and Atticus wasn't sure what to say. Did he apologize? Pretend not to know what Slade was messaging about? Or leap right into an explanation of his own so that Reese had both sides of the story?

He opted for the latter.

"I don't know what Slade told you, but if it's all the same to you, I don't want to change partners."

Reese's gold eyes skimmed his face. "I'm glad to hear you say that."

As for why Reese was glad, Atticus didn't know.

"There's no rule against dating in the workplace," Reese continued, "but—"

Atticus stopped him. "I know. And that's not a problem. Not anymore."

He could tell by Reese's expression that he wanted Atticus to elaborate, but he didn't feel like getting into it. For the moment, he had too much to deal with to worry about the status of his relationship with Slade or Carson. The only thing he knew for sure was that he was not going to let it dictate how he lived his life. The relationship was supposed to be fun, but Slade was ensuring it was anything but. And Atticus didn't think he was the only one feeling the pressure since Carson seemed to be keeping his distance, too.

"I plan to talk to Slade," Reese informed him. "I want him to know it's our preference that you work with Archer."

"Our?"

"Mine and Brantley's."

Atticus nodded. "I agree."

And that much was true. He'd officially worked with Archer for less than a day, but he got the feeling he was going to learn a lot from the man. Plus, it helped that Archer treated him like an equal, rather than a newbie who was lacking in the smarts department.

When Reese didn't say anything more, Atticus gestured toward the door. "We're about to head out, if that's cool."

Reese nodded. "Y'all be safe on the road. We'll let you know as soon as we have hotel info. And we'll shoot you a text when we get there."

With a quick thumbs up, Atticus headed for the conference room to pack up his things.

AFTER LEAVING BRANTLEY'S, TRAVIS HEADED FOR HIS parents', wanting to make a plan for where the kids would be staying while he and Gage were in Dallas. It was an impromptu trip, and while they were usually happy to let the kids stay the night, he did not want to bombard his mom and dad. Five kids were a lot for anyone to deal with, even if most of them were relatively self-sufficient at this point.

"Did you ever meet Kylie's mother?" Gage asked.

"No. She was gone by the time I met Kylie," he admitted.

"Did she ever talk much about her?"

Travis shook his head. "I got the impression she was angry at her, so I never pushed." He glanced at Gage. "She ever talk to you about her?"

"Not much. I tried a time or two, but she closed up whenever Meredith was mentioned."

Yeah, that was how Travis remembered those conversations going. According to the story, Meredith had up and left when Jessie turned eighteen, heading out for greener pastures and never looking back. Kylie and her sister were close with their father, and they didn't have a problem with their father's girlfriend.

Now that they had bits and pieces of Holt's conspiracy theory, Travis had to wonder whether Meredith had left in order to keep them safe.

Or maybe she disappeared because she was a selfish bitch and didn't give a shit about anyone.

It was far too early to tell.

"Did she ever mention her mom havin' an affair with a student?"

Travis's nose curled in distaste. He'd heard the same in Brantley's voice when he relayed that detail. If it were true, he hoped like fuck that woman had spent at least a portion of these past couple of decades in prison.

"No. I have to think she didn't know." At least he hoped she'd been spared that information.

"Do you think we should tell Jessie that her mom's in town?"

Travis jerked his head toward Gage. "No. Jesus."

"You don't think she might want to know?"

"Why would she? The woman ran out on them."

"True. But that doesn't mean she's given up on her altogether."

Travis didn't understand why not. Why would Jessie want to let Meredith back in her life when she couldn't be bothered to stick around when she should have?

"I don't think we should mention it," Travis told him. "Not until Brantley and them have more information."

"And you think Max is gonna just pass over details to enlighten them?"

Travis huffed a laugh. "Not a chance. But I want to see Max's reaction when he hears about it."

"Chances are once that happens, this Martin Calloway guy will end up missing or dead," Gage drawled, his attention out the window.

Yes, there was a good chance. That tended to happen to people who crossed Max Adorite. While Travis didn't condone what the man did, he had to admit he admired his ability to take care of his own. Right or wrong, Max protected what was his, and Travis couldn't fault him for that.

Not that he would share that with Gage. His do-gooder husband would never understand the darker side that resided in Travis. Nor would he want him to. That was why he loved Gage. The man made him a better person simply because Travis would do anything not to hurt him.

As he was turning into his parents' driveway, he glanced at Gage. "Let's see what my parents are up for, then we'll call my brothers to see who we can offload to them."

Gage laughed. "You talk about our kids like they're furniture."

"Yeah, well, sometimes I think they might need to be surgically removed from it. At least this way, they'll get out some of their energy."

"True. But you know good and well that Zane's gonna hop them up on sugar when we get back. That's his way of punishing us."

Travis grinned. Yeah, even at thirty-three, his baby brother was still a pain in his ass.

CHAPTER SEVEN

WHEN ATTICUS AND ARCHER WERE FINALLY ON the road just before noon, with a little less than two hundred miles in front of them, Atticus was able to relax a bit. From the time he got to HQ after leaving Slade's that morning, he'd been waiting for the man to show up and start in on him again. As it was, he'd had to turn his phone on vibrate a few minutes ago because the text messages had started. From both Slade and Carson. If Atticus had to guess, Slade had told Carson that Atticus was cheating, and now Carson wanted to know what was going on.

They would have to wait.

"Do you know Brantley's cousin?"

Archer's question pulled Atticus out of his thoughts, his focus returning where it was needed.

"Travis?"

"Yeah."

"I don't. You?"

"Only met him once before. Simon's talked to him a couple of times, I think. I can't quite figure him out."

Atticus kept his eyes on the road. "I'm sure this has to be hard on him. I mean, what would you do if someone told you someone you thought was dead might be alive? Someone you loved, at that."

"As much as I'd like to say I wouldn't get my hopes up... I'm not sure it's even possible."

Atticus understood that to a degree. "I'm not an expert on losin' people. Or loving someone, for that matter. The closest I've got to family is the task force and well..." He let the sentence trail off.

"That's one thing I like about the team," Archer said, relaxed in the passenger seat, his big arm draped on the center console, other elbow propped on the door. "Y'all are a close-knit group."

"I haven't been a part of it long," he admitted. "Came on board in May, so not even six months."

"You wouldn't know it."

Atticus tried to see things from Archer's perspective. From the outside, yeah, he could see that the task force appeared to be close. When it came to work, they definitely were. Regarding their personal lives, some of the team kept to themselves, while others were more interactive. No matter what, they had each other's backs. And sure, Atticus was part of that. They'd been far more welcoming to him than he had expected, so he couldn't complain.

They drove in silence for a few miles; the only sound was the random buzz of an incoming text on his cell phone. He was going to have to turn it off if Slade kept this up. Neither of them acknowledged that stupid buzz, but it was growing more annoying by the minute. Then, for some unforeseen reason, Atticus felt compelled to warn Archer.

"Slade doesn't want me partnering up with you."

Atticus kept his eyes on the road, unable to so much as glance Archer's way. He could only imagine how immature that sounded, and he hated that the words had tumbled right out of his mouth.

"What about you?" Archer prompted.

"What about me?"

"Would you prefer to change it up?"

"No," he blurted a little too quickly. Taking a deep breath, he said, "No. I'm lookin' forward to workin' with you."

"Likewise."

"It's just…"

Archer chuckled when Atticus trailed off. "It's okay. Spill. We've got a pact. As partners. You get to blow your verbal vomit all over the table, and I do, too, remember?"

Atticus snorted. Oh, yeah. He definitely remembered the conversation they'd had the night before. He'd found himself apologizing profusely after rambling incessantly about his fucked-up relationship with Carson and Slade.

"Shit. I really am sorry."

"Don't apologize. If we're partners, we'll pick on things in each other's lives. It's natural."

"Yeah?"

Archer nodded.

"Okay then. What about you? In a relationship?"

66

"Can't say that I am."

"Well, when you are, I'll listen if you pop your cork and spew all your shit all over the table."

"That's a deal."

Shaking off the memory, he huffed. "Yeah, but I can't seem to control it."

"Go on, spit it out. You'll feel better."

"I'm usually bein' told to swallow," Atticus muttered under his breath.

Archer's head turned so fast Atticus was surprised it didn't come flying off his shoulders. That was when he realized what he'd said. And that he'd said it out loud.

"I am—" Atticus cut off his apology when he saw what looked like heat flashing in Archer's turquoise blue eyes.

Jerking his attention back to the road, Atticus opted to forgo the apology and any talk of personal shit.

"So… how do you think it'll go talkin' to a mob boss?"

BAZ STOOD AT THE NURSERY WINDOW AND watched as his two babies slept soundly. Visiting hours were over for the moment, but he couldn't bring himself to leave. It was getting more challenging with each passing day. Didn't matter that they were staying in a hotel only a short walk from the hospital; it felt like it was a million miles away.

"Hey," a familiar voice sounded from behind him.

Baz turned and saw Dr. Justin Tinder, JJ's OB/Gyn, walking toward him.

"I was just coming to get an update on the little ones. How're they doin'?"

Turning his attention back to the babies, Baz smiled. "Good. They may get to go home earlier than expected."

"That's fantastic news."

Yes, it was. Not soon enough, but then again, despite how anxious he was to get them home, Baz didn't want to rush them.

Dr. Tinder joined him at the window. "Look at all that hair."

"My dad would tell you it's strong Buchanan genes," Baz joked. "But everything good in those babies is from JJ."

"Something tells me JJ would disagree with you there. According to her, you're quite the catch."

He couldn't stop the smile.

"Did they say when they'd get to go home?"

"The doctor said he'd reassess them on Monday afternoon and have a more definitive answer by then."

"I'll keep my fingers crossed." Dr. Tinder glanced both ways down the hall. "Is JJ around?"

"She's in the gift shop. They've got these pink and purple elephants she swears she can't live without."

"Sounds like her. Well, hey. I've got rounds, but if you or JJ need anything, give me a call."

"Will do." He offered a smile. "Oh, and my father's still insistent that you come to dinner sometime. He likes having company."

"Funny. I like having food, so I think it's doable. Tell me a time and a place and I'm there."

Dr. Tinder patted him once on the shoulder, then strolled off down the long hallway. Baz continued to watch his sleeping babies. It was weird how content he felt considering his newborns were in the hospital, yet for some reason, he did.

"You might give 'em a complex if you watch 'em too much."

The sound of JJ's voice lightened him even more. She had that way about her. Everything she did made him feel like a better man, a better human.

"Dr. Tinder was just here."

She smiled, waved behind her. "I passed him. He mentioned dinner with your folks. Wes is insistent about that, huh?"

"Oh, he definitely is."

When she moved closer, he put his arm over her shoulder and pulled her into his side. He kissed the top of her head.

"I thought maybe we'd work in the cafeteria if that's okay with you," she told him as they both admired the little miracles they'd created. "I'd like to look into the doctor who signed Kylie's death certificate. Since she was pronounced in this hospital, there's a good chance he's around here somewhere."

Baz peered down at her. "Provided you don't intend to confront him."

She plastered on a winning smile. "Why shouldn't I?"

That was a damn good question. One he couldn't answer. Or rather, one he knew he *shouldn't* answer. The fastest way to get on JJ's bad side was to stand between her and a goal. The woman was as independent as they came, and since that was one of many things he loved about her, it would make him an idiot to try to stifle that.

"Fine," he said, dropping his arm and taking her hand. "But if you talk to him, I go with you."

"If you insist."

"I do."

JJ peered through the window. "Sleep tight, peanuts. We'll be back soon."

They most certainly would.

"MIND IF WE GIVE TESHA A BREAK?" Reese prompted from the passenger seat.

Brantley grinned. He'd been waiting for it ever since they saw the sign for Hillsboro. In fact, he was surprised Reese had waited this long.

"You timed that perfectly, didn't you?"

"Timed it? For what?" Reese's words were thick with innocence.

"Buc-ee's."

"Are we near one?"

Brantley glanced over, cocked an eyebrow. He knew Reese was well aware of the location of every Buc-ee's in the state. The man was oddly obsessed with them. Not that Brantley would turn his nose up at one. They were just shy of being a superstore rather than a convenience store. Plus, it was rarely difficult to find an available gas pump.

Since they were currently driving on I-35, coming into Hillsboro, the next location wasn't too far ahead. And Reese's well-timed request gave Brantley plenty of time to exit.

Very thoughtful of him.

He sensed Reese's smile as he worked his way to the right lane to exit. When they pulled in a few minutes later, Tesha's head popped up, and her tongue lolled out of her mouth. She panted with excitement as she always did when they stopped during long trips.

"I'll drop you off in the grass, then fill the tank. When I'm done, I'll meet you inside."

Brantley pulled alongside a large grassy area that was a decent pet stop if he did say so himself. Plenty of gas stations had none, which was stupid if you asked him. A dog was no longer an animal people kept in their backyard and only spent time with when they remembered they had one. Dogs were now in charge of the humans, he was pretty sure. Theirs was. So, yeah, if Buc-ee's was looking to make any sort of improvement, they could add dog parks to their locations. Then they'd be just about perfect.

It took no time at all to fill the truck. Once he did, he pulled up to the front, parked. As he was getting out, his phone rang.

Travis.

His gut twisted. A familiar response anytime he dealt with Travis. Part guilt, part anxiety. He never knew what mood Travis would be in—only that it wouldn't quite be a good one.

"Yeah. What's up?" he answered, grinding his teeth.

"Gage is sending you the reservations now. We're about an hour out. I'll let you know when we get there."

Straight to the point. Shouldn't surprise him in the least.

"We're probably half an hour behind you," Brantley told his cousin. "But Atticus and Archer are ahead of you."

"Perfect. And Simon?"

"He was gonna ride with us, but decided to fly up there in case he needed to head back tonight. Harold's MIA."

"Harold's always MIA," Travis said, sounding bored.

True.

"We'll see you when we see you," Travis said before disconnecting.

Brantley glanced at the phone screen, shaking his head. And people said he lacked social skills.

A few seconds later, his phone chimed, signaling an incoming text. He checked the screen, confirmed it was from Gage, then shot the message off to Atticus, Archer, and Simon so they would have the details for check-in.

He found Reese and Tesha along the back wall where the drinks were kept in large refrigerators.

"Water or Ghost?" Reese asked as he approached.

Hmm. Good question. Water was probably the better choice, but an energy drink would help more.

"Both," he answered easily. He needed the caffeine if he was expected to deal with Travis and engage with Max Adorite later. They were both on his shit list, but for different reasons.

Reese grabbed several bottles and cans, passing them off to Brantley.

"Did you get—"

"Brisket sandwich and fudge," Reese filled in.

"Did I mention how much I love you?"

"Not today, you haven't."

"I could serenade you right here in the middle of the store if you'd like."

Reese's cheeks turned pink as he muttered, "Don't you dare."

Brantley grinned.

Fifteen minutes later, after Brantley had downed his sandwich and Tesha got water and another bathroom break, they were back on the road. Tesha was asleep in her seat, curled up with a blanket that Reese had bought her specifically for road trips.

"JJ messaged a little while ago," Reese said, positioning things in the cupholders to his liking.

"And?"

"They don't have anything yet, but she's lookin' into the doctor."

Good. Brantley wanted to know every fucking thing there was to know about that man. If there were even a smidge of proof that Kylie was alive, he would be a damn fine starting point. Since he signed off on her death certificate, he would be the first one to know whether she'd been breathing when he put pen to paper.

And if she was, God help him as soon as Travis or Gage found out.

CHAPTER EIGHT

"I was not expecting this," Archer told Atticus when they walked into their hotel suite.

Yes, it was a suite. Not a room like normal businesspeople booked when they checked into a hotel. This was a suite, complete with two separate bedrooms, each with its own bath, that were divided by a large living area and a small kitchenette.

"You want the left or the right?" Atticus asked, his gaze scanning the space.

"Doesn't matter. You choose, I'll take what you don't."

Atticus dropped his backpack on the couch, then went to the left, disappearing into one of the rooms, while Archer deposited his bag on a lone chair in the corner. Why it was there was anyone's guess.

"Is this the normal set-up when y'all are out of town?" he shouted so Atticus could hear him.

"Most of the time, no."

Archer figured.

"When we were in New York, I was sleepin' on the pull-out sofa in Slade's room because they were outta rooms," Atticus explained, returning to the living room without the bag he'd been carrying.

Archer had to wonder if that was when they first got together. Then again, if Atticus was on the couch…

None of your business.

Keeping with the theme that Atticus's personal life wasn't his business, Archer said, "Been there, done that."

Atticus chuckled. "Much easier for me to do, I imagine."

Archer fought the urge to look at Atticus. He'd been fighting that battle ever since Atticus made his comment in the truck.

Go on, spit it out. You'll feel better.

I'm usually bein' told to swallow.

Being that they were partners, it was completely inappropriate for Archer to have reacted the way he had to that statement. Luckily for him, Atticus had been too embarrassed to notice.

However, he had reacted. And for the first time, he had looked at Atticus. *Really* looked at him.

He noticed his dark hair, a little on the disheveled side, but the unkempt style suited him.

He noticed his green eyes, a color so intriguing, Archer wasn't sure he'd seen it before. Maybe a cross between celadon and emerald.

He noticed his neck and the way his Adam's apple bobbed when he swallowed.

He noticed the toned muscles and the dark hair spattering his arms.

He noticed the man's hands. More specifically, the strength he saw in them when Atticus was gripping the steering wheel as though it were a lifeline.

Yeah. He had definitely noticed.

Worse was the fact that he liked what he saw. A lot.

Not that he would ever act on it. Archer figured it was merely a side effect of his falling out with Spencer. After all, he hadn't heard from Spencer since the night things went terribly wrong on their date. Since that had been Thursday and it was now Saturday, he wasn't sure what to expect. There was a good chance he would never hear from Spencer again. He didn't like the idea, but figured it was better to end it now before they ventured into territory where feelings started to arise.

"We should set things up in here."

Realizing Atticus was attempting to move furniture, Archer got with the program. He pushed the coffee table closer to the couch so they could use it as a make-shift desk.

Archer grabbed his laptop from his bag and took a seat beside Atticus on the couch. The instant he sat, his arm brushed Atticus's. Like a dumbass, he shot to his feet, nearly sending the laptop across the room.

"I'll ... uh ... take the chair."

Atticus was staring at him like he'd grown a third arm, this one out of his face. "You okay?"

"Never better." It was a lie. But one he was determined to make true. "Why?"

"Never saw a guy your size move that fast."

"The couch was lumpy."

Based on Atticus's expression, he would believe Archer was an alien from another planet before he believed that.

"Let's map out a plan for while we're here," he told Atticus, wanting to get back on track. "Outside of the conversation with Max Adorite."

Atticus was still watching him, but he nodded, his gaze slowly shifting back to his computer screen. "I think we need to do some recon on Martin Calloway. We need to get an address for him so we can check out his home, his office, maybe shadow him for a few hours."

"That's a good idea."

Archer started a list, putting that as the first bullet point.

"I'd also like to talk to Allison Bogart or her parents. Or all of them. See if they can give us any information."

Archer added those to the next bullet point. "What about the team? Can they handle anything back at home?"

Atticus looked up, then leaned back and took a deep breath. "I guess it depends on who's available and what can be done down there."

"Let's start by listing out who's available."

"Okay." Atticus closed his eyes for a moment. "We've got Evan, Charlie, and Jay."

Archer noted them separately. "Okay."

"Becs and Holly. They could do deep dives."

"Good." Archer added their names.

Atticus's eyelids lifted slowly. "Jay and Slade."

"I already have Jay, but I'll add Slade."

"Oh. Right. Okay. Baz and JJ are lookin' into the doctor who signed the death certificate," Atticus said. "Reese messaged me earlier about that."

Adding that as a bullet point, Archer nodded. "That's a good lead. If he falsified it, they'll figure it out."

"Especially if they follow the money," Atticus noted. "No one does anything for free."

"True. I'll make a note for Luca. I know he's currently on another case, but if he gets done, we could utilize his skills. What about Darius?"

"Yeah. We can use him until Monday," Atticus said, sitting up and tapping his keyboard. "He sent an email earlier. The new hires are starting then. He's pushin' to get them set up by then, so he might be busy, but we could use him in a pinch."

"Will they be ready to pitch in? The new hires?"

Atticus shrugged. "I don't know much about them. I mean, I've seen the resumes, but I don't know who they hired."

Archer sat back in his chair when Atticus spun the notepad around, dragging his finger down the list as he read.

"We've also got Elana and Simon," Atticus noted. "What if we have him do a deep dive into Censorious? See what they've been up to for the past few years. She can help him."

"He'll want that information for his upcoming podcast, so yeah."

Leaning forward, Archer held the pen out for Atticus. When he reached for it, Archer made sure not to let their fingers touch.

"I don't bite, you know."

Is it wrong that I wished you did?

Dumbass, of course it's wrong.

Ignoring his internal rant, Archer sighed. "Sorry. It's not you. I swear."

"Yeah? You sure about that? Ever since I made that blunder in the truck, you've been actin' weird."

Figuring it was best to play dumb, but not too dumb, Archer said, "Have I?"

Atticus sighed. "Look. What I said was way out of line, and I apologize. If I somehow made you uncomfortable…"

"You didn't." Archer snorted. "Not the way you think."

Atticus looked horrified. "But I *did* make you uncomfortable."

"No," Archer blurted as he shot to his feet. He needed to move. "No," he said calmly. "It didn't bother me. I just … I reacted badly to it, and I think I owe *you* an apology."

Atticus snorted. "What? You realize that doesn't make a lick of sense."

Archer planted his hands on his hips, stared up at the ceiling, and choked on a laugh. "It doesn't, does it?"

ATTICUS FELT LIKE A COMPLETE IDIOT.

He knew exactly what comment Archer was referring to, and he'd been fretting over what he'd said from the second the words had tumbled out of his mouth. It had been completely inappropriate. He'd even considered talking to Brantley and Reese, admitting to having crossed a serious line.

"I'm new to this partner thing," he admitted. "And I'm not all that PC to begin with. I guess I should've warned you."

Still turned away, Archer shifted that piercing blue gaze his way.

God, the man had the most intense eyes he'd ever seen. They were just so … *blue.*

"Plus…" Atticus let it trail off because he wasn't sure it was a good idea to admit what the real issue was. Or even acknowledge it, for that matter.

Archer turned to face him, clearly waiting for him to finish his sentence. "Tell me."

Shaking his head, Atticus laughed. "No. It's stupid and really unimportant."

"Let me be the judge of that."

Leaning back on the couch, Atticus stared up at his new partner. Way, way up. The man was enormous. *Like break-me-in-half enormous.* And yeah, he was most definitely hot.

But so was Carson.

And Slade.

His reaction to Archer was simply his old habits coming to light again. Old habits that Atticus refused to give in to. He was not that guy anymore. More importantly, he did not want to be that guy anymore. Being with Slade and Carson, while not as fulfilling as he'd anticipated, had opened his eyes to possibilities. He wasn't broken. He could *feel* things. And he wanted to feel those things. He didn't want to hop from one bed to the next, walking away satisfied but ultimately incomplete.

He wanted … *more.*

One day.

When the time was right.

Sitting up straight, Atticus exhaled a harsh breath. "It's nothing. Really. I'm sorry for the comment. I assure you, it will *not* happen again."

He expected Archer to say something, but when he scrounged up the courage to meet his gaze again, he found the man staring at him. He wasn't sure whether that was disappointment or relief in those electric blue eyes.

Whatever it was, Atticus was ignoring it because it didn't matter.

"We should get back to work. I'd like to have an action plan in place by the time Brantley and Reese get here."

"Action plan." Archer's shoulders relaxed. "Right. Works for me."

"Okay, so we've got—" He stopped when his phone buzzed, glancing down at the screen to see Carson's name. "I need to take this."

Atticus grabbed his phone and headed to the bedroom he would be occupying. He didn't bother closing the door.

"Hey."

"Hey. You got a minute to talk?" Carson asked, his voice smooth, erotic almost.

Atticus walked over and sat on the edge of the bed. "Sure. What's up?"

"I heard you're in Dallas. Not even a goodbye, huh?"

Staring at the carpet, he said, "You've been MIA."

"You could've texted me."

Yeah, he could have. But he didn't.

"How'd you find out I'm in Dallas?"

"I got a call from Slade. He mentioned it. Right after he told me you spent the night with your partner."

Atticus could hear the curiosity in Carson's tone, but it lacked the accusation he'd gotten from Slade. It didn't escape him that there wasn't an ounce of jealousy in his words. Carson didn't get jealous. Probably not easy to do when you prefer to watch your significant other fuck someone else.

Shaking off the thought, Atticus sighed. "I didn't spend the night *with* him. We camped out at HQ last night. We're workin' on a case. It got late. I slept for two hours on the couch. By myself."

"So you're not movin' out so you can move in with him?"

Atticus rolled his eyes. "Of course not. Slade's just bein' Slade."

"He can get like this."

"Get like this? You mean he *is* like this. I haven't given him a single reason to doubt me, but that's all he does."

"He's been hurt before," Carson said, defending him.

"I know that. But I'm not the one who hurt him."

"But I am."

"He doesn't get to extend his insecurities about you onto me."

Carson didn't respond.

"I'm sorry. I didn't mean it like that." He took a deep breath, exhaled slowly. "I'm workin' an important case right now and I don't have time to hold Slade's hand and walk him through the forest of doubt. Hell, he tried to tell me I couldn't go to Dallas. That I needed to change partners."

"Give him some time."

"I don't have it to give," Atticus told him. "Between him watchin' every move I make, waitin' for me to screw up, and you bein' off doin' whatever it is you're doin', this thing we've got isn't fun anymore."

"You weren't complainin' the other night."

Atticus knew exactly which night he was referring to. And no, he hadn't complained because fucking was fucking, and done right, it was a damn good time all around. He would not deny that the best sex he'd had up to this point in his life had been with Slade and Carson.

"Doesn't mean I'm willin' to sacrifice everything else for an orgasm."

"Ah. I get it now."

"No, you don't. Where have you been, Carson? You come around when the lights are off. The rest of the time, you're comin' up with excuses why you can't hang out."

"I didn't realize I was doin' that."

Atticus wasn't going to argue. Carson sounded distracted and more than a little disinterested. Oddly enough, he'd noticed that had been the case ever since Carson and Slade had made up—or at least tried to. Before then, Carson had been fully engaged, acting as though he was interested. Since then... Atticus couldn't really describe it, but he worried that the chase was what Carson was really after. And once he caught his partner, he got bored.

"It doesn't matter right now. I need to focus on this case."

"When're you comin' back?"

"I don't know. A few days, I figure."

"Well, I'll check in with Slade, let him know I talked to you. Try to unruffle his feathers."

"Good luck with that."

After he disconnected, Atticus remained where he was, staring at his phone. Something told him that whatever conversation Carson had with Slade was not going to go over well. And if Atticus wasn't there to force them to be civilized, there was a good chance they would make the same decision he did. That it was just getting to be too difficult.

SIMON ARRIVED AT THE HOTEL A LITTLE after five. He'd gotten a late start, not wanting to leave Violet with her father missing. She was actually the one to urge him to go, claiming he'd been waiting for this interview for a long time.

She wasn't wrong.

Still, he felt guilty about leaving her, so he'd opted to fly up since it took considerably less time. Especially with his TSA PreCheck and no luggage to deal with. This way, he could go back tonight rather than stay at the hotel. Which was why he didn't bother checking in; instead, he texted Archer to get his room number.

By the time he was in the elevator to the top floor, he felt a little more like himself. More focused, at least. He wanted to get this interview out of the way because he had waited for it for so long. There were questions he needed answers to, and insights he hoped to glean from a conversation with Maximillian Adorite. Once that was done, he could get home to his fiancée, where he belonged.

Funny that. Before Violet, Simon's entire existence had revolved around stories. Other people's stories. Now, he was eager and excited to get started on one of his own.

Once he reached the last room on the top floor of the hotel, he rapped his knuckles on the wood. A moment later, Atticus opened the door, stepping back instantly to let him in.

"Hey," Archer greeted from his spot on a chair in what passed for a living room, he figured.

"Hey."

"How was the trip?"

"Quick and oddly quiet."

Archer chuckled. "You don't get much of that these days, huh?"

"No. And I'm certainly not complaining." Simon looked at Atticus, who was getting situated on the couch. "How's it going?"

Atticus looked up. "Good."

Not one for small talk, clearly.

"What're y'all working on?"

"Listing out some action items," Archer answered. "Figure we'll cover as many bases as we can while we're up here."

Simon nodded, setting his leather bag on the two-person dinette table. "I was able to do some digging on Meredith Prescott last night. I think I might know where she is."

Something shifted in the air. He wasn't exactly sure what it was, but he felt it as though it were tangible. When he glanced over, he noticed Archer and Atticus were looking at each other.

"What?" he prompted, waiting for one of them to tell him the secret that was passing silently between them.

"Uh…" Atticus looked his way briefly, then back at Archer.

"Meredith Prescott showed up at Brantley's this morning," Archer said, his tone reluctant and a bit sheepish.

Simon stared at him, confused. He opened his mouth, but nothing came out.

"I am so sorry, man." Archer sat back in his chair. "I swear to God I thought I told you."

"She just showed up?" he prompted when his brain kicked back into gear.

"Last night, apparently," Atticus said. "She went to the B and B."

"Where is she now?"

"Decker's keeping her in a motel outside of the town limits," Archer supplied. "I thought it would be safer to keep her out of Coyote Ridge."

Simon slowly sank into the extra chair, wrapping his head around the new information. He could feel Atticus and Archer watching him.

"Did she say anything?"

Atticus shook his head. "Not really. Other than to confirm she drove down from New York."

"Travis and Gage were there," Archer noted.

That piqued Simon's curiosity. "How'd that go?"

"About as well as can be expected," Atticus answered. "I don't think Travis likes her all that much."

"I didn't realize he knew her."

"I don't think he does."

Interesting.

"I really am sorry I forgot to mention it," Archer said, sounding sincere.

Simon waved him off. A few months ago, he would've been angry that he didn't have all the information as soon as it came in. Oddly enough, he was far more worried about Violet than about what Meredith Prescott was doing in Coyote Ridge. That was a first for him.

Hell, these days, he was experiencing a lot of them.

Made him wonder what that meant for his career. If he didn't get excited about the prospect of flinging himself fully into someone else's mystery, what good would he be to his audience?

That didn't mean he wasn't going to pencil in time to interview her.

CHAPTER NINE

BRANTLEY PULLED UP TO THE ITALIAN RESTAURANT that Max had directed them to, feeling a sense of foreboding as soon as he tracked the seven men positioned around the place. That was only what he could see from the front. He figured there were several in the back as well. All of them were dressed in black from head to toe, their uniforms very similar to Brantley's everyday casual wear.

They all wore weapons on holsters at their hip, and he got the feeling these guys weren't amateurs. They were alert, not on edge. Not once did they abandon their post.

Interesting.

"He's beefed up security, huh?"

"Looks like it," Reese muttered. "They're gonna pat us down."

"No, they're not." Brantley refused to kowtow to this asshole. Sure, Adorite had a reasonable expectation of safety in his own home, but here, in public, he wasn't going to get Brantley's full cooperation. And he damn sure wasn't going to get his weapon.

"And if they do?"

"They won't," he told Reese. "Let's get this over with."

Once out of the truck, Brantley ensured his weapon was visible as he approached the two guys flanking the front doors.

One of the two spoke softly with a hand to his ear, likely to engage a microphone on the earwigs they were wearing.

A moment later, the bigger of the two stepped forward. "Arms out."

"Sorry, guy. I'm not here to get felt up by one of Max's goons. I've got my holstered nine, a clutch piece at my ankle, and two knives you won't have a chance to see. As for the dog, she doesn't need a weapon. She is one. And if I had to guess, my husband's got his Glock and likely a clutch piece—a twenty-two, probably. I don't know for sure because I haven't had a chance to frisk him since I'm here to talk to your boss. But trust me, once I check that off my list of shit to do, I plan to go back to my hotel and do a very thorough strip search of this man right here." He pointed toward Reese and exhaled, still holding that inky black stare. "Now, I'd appreciate it if you'd let us in so we can get this over with. As you can see, I've got something far more exciting on my agenda tonight."

The two goons looked at each other. The one who had remained back by the doors lifted his hand to his ear again. A moment later, he nodded, both of them stepping aside to allow them through.

"Huh. Whad'ya know," he said as they walked into the restaurant. "It worked."

Expecting a response from Reese, Brantley looked over. He saw how red the tips of Reese's ears were and knew he was fighting the blush.

"It's okay, baby. I got it outta my system. I promise to be on my best behavior for the next…" He looked at his watch. "Ten minutes, at least."

Reese snorted.

The moment they stepped into the main dining room, a dozen men shifted into a stronger position around the perimeter of the space.

"They're not a threat," Max called out, getting to his feet and walking over to meet them. "I hear you've got plans later."

Brantley smirked, knowing that Reese's face was likely beet red.

"Are we the first ones here?" he asked, knowing they were, but wanting to get this underway. He wasn't in the mood for pleasantries or chit-chat.

"Three more just arrived. Travis called, said he'd be a few minutes late, and to start without him."

Interesting. The man hellbent on being there was now MIA. Hmm.

"Have a seat." Max stepped back and gestured toward the table that was set with linens and silverware, glasses and plates. "At the very least, you can eat."

"You cleared out the place, huh?"

"Not hard to do when you own it," he said dismissively, remaining on his feet as sounds came from the front.

Brantley took a moment to study Max. It still stunned him how young the guy was. When you think of *mob boss*, the images that come to mind were derived from movies and television. Most of those guys had age backing their experience. For Max, at thirty-six, he'd been the head of his family for going on a decade. What twenty-six-year-old could successfully run an illegal enterprise and make it considerably more profitable than when under its previous leader? Then again, his training would've come from childhood.

A few minutes later, Archer, Atticus, and Simon strolled in, none looking any worse for wear. Brantley could tell they'd been relieved of their weapons if they'd been carrying. He assumed they had because Atticus had been trained to keep his weapon with him at all times when working. Now Brantley needed to work on ensuring the kid learned how not to give it up if at all possible.

Max greeted each in turn, the four of them exchanging personal introductions. Brantley didn't even bother getting to his feet. He wasn't here to get cozy with a mob boss.

AFTER BEING OFFICIALLY INTRODUCED AND THEN SETTLING in at the table with the others, Simon had been informed that Travis and Gage were running behind. Since their presence wasn't necessary to get his questions answered, he figured it was as good a time as any to kick things off. Manners had him waiting until after drinks were served, but he didn't hesitate much past that.

"I'll preface this by asking if I can record," Simon watched Max, expecting a resounding no.

Max waved a hand. "Have at it."

Simon thought he hid his surprise well, but he wasn't entirely certain.

"But *I'll* preface," Max added, "by stating that if I don't like the direction, I'll confiscate the recorder before you leave."

Grinning, Simon nodded. "That's fair."

A few minutes passed while several servers came out to take orders and deliver another round of drinks and several appetizers. When the rush cleared, Simon turned to Max and tapped the button to record so that Max was aware.

"I'm not sure whether anyone has relayed our reason for being here, but I'll give you some of the details so we have a starting point."

Max nodded, then took a sip of what appeared to be scotch or whiskey.

"A friend of mine was doing research for one of his books, and he came across some information that referenced your family. There was an article quoting prior FBI statements claiming they had a witness who would testify to seeing you commit a crime."

Max didn't speak, but Simon had his full attention.

"This witness is Meredith Prescott. Does that name sound familiar?"

"No," he replied easily. "Can't say it does."

Simon had expected that. "She happens to be Travis's wife's mother."

"Estranged mother," Brantley noted.

"Yes, estranged. We don't have details yet"—at least Simon didn't think they did—"but it appears she might've left town to avoid testifying."

Simon knew that wasn't enough information to get Max talking. If he'd been in the man's shoes, he certainly wouldn't just start spouting about the past, fact or fiction.

"The issue we've run into is with the man who seems to be at the forefront of the investigation. Martin Calloway."

He could tell by the gleam in Max's eyes that he recognized the name.

"Do you know him?"

Max smirked. "I'm acquainted with Martin Calloway."

"We believe he's targeting your family and your businesses."

"That's been the case for as long as I can remember. I also know he hasn't come up with anything yet."

"Did Calloway know your father?"

"They weren't poker buddies," Max acknowledged.

"Is it safe to assume that Calloway's interest in you stemmed from an encounter he had with your father?"

"Why would you think that?"

"You mentioned he's been targeting your family for as long as you can remember. I assume that means since you were young."

Again, Max stared, not saying anything.

"From what we've found, he's personally targeting you."

"And your point?"

"It's got to be bad for business."

Max's dark eyebrows rose slowly. "I have ways of getting through the day without ruffling the FBI's feathers."

Simon wanted to ask for specifics, but decided to hold his tongue. He got the feeling his line of questions was starting to irritate the man. He did not want to risk setting him off before the main course.

FROM THE MOMENT ATTICUS WALKED INTO THIS restaurant, he felt as though he'd been tossed down the rabbit hole. Something about the entire thing felt surreal. Like he was witnessing it all from the safety and security of a dream.

Only, the guys standing sentry around the perimeter of the room really were wielding AKs and standing guard over their boss.

Funny that. Based on the way Brantley talked to Max—with absolutely zero respect—he wasn't aware of the army of men, or he simply didn't care.

Atticus knew he shouldn't, but he found that insanely hot.

"You don't sound worried," Simon said, watching Max as he'd been doing since he sat down at the table. It was like the guy was trying to catalog everything about Max so he could jot it down later.

"The FBI and every other alphabet agency have been out to take my family down for years. They've failed so far."

Another thing Atticus found hot and probably shouldn't … the way Max was so calm and so cool. For a man who needed an army to protect him from God only knows who, he was taking the whole thing in stride.

It was likely the reason the guy still looked so young.

Atticus had done his homework, so he knew Maximillian Adorite was thirty-six years old, and the current head of the Adorite Crime Family, a.k.a. the Southern Boy Mafia, having taken over when his father was killed a while back. Leyton Matheson, the acting underboss, was Max's childhood friend and was now married to Max's sister, Ashlynn. Over the course of the past couple of years, the organization had been restructuring, securing its foothold on the state in order to keep the Moroso Crime Family at bay.

According to data that Luca and JJ uncovered last night, the Adorites had control of a significant portion of northern Texas, including all routes into and out of all four bordering states—New Mexico, Louisiana, Oklahoma, and Arkansas. They did not control the pipeline from Mexico; however, they had established valuable relationships with several of the cartels.

Based on the fact that the media referred to them as the Southern Boy Mafia, Atticus had expected some sort of redneck hillbilly running the show. That was so not the case. Max and his five-thousand-dollar Armani suit were about as far from hillbilly as one could get. The man seemed to command respect by simply breathing. Add to that his somewhat laid-back personality, and this could've been any old Saturday night dinner among friends.

Minus the armed guards, of course.

"We don't need a dossier of your crimes," Brantley stated. "We know it's vast and long. What we need to know is whether you know anything about the guy leading the charge against you."

"What about Censorious?" Archer asked when Max didn't respond.

Atticus was watching Max, so he caught the slight tick in his jaw. Whether he would admit it or not, he definitely recognized the name.

"That's a name I haven't heard in a while," Max said with a grin. "They still around?"

"Seem to be," Simon said, his attention raptly focused on the mob boss. "They've been dormant for a while, but it appears they're fortifying ranks once again."

Atticus listened while they relayed all the information they'd uncovered in the past couple of days, clueing Max in on every single detail.

It wasn't until just then that Atticus wondered whether the whole relay of information was intentional. Give the mob boss the info and let him solve the problem himself.

Kinda genius if that were the plan.
But if it wasn't...

CHAPTER TEN

NEARLY HALF A MEAL AND HALF AN hour later, Travis and Gage finally showed up.

Brantley's frustration level was rising significantly, but he'd done a decent job of keeping it under wraps while he listened to Simon ask Max an endless list of questions. Surprisingly, Max had been relatively straightforward with his responses. Of course, Brantley had no idea how much truth there was to any of it, but he also didn't care. The last thing he was worried about was Max's business dealings. And definitely not those that didn't pertain to the case at hand.

However, when Travis walked in, the tension in the air seemed to rise. He found that interesting since Max greeted Travis with a quiet, private conversation, the two men shaking hands, the gesture longer than was usually appropriate.

Not that there was anything romantic about it, but there was certainly an intimacy between them. Shared history, perhaps.

Brantley watched his cousin as Travis took the seat across the table, Gage taking the one beside him. Neither revealed how they were feeling about this little get-together. Not by their countenance anyway.

"Have we broached the subject we came here for?" Travis asked, eyes zeroed in on Brantley.

Brantley met those hard, steel-blue eyes. "Did you think we were twiddlin' our thumbs, waitin' for you?"

Travis's gaze skimmed his face, but his expression didn't falter. It was clear he wasn't impressed with Brantley's sarcasm, but again, Brantley really didn't give a fuck. The last place he wanted to be on a Saturday night was having dinner with the man who had left Reese to bleed out on the floor of a restaurant in order to get his sister to safety. While Brantley wasn't known to hold grudges, he would never forgive Max for that. Not if he lived to be two hundred.

"Did you get the answers you were lookin' for?"

Brantley pointed at Simon. "You'll have to ask him."

Travis looked at Simon, raising his eyebrows in question.

"I'd like to continue the conversation." Simon looked at Max. "Perhaps privately when we're finished."

"I like that idea."

"Well, I've got a question for you," Travis said to Max.

"What's that?"

"When you were nineteen, did you kill a man?"

Max's eyebrows slowly rose, but he didn't answer.

"It's come to our attention that my wife's mother witnessed you kill a man. The FBI intended for her to testify against you, but she went MIA before that could happen."

Holding his fork over his plate, Max stared back at Travis, the silence in the space surprisingly loud. Brantley was mesmerized by the tension that seemed to stretch between the two men.

"We know she didn't witness it," Reese supplied, clearly concerned about the metaphorical rubber band that was being pulled to its limits, threatening to snap at any second.

Max's gaze slowly slid to Reese, but again, he didn't say anything.

"But we also know the FBI was lookin' to take you down by blackmailing her into testifying," Brantley said, wanting to get this conversation moving in the right direction.

Max nodded his head slightly. "Doesn't surprise me."

How did Brantley know the mob boss was going to say that?

IF WORDS WERE KNIVES, THOSE COMING OUT of Brantley's mouth would've slashed him to pieces.

Imagining that made Max smile.

On the inside, of course.

He knew Brantley was still pissed at him. Likely always would be.

Though Max was genuinely sorry about what happened to Reese that night, he wouldn't apologize for taking care of his family. He hadn't known Reese was in the restaurant when he sent Rock to get Madison. If he had … well, he wanted to think he would've done it differently, but he couldn't say that with any level of certainty.

"What is it you want from me?" Max asked, glancing at the group of men sitting at the table. "If you're here for me to give you my life story, it's not gonna happen."

"We're tryin' to determine whether Martin Calloway actually has somethin' on you," Brantley stated. "To take him down, we need to understand his motivations."

"I can assure you, I don't make a habit of taking care of personal matters in a way that might risk an audience," he told the big Navy SEAL. "I'm well aware that there are eyes on me constantly. So, no, your witness did not see me, or anyone I know, do anything illegal."

"Do you know of a reason why Calloway might have it out for you?"

"Aside from him leading the charge for the organized crime division of the FBI," Atticus added.

Max laughed. "Of course."

He took a sip of whiskey and glanced at all the faces looking to him for an answer. He didn't have one. Not one that they wanted to hear. Based on the curious glances, they expected him to offer up something that would make sense. But for that to happen, Max would have to admit that his psychopathic father had an affair with Calloway's wife many moons ago. And since Samuel had fucked pretty much anything with two legs and a pussy, it wasn't easy to keep up.

But Calloway probably would've dismissed that since he wasn't the faithful sort either. He had a penchant for prostitutes, and he was known to rough 'em up when the urge struck. But Max figured it was safe to say Calloway had been far kinder to his whores than Samuel had been. Not long after one of Calloway's whores gave birth to his bastard baby, Samuel had come along and strangled the life out of the woman.

So, no, Max had no desire to share that morbid tale of infidelity and sociopathic tendencies. The only reason he was even meeting with them was because he respected Travis. He'd already paid his debt to Reese by helping them to fake Tobias Land's death to protect him. Max didn't make a habit of being too generous. People tended to take advantage.

Rather than make up some bullshit that might help them sleep at night, Max said, "I don't know, gentlemen. You'll likely have to ask him."

ARCHER WALKED INTO THE HOTEL SUITE FEELING like he'd wasted the last three hours of his life. If it hadn't been for a damn fine meal, he would've wanted to get that time back. Aside from Simon's less personal questions, Max Adorite hadn't answered anything. Not with truth or fact, at least.

They had gotten nowhere, but Archer also wasn't sure what they thought they would actually get. Even if Max had admitted he did or did not kill a person when he was nineteen years old, there was no proof. Plus, they had a statement from Decker telling them that Meredith had not seen anything. She couldn't testify because she wasn't actually a witness.

Which meant Martin Calloway was out for blood and willing to do whatever was necessary to take Max down, and it likely had nothing to do with that fictitious reason. But murder would've sounded good to a jury, so that was likely why Calloway had come up with it in the first place.

Was kidnapping a woman and faking her death part of *whatever was necessary*? Or had Holt conjured up something that offered nothing more than wishful thinking and false hope?

"What's on your mind?" Atticus asked as the door closed behind them.

"I'm not really sure." Archer glanced at the minibar. "I sure could use a beer right about now. Want anything?"

"Beer's good."

Archer grabbed two beers from the small fridge. He used the bottle opener to remove the tops, then passed one to Atticus before taking a seat on the sofa.

"Did you learn anything tonight?" he asked Atticus as he tipped the bottle to his lips.

"I learned that a mafia boss can talk in circles."

Archer laughed. "That he can. But what did we think he was gonna say? *Oh, yeah. When I was nineteen? Sure. I killed a guy. A half dozen, in fact. Which one are we talkin' about?*"

Atticus grinned. "Well, he definitely did not say that."

"Nope. He told us nothing."

"But we told him everything. You notice that?"

Archer stared at Atticus. "That he managed to get every detail out of us? Oh, yeah. I noticed."

"You think that was the plan? To give him the info and let him deal with it?"

"I don't think that's what Brantley was hoping for. Travis, maybe."

They sat there for a few minutes, drinking beer. Archer replayed the conversation from memory, coming up with nothing of substance that would get them to their end goal—finding Kylie Walker, if she was, in fact, still alive.

Or perhaps their end goal was to take down Censorious.

Maybe both.

"We need a plan for tomorrow," Atticus said.

Archer glanced over, noticed his head was tipped back, eyes closed, his beer in hand, resting on his stomach.

"I agree. But I think we should tackle that in the morning."

"Good idea." Atticus made no move to get up.

Archer grinned. "Come on. Let's get some sleep. It's been a long coupla days."

As he spoke, he forced himself up, unable to take his eyes off Atticus. When the man shifted, eyes opening, Archer found himself staring into those interesting green eyes. He forced his gaze away, shaking off the strange feeling.

"See ya in the mornin'," he said abruptly before heading to his room.

"Set your alarm for six," Atticus muttered. "Let's try for an early start."

"Will do," he called back before closing the door behind him.

He leaned against the door, frowning. What the hell was wrong with him? He was not attracted to his partner. Not even a little.

Big ol' liar.

Fine. He found Atticus attractive. But that didn't mean he was *attracted to* him. Just that he was pleasant to look at. Plus, he enjoyed talking to the guy.

Shaking his head, he forced himself away from the door. Setting his beer on the dresser, he made his way to the bed, pulling his phone from his pocket. He checked his text messages, hoping he'd gotten one from Spencer in the past hour. He hadn't. He knew that as sure as he knew his own name.

Propping himself up on a pillow, Archer stared at his phone. He contemplated sending Spencer a message, then decided against it. He was not looking to play games at this point in his life. He wanted something real, something fulfilling, and while he'd hoped he might find that with Spencer, he knew better. They'd known each other such a short time, and Spencer had been playing games with him since the beginning. The writing was on the wall; he would do well to heed it.

Placing his phone on the nightstand, Archer stared at the door that separated him from Atticus. He wondered what the man was doing. Was he passed out on the couch? Too tired to get up?

Or was he in his room, talking to Slade?

And why the hell did he care?

"I don't," Archer muttered aloud. "I. Don't."

Maybe if he said it enough, he would believe it.

Or maybe he just needed some sleep because exhaustion had his mind going places it shouldn't.

CHAPTER ELEVEN

Brantley walked into the hotel room alone. He'd left Reese downstairs with Tesha, the two of them taking a short walk to give her time to do her business. Tomorrow morning, they'd toss the ball around after their run so she could get her daily dose of fun, but for tonight, Reese said a walk would be enough.

He probably should've remained with them, but he was having a difficult time harnessing his frustration. He was a live wire, flipping and flopping, ready to zap anything that he came into contact with.

Max fucking Adorite.

As was the case whenever he saw the man, or hell, whenever he so much as heard his name, he still wanted to wrap his hands around the bastard's neck and squeeze until the life slowly drained out of him. And it would be a slow, agonizing death. Brantley would make sure of it.

He hated himself for letting the guy get to him, but he couldn't help it. Seeing him reminded Brantley of everything he'd nearly lost. Worse, it pissed him off that he wasn't able to put it behind him, to stop dwelling on the past. He'd trained himself to do exactly that. To move forward without looking back. It had worked up to this point in his life, and he liked that he didn't hold grudges.

Yet for some reason, he couldn't let go of this.

Brantley sat on the edge of the bed, resting his elbows on his knees and dropping his head in his hands. He focused on breathing, trying to calm himself. They needed to sleep so they could put a plan into motion in the morning. He wanted to track down Martin Calloway and figure out what the bastard was doing. Determine whether he was holding Kylie in some safe house somewhere or if it was all a figment of Holt's overactive imagination.

The door lock beeped, signaling someone unlocking it. He sat up straight, watching as Tesha and Reese came in.

Without hesitation, Tesha trotted right to her bed on the floor and curled up in it, preparing for sleep. Exactly what Brantley should've done when he came into the room. The preparing for sleep part, at least.

Reese stood at the door, Tesha's leash in his hands. He seemed hesitant to come all the way into the room. Brantley didn't blame him. He felt like a caged animal about to chew through the bars.

Their eyes remained locked for several heartbeats, and Brantley had to assume Reese could detect the hunger flowing in his veins. And it damn sure wasn't for food.

"I need you," he told Reese, watching him, aching for him. "Can I have you, Reese?"

"Always."

"Then strip," he ordered.

One dark eyebrow cocked, but Reese didn't question the command or the brunt force with which it was delivered. He set the leash on the open suitcase before reaching behind his head and grabbing a fistful of his shirt, tugging it over his head.

Fuck, yes. That was what he needed. That sinful body. That *man*.

Brantley watched as Reese slowly stripped, removing every stitch of clothing that covered the body that was built for Brantley's pleasure.

From the first time he saw Reese naked, he'd been mesmerized. Long and lean, Reese was utter perfection. All toned muscle and sinew, he was strength and grace personified. From the planes and angles of his impressive chest to the perfection of his tapered waist and those chiseled oblique abdominal muscles.

Damn, but he made Brantley's mouth water.

And the fact that Reese belonged to him was not something he would ever take for granted.

"Come here," he instructed when Reese was naked.

His husband moved toward him, his powerful legs bringing him closer. When he was an arm's length away, Brantley reached forward, curling his fingers around Reese's erection, which was bobbing proudly, hard and thick. He pulled him by his dick, bringing him right where he wanted him.

"I'm hangin' by a thread," he warned.

Reese's golden eyes glittered with heat as he caressed the top of Brantley's head with one hand. "I know."

"I'm gonna fuck you."

The corner of Reese's mouth lifted. "I know."

"Hard. Deep."

Their eyes remained locked as Brantley stroked Reese's cock.

"I expect you to say my name when you come."

Reese shivered as he nodded.

Because he sensed Reese was trying to anticipate Brantley's next move, he decided to deviate from his original plan. Leaning forward, he took Reese's cock between his lips.

Reese palmed the back of his head as he moaned softly, his hips jutting forward, pushing deeper into Brantley's mouth.

Brantley sucked and licked, fondling Reese's balls for long minutes, distracting his husband until the time was right for him to do what he really wanted to do.

In one swift move, Brantley surged to his feet, grabbed Reese around the waist, and threw him to the bed, face down. A second later, he was on top of him, pinning him to the mattress with his full weight. He straddled Reese's thighs, pressing his aching cock against the hard muscles of Reese's ass, his chest against Reese's back. He nipped his earlobe, attempting to harness some of his self-control.

It wasn't easy. If it weren't for the fact he was fully dressed, he would've been inside Reese by now.

"I hate that bastard," Brantley said, his voice low and rough near Reese's ear. "I see red whenever I so much as think about him."

Reese tried to buck Brantley off, but it was clear he wasn't trying too hard. It took minimal effort to maintain control of the situation.

He pressed a kiss to Reese's shoulder, then clamped his teeth down.

"Oh, fuck," Reese hissed, his hips jerking.

"Hurt?"

"Yes." Reese gasped. "Do it again."

He did, biting Reese, leaving his mark on the man. For whatever reason, it pleased him to do so, made him feel a bit more in control. Every hiss, every moan that spilled from Reese was a reminder that the man was alive.

"Mine," Brantley groaned, licking the sting away.

"Yours."

Pressing his forearm across Reese's shoulder blades to keep him in place, Brantley reached down with his other hand, unbuttoning his pants, unzipping in order to free his cock. He shoved the cumbersome fabric down far enough so he could slide his dick between Reese's cheeks.

He spit in his hand, lubed the head of his dick as best he could, then began prodding Reese's hole, pushing in, retreating. Precum became a lubricant, allowing him to push in deeper.

"Fuck, you feel good," he groaned as Reese's body clasped him like a velvet fist. "So fucking good."

He was aware of Reese reaching beneath him, jerking his trapped cock in time to Brantley's thrusting hips. It didn't take long before his tenuous grip on his control snapped. He got to his knees, shoving his pants down more, then jerked Reese back with him. He dug his fingertips into Reese's hips as he held him in place and drove them both to that razor-sharp edge. He lingered there for long, blissful seconds as he chased that high that he only got when he was with this man.

When he reached the summit, he growled, "Come for me, Reese. Come." *Thrust.* "Right." *Thrust.* "Fucking." *Thrust.* "Now!"

With a groan, Brantley slammed into him one final time, his cock erupting, filling the man he loved. Reese's grunts and groans crescendoed at the same time, a signal that he'd launched headfirst into the abyss with him.

REESE LAY ON THE BED, BRANTLEY BONELESS on top of him. He was replete and content for the first time in hours.

Brantley kissed his shoulder. "Did I hurt you?"

"No," he said, because it was the truth.

"You sure?"

Rather than respond, he shifted his hand over Brantley's, where it rested on the bed. He played with the band on Brantley's ring finger, turning it slowly.

He'd known from the moment Simon had mentioned Southern Boy Mafia that this case was going to be difficult on all of them, but especially Brantley. He hated Max with good reason. Reese probably should, too, but his guilt didn't allow him to put all the blame on anyone else. And yeah, he still felt guilty about what he'd done: texting back and forth with Madison, meeting her for dinner. Looking back, he couldn't understand why he would've risked everything for a woman he hadn't loved. Sure, he'd thought he had at one point, but that was before Brantley came into his life and showed him what love really was.

So, no, he couldn't hate Max for sending Rock to Madison's rescue or for leaving Reese in that restaurant with a bullet in his chest. He blamed himself. He was the one who'd gone there, and that was the way the cards had fallen that night.

But here, now … he had let go of some of the guilt. Some, but not all. It would never fully disappear, but he didn't dwell on it anymore. He chose to appreciate what he did have and to be grateful he hadn't lost the most important thing in his life.

"I love you," he whispered.

"I love you, too, baby," Brantley replied, his hand moving so he could twine their fingers. "And I'm sorry."

"Don't apologize."

Brantley pressed another kiss to his shoulder. "You've got my mark on you."

"I'm sure I do." He would wear it proudly.

"What do you say we take a shower, then get some sleep. Maybe you'll wake me up for another round before we start the day."

"I think I can manage that," he said with a smile.

Six hours later, Reese was buried deep inside Brantley, staring down into his face as he fucked him. Slow, deep. It was the perfect start to any day.

"Good?" he asked, holding Brantley's stare in the mostly dark room.

Brantley nodded, not looking away.

Reese continued to rock his hips, pushing in deep, sliding out slowly. The friction on his cock was incredible, the tight clasp of Brantley's body perfection. He wouldn't complain if he remained just like this for the rest of his days.

Except that wasn't possible, so he continued driving them both higher until the plummet back down was inevitable.

"Come for me, Brantley," he whispered, his eyes shifting to where Brantley was stroking his cock.

"So close," he groaned.

Reese slammed his hips forward.

Brantley grunted. "Yes."

He did it again.

"Fuck, yes."

Again.

Brantley's jaw flexed as he gritted his teeth, his head tipping back. Reese continued to impale him, driving him right to the edge. He fought to hold on until…

"Reese!"

Brantley's orgasm triggered his, his hips slamming home one final time as he came with a rush that stole his breath.

He had no idea what the day had in store for them, but he knew for certain that nothing would be as good as that.

CHAPTER TWELVE

Sunday, October 2, 2022

TRAVIS STOOD IN THE HOTEL SHOWER, HANDS planted on the wall, the hot water beating down on the back of his neck. He kept his eyes closed, silently hoping for a moment's peace from the chaos that was running wild through his brain.

He'd slept for shit last night, tossing and turning, desperate for information while at the same time terrified of what it might entail.

Kylie alive? He knew it wasn't even possible. He'd *seen* her. Lifeless. Cold.

Dead.

His chest tightened the same as it had when Brantley hit him with that revelation yesterday morning. Since then, he'd been stuck in this mental vortex of memories. Everything was being stirred up by this warped sense of hope that he couldn't shake.

A single knock sounded, followed by, "You okay in here?"

Gage.

He didn't answer. He couldn't.

"Travis?"

Squeezing his eyes shut, he tried to shove off the memories that insisted on pummeling him. He refused to break down, refused to succumb to the pain that he'd finally managed to wrangle under control. For the most part.

There was only one way to fight his demons right now, so he stood tall.

"Get in here," he commanded Gage, his voice hoarse and rough. "Now."

His husband didn't respond, but he knew he was listening.

Travis waited patiently, focusing on his breathing, searching for that store of inner calm that he'd been depleting at a rapid rate in recent days. Just when he'd managed to settle into his new normal, to *accept* this fucked-up existence *as* normal, someone went and threw a wrench into the works.

He drew air in through his nose and blew it out slowly, turning when he heard Gage step into the large shower stall. Travis paused to look at the man. Really look at him.

At forty-two, Jason Gage Matthews was in his prime. He'd spent the past year and a half making drastic changes to his lifestyle, likely his only coping mechanism in the sea of chaos they now floated in. He was bigger, stronger, and yeah, more handsome than he'd ever been. And Travis only had to look at him to get hard, to ache, to need.

Travis grabbed Gage's forearm, slowly wrapping his fingers around it before pulling him close. Gage moved hesitantly, eyes skimming his face. It was clear he was attempting to gauge Travis's mood, to figure out what was about to happen.

He kept pulling until they were chest to chest, then he placed Gage's palm on his back, wanting to feel the man's touch. When Gage got with the program, his fingertips digging into Travis's muscles, kneading gently, he gripped Gage's jaw and slowly lowered his head.

"I'm holdin' it together with a rusted chain link," he admitted, his voice low.

"I know."

"I don't know how much longer I can do it, Gage."

"However long it takes."

Travis wished he had Gage's strength, his mental fortitude. "And if I can't?"

Gage pulled him closer, his other arm banding around him. "Then you let me catch you when you fall."

Those words caused his chest to tighten, his heart to swell. He loved this man with all that he was. Deep down, he knew Gage deserved better, and that was the reason Travis was fighting to be a better man. To be what his husband and kids needed. It wasn't easy when a piece of him was missing. A large piece of his heart had been chiseled off when Kylie died, and time did not seem to be healing those jagged edges.

Travis gripped Gage's face in both hands. Pressing his thumb to Gage's chin, he forced the man's mouth open. His eyes remained open until their lips met. Only then did he close them, giving himself over to the kiss as he slid his tongue inside Gage's mouth. He kissed him. Insistent, demanding. Showing Gage what he wanted, what he needed. As had been the case for years now, Gage already knew. He was right there with him, their tongues mating, hands roaming as the hot water poured down on them both.

As the kiss intensified, so did Travis's need. His hands became more insistent, clutching, gripping, controlling. It was his natural instinct to dominate, and he loved that Gage wasn't so quick to surrender. The fight in the man he loved stirred him, made him burn.

Before he even realized what he was doing, Travis had his hand around Gage's throat. He was squeezing. Not hard enough to hurt, but enough to control. Gage's eyes glazed, his lips parting as he stared back at him.

Without a word spoken, Gage stepped forward, pushing against Travis's hand, tightening his grip. When his back met the tile, Travis continued to watch him, waiting. The instant Gage went to his knees, Travis's control snapped. He grabbed two fistfuls of Gage's hair, staring down at him as his husband took his cock between his lips.

"Fuck yes," he whispered, loving that Gage knew what to do to soothe and torment in equal measure. "That's it, baby. Suck my dick." He grunted, pleasure surging in his blood. "Oh, sweet Jesus. Fuck that feels good."

Gage stared up at him as he took Travis to the root. Somehow, the eye contact made it hotter. Sparks of sensation danced at the base of Travis's spine as the pleasure took hold.

"You look good like that," Travis crooned. "On your knees. My dick in your mouth."

He inhaled sharply when Gage's hands cupped the back of his thighs, gripping firmly, kneading the muscles. His touch did that to him. Grounded him in the moment, kept him there.

The pleasure increased as the minutes ticked by. Travis let it build, pushing him closer and closer to the edge. When he was riding that fine line between pleasure and bliss, he tightened his hold on Gage's hair, stopping him. Fisting his cock with his other hand, Travis held off his release with sheer force of will.

"I'm gonna fuck your mouth. Hard," he warned.

Gage's eyes glittered hotly.

"Then I'm gonna come down your throat." He canted his head, studying Gage's face. "When I'm done, I'm gonna wash and you're gonna sit on that bench and jack off for me."

Gage's lips parted, his eyes rolling back.

Travis took the opportunity to shove his dick back into his husband's mouth. He did as he promised, holding Gage by the hair, he drove into his mouth, fucking his throat. He was rough, but he couldn't help it. He'd spent most of his adult life living with the frayed edges of his control. Somehow Gage managed to push him past that. Always had. And even now, after nearly nine years of marriage, he still did.

He didn't hold back, grunting and groaning as he sought the release that would reset him for a little while.

"Suck," he bit out. "Oh, yeah. Take me deep." He drove into Gage's throat and groaned. "Just … like … fuck yes. Take it all."

A rumble started in his chest and rattled its way up his throat, the sound rough as it echoed off the tile when he came down Gage's throat, his spine tingling from the electric current that arced through his body.

When he was spent, he helped Gage to his feet and kissed him. He gentled his touch, soaking up everything Gage offered.

"I love you."

"Yes, you do," Gage whispered, chuckling.

"Careful, baby."

"Or what?"

"Or I'll make you jack off until my dick's hard again. Then I'll bend you over and fuck you until neither of us can walk."

Gage's mouth turned up at the corner. "Promise."

With a groan, he kissed Gage. He felt reasonably better as he always did when he lost himself in the man he loved. The anxiety would return at some point—likely within the next hour—but for now, he would accept the reprieve.

GAGE WALKED INTO THE HOTEL RESTAURANT, LEAVING Travis in the lobby to take a call. He found Brantley and Reese at a table for four in the far corner, both with coffee in front of them.

"Hey," he greeted as he pulled out a chair. "Travis is on the phone with Sawyer. About the resort."

"Problems?"

Gage grinned. "Depends on who you ask. Travis'll say yes because he doesn't trust anyone to man the fort. Sawyer'll say no because he does a damn fine job of fillin' in for Travis when he needs to."

A waitress approached, smiling. "Can I get you something to drink?"

"Coffee." He held up two fingers. "Two, please."

"Sure." She glanced between the three of them. "Are you ready to order?"

"Not yet." Brantley nodded toward the empty seat. "We're waitin' for the lone holdout."

She giggled, though Gage wasn't sure it was meant to be funny. "I'll be right back with the coffee."

"So." Gage looked at Brantley. "I take it Atticus and Archer aren't joinin' us."

"They went to the training center. We'll meet up with them in a bit. I figured we could talk openly without them here."

"And by *openly*, you mean you'll give us your two cents on why you want us to go home."

Brantley lifted his cup, smirked. "Somethin' like that."

"Well, I'll tell you now that we *are* headed home. Shortly, in fact."

It was apparent that surprised Brantley.

"What you're doin' here ... it's important," Gage said, glancing between them. "And I know you're capable of doin' it without our interference." He held up a hand when Brantley would've talked. "I do want you to take the information I've got on Censorious. Give it a look. Maybe it'll help, maybe it won't. I don't know what your end goal is."

"Yes, you do," Brantley stated, his tone firm. "You don't want to believe it, and that's fine. I'm not sure I do either. But until I prove it one way or the other, I'll be workin' this."

Gage's gaze dropped to the table. He wanted to tell Brantley that there was absolutely no possibility that Kylie was alive. He knew because he had seen her after she died. He'd held her cold, lifeless hand. No amount of dedication to any cause would've brought her back to life. Not even a man who was hellbent on taking down a crime syndicate.

But he didn't say that. He couldn't. Denying what they were claiming felt sacrilegious. He was doing his best not to get his hopes up, but deep down, Gage couldn't help himself. He wished with all that he was that they were right. That somehow it could be true. That Kylie was alive somewhere, and they were going to find her and bring her home. By not denying that, Gage was putting it in God's hands.

"Here you are," the waitress said as she delivered two coffee mugs before refilling Brantley's and Reese's. "Are you still waiting?"

"No." Gage flashed a smile. "We can order."

The next few minutes were spent relaying what they wanted to the woman while she jotted it all down. Gage ordered for himself and Travis, knowing exactly what his husband preferred. They'd been together long enough, Gage pretty much knew what Travis wanted to eat on each day of the week. He was fairly predictable that way.

At least when it came to food. As for everything else, Travis was about as predictable as the stock market.

Travis appeared at the table moments after the waitress left.

"Sorry about that."

"No worries," Reese said. "Everything cool?"

"Probably. It's hard to know when I'm not there."

"I was tellin' them we're headin' back after breakfast."

Travis looked at Brantley. "I'm sure that makes you feel better."

Brantley smirked. "It does."

"Play nice," Gage said as he reached for his coffee cup. "Did you get anything worthwhile from dinner with Max?"

"Only that he likes to talk in circles," Brantley answered.

"That he does," Travis agreed.

"Keep in mind, he's got plenty of law enforcement in his pocket," Gage warned. "You don't get where he's at without it. He's got more than enough protection, which means he also knows who to talk to. If you were lookin' to incite the bear, you probably succeeded."

"That wasn't our intention," Brantley said. "But yeah. I see your point."

"I suggest you track down Martin Calloway before Max finds someone to wipe him off the map," Travis told Brantley.

"That's the plan."

Gage didn't bother asking whether he meant the former or the latter. Knowing Brantley, it could be either.

"I know y'all prefer we steer clear, and we will," Gage said before Travis could interrupt. "But if you need anything ... anything at all, you just need to call."

"Do you plan to talk to Meredith?" Reese asked.

Gage looked at Travis, who promptly answered with, "No."

"That's not necessarily true," Gage told Reese. "We're gonna talk to Braydon and Jessie when we get back. Let them know that she's there. If Jessie wants to see her, we'll figure out a plan."

"Just do your best to keep it on the DL," Brantley said firmly. "The fewer people who know about her, the better. We still don't know if feds are lurkin' about, waitin' for her to appear."

"We will," he confirmed. "You have my word."

"And if you get anything useful from her, I'd appreciate you lettin' us know," Brantley said, looking at Travis.

"Sure." Travis lifted his coffee cup. "Provided you do the same."

Gage noticed the way Brantley's features softened when he said, "Of course."

It was clear Brantley was on the defensive, but Gage didn't think it was because he didn't want them involved. If Gage were a betting man, he would've put big money on Brantley carrying around some misplaced guilt. Ever since Kylie's death, Gage had noticed the tension between Brantley and Travis. And while Travis didn't blame Brantley—none of them did—he got the feeling Brantley still saw himself as responsible.

He only hoped that one day that guilt would fade and they could get back to being friends.

That was all he could hope for because anything else ... was simply more heartache waiting to happen.

CHAPTER THIRTEEN

WHEN ATTICUS SUGGESTED THEY CHECK OUT THE Sniper 1 Security Training Center, Archer wasn't sure what to expect. He'd seen a number of facilities over the years used by operatives in one phase of their career or another. The only thing they had in common was that they usually had a gun range and some weight training equipment. Otherwise, the options varied.

But none of them looked like this one.

The large metal building housed what had to be the largest course he'd ever seen, not to mention a rather impressive simulation center, which, according to Atticus, was like a real-life experience.

"Let's see what you've got, Marine," Atticus joked as they stood in what could've passed as a warehouse with the stacks of metal box containers scattered throughout.

"I'm game if you are," he told his partner with a smirk.

Atticus quirked an eyebrow and flashed a smile. "You're on. Let's get the equipment."

He followed Atticus. "What equipment are we getting?"

"We'll do the virtual reality scenario. Not quite as impressive as the simulation room, but pretty damn cool. The gear is set to measure body temp, heart rate, and whatnot while you're in it. Plus, in the event you get shot, it'll let you know."

Interesting.

While they were getting set up with the gear—which included a dry-fit, long-sleeve shirt like the ones he wore to work out in and half a dozen sensors that were secured in strategic places to measure every move and every shot they took—RT and Z arrived.

"Good," Z said by way of greeting. "I was hopin' to get a demo of your skills."

"If you really want to see his skills, you'll have to put him in a perch a few thousand yards away," RT said, looking impressed.

Archer had never been interested in bragging about his shooting skills. Although Uncle Sam had trained him and honed his natural abilities, it wasn't something he was particularly proud of. While in the employ of the Marine Corps, he'd done the job they asked of him, and he'd done it well. Regardless of who had commanded him to take the shot, every kill was forever ingrained in his brain. And they weren't moments he relived if he could avoid them.

"Let's run the hostage drill," Z said, looking at Atticus. "You're in the lead on this one."

Atticus nodded.

Archer had to admit, he was impressed with Atticus's attitude. Didn't seem to matter to him who held the control in the situation; he was good at acclimating. According to the few stories Atticus had shared with him, that hadn't been the case until recently.

"Good luck," Z said before disappearing into a glass-enclosed control room, RT right behind him.

A moment later, Z's voice sounded through the earpiece Archer had inserted.

"The hostage is a twelve-year-old girl. Intel tells us she's bein' kept in a small room on the south side of the building, second floor. Heat signatures show three guards near the room, two making rounds on the exterior of the building, and five throughout."

"Exterior?" Archer asked.

Atticus pointed toward the large shipping containers that split the building in half. "This side of the containers is considered the exterior for the sake of the exercise."

"North, I presume?"

"Correct."

"Okay, then, team leader, what's your plan?"

Atticus walked over to a glass-topped table and tapped it. A blueprint of the "building" appeared, so he figured it wasn't a table, but rather a computer.

"If she's back here, I think our best bet is to move in from the east. As soon as this guard makes his next round, we'll slip in through here. We'll keep it quiet for as long as possible, so we don't alert them all."

Archer kept his attention on the screen as Atticus outlined exactly what they would do once inside.

"It's all virtual reality," Atticus explained, passing a pair of goggles that resembled the night vision ones he had at home. "And it's high tech. They will see you. They will shoot you." Atticus smirked. "And when they do, it hurts like a motherfucker."

"Roger that."

Once they were set to start, Archer found himself grinning. It had been a long time since he'd done anything like this outside of a video game.

A buzzer sounded overhead, signaling the start of the exercise.

Atticus started moving instantly, keeping close to the outer wall, ducking down behind several rows of metal barrels that were stacked three high.

Archer watched as a soldier passed by. He had an assault rifle propped against his shoulder, and he was puffing on a cigarette as he scanned his surroundings. He looked so real, Archer expected to smell cigarette smoke.

When the soldier continued his patrol, Atticus's voice sounded softly in his ear. "Three ... two ... Go."

Without hesitation, Archer moved with Atticus. He went on full alert, years of training kicking in. He kept an eye on Atticus, looking to take direction from the lead, while watching their six, ensuring no one was sneaking up from behind. When Atticus stopped, he stopped. When Atticus moved, he moved. They weaved their way through rows of storage containers set up to look like various rooms. They cleared them one at a time, encountering two soldiers. Atticus took one out with a knife, while Archer got the other in a choke hold and sent him to sleep it off for a bit.

He couldn't believe how real it felt, as though he'd actually met resistance when he was choking the guy out. How they did it, he had no idea. Wasn't sure he wanted to know because then it wouldn't be quite as cool.

Back in the hallway, they found a set of metal stairs that led up to the second floor. With hand signals from Atticus, Archer remained on the lower steps, keeping his eye out for anyone approaching on the first floor while Atticus ascended slowly, weapon at the ready. As soon as Atticus reached the first landing, a shot rang out.

Archer spun around in time to see Atticus take a bullet in the shoulder, knocking him back and down. He knew the blood was only a special effect from the virtual reality, but it was so fucking real, it caused Archer's blood pressure to increase.

From there, he went on instinct. He was up the stairs, positioning himself to protect Atticus, weapon aimed at the second floor. They were blown, so stealth was no longer an issue.

Mindful of the amount of ammunition he had, he traded gunfire with the man at the top of the stairs. He managed a shot to the guy's right leg, dropping him. As the shithead was falling to the floor, he got another shot to the head.

Then he was helping Atticus to his feet.

"I told you it hurt like hell," Atticus said, grunting.

"Don't take any more, 'kay?"

Atticus chuckled. "I'll do my best. Go on. Lead the way."

Archer headed up the stairs to the second floor. He followed the sight of his weapon, clearing the area. From somewhere nearby, he heard shouts and arguments, figuring it was the bad guys trying to figure out what to do next. Checking that Atticus was behind him, Archer continued forward, pausing at doorways, scanning the two rooms they bypassed for more baddies.

Before they reached their destination, they encountered another soldier, this one armed with a knife. Archer learned what Atticus was referring to when that knife sliced his right arm. He knew instantly that it didn't cause real damage, but the shirt he wore was designed to send a shock that simulated the pain he would've endured if it had been real.

To be honest, he would've rather taken the slice from the knife.

Ignoring the pain, he focused on taking the guy out. He was dodging and weaving to avoid another stick and lost his rifle in the melee. He spent far too much time entertaining the bastard before snatching his Sig from its holster and firing a shot to the guy's kneecap. Once he was on the ground, he put another in his head to end him once and for all.

With the threat eliminated, Archer holstered his Sig, picked up his rifle, and stepped over the body, continuing forward. He had the door in sight, but another soldier was standing in front, firing random shots in rapid succession and shouting obscenities. It would've been comical had Archer been watching it on TV.

"I'll distract him," Archer told Atticus. "You go low."

"Ten-four, good buddy."

It took effort not to laugh, but somehow he managed. He shouted at the soldier, surprised when the man stopped hollering incessantly.

"We'd just like to talk," Archer lied. "Do you think we could do that?"

"No!"

He should've known it wouldn't be that easy. It never was.

"What if I talk and you listen?"

"No!"

"All right. Don't say I didn't try." Archer leaned out of the doorway, flashing a grin at the soldier. The guy was surprised by the movement. Enough that he couldn't get his weapon raised before Atticus slid out into the hallway and took a shot that hit the guy center mass.

"Nice," Archer praised, wincing because his arm was still hurting from that virtual slice. He figured the shirt was continuing to send electrical pulses to simulate what an untended wound would feel like. He couldn't imagine what Atticus was going through.

When Atticus got to his feet once again, they hurried to the door of the room, flanking it on both sides. Archer met Atticus's gaze, waited for his instruction. When he got it, he reached down and turned the knob, shoving the door open. They took fire from inside the room. When it died down, the only sound was that of a girl screaming.

Because he didn't have eyes in the room, he couldn't take out the bad guy without risking hitting the girl. He needed a location to know where to aim.

Nodding his head toward the room, he silently urged Atticus to take a peek since he was in a better position to do so without taking a headshot. With his eyes on Atticus the entire time, he waited for a signal, informing him where the bad guy was.

Atticus used two fingers, signaling that he was on the right.

"And the hostage?" he mouthed.

Atticus signaled to the left side, then straight back.

Taking a deep breath, Archer took a chance, darting into the room, aiming his weapon, and firing. He took out the bad guy, dropping him with a shot to the neck. Atticus was right behind him, both of them holding their weapons at the ready. He had enough experience not to trust that the hostage was the one they were seeking. She could've easily been a plant—just another baddie looking to take them out.

Under the guise of loosening the ropes holding her, he checked for weapons. When he found none, he signaled to Atticus.

And the overhead lights came on. The pain in his arm disappeared instantly.

"Congratulations," Z said into his ear. "At least you're not dead."

Yeah. At least.

BRANTLEY READ THE STATS ON THE SCREEN as the exercise ended.

"Are you sure the sensor's readin' right?" he asked RT.

"It is." He pointed to the side of the screen reflecting Atticus's stats. "And look at this improvement. The kid's got somethin' a lot of people don't."

Yeah, he did. And surprisingly, Atticus was coming into his own in a very short time. Hell, since he'd gone through training, he'd done a complete one-eighty, and it was damn hard not to notice. It was one of the reasons Brantley had put him and Archer as leads on this case.

"They're comin' out," Z announced.

Brantley looked up to see both men grinning as they talked. He wasn't sure what was being said because the mics had been turned off, but whatever it was, it looked like they were having a good time.

Suddenly, Atticus stopped and began digging in his pocket. He pulled out his cell phone, frowned at the screen, then tapped it to take the call. He turned away.

Brantley headed out of the control room to talk to Archer, curious what the man thought about the training facility.

"Pretty impressive," he said as he approached the big guy.

Archer huffed a laugh. "You're tellin' me."

"I meant your score."

Archer's eyebrows rose slowly. "They were keepin' score?"

"Everything's scored or graded around here. Everything's measured."

"Figures."

"You and Atticus came in the top ten for that course and level."

"Lemme guess. You and Reese hold the number one spot."

Brantley grinned, not bothering to answer.

Archer shook his head, rolled his eyes, and grinned. "Of course you do. Navy SEAL."

Nudging his chin in Atticus's direction, Brantley asked Archer, "Who's he on the phone with?"

"One of his old contacts up here. We're tryin' to track down an address for Martin Calloway."

Brantley was impressed. "Any luck?"

"Hopefully. We thought we could have someone follow him while someone else does recon on his residence, if we can get an address. If not, I figure we'll have someone stake him out at his office, then follow him to see where he goes from there."

"Good idea." And Brantley liked that Archer hadn't assigned himself to the task. It showed his ability to delegate.

"We've also asked Evan to go to the motel and talk to Meredith Prescott. I'm not sure she knows anything, but it won't hurt to have him interrogate her a bit."

"Sometimes you don't even know what you know until someone asks the right question."

"Agree. And he's takin' Becs with him. Hey, man." Archer nudged his chin at someone behind Brantley.

"Hey," Reese said as he joined them. "What's up?"

"I was just tellin' Brantley that Evan's gonna go talk to Meredith today."

Atticus strolled up, causing Archer to pause.

"Any luck?" Brantley asked him.

Atticus frowned, then glanced at his phone. "Oh, yeah. Right. Actually…" His gaze slid to Archer. "He said there's been hush-hush rumors that Censorious is back in business and currently in the middle of acquiring a new top-level."

"Who said this? And how do they know?" Reese asked, his attention darting between all the faces.

"I've got a contact who works for the *Dallas Morning News*. He's one of their fact-checkers. I asked him about Martin Calloway. Rumors specifically. He said they've been lookin' into them for the past couple of months. Ever since word got out that they've regrouped." Atticus looked at Archer. "I think we should get Simon on it. See what he can find out."

Archer nodded. "Sounds good to me. I was just givin' them an update."

"Don't stop on my account."

Brantley fought the urge to smile. He was a bit surprised at how naturally the two of them worked together. He had expected some hesitation as they worked to determine which was the more dominant partner. It was interesting to see they were somehow managing a relatively balanced structure. It kinda reminded him of how he and Reese worked back in the beginning. Their personalities complemented one another, allowing them to get shit done without a lot of bickering.

"We've asked Charlie to do a thorough analysis on Allison Bogart, going back as far as she can. A conversation would be better, but we need to locate her first," Archer explained. "We're not sure if she's still in Coyote Ridge, but it's worth finding out. A sit-down with her is in order."

"Agree." Brantley glanced between them.

Archer continued. "Jay will be doing a deeper dive on any information the team comes up with. If we find out Allison's got a partner, he can dig into it. We might be able to get some info from them once we identify who they are."

"Oh, and JJ emailed this mornin'," Atticus added. "Said Baz is gonna talk to the doctor today. She's currently runnin' background on him, but what she's found so far is probably enough to nail him to the wall." He grinned. "Her words."

Yeah, Brantley was glad he decided to put them on this.

"What would you like us to do?" Reese asked.

Archer looked at Atticus, nodded.

Atticus was the one to answer with, "We discussed it this mornin' and we thought it best if the two of you stake out Martin Calloway. We're workin' to get a home address for him, but so far, no luck. We do know where he works, so if you want to start there."

Brantley looked at Reese, waited.

"I'm good with that." Reese looked at Archer. "I'll need you to take Tesha. She's good on stakeouts, but I hate to do that to her if I don't have to."

It wasn't the first time he'd seen a man's face light up the way Archer's did. Like a giant kid on Christmas morning. He saw a version of the same every day on Reese's face. It was almost amusing how excited a grown man could get about being partnered up with a dog.

"He's got a list of her main commands," Brantley told Archer, fighting the urge to laugh. He kept to himself the fact that the list was on a notecard. And it was laminated.

"What about you two?" Reese asked.

"We're gonna do some recon on Decker," Archer said without hesitation. "Thought we'd check out where he grew up, see if we can talk to anyone who knew them back then. Since he's the one who said Martin Calloway blackmailed his father as well as Meredith, it makes me believe he's the nexus. I want to see if we can get some clarification. Due diligence and all that."

"And we're hopin' to track down Allison Bogart's parents, see if we can get anything out of them," Atticus added.

Brantley nodded. "Sounds like y'all've thought of everything."

"Have you gotten an update from Luca?" Atticus asked.

And apparently, it wouldn't be long before Atticus was taking over the team. The kid was on top of everything.

"He texted me a little while ago," Brantley told him. "They don't have anything yet, but he's workin' with Slade. They'll be talkin' to some people today."

At the mention of Slade's name, Atticus's gaze shot to the ground. Brantley was curious what was going on between those two, but decided now was not the right time to inquire. They had too much to do to worry about personal bullshit.

Twenty minutes later, they were in the truck, headed to Plano to stake out an FBI agent.

"I find it interesting that this particular field office handles government corruption," Reese said, staring at his phone.

"Ironic, huh?"

"The fact that you used *ironic* correctly is ironic," Reese teased. "But yes, it's most definitely ironic. I guess if you're in charge of locating guilty parties, it's easy enough to cover up your own crimes."

"True. What information do we have on Martin Calloway?"

"Give me a sec." Reese grabbed his laptop from the back seat and propped it in his lap.

Brantley let the navigation system direct him where to go, glancing every so often at the screen to see how much time until their arrival.

"All right," Reese said. "Here we go. Holly started doin' a deep dive on this guy. Martin Calloway. Sixty-three years old. Married for the second time. First wife died in a car accident eighteen years ago. He's been married to the second for…"

Reese looked up.

"For?" Brantley prompted, not sure why the sudden silence.

"Seventeen years, eleven months."

Ah. Well, yeah. He could understand it now. That did sound a little … planned.

But rather than jump onto another conspiracy bandwagon, Brantley went with something less likely, but definitely a possibility. "Maybe he just falls in love fast. Could be completely coincidental."

Reese laughed. "Yep. Because we believe in coincidence."

"We believe that not everything's a conspiracy," he countered. "Like I said, maybe he falls in love fast. What else? He have kids? Grandkids?"

With his attention back on the computer screen, Reese continued. "He's got five kids. Two with the first wife, two with the second."

Brantley waited for the rest, but nothing came.

"Hey, I know I'm not a mathematician or anything, but I'm pretty sure two plus two does not equal five."

"I'm lookin'. Hold on."

Why did that seem to be the theme of his day?

CHAPTER FOURTEEN

REESE KNEW BRANTLEY WAS GETTING ANTSY. HE didn't like to sit still when they were in the middle of a case. Unfortunately, at this point in the investigation, they were pretty much starting over at square one each day. Until they had a strong line to pull on, they were sifting through the fibers one at a time, building something from nothing.

At least that was how it felt.

Which sucked.

However, the information he was searching for could quite possibly help explain a whole lot of things. If it was what Reese thought it was.

Reaching for his phone, he pulled up the contacts, found Holly's number, and dialed.

"Hey. How's Dallas?" she greeted, sounding far happier than he expected anyone to be on a Sunday morning when they had to work.

"Peachy," he said absently. "Sorry. No time for chit chat. I need you to do somethin' for me."

"Sure. What's up?"

"In your notes on Martin Calloway, you've referenced a sealed adoption. I need you to reach out to JJ and see if she can get the information for me."

"Your faith in me is humbling, Reese."

Frowning, he looked up, stared out into the bright morning sun as Brantley drove down the highway. "I'm sorry. I just figured you hit a wall since you left it like that."

He could hear the smile in her voice. "When have you known me to hit a wall?"

"Umm…"

"It was rhetorical. I did actually hit a wall, but I went down another path, not wanting to bother JJ or Luca yet. I wanted to give it the ol' college try before I threw in the towel."

"And...?"

"And I came across a dark web forum that—"

"Hold that thought," he interrupted. "Let me put you on speaker." He tapped the button to shift the call to speaker. "Okay, Holly. Go ahead."

"Hey, boss," she greeted Brantley. "Anyway. I came across a dark web forum. It's packed full of people lookin' to find the identity of their birth parents. Some lookin' for the child they gave up. For a price—sometimes hefty—someone'll do the work for you."

"Why would someone do that? Why not just have the record unsealed?" Reese inquired. "Or isn't there some form you fill out that notifies the other party that you're lookin'?"

"Maybe you go here when you don't want to tip off the parent or the kid? I don't know. Whatever the reason, I was able to chat up a couple of people, and they pointed me in the right direction. From what I can tell, Martin Calloway had a child with a prostitute named Shawna, no last name. She gave birth to a girl on April 6, 1995, in Kent, Louisiana. According to notes from a social worker ... I managed to sweet-talk my way into gettin' those ... neither Martin nor Shawna wanted the baby. She was given up for adoption and placed with her new parents when she was three days old."

"Do you have the parents' names?" Brantley asked.

"I do."

Reese ground his molars together, hoping against hope that she did not say—

"Fred and Tracey Aronda."

Brantley's gaze snapped over so fast, Reese was sure the guy was dizzy.

"Did she say what I think she just said?"

Reese nodded.

"I take it those names mean somethin' to you?" Holly asked.

"Fred and Tracey Aronda are Juliet Prince's parents."

He was met with silence for a few seconds before Holly said, "Holy schnauzers. Are you sayin' that Martin Calloway is the biological father of Juliet Prince?"

"That's what *you're* sayin'," Brantley corrected. "Are you sure that information's correct?"

"Yes. But I'll gladly reach out to JJ with what I know. I'm sure she can backdoor her way into the adoption record to confirm."

"Do that," Reese said. "Please. We need to be solid on this."

"Does it make that much of a difference?" Holly asked. "I mean, Juliet Prince is dead."

"Yeah. And there's a better than good chance that Calloway's aware of that."

"I'm sorry. I'm lost. How does that change things?"

"Well, it's rather simple, Holly," Brantley said slowly. "If Kylie—"

Reese reached over and smacked his palm against Brantley's chest, cutting him off. He shook his head, warning him. They hadn't clued the team into the information they had on Kylie.

"Are you there?" Holly asked, sounding confused. "Did I lose you?"

"We're here," Reese said. "Sorry. There's an accident on the highway. Brantley needs to focus."

"Oh. Okay."

"Send that over to JJ. Have her confirm it."

"Will do. I'll let you know what we find out."

"Later," he said, then disconnected the call.

Before Brantley could instruct him to do so, Reese dialed JJ's number. It went to voicemail, so he left a message regarding the information Holly had relayed to them. He informed her to do the search, but to keep the information from Holly for now. He hated to do that, but until they had some sort of confirmation that Kylie Walker was alive, he didn't want to get anyone else's hopes up.

"I think it's safe to say this isn't a coincidence," Reese told Brantley.

"No. It's not. It's motive."

Yeah. And that meant Kylie—provided she really was alive—could've been taken for reasons far more sinister than to take down the Southern Boy Mafia. If Martin Calloway took her for that purpose, then that meant he'd been aware of what was going on when they were attempting to find Juliet.

"What if Calloway took Kylie to cover up Juliet's crime?" Reese mused aloud.

"Makes sense. He could've done it to keep her from bein' prosecuted. His attempt to protect her."

Reese nodded, seeing how that could be possible. "And if he found out that Max had a hand in Juliet's death..."

He didn't need to finish that sentence. Based on Brantley's expression, he was on the same page. Which would mean that Calloway could've suspected that Travis had a hand in it, too. They were friends, right? Which meant there was a damn good chance Calloway had kept Kylie as payback.

And wouldn't that be a bitch?

BRANTLEY FOCUSED ON THE ROAD AS HIS mind raced, tossing around this new information in an attempt to make sense of it all.

He didn't believe in coincidence. There was no fucking way that any of this shit simply fell into place. Hell no. Not this.

"Back to our initial assumption… Let's say Calloway jumped on the opportunity to lure Meredith out by fakin' Kylie's death," he mused, tapping his finger on the steering wheel. "He took her, intending to give her back if and when he strong-armed Meredith into testifying against Max."

"I'm with you," Reese said.

"Considering her injuries—" His phone rang, cutting him off. "It's JJ." Brantley tapped the navigation screen to answer the call. "Yeah?"

"Hey," she greeted, sounding like JJ: no-nonsense with a hint of a smile in her voice. "I've got some info on the good doc."

"What is it?" he prompted, trying not to sound too urgent.

"Well, let's just say he's a man who lives above his means. Way above. Probably has to do with the fact he's got two ex-wives and six kids. Pays a pretty penny in child support and alimony. Add to that a couple of mortgages and an affinity for fast cars…"

Brantley waited, knowing she would eventually get to the point.

"What's interesting is that on January 9, 2021, the day Kylie *died*, Dr. Timothy Weaver got a quick fix to his money woes in the amount of five hundred thousand dollars. It came from an offshore account that's listed under a shell company that's tied to half a dozen more. I'll get to the root, but it's gonna take me some time."

"Does he still work at the hospital?"

"Oh, yeah. Like nothin' ever happened. Baz is on his way to talk to him now. He told me I had to sit this one out when I threatened to put him in a box until he agreed to tell me everything."

"A box, huh?" Reese chuckled.

"A small one. With only a teeny hole for air."

Brantley shook his head, smiled. Leave it to JJ to add some levity to the situation.

"What are you two up to?" she asked.

"We're headin' to the FBI headquarters to see if we can get eyes on Calloway."

"On a Sunday?"

"It's a long shot, but it's all we've got right now. If we get lucky, we'll follow him for a bit, see if he takes us anywhere interesting."

"Like directly to Kylie?"

"We don't know that he actually took her," Brantley reminded her. *Or that she is alive.*

"Then I guess it's one giant coincidence that Dr. Weaver got a boatload of money on the day she died. Maybe he got it from the estate of his long-lost friend, the Nigerian prince who was so indebted for his friendship that he left him everything."

"What Nigerian prince?"

Reese snorted. "She's bein' facetious. It's an email scam."

Brantley frowned. "Or maybe it's a legit inheritance."

"I was joking, B."

"No. I'm not talkin' the Nigerian prince." He waved a hand. "I'm talkin' a legit inheritance. You might check to see if his mother or father passed away."

"I did and they didn't," JJ insisted. "Trust me when I tell you that money did not come from anything legal."

"Doesn't mean he'll cop to it," Reese noted.

"Baz can be persuasive," JJ said, a smile in her voice.

Brantley let Reese take over the conversation.

"Did you get my message about Juliet Prince's adoption records?"

"What adoption records?"

Clearly she hadn't listened to her messages.

"Holly uncovered some information that shows Martin Calloway had a baby with a prostitute, and Fred and Tracey Aronda adopted that child."

"Holy shit. I guess I *should* listen to the message."

"Do that," Brantley instructed. "And then find out if it's legit."

"If it is, that makes it even more likely that Kylie's alive," JJ surmised aloud. "Calloway might be holdin' her as payback."

"What's he gettin' out of it by keepin' her?" Brantley asked, genuinely curious. "At this point, he should've used her as leverage."

"Maybe he's waitin' for somethin'," JJ answered. "If he's banked everything on Meredith testifying—which he'd have to be really stupid or really desperate to do that—then maybe he's got her stashed away somewhere."

Or there were a dozen other plausible explanations. None of which Brantley wanted to think about. At the moment, they were running on blind faith that she was alive. Until he had some sort of proof, he had to stick to the facts.

"If he does, we'll find her," Reese said.

Brantley heard the doubt in his husband's tone.

"Let me do some diggin' and I'll get you what I can," she replied. "When Baz gets back, I'll have him call you with an update on Weaver."

"Thanks, JJ," Reese said.

"Yup."

The call disconnected.

Brantley glanced down at the speedometer, realizing he was doing nearly twenty over the speed limit. He lifted his foot off the gas pedal, dropping back down.

"We're gonna figure this out," Reese said. "Let's deal with the information we have first. We'll proceed from there."

Brantley nodded. "Call Archer and Atticus. Give them an update. They're the ones leadin' this shit show."

Reese's warm hand landed on his arm. "We're gonna figure it out."

"I fuckin' hope so."

Baz walked into the private office of Dr. Timothy Weaver.

He'd already been through the emergency department in search of the man, but was told he wasn't on duty for another hour. According to one of the helpful nurses, Dr. Weaver was handling a few calls in his office.

And sure enough, the doctor was sitting behind a big mahogany desk, glasses perched on the tip of his nose while he stared at his computer screen.

"Dr. Weaver?"

The man looked up, eyes wary. "Yes?"

"My name's Sebastian Buchanan. I work for Sniper 1 Security. We're lookin' into a case and your name came up."

His salt and pepper eyebrows dipped low as he pulled his glasses off his face. "I'm not sure I can help you. Doctor/patient confidentiality and all that."

"Oh, I'm pretty sure that doesn't apply in this case."

Since the good doctor didn't suggest he take a seat, Baz took it upon himself to get comfortable, a move that clearly made Dr. Weaver nervous.

"A little over a year and a half ago, a woman was brought in after she was struck by a car. According to what you told the family, you did everything you could, but you could not save her."

That got his attention, but it only added more worry lines to his brow.

"Kylie Walker." Baz paused, waiting to see if Dr. Weaver would recognize the name.

He did.

Yeah, he definitely did, but he attempted to hide his initial reaction with a frown. "I'm sorry. That was quite some time ago. I don't recall."

"Oh, come on now, Doc. I can tell by those deep grooves"—Baz rubbed his forehead for emphasis—"that you know exactly who I'm talking about."

The doctor smoothed his expression. Or tried to. "No, I'm sorry, I really don't."

"Well, let me see if this helps." Baz leaned forward, resting his elbows on his knees and pinning the doctor with a cold stare. "On January 9, 2021, the same day you pronounced Kylie Walker dead, you received a hefty chunk of change into your bank account." He cocked an eyebrow. "Does that ring any bells for you?"

Dr. Weaver had the good sense not to comment.

"Yeah. I thought it might." Baz took a deep breath, reined in his anger. "See, here's the thing. Kylie Walker's husbands—she has two, that wasn't a blunder on my part—and her five kids … well, see, they miss her. And we came across some information that leads us to believe she's not in that coffin in the ground like we originally thought."

That hint of worry turned into a full-blown case of fear. Dr. Weaver's eyes widened, and his mouth opened, but no words came out.

Baz sat up straight. "I take it you know something."

Dr. Weaver shook his head adamantly. "No. No, I don't." He pushed his chair back and shot to his feet. "I've got rounds. You really need to leave now."

Baz slowly stood up, looked at the door. "Rounds? Oh, okay, sure. Let's go make rounds. I can follow you while you work. We can continue our conversation."

A sheen of perspiration broke out on his forehead, and the doctor was talking fast when he said, "You can't. That's not allowed. I don't know anything. I don't even remember who you're talking about. That was so long ago."

Baz smirked, waiting for the doctor to run out of excuses.

"And I never got a deposit of five hundred thousand."

Holding up a finger, Baz cocked his head. "See, I never said how much that deposit was for."

"Yes, you did. You said a hefty chunk of change. Five hundred thousand."

"No. I purposely left that part out."

Dr. Weaver moved toward the door, but Baz intercepted, blocking him before he could make his escape.

"I have rounds," the doctor repeated.

"As long as you don't mind having a shadow because I'm not leaving until you tell me what I need to know."

"I don't know anything."

Baz stared into his eyes. His pupils were dilated, and a single drop of sweat started to trickle down his left temple slowly. He would bet good money that the man's heart was racing and his palms were sweating.

"What was the money for, Dr. Weaver?"

"I don't know about any money," he said, his voice trembling.

Baz took a step back. "Is that your final answer?"

Dr. Weaver looked relieved when he said, "Yes."

Nodding, Baz turned toward the door. "When you're ready to talk, come find me. I'll be talking to the nursing staff and the hospital's administration. I'm sure someone can tell me what that deposit was for."

He took one step forward before Dr. Weaver barked, "Wait!"

Baz slowly turned around to see the man wiping his forehead. "Look. I was sworn to secrecy, so there's not much I can tell you."

"Sworn to secrecy? By who?"

"The federal government. The person you're talking about was a federal witness who was taken into custody."

Son of a bitch.

Baz tried to keep his heart from galloping out of his chest, but it wasn't easy. "Why?"

"The FBI didn't say. They just told me that it was pertinent that she *died* that day. They were setting her up with a new identity. I don't know what it is."

"You're telling me that Kylie Walker did *not* die that day?"

"I'm telling you that the FBI told me I couldn't talk about it."

"What proof do you have?"

Dr. Weaver's eyebrows slammed down. "What proof? There is no proof. When someone goes into witness protection, they do what's necessary to keep it under wraps. No paperwork."

Baz snorted. "Are you saying you falsified a death certificate on good faith that they were telling you the truth?"

"I had to."

"And you didn't find it strange that the *federal government* was willing to pay you five hundred thousand dollars for your cooperation?"

"They said it was the normal fee."

Oh, Jesus Christ. Surely this guy wasn't as stupid as he pretended to be.

"Who did you work with at the FBI?"

Dr. Weaver turned back to his desk. "I don't remember. But I've got his card."

Baz waited while the doctor shuffled through papers in one of his desk drawers. A minute later, he produced a card, passed it over.

MARTIN CALLOWAY

ASSISTANT SPECIAL AGENT IN CHARGE

Yep. That would be the guy.

Fuck.

Gesturing toward the office, Baz urged Dr. Weaver backward. "I've got a few more questions, and you'd better have some damn good answers."

On his way out of the hospital half an hour later, Baz called JJ.

"Tell me you found something," she said, sounding chipper.

"I definitely did."

"Did Dr. Weaver cop to bein' paid off?"

"He did. Said he was given instructions to stage her death because she was a federal witness going into witness protection."

"Holy shit. What do we do now?"

"Well, I think you should call Brantley and give him a heads-up. Since we've got some time before we can see the babies, I'm gonna run over to the funeral home."

"I'll do some diggin' real quick. See what I can find. They would've gotten a payoff, too, huh?"

"I can't imagine they could've gone through the process without realizing they didn't have a body."

"What if they did? Have a body, I mean."

Baz frowned, pausing at the door. "You think they sent one in her place?"

"It makes sense, right? They'd have someone to bury so they wouldn't ask questions."

He shook his head, pushing the door open. "And what? They just convinced the family not to have an open casket? No, I think they were in on it."

"You're probably right. Let me work on it. I'll let you know. Love you."

"I love you, too."

CHAPTER FIFTEEN

WHEN ATTICUS PULLED INTO THE TRAILER PARK, a flood of memories hit him as he navigated through the potholes and cracked concrete, passing the rusted metal houses. This place felt eerily similar to the trailer park his grandmother had lived in when he was a kid.

Most of these were in desperate need of repair, some likely should've been condemned already. Every sixth one looked as though someone cared for it enough to add some homier touches, such as the bright yellow flowers in a homemade window box or mulch around a skinny tree in the yard.

He wondered what it had looked like when Decker lived there. The same? Or was it now rundown from time and lack of interest or means?

"You see any numbers?" Atticus asked Archer.

Tesha's head popped up between the seats as though she was going to be the one to give him direction.

"A couple. Keep going." Archer scratched Tesha's head. "Based on what I'm seeing, it'll be at the end of this street on the right."

They could've walked the neighborhood easily. All three streets ran parallel to one another, roughly ten houses on each side, for a total of fifty to sixty trailers. Maybe less because there were a few empty lots sprinkled in. Or perhaps they weren't empty, and the grass was just too high to see what was buried within.

"According to what Luca found the other day," Archer noted, "Decker's father passed away two years ago. The house shows to be in Decker's name now, and it looks like someone's paying the rent on the lot. Trailer is paid for."

Was Decker paying for it? Did he have a sentimental attachment? Or just didn't have time to get by and clear it out?

Those were questions Atticus didn't think they would get answers to. Decker Bromwell did not seem like the forthcoming type.

"This is it," Archer said, pointing toward a freshly painted trailer with cream-colored siding and maroon trim. This particular single-wide mobile home was considerably newer and not metal. By *considerably*, Atticus figured it had been new sometime in the late 90s, while the majority of the others would've been constructed in the early to mid-80s.

"Looks like someone's keepin' up with the place," Archer said. "And keeping the yard mowed."

There weren't any homey touches on this one, but the yard was mowed, the shrubs—what few there were—had been trimmed.

Was Decker doing that? And why bother when the rest of the neighborhood looked like the weeds were attempting to swallow it up?

The driveway was wide enough for two cars, but there weren't any parked there. The concrete was stained from years of leaking oil. Beside the driveway was a mailbox that looked like it had been replaced recently.

Archer got out first, helping Tesha out of the back seat. Atticus moved more slowly, glancing at the trailers across the street, wondering if any of the current occupants had lived there when Decker was a kid.

When he joined Archer and Tesha on the path to the door, he said, "Let's knock. Maybe he's rentin' the place out."

Archer remained on the path with Tesha while Atticus walked up on the small wooden deck that passed as a porch. The storm door looked new. Cheap, but new. There was no doorbell, so he opened the screen and knocked on the front door.

After a minute, it became evident that no one was going to answer.

"We'll check the back," Archer said, slipping around the side of the house with Tesha prancing at his side.

Again, Atticus looked around, attempting to act as though he was supposed to be there. A short time later, the front door opened, and Archer appeared.

"Definitely vacant." Archer stepped back so Atticus could join him.

"Did you pick the lock?"

"Well, I wasn't crawling through the window."

That particular mental image made Atticus smile. He could just see Archer stuck in the window, giant shoulders wedged, his ass hanging out.

Closing the door behind him, Atticus stepped into the dimly lit room. New blinds covered the windows, keeping the sun at bay. Or maybe they'd put them up to keep prying eyes from checking out the place. There was new carpet in the living room, and new laminate wood flooring in the kitchen and hallway. It smelled like fresh paint.

"Not much to it," Archer said from somewhere off to the right. "Two bedrooms, one bath. There's furniture back here."

Atticus made his way down the narrow hallway, past a bathroom which looked like it had been gutted and redone, and a small, recently carpeted bedroom on the right. At the end was another bedroom, likely considered the primary in a house of this size. It had been painted, and the new carpet extended in there as well. The furniture was new: a full-size, white lacquer bed, a matching dresser, and a nightstand. On the dresser, a black jewelry box sat on top of a white doily. On the nightstand, there was a pink, wind-up alarm clock and a lamp with a frilly shade. The plush white comforter and pillows decorating the bed still had creases from the packages they'd been in.

"I don't get it," Atticus said, slowly spinning to take it all in. "Why furniture in here?"

"Looks like it's girl's furniture, at that," Archer noted. "And I already checked, the kitchen's empty. No dishes. There's some toilet paper under the sink in the bathroom and a set of towels—new with tags—hanging on a bar. Other than that, nothing. No soap or toiletries."

Why would Decker keep this? And why would he furnish only one room?

"Do you think this was his room when he was a kid?" he asked Archer.

"Could've been. If his dad was on the road all the time, maybe he got the big room."

Atticus could see that. But it didn't explain the furniture. He doubted this was the style Decker had when he was a kid, so he likely wasn't trying to recreate memories.

Archer went to the nightstand, opened the top drawer. Atticus watched as he reached in and pulled out a picture frame. After glancing at it, Archer passed it his way.

"That looks like Meredith," Atticus said, studying the image of a woman holding a baby. "Why does he have a picture of her holdin' a kid?"

"Only one she had?" Archer mused.

Yeah, maybe. When Kylie or Jessie were babies? Maybe Decker wanted a picture of her, and that was what she opted to give him? Seemed odd, but so did a lot of other things about this case.

And this room.

"Check the back of the picture," Archer suggested. "See if there's a note on it."

It took only a second to pry the photo from the frame. He flipped it over. "Someone noted the year as 2006. And there's a name. Cicily Rose. Three months," he read.

"Definitely not Kylie or Jessie." Atticus looked up at Archer. "Is that…?"

"Decker and Meredith's kid?"

"Yeah." Could it be?

"2006 would've been the year after she left," Archer stated. "And that would make the kid about sixteen now."

Atticus looked back at the photo. "Decker would've been what? Twenty-one, twenty-two when the kid was born?"

"Something like that," Archer confirmed. "But we didn't find anything about a kid."

No, they hadn't. And they'd done a reasonably thorough investigation on Decker and Meredith. At least he thought they had.

Atticus looked at the room. "Surely he isn't keepin' this house for her."

"I'll send the information to Evan and Becs," Archer stated. "See if they can talk to them about the girl."

Nodding, Atticus took a quick picture with his phone before putting the photo back in the frame and into the drawer before closing it. He texted the image to Becs so she would have it.

"If he has a kid, do you think he's been in her life?" Atticus mused, not expecting a response. "Did Meredith raise her? While on the run?"

"Maybe she wasn't on the run," Archer said, following him as they made their way to the front door.

"You think she ran away to have the kid?"

"A question we should probably ask her."

Yeah. At least with the photo, maybe Evan would have some leverage to make the woman talk.

"Come on, girl," Archer said to Tesha as he pushed open the front screen door. "Let's see if anyone in the neighborhood'll talk to us."

"I'll go across the street," Atticus told him. "You take this side."

131

They went their separate ways, but their attempt to talk to people proved futile. Either no one was home, or they simply didn't want to be bothered. Atticus tried four houses before giving up. When he returned to the truck, Archer was giving Tesha water.

Archer stood when he approached. "How'd it go?"

"Nothin'."

"Same here."

Atticus looked around one more time, swearing he saw a curtain move in the trailer across the street. He stared until he assumed his eyes were playing tricks on him.

He made a mental note to swing back through if they didn't come up with a better lead to follow.

"Where to now?" Archer asked when they were back in the truck.

"I want to drive by the high school." He started the engine, began navigating the bumpy road again. "Get a feel for where those two met."

"You're a visual guy, huh?"

Atticus glanced over, smirked. He was proud of himself for not popping off the first thought that came to mind. *I prefer to be the watchee, not the watcher* didn't seem like the appropriate thing to say to your new partner. No matter how hot the guy was.

And damn if Archer Halligan wasn't fucking hot.

EVAN WALKED OUT ONTO THE FRONT PORCH when he heard Becs's car pull up. He had called her half an hour ago and asked if she wanted to go with him to talk to Meredith Prescott. With Slade off helping Luca, he would've had to go solo otherwise. While he wasn't opposed to working alone, he found that they could cover more ground when there were two of them. And in this case, it would likely work in his favor to have a female with him. Becs might put Meredith at ease.

"Hi, Mr. Vaughn," Carly, Becs's nine-year-old daughter, said as she skipped by him into the house.

"Hey, kid," he greeted, his attention lingering on the driver's side, waiting for Becs to make an appearance.

When she stepped around the car, coming into full view, he did his best not to ogle. Not an easy feat for a man who'd been lusting after this woman for months now. It took every ounce of his self-control to pretend otherwise, and from what he could tell, he was doing a relatively good job. Becs was still giving him the cold shoulder after the argument they had in New York back in August.

Not that he blamed her. It had taken a conversation with Kaye for Evan to realize how badly he'd fucked up. Since his mother wasn't an idiot, she'd picked up on the tension between him and Becs and had called him on it. He'd explained it rather poorly, in his opinion, but that hadn't stopped Kaye from telling him he was at fault for sending mixed signals. Evan had been angry with her at the time, probably because she'd told him something he already knew, and the guilt was weighing him down.

However, he was doing well to stick to his guns when it came to keeping her at a distance. Becs needed someone who could give her everything she wanted, not merely the things she needed. Since the death of his wife, Evan hadn't felt like he was capable of giving anything to anyone.

"You ready?" Becs asked, not looking directly at him.

That was her thing now. Ever since New York, Becs had done her best not to be alone with him. He'd fucked that one up but good. And he was paying for it every single day, having to see her, having to work with her, and not being able to get close again.

It was nothing less than what he deserved.

"Yeah. Let me tell my mother."

He pivoted on his heel and headed back into the house. He went directly to the kitchen, pouring out the rest of his coffee and rinsing the cup before setting it in the sink.

"You need anything before we go?" he asked Kaye, who was sitting at the table with Sophie and Carly, getting ready to put together a puzzle.

"We've got it all under control," she answered, peering up at him. "You two have fun."

"It's work, Mom."

She smiled. "Doesn't mean it can't be fun."

Shaking his head because he knew what she was really saying, Evan glanced at his daughter. "Bye, Soph."

"Bye, Dad. Have fun," she said without looking at him, her full attention on getting the puzzle pieces spread out.

"We should be back in a couple of hours."

When no one responded, he assumed they had it covered, so he made his way back outside, where Becs was waiting for him.

"My car or yours?" she asked, her gaze shifting just over his right shoulder.

"Depends. You want to drive?"

"Not really."

"Then we'll take mine."

The forty-minute drive to the motel where Meredith Prescott was holed up was as uncomfortable as the conversation about who was driving. He tried to make small talk at first, but when it became as tedious as threading a needle with your eyes closed, he gave up. It wasn't until they were pulling into the motel parking lot that Becs finally spoke up.

"I guess they didn't spring for luxury accommodations."

No, it didn't appear they had. "Maybe Travis is a penny-pincher."

"Not according to Atticus," Becs said with a grin. "They've got a suite in a fancy hotel."

Did they now? "You talked to Atticus?"

"I talk to him all the time," she said absently. "We're friends."

Of course they were. Why wouldn't they be? That was another thing that had changed since New York. After Becs had invited Atticus to check out the sights with her, they'd become tight. He told himself there was nothing to be jealous of since Atticus was gay, but sometimes his better angels simply didn't listen to him. He was. Jealous. Not because he worried she'd fall in love with Atticus. He was jealous because Atticus got to see her smile, hear her laugh, talk about the things that were important to her. Evan wanted that back, but he was too much of a coward to admit it.

"You ready?" she asked, her hand on the door handle.

"Yeah," he said reluctantly, wishing he could find a way to get their relationship back to the way it had been before he'd felt the pleasure of her kiss. Unfortunately, he'd spent hours and hours trying to come up with a way, but he never got very far. Whenever he thought about Becs, he thought about kissing her, about the way he wanted nothing more than to strip her clothes from her body and ravish every inch of her.

Not that he would let her know that. He preferred for her to go on being mad at him while he secretly pined for her. She was safer that way.

With a sigh, Evan got out of the car when Becs did. He followed her up the stairs to the first weathered door on the second floor. She knocked softly, then took one step back and a few to her right, keeping space between them while they waited for Meredith to answer.

The door opened, and Decker's face appeared. He looked the same as usual. Like he'd been sucking lemons for the better part of his life.

"What do you want?" His gaze snapped back and forth between them.

"To talk to Meredith."

He shoved the door open, letting it hit the wall. "Have at it. I'm done talkin'."

"Where are you going?" Meredith called after him when he stepped outside.

"To get some air. Talk to them, Eddie. Let's get this done so you can go home."

Evan was watching Meredith, noting how she looked like he'd punched her in the stomach with those words.

He found their interaction interesting, to say the least. After how defensive Decker had been about his relationship with her, Evan would've put money on them still being together.

That did not appear to be the case.

"My name's Rebecca, and this is Evan," Becs introduced, keeping her voice soft, non-threatening. "We work for Brantley and Reese. Would you mind if we came in?"

"Of course." Meredith gestured toward the small table and two chairs. "Please. Have a seat."

Becs stepped around the table, taking the chair closest to the wall, leaving the one near the door for him. Evan shifted it around, then eased into it while Meredith perched on the edge of the bed, her attention lingering on the door as though Decker might come back through it.

"How are you doing?" Becs asked, sounding sincere. "This must be difficult for you."

Meredith's eyes skimmed Becs's face, as though she was looking for her ulterior motive. "I'm fine. I'd be better if I wasn't confined to this place."

"Hopefully it won't be for long," Becs said. "Brantley and Reese just want to take the appropriate precautions to keep you safe."

"So I hear."

"We need to ask you a few questions," Evan told her, wanting to get this over with.

"About what? I really don't have anything to tell you."

They'd see about that.

"When you left—originally—why did you leave?" He figured it was best to just lay it out there. He didn't want to pussyfoot around, pretending he was here as a friend. He wasn't. They had a job to do, and in order to do it, they needed to get this woman to open up.

"I needed a change," Meredith said, not looking him in the eye.

"From?"

"My life."

"You up and left two kids and a husband because you were what? Bored?"

Meredith shrugged. "Maybe."

"Lie."

Her eyes snapped to his face.

He got her attention at least.

"Look. We don't have time to play games. I get that you don't know who to trust, but right now, we're about as good as it gets. Now let's try this again. Why did you really leave?"

She took a deep breath and let it out in a huff, her shoulders slumping as she did.

Just when she was about to answer—with another lie, based on the purse of her lips and the glance to the left—Becs's phone buzzed. She would've ignored it, but Evan nodded toward the device sitting on the table between them. From where he sat, he could see Atticus's name on the screen.

Becs picked up the phone and tapped it. Her eyes widened, and she turned it toward him so he could see a photograph that Atticus had sent.

He had received a text from Archer earlier, but no picture to go with the brief details. Before he could ask Archer about it, Becs had pulled up in front of his house.

Turning the phone, Becs flashed the screen in Meredith's direction. "Who's the baby in this picture?"

Meredith's eyes widened, and her hand went to her mouth. "Where did you get that?"

"Who is it?" Becs repeated.

Tears formed in Meredith's eyes when she looked up, meeting Evan's gaze first. "That's—"

The door opened and Decker stepped inside. His attention shot to the phone Becs was holding up, then his expression shifted, morphing into something you'd see in your nightmares.

"Where the fuck did you get that?" he bellowed at Becs, taking a step toward her.

On instinct, Evan got to his feet, making it impossible for Decker to get to her. "Back off."

Decker glared at him, then lunged to the right. "You back off. Where the fuck did you get that?"

Evan blocked him again, this time putting his hands on Decker's chest and shoving him back. "I said. Back. Off."

From behind him, Becs said, "Cicily Rose. 2006."

If the kid was born in 2006, that made her sixteen or so.

"Is that your daughter?" Evan asked Meredith.

"No," Decker answered, still glaring at him.

It was then that Evan realized Decker's eyes didn't hold anger or fury as he'd initially thought. Oh, no. What he saw there was significantly worse.

That wasn't rage. It was pain.

Which meant he'd nailed it in one. That child in the photo wasn't just Meredith's daughter. She was Decker's.

CHAPTER SIXTEEN

BACK IN THE HOTEL ROOM, JJ HAD her laptop and Baz's set up on the desk. She had a search running on his for any information on Juliet Prince's adoption. Someone hadn't wanted that information to be found based on how deep she had to dig. The fact that Holly had gotten as much information as she had proved that she was coming along in her training.

It made JJ proud.

But it wasn't enough to acknowledge that Martin Calloway and Shawna had a child and gave her up for adoption. They needed to know more. Like who Shawna was and what happened to her. If they could find her, she would likely have a wealth of information to share. And if she was still a prostitute—probably old and withered at this point—it would likely only take money to get her to spill.

Unfortunately, JJ was having no luck finding the woman who had birthed that child. She'd found a social security number, but it appeared someone had stolen her identity at some point, so what she was finding didn't appear to belong to Shawna at all.

Which meant she needed to dig deeper into Martin Calloway.

But not yet.

At the moment, she was manually sifting through the life of one Walter Gallagher, director of the Gallagher-Hightower Funeral Home.

It was an exciting life from what she could tell. Walter was divorced from wife #1—had been for six years—and in the process of getting a divorce from wife #2, whom he'd been married to for less than three. At seventy-two, it appeared good ol' Walter had another future Mrs. Gallagher already picked out if his social media was anything to go by.

"You dog, you," she muttered, tapping some keys to get into the really interesting part of his life: his finances.

It took a bit of creativity to cut through some firewalls, but JJ managed, as she usually did. And when she reached her final destination, she sat back and grinned.

"Pay dirt!" JJ thrummed her fingers on the desk. "Man oh man, Walter. You're not only rollin' in it—which explains the thirty-year-old girlfriend—but you've got your hand in some yucky, yucky pies."

Grabbing her phone, JJ pulled up Baz's number and dialed.

"Tell me you found something," he said in greeting.

"I found something."

"Is it gonna make this conversation enjoyable?"

JJ smiled. "I'd like to think so."

She rattled off the details she'd unearthed as quickly as she could, not wanting to keep Baz from talking to the man. They only had so much time before visiting hours, and she knew he wanted to spend as much time with the babies as she did.

"That works," Baz told her when she finished. "I'm gonna head in now and insist he talk to me."

"Good luck. Call me when you're done."

"You can count on it."

When the call disconnected, she stared at the screen, wondering how the hell so many crooked people could exist in the world.

"Once we've found Kylie, I think I might revisit you, Mr. Gallagher. You and Dr. Weaver. It's high time you both made a considerable contribution to a worthy charity."

Stretching her fingers, JJ settled in to do a little more digging. This time, she was going to go right for the devil himself.

WHEN HE DISCONNECTED THE CALL WITH JJ, Baz got out of his truck and looked around. The parking lot of the funeral home was large enough to cater to big groups. There were a few spots up near the building marked for family, and a few that didn't have a designation. He had opted for one of them. Based on how empty it was, he didn't think it would be a problem.

He considered going in and pretending to be interested in a funeral package. But if he did that, he would likely have to talk to a salesperson, and he was interested in going directly to the top. A quick call a short while ago had told him that Walter Gallagher was in, so he hoped he didn't get the run around.

Opening the door, he was greeted by soft music and a large open space. In front of him, at the far back of the building, he could see floor-to-ceiling, stained-glass windows through a set of large wood doors that were propped open. The room also had rows of pews sitting in front of a podium.

On his side of those doors was an enormous lobby with a few decorative chairs and tables on each side for people to sit should they need to. Off to the left, there was a desk currently occupied by a blonde with big blue eyes and a wide, friendly grin.

She got up from her seat and started toward him. "Good morning. My name's Lacey. Can I help you?"

"I'm here to speak to Mr. Gallagher."

She smiled brightly and sounded cheerful when she asked, "Do you have an appointment?"

"I do not."

That smile immediately flipped upside down. It was a dramatic flip, the kind one might use when talking to a small child. "I'm so sorry. Mr. Gallagher doesn't take meetings without an appointment."

Baz kept his smile in place, though he knew it didn't reach his eyes. "He'll need to make an exception today."

"I'm sorry, but—"

"Lacey?"

"Hmm?"

"Could you please get Mr. Gallagher? You can tell him I'm here to discuss Kylie Walker."

"Is she scheduled for a funeral?"

Baz considered pushing past her, but maintained his cool. "Please. Mr. Gallagher. Now."

It was obvious that it pained her to do so, but Lacey turned and walked away. She disappeared down a long hallway, then through a door on the left. Because he wanted to ensure Mr. Gallagher didn't make a run for it, Baz stood at the mouth of the hallway and watched the exits, both the one he came through at the front and the one at the end of the hallway.

Lacey appeared a moment later, nodding her head as she backed out of the room. She hurried toward him, her smile long gone.

"He'll see you." She pointed down the hall. "First door on the left."

"Thank you."

Not wasting time, Baz followed her directions and ended up at the doorway to a large, elaborately decorated office. And by *elaborate*, he meant ugly.

The older man—he presumed Walter Gallagher—pushed back his chair and slowly got to his feet. His nearly snow-white hair was brushed back, his thick eyebrows ungroomed. His dark blue suit had thin silver pinstripes that matched the silver shirt beneath. His silk tie was slightly askew, but a perfect match to the suit.

"I'm Walter. How can I help you today?"

Baz stepped forward. "My name's Sebastian Buchanan. I work for Sniper 1 Security. Your name came up during one of our investigations. Would you mind answering a few questions?"

"I can certainly try, but I can't promise I'll know anything. Lacey informed me that you want to talk about—" He waved a hand. "I apologize. I've already forgotten the name."

Baz watched Walter's face closely when he said, "Kylie Walker."

There. The way his eyes squinted and his jaw ticked. It told Baz that he recognized the name. It also told him that the next words out of Walter's mouth would be a lie.

"I'm sorry. The name isn't familiar."

Baz gestured toward one of the chairs. "Mind if I sit?"

He didn't wait for Walter to answer before stepping around him and sitting in the chair closest to the door. It forced Walter to come around his desk.

"What is it you need to know about … is Kylie a female name? Or male?"

Baz sighed as he leaned back and propped his ankle on his knee. "You can cut the shit, Walter. We both know you're well aware of Kylie Walker. Or maybe you just remember her name because it came with a rather large sum of money into your bank account on January 9, 2021."

Walter's bushy eyebrows snapped down. "I beg your pardon."

"Beg all you want. I know you received the money. And I can likely assume you've got a business card in that desk of yours. It'll be from an FBI agent who asked you to do something for him."

Walter stared at him for a moment, his light blue eyes skimming. He was buying time, probably trying to figure out if he should keep lying or give up the ghost.

Baz knew which he preferred.

Unfortunately, Walter went the opposite route. "Again, I'm sorry. I don't recognize the name."

Baz stood and walked to the door. He leaned out, projecting his voice down the hall. "Lacey! Could you please come in here?"

"What are you doing?" Walter asked as he got to his feet.

He moved much faster than he had when Baz walked in.

"Since you don't remember, I figure I'll ask Lacey. I'm sure she can look at the books, can't she?"

"Of course not. She handles sales."

"Did you need me, Mr. Gallagher?" Lacey asked when she came to the door.

Baz watched the interaction. Lacey definitely wasn't the future Mrs. Gallagher. For one, there wasn't a ring on her finger, and two, she looked terrified to talk to Walter.

"Never mind." Walter waved her off. "Go back to your desk."

"Yes, sir." She backed out, her gaze darting to Baz briefly before she looked down and hurried back down the hall.

"Close the door," Walter insisted.

Baz stepped back into the office and closed the door.

"I just remembered who you're talking about. She was a special project that I dealt with. No one else on staff was aware. I was working with the FBI and was ordered not to share any information with anyone."

"And they paid you?"

"Yes. A very small, reasonable amount to handle the appropriate paperwork. Five thousand, if I recall correctly."

Baz sighed. "Try seventy-five thousand. And you didn't handle paperwork, you faked a funeral."

For the first time since Baz walked in, Walter was speechless.

"Tell me this: how did you manage to convince the family to keep the casket closed?"

Walter pursed his lips for a second. "I informed them the family would likely be upset by the condition of the body. There were small children, I believe. They would've likely been distraught if they saw her."

"Is that what you were told to say?"

"Yes."

"Is there a body in the coffin that your crew lowered into the ground?"

He shook his head as he opened the top drawer of his desk. He rummaged for a moment, then produced a card. "This is the man you need to speak with. He informed me this was a matter of national security."

Baz took the card, but he didn't bother to look at it. He already knew Martin Calloway's name was on it.

He was the bastard responsible for all of this.

MARTIN CALLOWAY WAS SITTING AT HIS DESK in his home office when his phone rang. When he wasn't at the FBI field office, he had the calls rerouted to his private line or his cell phone, depending on where he was. Since the private line was ringing, he knew the call wasn't personal business.

"What?" he barked.

"Mr. Calloway?"

Forcing calm into his tone, he said, "Who is this?"

"Walter Gallagher. I'm with Gallagher-Hightower Funeral Home."

Martin didn't recognize the name. "What can I do for you, Mr. Gallagher?"

"You told me to call if anyone came around asking about Kylie Walker."

He sat up straight, an odd buzzing in his ears.

Gallagher. Gallagher.

Ah, yes. The funeral home director who'd been more than happy to accept a generous bribe to do his bidding.

Choking back the anxiety that threatened to choke him, he said, "And did they?"

"Yes, sir. He just left. Said he was with a security firm. They're investigating something. He didn't say what, just asked a bunch of questions."

"Did you tell him anything?"

"I told him the truth."

For fuck's sake. Was it too fucking difficult for people to make shit up these days? When you told them not to mention a thing, they somehow heard the opposite.

But there was nothing he could do about it now.

"Thank you for letting me know," he told the man whose name he'd already forgotten.

"Is there anything I need to do?"

"Yes. Don't talk to anyone else. Send them my way."

"Of course, sir."

Martin hung up the phone without saying goodbye. He was reaching for his keyboard when his cell phone chimed with a sound he wasn't familiar with. He glanced at the screen to see a security alert.

"What the fuck?"

He tapped the link in the notification, and it brought him to a service he had signed up for a long time ago. It would tell him if and when someone ran a search on him. Something beyond what the usual credit bureaus allowed.

"Son of a bitch."

He grabbed the phone receiver and dialed.

"Hello?"

"Allison, I need your help."

As usual, she sounded entirely put out by him. "With?"

"Someone's running a search on me."

"And this surprises you?"

"Look, girl. You can stop with the smartass comments. You know what's at stake if you don't do what I need you to do."

Her response was silence.

"Now, I want you to figure out who's running the search and what they're trying to find."

"I'll see what I can find out."

"Don't fuck with me, Allison."

She sighed. "I'll call you back, Martin."

He didn't get a chance to tell her that she'd better. He heard the telltale click of the disconnect, causing him to slam the receiver into the cradle.

He did not like people digging into shit that was none of their business. Especially not now when so much was going wrong.

CHAPTER SEVENTEEN

ATTICUS GLANCED AT HIS PHONE WHEN IT buzzed. It was a text from Becs.

> 💬 I'll get back to you. Meredith and Decker went nuts when they saw the photo.

He read the message out loud to Archer.

"Wonder why?"

"Maybe he knows we got it from the trailer." That was the only logical conclusion Atticus could come up with. If Cicily Rose was their daughter, there would be no reason to get upset about it. Unless, for some reason, no one was supposed to know about her.

"Yeah, maybe. We need to do some background on her," Archer suggested. "See if we can find out where she is."

"I asked Becs to do that, but it sounds like she's busy."

"What about Charlie?"

"She took on looking into Allison. She texted about an hour ago, said she was following a lead on her location."

"That sounds promising."

Atticus had thought so, too. He wasn't sure what information Allison could provide, but she was tied into this somehow. Considering they'd determined Calloway was blackmailing her, there was a good chance she wouldn't tell them anything.

"At the very least, we'll know where she's at. Anything from Brantley or Reese yet?"

"Nope."

"Well, it is Sunday. I'm not sure there's a lot going on at the FBI office."

Yeah, Atticus had thought of that already. They'd come up on a weekend expecting to nail down leads without much to go on. Besides what they'd found at Decker's trailer, they weren't getting very far.

"You hungry?" Archer asked.

"Yeah. Sure. What sounds good?"

"You like Mexican food?"

"It's one of the main food groups, right?"

Archer chuckled. "I knew there was a reason I liked you."

Doing his best to ignore the way those words made him feel, Atticus grinned. "You have a place in mind?"

"Actually, I do."

A couple of minutes later, after Archer had entered the information into his phone's navigation, they were following the instructions to a place Archer said would knock his socks off. Atticus wasn't sure about all that, but he figured it beat fast food burgers and fries.

Nearly an hour later, they'd all but licked their plates clean and were getting ready to pay the bill when Charlie called.

"Hey," Atticus greeted, putting his finger in his right ear to block out the noise. "Hold on just a sec. I can't hear."

"I'll take care of this," Archer said. "Meet you outside."

Nodding, Atticus headed for the door. When he stepped outside, the din of conversation subsided, replaced by the beep of a horn, the gunning of an engine, and the occasional shout from nearby. Typical Sunday in downtown, he figured.

"What's up?" he asked Charlie as he stepped away from the restaurant door.

"I found her," she said, sounding excited.

"Do you have eyes on her?"

"No. Sorry. I … uh … I'm at home with my mother. But I was able to track one of her credit cards. She's here."

"Here as in…?"

"The Austin area. South, to be exact."

"How far south?"

"I don't have it nailed down just yet, but she's used her credit card at a couple of places in Johnson City and at another in Dripping Springs. I'm not familiar with those areas, but I can tell you they aren't too far apart on the map."

"Can you tell what's down there?"

"I'm guessing a member of Censorious. I was looking at the spreadsheet Simon started this morning, and he shows one of the members lives in Blanco. Maybe she was hanging out down there."

Maybe.

"Can you tell when she was in Coyote Ridge last?"

"She doesn't have any charges here or close to here that I can tell. If she's been in town, she's payin' cash or not spending anything. I'm gonna see if I can get her cell phone pings next."

So she wasn't keeping an eye out for Meredith? Was someone else? Were they even worried about Meredith anymore? It had been nearly two years since Kylie died. What would make them think she'd come back now?

"Atticus?"

"You happen to get any information on her parents? I was hopin' we could chat with them while we're up here."

"From what I can tell, her mother moved to Arkansas a couple of years ago. And her dad … he's in prison."

"Prison?" How the hell had he missed that during their initial search?

"Yep. Armed robbery."

Sounded like a great guy.

"If you track Allison down, do you think you could trail her for a bit?"

"I wish I could," she said, sounding sincere. "I need to stay here with my mom."

Atticus knew Charlie's mother suffered from dementia and they'd had problems with her wandering off.

"Understood. I'll give Slade a call," he told her. "See if he can spare some time."

"I'll send you the stores where she used her card. If I can shuffle some stuff, I'll let you know."

"No worries. Thanks, Charlie."

As soon as the call ended, he dialed Slade's number. He was surprised when the man answered. He thought for sure he was going to be ignored.

"Hey. Any chance you can follow up on a lead for me?"

"What lead?"

"Allison Bogart. Charlie was able to track her down. I'd like to get eyes on her."

"Sorry. No can do."

"Why not?"

"I'm busy. You know. Doin' my job."

Frowning, Atticus tried to rein in his temper. "This case takes precedence."

"And you've got the whole team at your beck and call. Everyone but me. Sorry. I'm workin' with Luca."

Atticus was about to argue when Archer stepped out of the restaurant. Not wanting his partner to hear him go off on Slade, he decided to let it go.

"I'll find someone else. Thanks."

He didn't wait for Slade to say anything before disconnecting.

Archer eyed him cautiously as he approached. "What's goin' on?"

Atticus relayed the information Charlie had given him, explaining that she wasn't able to follow up, and neither could Slade.

"What about Evan?"

"I'm gonna try him next."

"You care if I drive?" Archer asked.

Atticus palmed his keys, considering it. "Sure. Why the hell not?"

He tossed the keys to Archer as they made their way down the sidewalk toward the lot they'd parked in a couple of blocks over. By the time they got to the truck, he'd gotten a response from Evan letting him know that he and Becs would be glad to assist as soon as they were finished talking to Meredith and Decker.

"Hopefully they'll find her and get her to talk." Archer moved the seat back to accommodate his long legs. "And if not, we could always check out early, head back down, follow her ourselves."

Yes, they could. They were in charge of the case, and since Brantley and Reese were currently tasked with finding and following Martin Calloway, there wasn't much for them to do in the area.

Since their options were extremely limited, Atticus said, "Let's go back to the hotel, review what we've got, and figure out a plan of action."

"Sounds good to me."

As Archer drove, Atticus stared out the window and thought about Slade. More specifically, his lack of respect when it came to his authority on this case. It shouldn't matter that they were sharing a bed on occasion; Atticus deserved more than to be dismissed because Slade was in a mood.

Then again, did he expect anything less?

Becs had been surprised when Evan called that morning, asking if she would accompany him into the field. They hadn't talked much lately. Not unless it pertained to work. As his analyst, she did her best to accommodate his needs while being mindful that her personal feelings for him had no bearing on her ability to work with him.

She had to give herself credit. She was doing well to pretend she didn't have a dull ache in her chest where he was concerned. It was completely inappropriate for her to have fallen for him, but there was no denying it had happened. At the same time, she wasn't willing to sacrifice her own needs for a fling, so she was keeping her distance even though it was killing her to do so.

She listened while Evan and Meredith exchanged questions and answers. Although they hadn't gotten a straight answer about the photo Atticus had sent, Evan was chipping away at Meredith slowly. They now knew that she had left her husband and daughters because of Martin Calloway. According to her, he had threatened to tell her husband about her affair with her student, and she did not want to hurt him like that. It had been her only option.

Only problem was, she was lying.

Becs didn't know how she knew that, but she did.

What she didn't know was how to get Meredith to open up and tell the truth. It was the only way they could help. Not knowing Calloway's motivation where Meredith was concerned kept them at a disadvantage.

"I told you, I don't know," Meredith repeated, sounding irritated.

Becs reached over and touched Evan's arm. She felt his muscle tense beneath her fingertips, but he didn't jerk his arm away.

"I think we should come back later," she suggested. "Give Meredith some time to process. Maybe she can come up with more once she does."

Evan's dark brown eyes lacked sympathy, but he nodded. "Fine." He looked at Meredith. "You two should get some food. We'll check back in a couple of hours."

"That would be good," Meredith said, her arms wrapped around her middle as though she was holding herself together.

149

Becs got to her feet, grabbing her phone from the table. When Evan opened the door, he stepped back so she could walk out first. The brilliant sunshine hit her like a spotlight.

"Wow. Was that room really that dark?" she asked, shielding her eyes with her hand.

"It was."

She needed to invest in some sunglasses.

"Where to?" Evan asked when he got in the car.

"Atticus sent the addresses Charlie gave him for Allison. Said one's a gas station, another's a hotel, I think." She tapped her phone, pulling up his last message. "It's worth a trip to see if we can catch up to her."

Evan didn't say anything, just started the car.

Becs put the address into the navigation on the phone and got the directions. Although the silence was suffocating, she settled into her routine and pretended she had nothing to say to the man who'd given her hope for the first time in a very long time and yanked it away almost in the same breath.

BRANTLEY SAT WITH HIS ARM RESTING ON the steering wheel.

"This is a bust," he told Reese when it was clear Martin Calloway was not at work on a Sunday.

"Probably." Reese sounded distracted, his attention still fixed on his computer screen, where it had been for the past hour and a half, ever since they pulled into the parking lot across the street from the FBI headquarters.

Unable to take it any longer, he leaned toward Reese to see the screen. "What are you lookin' at?"

"Atticus sent this photo over. There's a year—2006—and a name—Cicily Rose—on the back. He thinks Meredith and Decker had a kid."

"Did someone bother to ask them?"

"Yeah. Becs and Evan. She said they didn't confirm or deny, but both were visibly upset when they realized she had the picture."

Interesting. "Did you figure out who she is?"

"I need JJ to do some digging. I can't even find a birth certificate."

"Maybe they put her up for adoption," Brantley suggested.

"That's my assumption, too."

While Brantley was waiting for Reese to say more, his phone rang. He saw Baz's name on the screen and answered. "Tell me you've got some good news."

"Depends on how you define good."

"Anything that will move this case forward at this point."

"I spoke to Dr. Weaver."

"And?"

The pause that ensued was nearly deafening.

"He told me that the *federal government* paid him five hundred thousand dollars to fake the death of a federal witness."

It was a damn good thing Brantley wasn't driving. He was positive he stopped breathing.

"Kylie's alive?" Reese asked.

"According to Dr. Weaver, she was alive that day. He gave me the card of the agent he worked with. It was Calloway."

"What do you mean she was alive that day?" Brantley asked.

"When I pressed him for details, he told me that her condition wasn't stable, but they insisted on moving her anyway. They assured him she would be taken to another medical facility."

"Any chance he got a name?"

"Home and Hearth Nursing and Rehabilitation," Baz answered. "But before you ask, JJ already looked it up. It doesn't exist."

"Fuck."

"Dr. Weaver did say that he emphasized how critical it was that they get her settled. He said Calloway asked if she could endure a ride to Dallas. He told him no."

"He kept her down there?" Brantley mused.

"I don't know. I also went by the funeral home. Talked to the director. He, too, got a lump sum on that day. He tried to lie to me about it, but finally admitted he was paid to inform the family they shouldn't view the body because of the condition it was in. Also told me there is no body in the casket."

Son of a bitch.

"Hold on. JJ wants to talk."

"Hey," she said. "Let me put it on speaker, just a sec."

Brantley waited patiently.

"Okay. The card Dr. Weaver gave Baz has a number on it. I pulled it up. It's a cell phone. Not government-issued."

"Let me guess. It's a burner."

"It is. But get this. It's still active. I was able to ping its last location."

"Tell me it's in Dallas."

"It wasn't the last time it was turned on six days ago. It pinged a cell tower near Johnson City."

"That's south of Austin," Brantley told her.

"It is. About fifty miles southwest. Sixty-five miles north of San Antonio. And it's also the same location where Charlie found credit card charges for Allison."

Definitely not a coincidence.

Brantley sighed. "Which means we're now too far north."

"That doesn't mean she's there," Reese said.

JJ's tone was crestfallen. "No, it doesn't."

"It might not pinpoint anything, but it's more than we had a few minutes ago," he told them, refusing to give up. "Have you given this information to Atticus and Archer?"

"I did. Just a few minutes ago. Atticus called to check in, said they're updating their data, wanted to get a feel for where everyone was at."

Brantley had to admire the kid.

"All right. Let me call Atticus," Brantley told them. "See what he wants to do."

"I know Dallas seems logical, since Calloway lives and works up there," Baz said. "But if he has her, I don't think he'd want to keep her close to home."

Probably not. Then again, Brantley had no idea what the bastard was thinking.

"Let us talk to Atticus. We'll get back to you."

"Talk to you later," JJ said before ending the call.

"Call Atticus. Find out where they are." He put the truck in gear. "Tell him we're headin' back to the hotel."

While Reese took care of that, Brantley drove. He was glad he only had to navigate this area on a Sunday. He couldn't imagine what it was like on a weekday. The overabundance of people and traffic made him homesick for his small town.

He smiled. It was funny how different he was now than he had been when the Navy sent him on his way. He'd spent the majority of his adult life following direction, going wherever he was told. He hadn't had a solid place to land, and he'd been okay with that. Then he came back to Coyote Ridge, met Reese, fell in love, and found that he liked being in one place, near family.

"They're at the hotel. We'll meet them in their room."

With an agenda, Brantley focused on the road in front of him.

CHAPTER EIGHTEEN

SIMON SAT WITH HIS LAPTOP BALANCED ON his legs, his feet on the coffee table.

Every so often, Harry or Hermione would pass by, rubbing against his calves or stepping over his feet. They seemed content that he wasn't doing anything, which was a far cry from the way their favorite human had been wearing a path in the hardwood for most of the morning. Violet had taken her pacing and sighing to the bookstore, leaving him at home to work.

In his defense, he did offer to go with her or help with the search for her father. She adamantly insisted that he not do either, telling him it was more important for him to do something other than babysit her or look for a man who had a tendency to disappear when the mood struck.

He wasn't so sure that was what happened this time, but they were getting updates from Luca and Slade, who were both working to find Harold. Last he'd heard, they were following a lead and would let them know what turned up.

Simon wasn't holding his breath. He hoped like hell Harold was okay, that he wasn't locked in some asshole's dungeon somewhere, but he'd been told not to fret, so he wasn't.

Yet.

He toggled to the spreadsheet he'd started building with the names of previous and current Censorious members.

As soon as he had seen his name on Archer and Atticus's task list, he'd been relieved that they were giving him something to do. Granted, his assignment included finding members of Censorious as well as the history of the group, so it wasn't anything really glamorous. Unlike Evan and Becs, who were tasked with getting information from Meredith, or Holly, who was digging into Martin Calloway's life. But he figured everyone had to play their part, so he was doing what he'd been told.

He had some details on Censorious from his brief investigation when Holt first told him about his theory. But they needed more. A lot more. Especially if the goal was to take them down once and for all.

And while he was running searches and identifying the connections between members, he was getting updated on what the rest of the team was working on. Per Archer's instructions, each person was uploading the data they had as soon as they got it, making detailed notes. It wasn't exactly what he needed to build a story outline for the future podcast, but it was something. It provided him with names that he was adding to his interview list.

Using the database that JJ had supplied him with, Simon searched known associates of Martin Calloway just for shits and giggles. To his surprise, it kicked back a list that was far more extensive than he expected. It also provided links that gave him summaries of those associates, most of whom were FBI or former FBI agents that Martin had worked with over the years.

A ping sounded, signaling another update to the spreadsheet. Because it was fueling his addiction to data, he toggled over to the sheet and noticed an update from Charlie.

"Holy shit," he muttered, leaning in to read the notes on Allison Bogart. "They found her."

Well, not exactly, but they had more to go on now that they'd traced her credit card.

He grabbed his phone. He needed to know who was going to talk to her and when. He wanted a chance to pick the woman's brain, to find out just how close she was to Martin Calloway.

Simon was about to dial when he paused, staring at the screen. If he called Archer, he would look like he wasn't pulling his weight. They'd given him an assignment, and it didn't involve talking to Allison.

He dropped the phone on the cushion beside him.

This whole working with a team thing was going to take some getting used to.

As he stared at the phone, continuing to debate whether to make that call, he wondered whether this was something he could do long-term. Or if he would always be overwhelmed with a need to quench his thirst for information by going to the source himself.

For right now, he would be a team player. Once they'd determined whether Holt's theory had a ring of truth to it or not, he'd decide how he wanted to proceed.

Harry walked over, rubbing his back against Simon's calves.

"I know, Harry. It's not easy, but it's the right thing to do."

His inner journalist heard the words and rolled his eyes.

Archer was staring at his computer screen, wondering if his eyes were beginning to cross from information overload, when there was a knock on the hotel room door. Tesha was instantly on her feet, her full attention on the door.

"It's all right, girl. Probably just your dads," he told her as he set his laptop aside and got to his feet.

"It should be Brantley and Reese," Atticus noted, not looking up from his screen.

He chuckled. Apparently, Atticus was too focused to know what was going on around him, too. He appreciated the interruption because it allowed him to switch gears. It also reminded him that Brantley and Reese hadn't gotten anywhere with tracing down Martin Calloway, which had been disappointing all around.

This trip was netting them very little when Archer had been so hopeful in the beginning.

"Hey," he greeted as he opened the door.

Brantley whistled long and slow as he strolled in. "This is fancy."

"Unexpected is what it is," Atticus said from his perch on the couch.

Tesha's tail began to wag excitedly, her butt following suit as she waited for Reese to acknowledge her, which he did with a huge smile.

Reese crouched down. "Hey, girl. I know. I missed you, too." He looked up at Archer. "How'd she do?"

"She's perfect." And she really was. Having spent the day with her had sealed the deal for Archer. He wanted a dog. Of course, he wasn't sure now was the right time to get one, considering he didn't have a place of his own, but he could still hope.

"No luck with Calloway?" Atticus prompted.

"It's Sunday," Brantley answered. "I didn't expect much. What about y'all? Did JJ find anything out on the kid?"

"We haven't heard from her yet."

Brantley looked at Reese. "Can you talk to Z? See if he knows anything about Decker havin' a kid."

Reese nodded and pulled out his phone.

"You can use my room for quiet," Archer told him.

"Thanks."

"Charlie was able to produce a lead on Allison," Atticus spoke up. "She has some credit card transactions somewhere south of Austin."

"JJ mentioned that," Brantley noted. "Johnson City or somethin'?"

"There's a ping in…" Atticus paused, looking at his screen. "It says Dripping Springs *and* Johnson City. Evan and Becs are headed to Dripping Springs now. She shows to've stayed in a hotel there. They're gonna start talkin' to people. If that doesn't net them anything, they'll move on to Johnson City."

Brantley frowned. "That's the second time Johnson City has come up."

"When was the first?" Archer asked.

"JJ said the last tower that Martin Calloway's burner phone bounced off of was in Johnson City."

"That can't be a coincidence," Archer mused.

"Definitely not."

Brantley sighed, glancing toward the bedroom where Reese had disappeared. When he looked back, Archer got the impression he was ready to get down to business, but was waiting.

"I also talked to Baz about his convo with the doctor and the funeral home," Atticus said, leaning back on the couch, his attention on Brantley. "It sounds like Calloway had his story all lined up."

Brantley nodded. "Protecting a federal witness by staging her death."

"Exactly."

157

Archer had been shocked to the roots of his hair as soon as he heard that. It pretty much backed up Holt's theory that Kylie was alive. Of course, until they had eyes on her, no one knew for sure, but it proved they were heading in the right direction.

Figuring it was his turn to contribute, he said, "It sounds to me like he had it all planned out. Right down to where he was going to take her."

"The rehab place is bogus," Brantley said.

Acher nodded. "We heard that. But it did list a Johnson City address. Could be she's in that vicinity."

"Your guess is as good as mine," Brantley muttered.

"It's a good place to start," Atticus chimed in. "I don't think we're gettin' much done up here."

"Y'all get anything other than the picture at Decker's?"

Archer shook his head. "The place was cleared out, but someone's doing the upkeep. We tried to talk to some neighbors but were stonewalled."

"Doesn't surprise me. People don't like to get involved if they don't have to."

"It sounds to me like we're a few hundred miles too far north," Atticus said, still watching Brantley.

"I think so, too."

"We headin' back, boss?"

"That's up to y'all," Brantley said, glancing between them. "You're runnin' the show. If you think there's somethin' we can find up here, we can stay."

Archer looked at Atticus, wanting him to lead. He was the one who'd compiled the information they had. It was only fair for him to decide what path they took from there.

Atticus glanced at his computer screen. "I think we got what we needed from here. Talkin' to Max and checkin' out Decker's place. We should focus our attention on locating Allison and findin' out if Calloway's still in the area." Atticus's gaze cut to him. "What do you think?"

Nodding, Archer said, "I agree."

Reese joined them a moment later. "Z's lookin' into it, but they don't have any record that Decker's got a kid."

Archer figured there could be several reasons for that. To protect the girl, since Meredith had been on the run from the FBI at the time. Or to protect her from the mob, if Max had been looking for her. Or Meredith had kept her a secret to protect herself since the baby's father had at one time been her student. A child, at that.

Personally, Archer did not like thinking about that part. It gave him the creeps.

"They've decided we'll head back," Brantley told Reese.

Reese glanced between Atticus and Archer. "Now?"

"Yeah. We can be back in Coyote Ridge in time for dinner," Atticus said.

"Then we can gather the team first thing tomorrow." Archer looked at Brantley. "We think it's time we bring them all up to speed. On everything."

Brantley stared back at them and it was obvious the gears were spinning. Archer understood the man's need to protect his team, but there was only so much they could get done without them.

Finally, Brantley nodded. "Fine. We'll leave it to you to let them know. I suggest we start early. We're not gonna slow down until we have proof that Kylie's alive."

Archer liked that Brantley was thinking in the positive, rather than the negative. They had all questioned Holt's line of thinking in the beginning, but the more they uncovered, the more Archer believed Kylie was alive. He desperately wanted her to be.

"We can do that," Atticus told them.

"Come on, girl," Reese called to Tesha.

"We'll see you back in Coyote Ridge," Brantley said on the way to the door.

When they were alone again, Archer turned to Atticus. "It'll take me just a few minutes to pack, then I can go down and check out while you get the truck."

Atticus closed his laptop and stood. "I'm ready when you are."

CHAPTER NINETEEN

"THIS IS A RURAL AREA," BECS TOLD Evan as he drove them through Dripping Springs's main drag. "Which means the cell radius for the tower Charlie tracked her to can be up to twenty-five miles away."

She wasn't even sure the town was that wide. Granted, it wasn't as small as Coyote Ridge, but with less than five thousand people, she figured it was still considered small-*ish*. They had big-name stores like HEB, Tractor Supply Co., and Home Depot. Sprinkled in with the various retail stores were all sorts of fast-food joints, including McDonald's, Dairy Queen, Taco Bell, and Whataburger. And of course, there was a Starbucks.

Becs wasn't positive, but she had read somewhere that Jensen Ackles and his wife had a brewery somewhere in town. Family Business Beer Co. or something like that. Admittedly, she didn't drink much beer, but she was a huge *Supernatural* fan. She wondered whether he hung around there much.

Not that they had time to find out.

This town, with its plethora of businesses on the main thoroughfare, was nothing like Coyote Ridge, but she liked the feel of it. If only it were smaller, perhaps they stood a chance of finding Allison Bogart.

Becs sighed. "She could be anywhere."

"Or nowhere."

"Maybe a little optimism'll get us further," she said, not looking at Evan.

"Oh, sorry. She could be right around..." Evan took a right. "...This corner. Oh. Nope. Not here."

She understood his frustration, even if it annoyed her. There were far too many large businesses along a bustling highway for them to do any sort of door-to-door.

"I'm runnin' a property search, but I doubt I'll come up with anything."

"What about her parents? Do they own any property around here?"

"Oh, well, why didn't I think of that?" Becs quipped. "I've already checked. And no, they don't. Her mother remarried after divorcing her dad when he went to prison. Looks like she's relocated to Arkansas. And Allison's father's residence is behind secured bars and walls in Abilene."

"She have any other family?"

"Already looked. And no." She held up her hand to stop him when he opened his mouth. "And if you tell me to ask JJ to check, I'm gonna punch you in the arm."

When he reached the intersection, Evan stopped and looked over, his smile growing.

She hated that smile. Hated it because she loved it so damn much. More than she was willing to admit to anyone. Including herself.

"Stop that," she said, holding up a hand to block his face.

"Stop what?"

"Smiling."

"You don't like it when I smile?"

"No."

"Why not?"

"I just don't."

"I think you do. You just don't want to admit it."

"You think wrong." She pointed at a parking space. "Let's find the hotel she stayed at. See if anyone recognizes her."

"Thinking like a detective already," he said with a laugh.

What she was thinking was she needed to get out of the car and away from him for a few minutes. It was difficult enough to sit beside him, to smell his light musky scent. It reminded her of the night they'd made out on the couch in his office. She'd been beside herself with lust that night. Never had a man made her feel the way Evan had. Not that she had a lot of experience. Her ex-husband was the extent of her history with men. He'd been her first boyfriend in high school, and she'd gone on to marry him like an idiot. And since the divorce, she hadn't bothered to date. It seemed futile at this point in her life when the only thing she wanted to focus on was her daughter and her job. In that order.

Once out of the SUV, Becs armed herself with her cell phone, which had a picture of Allison Bogart on it. It was all they had to go on and she only hoped someone here would recognize her.

Unfortunately, they came up empty on that front. After talking to the desk clerk at the hotel, they went to fourteen smaller businesses—she'd counted—including the gas station where Allison had made a purchase, and not a single person recognized the woman in the photograph. And every person they'd spoken with had seemed sincere.

"That was disappointing," she told Evan when they were back in his SUV. "What do we do now?"

He backed out of the parking spot and headed toward the stop sign.

"Should I go left or right?" he prompted.

"For what?"

"To get to a back road."

"Why?"

"Because we've driven this far. Might as well check it out."

Becs wasn't sure why that would help, but she used the map on her phone to direct him. They spent the next half hour driving around. Once they passed the mix of older homes and new businesses being built, the only things to look at were grass, trees, and hay. There was no way they were going to find Allison Bogart this way.

Her phone buzzed with an incoming text.

"That's Atticus. He said they're on their way back. Everybody. And to meet at HQ by six o'clock in the morning." She looked at Evan. "Do you think they found something?"

"If they did, they probably would call us in tonight."

True. Maybe. It was Sunday, and they would have a three-hour drive ahead of them.

"I really hate that we don't have anything to give them," she said, watching out the window. "We learned nothing from Meredith and Decker."

"That's not true."

Scrunching her face, she thought back to the conversation, trying to recall what she might've missed. She came up with nothing.

"Okay, I give. What did *you* learn?"

"Well, for starters, they're hiding something."

"I'm not sure that counts."

"Trust me, it does. We just need to come up with the right questions to get them to open up."

"Based on Decker's death-ray stare, I'm not sure that's even possible."

"It is."

"Well, I guess that's why you're the detective and I'm the analyst."

"Don't sell yourself short, Becs. You're a valuable member of this team. Without you, we wouldn't have made it this far."

She wasn't so sure about that, but she was not going to argue and make him think she was fishing for compliments. She wasn't. And certainly not from him.

She felt his eyes on her when he said, "You want to get a bite to eat before we get back?"

The two of them at a restaurant? Alone? No, thank you.

"I need to get back to Carly. Get her home and ready for school tomorrow."

"Fair enough."

Becs was grateful he didn't argue. At the same time, she wondered whether he thought she'd ever been worth fighting for.

163

ALTHOUGH THEY'D HAD THE CHANCE TO APPROACH Jessie at dinner, Travis had opted to wait. Sunday evenings were reserved for dinner with his folks, a tradition his mother had been carrying on for as long as he could remember and likely before that. Disrupting it with personal crap didn't seem fair to everyone there. Not to mention, there had been too many ears surrounding them, too many people who would ask questions that Travis couldn't answer.

At least that was the excuse he had used. Truth was, the idea of talking to Jessie about something so sensitive didn't sit right with him. Didn't matter where they were.

Unfortunately, Gage thought it needed to be done.

So they had waited, then waited a bit longer after Braydon and his brood finally left, giving them a chance to make it home and unload. Then, after talking his parents into watching the kids for a bit longer, they'd set out to get this over with.

Now Travis was pulling into Jessie and Braydon's driveway, trepidation filling his gut.

"This needs to be done," Gage said from the passenger seat. "And the sooner, the better."

"And if this news hurts her?" He looked at Gage. "What then?"

"At least she'll know."

Travis wasn't sure that knowing the mother who had abandoned you nearly two decades ago was in town was something anyone wanted to know. And no, he had nothing to base that opinion on because his mother and father had been there for him and his brothers since the day they were born. They had supported them when they needed it, disciplined them when they needed that, too. And not a single day had gone by that Travis hadn't known that his parents loved him unconditionally.

It pained him to think that Kylie and Jessie had spent a portion of their lives wondering why their mother had skipped out on them. Sure, maybe Meredith had waited until they were old enough to take care of themselves, but that shouldn't have mattered. She should've been there through every heartache, every celebration.

"Come on. Let's get this over with. I'm sure your parents want to get to bed at a decent time tonight."

They still had to pick up the rugrats when they were finished here, so yeah, he probably needed to get a move on.

He got out of the SUV and closed the door quietly, wanting the next minute or so to get his thoughts in order.

Of course, Braydon had supersonic hearing because he walked out of the house before they reached the porch.

"Hey." His smile was bright. "I know we didn't leave a kid behind. I counted."

Travis smiled. It was forced, but he figured it counted.

As they neared, Braydon's forehead wrinkled. "What brings you by?"

"We need to talk to Jessie."

Travis wasn't imagining the way Braydon stood taller, his shoulders squared. He was preparing to protect his wife from whatever bad news they might have.

"It's not bad," Gage said, clearly sensing the same thing.

Travis stopped beside Gage. "It's just news."

Braydon shifted, blocking the door. "About?"

"Come on, Bray. Let us talk to her."

"Are the kids still up?" Gage asked.

Braydon looked at him. "Jessie just put Waylon to bed. Zach and Rhett are watchin' TV."

"We won't be here long," Travis promised.

With a long exhale, Braydon stepped back and opened the screen door. "Hey, Jess! Travis and Gage are here."

"Shh," she hissed, stepping out of the kitchen. "Waylon finally fell asleep."

"Sorry, baby."

"Come on in," Jessie invited. "Y'all want coffee? Tea?"

"I'm good," Travis told her. He didn't intend to stay long.

"I'm good, too, thanks." Gage walked ahead of him into the kitchen.

"What brings you by?" She frowned when Braydon stepped up beside her, a lion preparing to protect its pride.

"We have some news," Travis said, glancing between the two of them before settling his gaze on Jessie. "It's about your mother."

Jessie's smile slid right off her face. "Meredith?"

He nodded.

"What about her?" Braydon asked.

Travis looked at Gage, who nodded in encouragement.

"She's in town," he said, forcing himself to hold her gaze. "Brantley and his team are lookin' into a case that they think she's involved in. She showed up unexpectedly last night."

"Have you seen her?" Jessie asked.

"Briefly. I've put her up in a motel in Taylor," he explained.

Her expression went from surprise to disinterest almost instantly. "Well, I hope she takes care of business and leaves as quickly as she came."

"You don't mean that," Braydon said softly.

Jessie took a step back. "Oh, trust me, I do. She hasn't been my mother for a long time."

"Do you plan to see her?" Braydon asked him.

Travis shook his head. "Not if I don't have to, no."

"You're not gonna introduce her to her grandkids?"

He swallowed past the lump that formed in his throat. He wasn't sure how to answer that because he didn't know what Kylie would've wanted. She never really talked about her mother, and the few times she had, it was with the same distaste for her that he could see on Jessie's face now.

"Probably not." Travis glanced at Gage, then looked back at Jessie. "We just wanted you to know, in case you see her in town."

Jessie turned away. "Well, thanks for tellin' us."

Travis met Braydon's gaze and hoped his brother saw the apology in his eyes. He didn't come here intending to upset Jessie, but they'd thought it best that she hear it from them first.

"We'll get outta your hair," he told Braydon. "Let me know if you need anything."

With that, Travis walked out of the house, wondering whether he should've told them about Brantley's ridiculous notion that Kylie might be alive. By the time he got in the SUV, he decided that information was better kept to himself. Just because he was holding out hope that a miracle was possible didn't mean it would come true. And the last thing he wanted was for anyone else to have to grieve Kylie's death a second time.

CHAPTER TWENTY

BY THE TIME BRANTLEY AND REESE MADE it home, it was just after eight.

They hadn't rushed, taking the opportunity to eat at a restaurant so Reese could have a salad—his request—and they'd stopped at not one, but two Buc-ee's on the way back, although they only needed gas at one of them. Traffic was heavy, but that wasn't unusual through the I-35 corridor on a Sunday evening.

They'd filled the time with conversation, rehashing what they knew, and tossed around a few hypotheticals. But that was all they were. They had very few facts that would get them the answers they were seeking. But Brantley wasn't giving up hope. Not yet. They'd gotten this far, and though progress was slow-going, they were inching forward.

Needless to say, he was glad to be home.

Once inside, Brantley dumped their bags in the front room, intending to deal with them tomorrow. Reese made sure Tesha had fresh water, then prepared her dinner.

"When you're done, come join me in the shower," he told Reese before making his way to the bathroom.

Brantley didn't wait, figuring his husband would show up when he was ready. He stripped and stood beneath the hot water, shoving all thought from his mind. He needed the mental break, a little reprieve from everything bouncing through his gray matter. He didn't want to think about Kylie or her mother or some corrupt government officials. Not right now.

Closing his eyes, he focused on breathing. In, out. Slow and steady, while the hot water beat down on his tired muscles. He forced himself to relax, to clear the jumbled mess of information rattling around in his head. He wasn't big on meditation, but he could see the appeal.

When he heard Reese, he lifted his head and opened his eyes, watching as the man he loved discarded his clothing. Funny how he never doubted that Reese would show up for him. The man seemed to know what he needed, and he was always there.

Goddamn, he was the sexiest thing he'd ever seen.

When Reese stepped into the shower, Brantley reached for him, pulling him closer. He wasn't in a rush, wasn't inundated with chaos. He simply wanted to savor this time with his husband and to block out all the rest for a little while.

"Thirty minutes," he told Reese. "No work, no worries. Only us."

Reese's honey-gold eyes glittered. "I like that idea."

Brantley cupped Reese's face, enjoying the way the stubble on his jaw scraped his palm. He leaned in, sealing their lips. The kiss started slow, sensual, then took on the heated edge it always did when they were together. Still, they maintained a leisurely pace, one fueled by passion that never seemed to burn out.

For long minutes, they teased and fondled, hands roaming, tongues and lips searching.

Feeding his need to touch, Brantley proceeded to wash Reese, ensuring he got every smooth surface, every crevice. When Reese returned the favor, Brantley sighed and moaned, giving himself over to the man he loved. By the time they were finished, their thirty minutes were up, but Brantley wasn't even close to being finished. He turned off the water, grabbed two towels, and passed one to Reese.

He gave his body a good rub with the cotton, then dumped the towel on the floor and took Reese's hand, leading him to the bedroom. Within seconds, he was plunging into the heated depths of his husband's body, pleasure accosting him as Reese stared up at him with heat and love burning in that golden gaze.

"I love you," Brantley whispered, pushing in deep, sliding out slowly. "So fucking much."

Reese's eyes remained locked with his as Brantley drove them both to that inevitable place where they would linger until they soared. And when he came, it was with Reese's name on his lips.

"Feel better?" Reese asked as they lay in a heap on the bed.

"For now."

"Me, too."

"Mmm." Brantley wanted to remain like that forever, just the two of them, skin to skin.

"Do you have a headache?" Reese whispered after several minutes.

"It's not too bad," he admitted.

Brantley thought he'd hidden it better. Thankfully, it hadn't exploded into full migraine territory, but it was gradually increasing. Oddly enough, sex derailed it momentarily, something about endorphins or whatnot. At the same time, it usually came on full force afterward.

"You stay here," Reese said. "I'll get you a pill and make sure everything's locked up."

"You sure?"

Reese responded with a kiss on his lips, causing Brantley to smile.

"I love you," he told Reese.

"I know. Now be quiet and get some rest."

Because his husband was insistent, Brantley did exactly as he instructed.

IF HE'D HAD ANYWHERE ELSE TO GO, Atticus would've gladly gone there. He had dropped Archer at the B and B, and only half wished he had a room there for the night.

Instead, he found himself pulling into Slade's driveway a little after eight, tense from the thought of arguing with the man.

Ever since Slade shut down his request for help, Atticus had given considerable thought to where they were in their relationship. More accurately, he'd been trying to figure out how it had gone so horribly wrong so quickly. One minute, the three of them were fucking like rabbits, agreeing to keep things casual between them; the next, Slade was on a tear, accusing Atticus of cheating.

And Carson hadn't seemed all that worried about anything. Not Slade's constant accusation, not Atticus's concern over it. No, if he didn't know better, he would say Carson had already checked out. But why? He was the one who had pushed for this.

Right?

Or had that been him? Had he gone and fucked it all up by wanting more than he should have?

He wished he understood what had prompted Slade to become so defensive. And what had made Atticus think they could somehow make this off-balance threesome work. It wasn't working. Not for any of them.

He parked his truck beside Slade's and killed the engine. He got out, considered leaving his bag, but figured he needed to do laundry at the first opportunity.

By the time he made it to the door, he was grinding his teeth, hating that he was dreading this.

The door was unlocked, making it easy to let himself in. He noticed the house was dark and quiet. Since he hadn't let Slade know he was on the way, he wasn't sure who Slade was expecting. Maybe Carson?

Oddly, he found he didn't care. Without making a sound, he made a detour to the bathroom to take care of business. He decided he would wait to shower until morning. In order to be up at the ass-crack of dawn, he would need the cold wake-me-up.

Once in his room, he closed the door, again making no sound. He stripped down to his boxers, plugged his phone up to charge, then fell into bed. He stared up at the dark ceiling, hoping sleep came quickly.

It sucked that things had gotten to this point. That he was hiding out from Slade, while at the same time wishing the man would come to him. And Carson ... it felt like just yesterday that Atticus had been blown away by the man. He'd been taken aback by Carson, intrigued. He came along at a time when Atticus's entire world was changing for the better, and he had mistakenly believed that it would go somewhere. That was the first time he'd ever thought long-term about anyone.

Then Slade had disrupted that little picket-fence dream when Atticus had stumbled upon the guy jacking off and calling out Atticus's name. From that point forward, he'd been confused. Well, confused and excited by the prospects. Especially when he learned that Carson and Slade had history. Unfortunately, it was more like bad blood than days gone by. Yet Atticus had pushed to see where things went because he'd been selfish, not wanting to give up either of them.

And here he was, sneaking into the house while Slade was likely sitting in his bedroom, watching TV or playing on his phone.

It was sad when he thought about it.

Sad, but, at the same time, it felt inevitable.

CHAPTER TWENTY-ONE

Monday, October 3, 2022

ARCHER ARRIVED AT HQ WELL BEFORE 6 a.m., thinking he would be the first one there.

He learned quickly that *on time*, in this case, would've actually been late, as Vince Lombardi was known to say. The parking lot was full of vehicles, some he didn't recognize, others he did. He was half an hour early, wanting to get things set up for a meeting with the entire team, but apparently, he would have to get an even earlier start if he wanted to beat them to the punch.

When he was halfway to the barn, he heard a sound behind him. Turning, he saw Tesha bounding out of the house, soaring over the steps of the deck to the ground as she raced toward him. The instant he saw her, his face split in a wide grin.

Unable to help himself, he stopped, squatting down so he could pet his new friend. "Hey, girl. What's up?" She wiggled excitedly. "I think so, too. It's gonna be a busy day."

She hopped around, tongue hanging out of her mouth, clearly happy to see him. For whatever reason, that made his day. He liked the idea of someone being that enthusiastic about his arrival.

"You ready to get to work?" he asked as he stood to his full height. "Well, come on."

They walked the remaining distance to the barn side by side.

After punching in his code, he pulled open the door, allowing Tesha to race in first. Inside, he found a buzz of activity. Atticus, Becs, and Evan were busy rearranging the equipment so that what they'd moved to the conference room was back in its rightful place.

"Morning," Evan greeted, depositing a pile of cords on Slade's desk.

"Good morning. What can I help with?" he asked after dropping his backpack in his chair.

"You could make the coffee," Becs told him with a wide grin.

If he didn't know better, he would think she was trying to set him up.

"You sure you want me to do that?" he asked. "It'll only be the best coffee you've ever had."

Atticus chuckled. "If you can turn Folgers into the best coffee ever, have at it, buddy."

"Watch and learn, partner."

While they continued to arrange, Archer got busy making coffee. He searched through the cabinets in the small kitchenette until he found what he needed. There wasn't much to work with, but they had cocoa powder and cinnamon. Once the coffee was brewing, he placed cups on a tray sitting beside the sink. He gathered the sugar packets and tiny creamer tubs, arranging them in small bowls, then adding them to the tray.

When the first pot completed, he dumped the grounds, added a new filter and fresh grounds, then put a clean pot under the spout and started the process all over again. While that was underway, he carried the tray out, set it on a desk where someone had placed a box of donuts and kolaches. He returned to the kitchen and waited. Once the second pot was complete, he carried both into the main room of the barn.

At that point, several more people had arrived, including Darius, Elana, Holly, and Charlie. They were assisting however they could, moving chairs from the conference room to provide additional seating.

Jay was the next to arrive, five minutes early. Brantley and Reese strolled in behind him a minute later.

"When are the new hires arriving?" Brantley asked Darius as soon as he was inside.

"I have them coming in at eight. Didn't want their arrival to disturb this meeting."

"Good. By then, you should have plenty for them to do."

"Do we have a new case?" Charlie asked. "Or are we still working on Censorious?"

Archer felt all eyes on him. He glanced at Atticus, then back to Brantley. When neither of them jumped to provide an answer, he directed his question at Brantley. "We're opening this up to everyone, right?"

"We are," he confirmed, then looked at Charlie. "Same case, but we have some new developments."

Movement on the large television caught Archer's eye. He looked over to see a car pulling up.

"That's Simon," he told everyone. "I called him last night. Asked him to join us."

"Good thinkin'," Reese said. "He's got insight, and we need all the help we can get."

"Have they found Violet's dad yet?" Darius asked.

"Not yet." Archer didn't know all the details, but Simon had mentioned that Luca and Slade were still working on it. The longer he was gone, the more worried Violet was getting. What Archer found more interesting was that Simon hadn't bothered to interrogate him about what information they'd gathered. Apparently, Simon was content to do some research and review the notes the team was updating, but he didn't seem too worried that they were moving along while he dealt with more pressing issues.

Love. It had the ability to fry the brain.

"Where's Slade?" Reese asked, glancing from face to face before stopping on Atticus.

"He said he'll be workin' with Luca until they find Harold," Atticus said, looking none too happy with that information.

"Do you want us to call him in?" Archer asked.

Reese looked at Brantley, who turned to Evan. "I guess we should so you're not—"

Evan spoke up, cutting him off. "If it's all the same to you, I'd like to keep Becs as a partner for the duration of this case."

Brantley looked at Becs. "You okay with that?"

She appeared surprised by the request, but at the same time, pleased. "Yeah. Sure."

Brantley addressed Archer and Atticus when he said, "We'll let the new hires make up the difference."

173

Archer moved to the door to let Simon in. As he was walking in, a ringing sound came from one of the computers. Becs hopped up, a smile on her face. She hurried over and tapped the keyboard. A moment later, JJ appeared on the screen. Baz's face popped up right after, when he moved into camera range.

"We're here," JJ announced.

"Good mornin'," Reese greeted.

"Mornin'."

"Any news on Naomi and Noah comin' home?" Holly asked, her voice filled with hope.

"We're meetin' with the doctor later this afternoon."

"We're keepin' our fingers crossed."

JJ smiled.

"If you want coffee or donuts, get them now. I want to get this show on the road," Brantley said, moving to take one of the chairs they'd moved from the conference room.

Archer walked over to Atticus. "You should take the lead on this."

Atticus peered up at him, looking as though he might argue. But he didn't. He simply nodded, then walked over to his desk and grabbed his notepad.

When he returned, he passed it to Archer. "Take a look at this. Make sure I'm not missin' anything."

Archer skimmed the pages. Atticus had detailed everything they'd accomplished so far, as well as everything they had left to do. There were notes in the margin, some things marked with asterisks, a couple crossed out. On the third page was a list of next steps, including which team member was assigned which task.

On the last page was a diagram with lines connecting various incidents. It was a basic outline showing the correlation of events.

"When did you have time to do this?"

"This mornin'. Couldn't sleep."

Archer was impressed. He skimmed it quickly and only had one thing to add. He grabbed a pen, made a notation, then passed it back to Atticus as everyone was taking their seats.

"Oh, my God. Who made this coffee?" Holly asked, eyes wide.

Becs and Evan pointed at him.

"Did you bring it from home?"

He shook his head. "Just fancied up the Folgers."

"It's amazing," Holly said dreamily. "From now on, it's your job."

"Let's get this underway," Brantley said from behind him. "Atticus? Archer?"

"You've got this," Archer told Atticus quietly, adding a smile.

Atticus hated public speaking.

Granted, this wasn't exactly the public he was addressing, but it was close enough. All eyes were on him, making him feel like a bug under a microscope.

"What I'm about to tell you might not be easy for some of you to hear," he began, forcing himself to make eye contact with his team, which was a hell of a lot harder than looking at yourself in the mirror when practicing. "You're aware we've taken on a case outside the norm for this team. We're lookin' into a conspiracy involving the FBI's desire to take down the Southern Boy Mafia. At least that was our original thought process when Simon came to us with this theory."

He took a breath, glancing down at his notes, although he didn't need them to continue. Oddly, he felt a sense of empowerment standing at the front of the room, addressing these people. He had expected to hear snickers and see amusement in their gazes. Instead, he found them all to be paying attention, listening to what he had to say. That gave him the strength to keep going.

"Archer and I were tasked with creating a timeline based on the notes we were given," he continued. "That timeline's available for anyone who needs or wants to look at it. If you have more information you think should be added, feel free to update it. We want to ensure we've covered all the bases." He took a breath, stood taller. "While we were updating it, we came across notes Holt made that gave us pause. We looped in Brantley and Reese immediately, knowing the information we had was sensitive."

He definitely had their attention.

"Some of you, mainly those who grew up in this town or have been here since the beginning, know Kylie Walker. For those who don't, she's the woman whose life was cut short by Juliet Prince, the woman who kidnapped Kylie's daughter, Kate." He looked from one face to the next. "Only we no longer believe her life was ended, but rather her death was staged to further the agenda of the rogue group of law enforcement known as Censorious."

The very air seemed to stop moving, all eyes still locked on him.

Holly gasped. "Kylie's alive?"

"At this time, we believe that to be the case," he explained. "Baz, would you mind sharing the details you have after your conversation with Dr. Weaver and the funeral home?"

Everyone shifted to look at the television at the back of the room while Baz filled them in, explaining the deposits that JJ had uncovered, as well as the FBI using the ruse of a federal witness in order to get away with kidnapping her.

"Oh my God," Elana said on a choked sob. "She's alive."

"We don't know that for sure," Brantley said, standing up. "I will say this. The information we're giving you does not go any further than those in this room. Not until we have proof of our theory. And only after I share whatever we find with her family. Understood?"

"Travis doesn't know?" Holly asked.

"He knows some of it. We haven't given him all the details yet. I won't be comfortable until I get eyes on her or find someone who knows where they took her. Like I said, we keep it within this team."

A round of nods and affirmative mutterings moved through the room.

"How long have you known this?" Evan asked, his tone holding a slight edge, as though he was bothered that he hadn't been included.

Atticus didn't blame him. He'd tried.

"Since Saturday morning," Atticus told him. "We shared our findings with Brantley, who took the information to Travis. With his permission, we moved on it. Our trip to Dallas was to talk to Max Adorite, the head of the Adorite Crime Family."

"That was about Meredith Prescott, right?" Jay asked.

"Correct. We wanted to get clarification on the events that supposedly took place nineteen years ago. As you know, Decker stated that Meredith did not witness a hit, although she was being blackmailed into testifying."

"But we don't know that for sure, right?" Charlie asked. "We have secondhand information from Decker."

Atticus glanced at Brantley, received a nod to continue.

"Meredith showed up Saturday morning," he said, realizing some of the team wasn't aware of her presence. "Evan and Becs were able to talk to her yesterday." He glanced at Evan. "Would you mind sharin' the information you have?"

While Evan filled the team in on their conversation, Atticus listened intently, hoping to hear something that he might've missed from reading Evan's notes.

"Meredith isn't very forthcoming with details," Evan explained after he summed it up. "I think she's hiding something, but we don't know what yet."

"What makes you think that?" Charlie asked.

"We received a photograph from Atticus," Becs answered. "And showed it to Meredith and Decker. Neither of them claimed to know who it was, but they were both visibly upset when they saw it."

The picture appeared on one of the wall screens.

"We've yet to determine who the child is," Atticus explained. "But the name on the back of the photograph is Cicily Rose. We assume she was born in 2006 since that's the year beside the name."

"The woman looks like a young Meredith," Becs stated. "I pulled up old yearbooks from the high school she worked at and compared them."

"Do we have a location on Cicily Rose?" Charlie asked.

"Not yet. We're weeding through a long list of possibilities," JJ said. "Believe it or not, it's a very popular name."

"Where did you find this picture?" Elana asked.

"From a previous address for Decker," Atticus answered, clicking a button on the remote to pull up the pictures he took while they were at the trailer. He flipped through them, giving the team a visual of what he and Archer had seen the previous day. He stopped when he got to the photo of Archer and Tesha mugging for the camera. Laughter erupted along with a few *awww*s.

"That's where he grew up?" Evan asked. "In that trailer?"

"We believe so."

"There's furniture in only one room?" Becs asked.

"Yes. And it looks new. The rest of the house was empty, except for some toilet paper and new towels in the bathroom," Archer supplied. "We attempted to talk to neighbors, but either they weren't home or they weren't willing to chat."

"We've added these to the case notes," Atticus informed them.

"Does Travis know his mother-in-law is in town?" Elana asked.

Atticus looked at Brantley, not sure he should answer that.

"He does," Brantley confirmed. "He was here when RT and Z brought her Saturday mornin'."

"Is there anything else you're keeping from us?" Charlie asked.

Before Atticus could answer, Brantley stood up.

"The only things we've purposely held back were the details around Kylie's death. It wasn't until yesterday that we had valid intel to back up Holt's theory that her death was faked. We still do not have any proof that she is alive, only that Martin Calloway paid off the doctor to forge her death certificate and that the funeral home knowingly buried an empty casket."

"Do Travis and Gage know that last part?" Holly asked.

"They know we're lookin' into the possibility that she's alive. Like I said, until we have concrete proof, we'll keep this to ourselves."

"What's our main objective here?" Evan asked.

"It's two-fold," Brantley said.

Atticus stepped back because it was clear Brantley was taking over. He didn't mind at all.

"First and foremost, our goal is to find Kylie," he said firmly. "Once we do that, we'll focus on taking down Censorious. We have the go-ahead from Z to officially tackle this and to see it through to completion."

"You make it sound easy," Becs said, looking skeptical.

"Trust me when I tell you, it'll be anything but."

Yeah, Atticus had a feeling he was going to say that.

REESE LISTENED WHILE THE TEAM PONDERED OVER the information they'd been given.

To be honest, it went better than expected. He thought for sure there would be more hurt feelings. He did pick up on some subtleties in Evan's and Charlie's tones. Since they'd been with the task force the longest, it was only logical that they would feel slighted. It hadn't been their intention, but they had held back valuable information.

Now that everything was out in the open, the team seemed determined to do what was necessary to find Kylie and take down a group of rogue law enforcement agents. The first seemed relatively easy compared to the second. Reese had no idea how to even begin cutting off the head of a very powerful snake. And that was what Censorious was.

Last night, after he'd dosed Brantley with his migraine medicine, Reese had done some research of his own. He had wanted to know what they were really up against. Simon, with help from Elana, had made decent headway in getting information on the group that had been formed to mete out their own brand of justice when they weren't content with the results of the US judicial system. They had a growing list of names, as well as information on their families, occupations, and political affiliations.

But they didn't have enough information. Not for his liking, anyway. So he had started digging deeper. What he found on his own had made his stomach churn. And to think, Martin Calloway claimed Max Adorite was the one who needed to be put down. From what Reese found, the opposite was true. At the very least, they both needed to be stopped.

Not that Reese had any intention of taking down Max. He might not believe in what Max stood for, but he understood it to a degree. His motivations, anyway. He was building an empire, fueled by money and power. Yeah, people got caught in the crossfire, but the collateral damage was minimal.

The same could not be said for Censorious. Martin Calloway was fueled by power and greed, using whatever means necessary to get what he wanted: justice. His perverted version of it. Censorious had distorted the definition of justice to achieve their goals. And they weren't above taking down innocent people in the process.

"What should we focus on?" Charlie asked, drawing Reese's attention.

Archer was now standing up, moving to the front of the room. "As Brantley said, our main objective is to find Kylie and take down Censorious. And yes, in that order. Our focus should be on finding Kylie."

"I guess there's no reason to exhume the body, huh?" Charlie asked.

"What's the point? The funeral home said there isn't one," Jay stated.

"And what if they're lying?" Elana countered.

"And if they are?" Jay argued. "Then we will have disturbed the woman's final resting place for no reason."

"But we won't know for sure unless we do," Charlie argued.

"Right now, I'm not worried about that," Brantley said. "If we get nowhere in the next twenty-four hours, I'll consider approaching my cousin with that request. For now, let's focus on following the leads we have."

"Where do we start?" Holly asked.

"The task list is up to date," Archer explained. "Make sure you add anything you get as you get it. This is our playbook right now, so you'll see we're adding things as we go. If you determine there's something that plays to your strength, assign it to yourself. But if you do that, it's yours. And we want hourly updates from everyone."

"I've got a lead on a member of Censorious," Reese told Archer. "He's got an Austin address. Charlie, Jay, if one of you could pay him a visit this mornin', see what you can get outta him."

He could tell that statement surprised Brantley, but he didn't say anything.

"I can do that," Jay offered.

"I've asked JJ to continue to monitor Allison Bogart's cell phone," Atticus said, stepping up beside Archer. "I think she's key to finding out more on all fronts."

"I agree," Brantley added. "If and when you find her, I want to talk to her."

"Charlie is gonna continue her research on her," Atticus added. "See if we can find out who she's workin' with. I can't imagine she doesn't have a partner."

"Depends on what her role is," Reese told him. "If she does, there's no guarantee that person knows what she's up to."

"True. But it's worth a conversation," Atticus countered.

"It is," Brantley agreed. "If you need someone to do legwork in Dallas, reach out to Z. He knows what we're focused on. Said he'll have agents at the ready if we need help."

Atticus gave a thumbs-up. "Noted."

"We're headed to Johnson City," Reese informed the team. "While Atticus and Archer head to Dripping Springs. We've got enough connections in those two cities to be more than a coincidence. It's worth doing some recon. If you need us, call, but remember, Atticus and Archer are runnin' this op. Go through them."

"You ready?" Brantley asked.

Nodding, Reese whistled for Tesha. He was eager to get this underway. Finding Kylie was all he could think about, and he knew he wouldn't rest until they did.

One way or the other.

CHAPTER TWENTY-TWO

BRANTLEY FOCUSED ON THE ROAD AND THE navigation instructions as they turned off the main highway onto another. There were no flyovers or exits on this stretch of road, simply stop lights in the middle of busy intersections.

When he'd first looked at the map, he'd expected another long, mind-numbing drive. Thankfully, their destination was closer than he anticipated, clocking in at a little over an hour from Coyote Ridge. Having made the trek from Dallas the day before, it felt significantly shorter. But it was still long enough for his anxiety to build, and the restlessness to settle in.

According to Reese, there was a pattern with the movements of the players they had identified up to this point, and it all seemed to be centralized in this location. As for whether they could nail down anyone, that was to be seen. Becs and Evan hadn't had any luck when they'd spent a good part of their Sunday in Dripping Springs flashing Allison's picture to the shop owners and customers. But Brantley was willing to do whatever he needed in order to get Kylie back and nail the bastards who'd disrupted the lives of so many people with their greed. If that meant knocking on every door in every small town, by God, he would damn well try.

Fuckers.

Oh, yeah. He was more than pissed, and thinking about how Martin Calloway had single-handedly fucked up a good family only exacerbated his rage. Kylie was the glue that held that family together, and Calloway had taken her away. For what? It still seemed ludicrous that he would think faking her death would draw her mother out of hiding or that Meredith Prescott's testimony would even hold up in court. It made no fucking sense.

"What's on your mind?" Reese asked.

"I don't get it. I just don't understand how Calloway can hinge everything on one woman's testimony. Especially a woman whose morals are as corrupt as his. Wouldn't a defense attorney shred anything she had to say?"

However, it did make sense that he would use Kylie if he was looking for payback for Juliet's death. That theory wasn't as far-fetched, although he couldn't quite wrap his head around it since Calloway had put his kid up for adoption when she was born.

"I think he's past that now."

His gaze darted to Reese briefly. "What?"

"I was up most of the night doin' research. I came across Censorious's manifesto."

"Oh, fantastic. Can't wait to hear it."

Reese clicked something on his phone, then began to read, "Our mission is clear: to eliminate crime and create a safer society for all. We are committed to protecting those who cannot stand up for themselves and stepping in when the government fails. United, we strive for justice—building a world where evil is eliminated, no matter what it takes."

Shaking his head, Brantley sighed. "Sounds like the musings of a madman."

"You're not far off. That was just the beginning. It goes on to explain how they intend to eliminate those they feel are a threat to society. They've got a list of offenders."

"By name?"

Reese nodded. "But they don't just target those they determine to be criminals. They've got specifics by race, gender, religion, and sexual orientation."

"Seriously?"

"Oh, yeah. They're racist, sexist, homophobic… It's ugly."

Great. Censorious was made up of a group of assholes who put targets on the backs of those who weren't like them. Just what this world fucking needed, another hate group hellbent on proving they were superior.

Fuckers.

"I want this bastard," Brantley said under his breath. He didn't give a fuck if Max Adorite and Martin Calloway challenged one another to a duel in the middle of downtown Dallas. That was their prerogative. But he did care that Censorious was targeting innocent people.

183

"You're not the only one," Reese said, his tone harsher than Brantley'd ever heard it.

Taking a deep breath, Brantley glanced at the navigation. Their turn was coming up.

"Becs and Evan showed Allison's picture at a few businesses in Dripping Springs," Brantley told Reese. "I think they had the right idea. Just the wrong photo for this town."

"You want to show Calloway's photo."

"Yeah. The team keeps comin' up with this as a central location. I can't imagine Calloway hasn't been here. And because he would, I doubt he's kept a low profile. That would draw attention."

"Not if he's hidin'."

"Trust me. These people pay attention. Small towns keep an eye out for each other. If one person noticed him tryin' to keep from bein' seen, they would tell someone. Then it would become a thing. He would have to blend in—or try to—to stay off their radar."

"He could have cronies doin' his dirty work."

Brantley had considered that. "No doubt about that. But Calloway would want to be front and center. Prove he's the dick-swingin' boss."

Reese huffed a laugh. "Quite the picture you paint there."

Brantley laughed. "You're startin' to sound like Atticus."

Ten minutes after they crossed the city limits, they'd parked the truck on Main Street and started making their way from business to business. To cover more ground, they had split up. That was nearly two hours ago. Reese and Tesha were across the street, and based on the look on his face, Reese was having about as much luck as Brantley.

But it wasn't time to give up yet.

Opening the door, Brantley stepped into a store that boasted fine art for sale. What he found when he walked inside wasn't quite what he was expecting. This wasn't the gallery of white with paintings highlighted by small beams of light as he'd thought. No, the floor was dark-stained concrete with imperfections throughout, and there were large, round tiered tables from the front to the back, all holding what appeared to be a variety of tchotchkes and trinkets.

"Hey, there," a deep, rusty voice called from the back. "Mornin'. What can I help you with?"

Brantley skimmed the rows of knick-knacks before turning his attention to the man walking his way. He was a bear of a guy, sporting a fluffy gray beard and a shiny bald head. The laugh lines around his eyes said the man had spent his years enjoying life.

"Mornin'," Brantley greeted in return. "Nice place you have here."

"Thanks." He peered around, clearly proud. "We like it."

Brantley wasn't sure who *we* were, but he smiled, phone at the ready. Before he could show the picture, the man thrust out a hand.

"Bobby McEntire. And you are?"

He reminded himself that small towns were friendly and shook his hand in return. "Brantley Walker."

"Nice to meet ya, Brantley."

"Likewise."

"What brings you in today? Need somethin' for the wall? Or maybe the mantel?"

He gave the items a cursory inspection, then looked at Bobby. "I was actually wonderin' if you've seen any of these people around here."

"Hold on a minute," the man said, digging in the bib of his overalls. He produced a pair of reading glasses and perched them on his nose.

The man took Brantley's phone, all but kissing the screen.

He recognized that look—the one that said he was searching the deep recesses of his brain but coming up empty—so Brantley expected the same response he'd gotten from every other person he'd talked to, those who bothered to look at the photo or not.

"Can't say I've seen her," Bobby said, looking up. "She's a pretty little thang, though."

Brantley reached around, swiping the screen.

Bobby's head tilted. "He looks kinda familiar. Not sure."

Brantley swiped the screen one more time.

"Oh, yeah." Bobby looked up, bushy eyebrows raised as he pointed at the screen. "That looks like ol' Marty Callahan."

"Calloway?" Brantley corrected.

Passing the phone back, the man grinned widely, showing straight white teeth. "That's it. Marty Calloway."

Pay dirt.

"Do you happen to know where he lives?"

Bobby shook his head dramatically. "Oh, he ain't from around these parts. Just visits his niece, I think he said."

Brantley waited patiently, not wanting to repeat himself. He didn't give a shit if good ol' Marty visited the spirit of the elephant out in an empty field. He just needed to know where to look.

"Lemme think," the guy said, turning and looking at the nearby table. He picked up a statue of a crow, admired it, then put it back. He picked up another statue, this one of a wagon wheel leaning against a wood fence. "This is more your style."

When Bobby passed the statue his way, Brantley was forced to take it. He smiled, obliging the man. "It's uh…" In truth, it looked like it had been made by someone who knew what they were doing, but then painted by that person's four-year-old kid.

"Nine ninety-nine," Bobby said. "That's a steal."

Considering the information he would get out of it, Brantley thought so, too. "I'll take it." He saw a matching one and pointed it out. "And that one, too."

"Oh, it's lovely." Bobby picked up the other statue and carried it toward the back.

Brantley followed.

"I'll get you rung up."

He was about to remind Bobby that he was looking for someone, but he didn't need to.

"And I'll see if I can remember where Marty said his niece lives. I've got a map. Give me a minute."

"Sure thing." He was starting to think the oblivious ruse was an act to sell the crap he was peddling.

No one said small-town entrepreneurs didn't know what they were doing.

WITH ANOTHER BUST, REESE WALKED OUT INTO the brilliant Texas sunshine, Tesha trotting at his side.

"Someone's gotta know them, Tesha," he said absently. "That or we're lookin' in the wrong damn place."

Which was a good possibility. Although plenty of their findings pointed directly to this area, Reese knew it could all be smoke and mirrors, all set up to give the illusion of progress. With their luck, this was just another distraction they didn't need.

"You wanna go in the hair place?" he asked Tesha, wishing like hell they could avoid it. Having his nostrils assaulted by a myriad of chemicals was not high on his list of enjoyable things to do on a Monday morning.

He could tell by Tesha's hesitant gait that she wasn't looking forward to it either.

"It's the job, girl," he said, starting down the sidewalk.

His cell phone rang, causing him to stop, praying it was someone who wanted him to do something besides go in that place.

"I got somethin'," Brantley said without greeting.

Reese glanced across the street, saw his husband coming out of the fine arts store.

Brantley lifted a hand to wave, then pointed in the direction they'd come from. "Meet me at the truck."

The call disconnected.

"Looks like he loves us, girl. Come on. Let's go."

Excited by the prospect of something new, Tesha's tail wagged as she worked diligently to remain at his side and not follow her instincts that told her to race ahead. Her training was ongoing, and with every passing day, she was learning more and more. The best part was that she was eager to learn. Well, the best part was that he got to train her, but he'd let her think it was all for her.

"Tesha, wait," he instructed when they reached the corner to cross the street.

She waited, her full attention on him. He knew he could walk across that street and she would remain right where she was until he gave her the command to go. It took a lot of repetitive work to get her to that point, but he no longer had to worry that she would dart out into traffic.

The light finally changed and the Walk sign began to flash.

"Go," he said, the signal to release her from the wait position.

She trusted him implicitly, starting forward at the same time he did. They made it across the street as Brantley was putting something in the backseat and closing the door.

"I've got an address." Brantley gestured toward the truck. "Let's go check it out."

Reese didn't ask what he'd just stashed inside under the radar. He wasn't sure he wanted to know.

"An actual address?" He was having a difficult time believing that. It was never that easy for them.

"Well, not an *actual* address, but a vicinity. Just as good."

No, it wasn't. Johnson City was a vicinity, and they'd spent more time in this small town than Reese cared to.

However, it kept him from having to go in the hair salon, so he wasn't going to argue.

After getting Tesha water, Reese helped her into the truck, connected the seat belt to her harness, then joined Brantley. He had the air conditioner on full blast, his attention on the map showing on the navigation screen.

"Bobby said Marty's been around here visiting his niece."

"Marty?" Reese grinned. "A killer named Marty."

"We don't know that he's killed anyone. He simply pretends they're dead."

"Oh, right. Yes."

"Anyway. He said to take 290 west to Flat Creek Road."

"Well, you drive and I'll enter the address," Reese instructed.

A few minutes later, with the navigation system showing how far they had to go, Reese stared out the window as they made their way out of the small town and into the more rural area. They were pretty much leaving civilization and heading into the great unknown.

"I hope you're not plannin' on goin' door to door," Reese said when they'd been on Flat Creek Road for a minute or so. There were dirt driveways every so often, all protected by closed and locked gates. The only thing that gave away that there were houses somewhere off in the distance were the mailboxes with reflective numbers on them.

"Nope. Just gettin' a feel for the area."

That didn't help much.

They passed a dry creek bed. When there was water, it would've flowed right over the road, which explained why it had been repaired more than once.

Just past that were a couple of sections of fence that seemed entirely out of place. Then more grass, more trees, and another gated property with a mailbox.

"And you think Calloway's holed up somewhere out this way with Kylie?"

"If we're lucky."

Reese didn't bother asking how he expected to find her if that were the case.

They passed several houses that were closer to the road, then a gated entrance to a farm, as well as a sign that warned of loose livestock. They kept going. There were fewer driveways the farther they went. The road narrowed, the outer edges washed away by water that flowed along the sides when the rain came.

When they drove over a cattle guard, Reese had to wonder how far they were going to go.

He observed out the window, noting more cattle guards, more trees, less grass, and fewer homes. The road continued to deteriorate, clearly not a priority for the county.

And then they reached the end of the line. The road they were on dead-ended into another. At least they didn't have to turn around.

Reese peered over at Brantley. "Which way now?"

Brantley didn't respond, but he took a right as though he knew exactly where he was going.

Since it was clear the man wasn't interested in chatting, Reese made note of the road they were on—County Road 205—and how far they were going. The good news was that the area wasn't abandoned. The fences along the road were maintained, and large parcels of land were dotted with recently baled hay. Still, most houses weren't visible from the road, although there were garbage cans every so often at the end of the driveway.

Reese glanced at the map on the screen.

"You realize we're comin' up on 290 again, right?" They'd pretty much taken a fifteen-mile roundabout, rather than going straight through.

Again, Brantley didn't respond. This time, Reese got worried.

"Okay. Pull over," he insisted, staring at Brantley.

With a huff, Brantley shook his head. "Can't."

"What? Why not?"

"Because we've got a tail."

Frowning, Reese glanced in the sideview mirror, looking behind them without turning around. "I seriously doubt someone followed you down a long, never-ending road. I think you're tired."

Brantley chuckled. "Definitely not tired. In fact"—he smiled over at Reese—"I'm energized for the first time since the last time I fucked you."

Reese felt his face heat as it always did when his husband made a comment like that.

CHAPTER TWENTY-THREE

BRANTLEY FELT HIS BLOOD HEAT.

It had started a ways back, when he noticed a red truck following them onto Flat Creek Road. At first, he figured it was someone who lived down there, so he waited until they turned off. Three minutes into the drive, they did. But strangely enough, a black, older model SUV pulled out not much later, this time from the other side of the road from where the first guy turned.

Since he wasn't the paranoid sort, Brantley had merely kept an eye on them, but he kept driving, doing the speed limit, taking stock of their surroundings.

But it was the third guy, this one in a silver Honda, that had given away their little game. They had been waiting at a stop sign, making it obvious what they were doing. Especially when Brantley paused long enough to let them go, only for the guy to wave him on. Brantley had waved back, flashing a good ol' boy grin.

"They think they're stealthy," Brantley told him. "Probably trained by the FBI."

"How do you know they're followin' us?"

He had to give Reese credit for not looking back and making it obvious. Although his truck's windows were tinted, he didn't doubt the guy was close enough to see if Reese turned around.

Brantley explained the leapfrog game they'd done.

"How would they know we're here?"

"My guess is Bobby was asked nicely to let good ol' Marty know if anyone came to town lookin' for him."

"Wouldn't that make him look suspicious?"

"Sure. But flash some cash and you can buy yourself some buddies who'll keep you apprised."

"True." Reese looked over at him. "Where to now?"

"Figure we'll stop at a gas station up here," he said when he turned right on 290, which would take them back the way they'd originally come. "See what they do next."

"And then?"

Brantley smiled. "If they follow, we'll lead them outta town, circle back."

"And if they don't?"

"We'll grab some lunch, wait a bit, then double back."

"To where?"

"The safe house."

Brantley could feel the intensity of Reese's stare. "What safe house?"

"The one they don't think I know about."

"And how *do* you know about it?"

"I was trained by Uncle Sam's Navy. How do you think I know about it?"

He could tell Reese wasn't impressed by his response.

"Did the store owner tell you?"

"No."

"You saw a sign? *Safe house here* with an arrow pointing to it?"

Brantley chuckled. "No. Now hold your questioning until we're done. You get Tesha out, let her do her business. I'll get gas."

"Want somethin' from inside?"

"Energy drink."

Brantley watched the silver Honda that was following them pass when he pulled into the parking lot. He kept his eye out for the others as he got out and pumped gas. The red truck drove by going in the opposite direction. He was moving slowly. Slow enough to earn a honk from someone trying to pull out of the parking lot.

By the time Brantley was finished, Reese was coming out of the store with Tesha and two energy drink cans.

"Do we still have company?" Reese asked when he climbed into the truck.

"No. Doesn't mean they're not waitin' up the road."

"For what? Us to leave town?"

That would be a reasonable assumption. Since Brantley hadn't stopped during their scenic drive, it was likely their pursuers thought he hadn't found what he was looking for. Little did they know, but they could've flashed bright neon signs with arrows pointing and not been as obvious as they were.

"Do me a favor," he told Reese when he put the truck in gear and pulled out of the lot. "Pull up an address for me. I need to know who owns the property."

When he had his laptop open, Brantley rattled off the address.

While Reese did the search, he continued to drive, making a few turns, left, then right, then right again. He saw no one following, and he was confident they believed he'd given up. But he still wanted to stall, to give them time to get comfortable again, so he drove toward the city limits, heading north. He figured there would be a decent enough restaurant up ahead, and they could have lunch, talk through what their next steps were, and give Atticus and Archer a heads-up.

"It's owned by a corporation. Looks like it's leased out as a hunting retreat." Reese looked at him. "Why?"

"How long's it been on the market?"

Reese typed, Brantley drove.

"They put it up for sale in November of 2018. Haven't changed the price since they did."

"Almost four years ago," Brantley noted.

"And?"

"And the for-sale sign is rusted and bent, which means they clearly aren't marketing the property with any sort of priority. The gate was leaning and barely latched with a rusted chain looped around it, but no lock."

"You saw all this while driving by?"

Brantley decided not to be offended by Reese's lack of faith in his abilities. "But two brand new trash cans were sitting at the edge of the street, one with the lid open and some takeout containers on top."

"Could be someone decided to clean out their car when they drove by. Figured it was a safe bet no one lived there."

"Oh, yes. Let's go with that."

"What? It could happen."

"It could. But it didn't."

"How do you know?"

"I just know."

"The store owner told you, didn't he?"

Brantley chuckled. "No. I swear. Speakin' of the store owner, I bought you somethin'." He reached into the back, grabbing the bag he'd stashed when they first got in.

"What is it?"

"Good ol' Bobby drives a hard bargain when it comes to givin' up information."

Reese pulled out the statues. "You actually paid money for these?"

"I did."

"How much?"

"Probably more than I should have. But it was worth it."

Reese frowned, peering over at him. "How do you figure?"

"Do you really think we would've had people tailin' us if we were goin' in the wrong direction?"

Reese was quiet for a moment, then said, "Fair point."

"I know it is. Now let's get some food and figure out how we're gonna get into that house."

"Where're we gonna eat?"

"I saw a sign for a barbecue joint back in town."

"Barbecue. Of course."

"Hey. It's a small town. You gotta try the barbecue."

"HEY. WHAT'S UP, BOSS?" ATTICUS ANSWERED WHEN he saw Brantley's name appear on his phone screen.

"Where're you at?"

"We are in… Where are we?" he asked Archer, putting the call on speaker so he could drive without crashing into someone or something.

"Somewhere between Austin and Blanco."

"I don't think that narrows it down much," Atticus told Brantley.

"We're almost to Dripping Springs," Archer clarified.

"How long will it take you to get to Johnson City?"

Another question Atticus couldn't answer while driving, so he looked at Archer.

Archer was staring at his phone when he said, "I'd say half an hour. Maybe less since Atticus is driving."

"Good. Head this way. Have you had lunch?"

"Nope. And I think Archer's stomach's startin' to get pissy."

Archer chuckled. "Heard that, did ya?"

Oh, yeah. Atticus had heard the rumble of Archer's stomach about twenty minutes ago. He'd been expecting the man to suggest they grab some food, but since he hadn't, he figured he wasn't quite ready for lunch. Apparently, he was wrong.

"We're at Pig Pen Barbecue in Johnson City. Meet us here."

"Don't have to tell me twice," Atticus said with a grin. "See you in a few."

"Did it sound like they've got something?" Archer asked from the passenger seat.

"You mean somethin' besides food?"

Archer chuckled. "Yeah."

"I can't imagine they'd have us drive that way unless they did." Since they'd gotten nowhere in their search for Allison Bogart—despite a cell tower ping near Dripping Springs—Atticus was more than happy to follow a hot lead. Flashing her picture door-to-door was not as much fun as it sounded, even if it was the quickest way to find someone when you didn't know where to look.

The rest of the drive was done mostly in silence, except for the radio, which was tuned to a country station. Not exactly what Atticus would've selected if he'd been alone, but when he found the channel, he got the feeling Archer liked it, so he went with it.

"Jesus," Archer said when they pulled into the parking lot of the barbecue place. "Can you smell that?"

"I smell it," he confirmed.

The air was fragranced with mesquite wood and meat. Lots and lots of smoked meat.

"I swear that's what heaven's gonna smell like."

Atticus laughed. "If you say so."

"I do."

They got out and made their way inside, finding Brantley and Reese at a wooden picnic table, plates of food half eaten in front of them.

When they walked up, Brantley raised a hand, signaling someone. "I didn't know what y'all wanted, so I got a little of everything. Take a seat."

Atticus waited for Archer to get his long legs under the table, then did the same, mindful that Tesha was down there.

"Did y'all find somethin'?" he asked, accepting the glass of water with lemon that the server brought him. "Thanks."

"We spent part of the mornin' shakin' a tail," Brantley said, wiping his mouth with a napkin.

"Oh, yeah?" Archer directed his full attention to the man. "That sounds promising."

"One of the shop owners sent us on a wild goose chase," Brantley explained. "We took a twenty-mile detour, but got some interesting information along the way."

"We *think* we got some information," Reese corrected.

"Trust me. That's a stash house."

"You think you know where Kylie is?" Atticus asked, feeling hope swell inside him. The idea of finding this woman who was clearly important to so many people was what fueled him right now. He wanted to find her—alive and well—and assist in bringing her back to her family. At the same time, he wanted to do serious bodily harm to the bastard who had taken her.

Brantley shook his head. "I didn't say that. But it's worth a look."

"What about the tail?" Archer inquired. "You shake him?"

"Them," Brantley corrected. "They played leapfrog with us for a while. There were three that I spotted. Someone must've tipped 'em off because they picked us up right after we turned onto Flat Creek Road. Followed for a while, then swapped. We came to the end of that road, and they swapped again. We pulled off for gas to shake 'em. Haven't seen 'em since."

"What are *we* here for?" Atticus hoped Brantley would say they would be going in to search the house with them.

Brantley looked at Reese. "How do you wanna play this out?"

Atticus waited while Reese chewed, swallowed, then downed some of his iced tea. His gaze slid from one person to the next.

"I'll take Archer with me," Reese said. "In our truck. You and Atticus take his truck. We'll go in first, see if we can catch the tail again, lead them out while you two go in from the opposite direction."

Atticus stared at Reese, wondering if he could've come up with a plan like that. He was thinking they'd all go in, check it out. Reese's plan was much more … coordinated and took into account that someone could still be watching them.

"We might have to walk in," Brantley said.

Atticus wasn't opposed to a hike. "How far?"

"I don't know. A mile, maybe."

Well, at least the Navy SEAL didn't say fifteen miles. Or klicks, as he'd heard Brantley say before. Hell, Atticus wasn't great at math, and trying to convert kilometers to miles, or vice versa, would take up a good part of his day.

"You armed?" Brantley asked him.

Atticus nodded. It had become second nature ever since he'd gone through training in Dallas.

"Good. Now eat. We've got some recon to do and we're burnin' daylight."

An hour later—because apparently Brantley wasn't in as much of a hurry as he had sounded—the five of them were walking out of the restaurant. Atticus had managed to eat, but he'd been wary of how much, not wanting to chance getting sick. As it was, the temperature had just broken eighty degrees Fahrenheit, and it was going to climb a bit more before the day was out. Not bad, but he would've appreciated some cooler weather.

"Give us twenty minutes," Reese told Brantley as he was loading Tesha into the truck. "We'll keep you updated."

Atticus nodded, then waited until Archer got in the truck before opening the driver's door. He had expected Brantley to insist on driving, but he never did. And since he was already sitting in the passenger seat, Atticus figured he would be.

"You want me to key an address into my phone's navigation?" he asked Brantley.

"What I want you to do is start the truck."

"Oh. Right." Atticus grinned, then inserted the key and started the truck.

Brantley adjusted the air vents. "Waste some time drivin' around here, then head west on 290. We'll come in the back way if we don't hear anything from Reese."

Nodding, Atticus put the truck in reverse and backed out of the spot.

For the next twenty minutes, he navigated through downtown Johnson City, being mindful of traffic laws. There weren't many people out on a Monday, but there were enough that he had to stop a couple of times and wait for them to cross the street.

When he finally got on the highway and headed west, he could feel his anxiety ratcheting up a notch or two. He was excited, but also fearful he would do something to fuck this up. Since he was partnering up with the big boss, the idea of screwing it all up was making his stomach churn.

"Relax," Brantley said. "It's not rocket science. We're gonna go in, do some recon, and come right back out."

Unless Kylie's there, Atticus thought. Then they'd have to alter their plans to save the girl.

He really hoped they got to save the girl today.

"HEY, BOSS. I THINK WE'VE GOT A problem."

Martin waited for the guy to elaborate. When he didn't, he did his best not to grind his molars to dust.

"And what problem would that be, Able?" he asked, somehow managing to keep his tone civil.

"Those guys that were askin' around about you are still here."

"Still here, where?"

"Well, right now, they're turnin' on Flat Creek Road again."

"Have they done anything newsworthy?'

"Uh... What's that mean?"

Martin ground his teeth until he thought one would crack. "Have they done anything I should be worried about?"

"Like what?"

Oh, Jesus Christ. "For fuck's sake, Able. Have they gone to the house?"

"Not that I know of."

"Well, then, I suggest you keep an eye on them."

"What if they go to the house?"

"Did Jerrel clear it out?"

"As best he could."

"Then I guess they'll go to the house and not find anything." When Able remained quiet, Martin got nervous. "They won't find anything, will they, Able?"

"No, boss. Jerrel cleared it out."

This was what he got for hiring locals to take care of things.

"Keep an eye on them."

"Will do."

Martin ended the call and dialed Allison's number.

As soon as she answered, he said, "Where are you?"

"Taking care of some things."

"Are you in Johnson City?"

"No."

At least she didn't lie to him. The bitch was known to push his buttons, and she was getting worse the older she got.

"You need to get back there."

"Why?"

"Looks like we've got company."

"I need to take care of something first. Then I'll head that way."

"Where's your partner?"

"He's getting things set up."

"Good. I'm glad to know you convinced him to do the right thing."

She remained quiet.

"Call me when you're back there."

"Sure."

The call ended, and he resisted the urge to throw his phone into the wall. He wasn't sure how the fuck those backwoods rednecks had managed to find him. He'd been careful. Extremely. There should've been no way for them to narrow down his whereabouts to a city.

That was assuming they were looking for him. If they were looking for someone else … well, he hated to be the bearer of bad news, but that was no longer a problem he had to deal with.

It paid to have someone on your payroll who knew how to disappear people in a way they could never be found.

CHAPTER TWENTY-FOUR

"I'm not sure why you think she would be here," Becs told Evan when they walked into the diner.

"She's looking for someone," he replied, appearing cool and casual, like this was an everyday occurrence.

"Good mornin'," the hostess greeted cheerfully. "Just two?"

Was it really still morning? Becs looked at her watch. 11:47 a.m. Yep. Still morning.

"Yes, ma'am," Evan replied to the woman. "By the window, if you don't mind."

She smiled and said, "Right this way."

"Are we really gonna have lunch?" Becs asked, keeping her voice low.

"We really are."

Rolling her eyes, she sighed and followed the woman to the table for two at the front of the restaurant. She had to admit, this was a pretty good spot to keep an eye on the restaurant as well as the parking lot.

Evan paused at the booth and gestured for her to sit. Before she could disguise her response, her surprise registered, and she knew he saw it. Playing it cool, she forced a smile and took a seat.

When he joined her on the other side, she realized he'd purposely positioned himself so he could see everything, while she was forced to look at him or the wall behind him. Sneaky butthole.

"Have you eaten here before?" he asked.

"Once or twice." She'd actually been here a few more times than that, but Becs wasn't interested in sharing that with Evan. She had come here with Atticus a few times for lunch. The diner was the closest to HQ and had better food than the fast-food joints they'd find farther up the road. Plus, Atticus seemed to like it. Or maybe he pretended to for her benefit. She made a mental note to ask him.

She and Atticus had established a friendship after the trip to New York, and she found he was easy to talk to. Not to mention, he was funny, and she didn't spend the majority of her time wondering whether he liked her.

Unlike Evan. Talking to him required her to get past the butterflies doing the cha-cha in her belly. And every second was spent wondering if her makeup needed to be fixed, or her hair, or whether she had something in her teeth.

They sat in silence for a few minutes while they perused the menu. When the server came around to take their order, Evan had her go first, so she ordered the chef salad and a glass of water. Evan ordered the same. When she left, the silence descended again, though this time it was thick enough to choke.

Sitting there with Evan, sharing a meal, was something Becs had fantasized about more times than she could count. Only in her fantasies, she wasn't staring out the window or nervous. She usually imagined herself carrying the conversation, making him smile and laugh.

She chanced a glance at him, noticing he was staring at her. "What?"

His expression softened. "Nothing."

"Then why are you starin' at me?"

"Because you're sitting in front of me."

Look at him being all logical. "Well, stop it."

He chuckled and she felt the pleasure bubble and fizz in her bloodstream. She loved to hear Evan laugh. He didn't do it all that much, so when he did, it was a treat.

Reminding herself they were working, Becs shifted gears. "What do you plan to do if we do see Allison?"

"Talk to her."

"About?"

"Her reason for being in Coyote Ridge."

"What if she says she's visiting family?"

"Would you believe that?"

Becs shrugged. "Maybe."

He smiled. "If she does say that, we'll ask who."

Again, he was being far too logical. "I can't imagine she'd just walk in here. Charlie's been lookin' for her since Sunday."

"Baz and JJ saw her in here."

Becs recalled reading that in the notes. It had been right before Brantley and Reese's wedding. Which meant Allison hadn't been too worried about anyone seeing her. Considering how small this town was, she had to know someone might recognize her.

Then again, maybe she thought no one would remember her since she only worked with the task force for a very short time.

"Fair enough. But JJ's pinged her phone dozens of times. She can't get a location, so it must be turned off."

"I'm sure she's got more than one phone. The number we have is likely for a burner she used specifically for us."

Yeah. She'd considered that too. Since Allison had purposely targeted the task force, it would make sense for her to have compartmentalized the role.

"You worked with Allison," Evan said casually. "What did you think of her?"

"I didn't work with her long enough to form an opinion." That was the truth. Mostly. She'd spent a little time with Allison at HQ, and she remembered the woman was bitchy, determined to get her way in all things. Her heart certainly hadn't been broken when she learned that Allison skipped out on the job.

"Why do you think she left?" she asked Evan. "She only worked one case. And didn't even finish it. Why would she up and quit so quickly?"

"Maybe Calloway called her in. Or maybe she figured out we didn't know anything."

"I can't imagine she had enough time to figure out anything. Not when we were focused on the case." The first big one that Becs had worked on, in fact.

Evan took a sip of water. "I worked with Trey that day, but according to Baz's notes, she was confrontational and too rigid when it came to how to handle things. I doubt he opened up to her about whatever it was she was lookin' for."

"I don't think he did, either." Becs couldn't see Baz spilling details to someone he didn't know. "But somethin' spooked her. Why else disappear the way she did?"

Becs remembered wondering whether she'd had a family emergency or simply didn't like the way the team worked together. Or maybe Allison had seen or heard something that sent her running. But what? It had been a fairly straightforward case. Cedric Hawkins had gone missing, and Governor Greenwood contacted Brantley for their assistance. In the end, it turned out that a group of wives had conspired to kill each other's husbands. Charlie was the one who talked down the wives, and they were all arrested. But based on Baz's notes, Allison hadn't approved of the way they were handling things, and at some point, she walked away, never looking back.

"Maybe she didn't want to stick around because we expected her to work," Becs considered. "If she already had a job as a spy for Calloway, she probably thought she had enough to do already."

Evan grinned. "Possibly."

Whatever her reasons, Becs wished they could find her. If she was tied in with this, they needed to know. They had very little to go on, and the thought of never finding out what happened to Kylie Walker didn't sit well with her.

"Let's have lunch, then we'll talk to some more people," Evan said, his tone smooth and easy. "And if she happens to walk in while we're eating, it'll make our jobs that much easier."

Yeah. If only.

WHEN EVAN COMMENTED THAT THEY MIGHT STUMBLE on Allison, he'd been joking. He'd used the excuse to get Becs to have lunch with him because he wanted to spend more time with her outside of HQ. Yesterday had been an eye-opener for him, and he realized how much he enjoyed talking to her, listening to her theories, watching her expressive features when she tried to work out a problem.

It was a ruse, and sure, his mother would likely accuse him of sending mixed signals again. She was probably right, since when it came to Becs, his only objective was to do right by her.

Did he want more? Absolutely.

Could he risk it? No.

More accurately, he couldn't risk her.

So, yeah, he was hoping they would run into Allison so that it didn't look as though he'd manipulated the situation. He had, but he didn't want it to appear that way.

And what do you know? That was precisely what happened as they were finishing their meal.

The waitress had just removed their plates when Allison Bogart walked into the restaurant, her eyes scanning every inch. As she looked his way, Evan purposely turned his attention to Becs, smiling at her as though they were enjoying a lunch date and not suffering through a silent meal together.

She looked nervous.

Not Becs.

Well, not *only* Becs. She looked nervous, too, but he was referring to Allison.

Leaning in, Evan touched Becs's hand, keeping his smile planted on his face. Her eyes widened with what he could only describe as shock, but she didn't pull away.

"She just walked in," he said softly, pretending he was telling her how pretty she was.

"Nuh-uh."

"Yes-huh," he chuckled. "Do not look."

Becs managed a smile, but he could tell it wasn't easy. "Is she with anyone?"

He shook his head, caressing her hand, hoping they looked like a couple enjoying a romantic meal together. It wasn't difficult to pretend since Evan had been thinking about it endlessly ever since New York, when he fucked everything up. The friendship they had established prior to the kiss that blew his mind had disappeared completely, thanks to all his mixed signals.

Becs leaned in. "What about outside? See anyone suspicious?"

Evan glanced out the window, scanning the parking lot. He didn't notice anyone lurking or anyone sitting in a vehicle waiting for her.

He looked at her again. "All clear."

"We need to talk to her."

"I agree." He patted her hand, sat up straight. "You should do that. I'll take care of the bill."

Becs frowned. "Me? Why me?"

"Because you can go to the restroom, then pretend to recognize her on the way there."

"It's not hard to pretend. I *do* recognize her." Becs lowered her voice. "And I'm sure she recognizes me. We didn't exactly become friends when she worked with us."

"Do you hold a grudge?"

Her red-gold eyebrows dipped low. "Of course I do. She's workin' with Calloway."

"Would you hold one if she didn't?"

Becs shrugged one shoulder. "Probably not."

"Well, then, pretend she's not workin' with anyone. Stop and chat, see how she's doing."

"That makes far too much sense," she muttered.

Evan laughed. God, he missed this woman so much.

Not that he could tell her that. She would shut down so fast it would likely make his head spin.

"While you do that, I'll text Atticus and let him know we've got eyes on her."

"Fine." Becs took a sip of her water, then placed her napkin on the table. "I'll do my best."

"Just pretend you're Gladys Overwith."

Referring to her fake persona that she used to get information over the phone made her smile. Her beauty blinded him, and he had to ignore the warmth that stirred his blood.

"Okay. Wish me luck," she said as she got to her feet.

"You don't need luck. You're a natural."

As he watched her walk away, he did his best not to stare at her extremely fine ass. It wasn't easy.

ARCHER DROVE AT REESE'S INSISTENCE. ACCORDING TO the man, he and Brantley resembled one another in size, at least from the perspective of anyone who might be following. He wasn't wrong.

"If you don't mind me asking, how'd you and Brantley meet?" It was his attempt to make casual conversation while they waited to see if someone would race up behind them. Since it was a long, relatively straight road, Archer figured he would be able to see them coming. Unless they were to come from one of the rare side roads that branched off.

"In town," he said simply.

Hmm. Was that Reese's way of shrugging off the question?

"Coyote Ridge, you mean?"

"Yep."

"Were you born and raised there, too?"

"Yep."

Archer grinned, checking the mirrors for anyone behind them. So far, they were clear.

"Is it like a secret or something?"

He felt Reese's eyes on him, so he glanced over. "One-word answers aren't usually your style."

Reese sighed. "Sorry. I can't help but worry about Brantley."

"In what way?"

"He's determined to find Kylie, and we still don't know that she's alive."

Archer had noticed that, too. In the past twenty-four hours, Brantley had shifted gears. He'd gone from adamant disbelief to unwavering hope. In a way, Archer understood why. The woman was ultimately family, so it would make sense that Brantley would jump in with both feet. However, as he'd learned a few times in his life, that was a quick way to come up against a wall of disappointment.

"I went on a date with JJ first," Reese said.

It took a moment for Archer to connect the dots. When he did, he laughed. "Before you and Brantley?"

"Yeah." Reese grinned. "I'd never been with a man before."

The way Reese said it sounded like he was embarrassed to admit it.

With his eyes scanning the rearview, Archer said, "I happen to believe we're pre-programmed for a deep, emotional connection rather than sexual orientation."

"So you've been attracted to women before?"

"Sure. Not the same way I'm attracted to men, but I've met a few who could keep my attention."

"Did you sleep with them?"

"One. When I was young and dumb. It was awful, but I figured that was mostly my fault since she was my first and I didn't know my ass from a hole in the ground." He checked his mirrors. "I've only been with men since. But I considered the possibility of it a couple of times. When it came down to it, I knew it wasn't going to satisfy me or her on a physical or emotional level, so I didn't."

"That's pretty deep, Archer." Reese laughed. "I'm impressed."

"Just because I'm hot doesn't make me shallow," he joked. "And I really do believe that." He barked a laugh, realizing how that sounded. "Not the hot part. I believe we make connections with *people*, not necessarily their gender."

"True." Reese pointed out the window. "When we get to the end, we're gonna turn right. Unless we've got a tail. Then we'll go left."

"Roger that."

Archer continued driving, keeping his full attention on their surroundings. That was how he noticed the silver Honda parked on the side of one of the feeder streets. As soon as they passed, it pulled out.

"I think we've got one," he told Reese, keeping his speed steady.

Reese shifted in his seat to check the sideview mirror. "Yep. That's the last guy we ran into." He grabbed his phone, dialed.

"Talk to me." Brantley's voice came through the truck's speaker.

"We've picked up a tail."

"Which one?"

"Silver Honda."

"They're waitin' for us?"

"Looks like it."

"Any way you can provide a distraction?"

Reese looked his way.

Archer grinned. "I'm sure that can be done."

"Good. We parked the truck in some trees off a side road. We're gonna walk in from here. I'll keep you updated."

"Be safe," Reese said, a slight plea in his tone.

"Always."

The call disconnected.

"Is Tesha buckled in?" Archer asked.

"Yeah."

"Good."

"Tell me you're not gonna—"

Reese's words were cut off when Archer slammed on the brakes. The truck came to a jarring stop, causing the car behind them to swerve to miss them. As soon as the guy drove past, Archer threw the truck in *reverse* and put his foot on the gas. He twisted in the seat to watch out the back window as he steered backward until he reached the last feeder street they'd passed.

"He's turnin' around," Reese said, sounding calmer than Archer expected.

Archer hit his brakes again and turned off on the side road, picking up speed so their tail would be forced to keep up. A few minutes later, he noticed an SUV had fallen in behind the Honda.

"There's a dark SUV back there."

"Yep. That's one of 'em."

"Does this road end?" Archer asked, wanting to know what his next step was before he got there.

Reese began tapping his phone. "It does, but there's another road that branches off just before."

"Left or right?"

"Left."

That would at least take them away from where Brantley and Atticus were.

"And the last tail? What color was it?"

"Red."

"Not too conspicuous, huh?"

"I'm not sure we're dealin' with pros."

Based on the way the guy behind him was keeping up, Archer wasn't so sure. The guy would fall back, giving himself time to see where Archer would go next. He was patient, calculating.

Which meant Archer needed to be, too.

CHAPTER TWENTY-FIVE

"WE'RE ALMOST THERE," BRANTLEY TOLD ATTICUS AS they threaded their way between a cluster of mesquite trees with low-hanging branches.

"Can't say I'm disappointed," Atticus huffed, grunting and cursing.

Brantley grinned. He couldn't help it. Then again, he'd chosen this particular field because he knew it would keep them hidden from the road. Of course, they also risked encountering an animal determined to keep them out. So far, they'd been lucky, but the birds had already sensed their presence, so it wouldn't be long before larger, more insistent wildlife figured it out.

"Do we know what we're walkin' into?" Atticus asked, slightly out of breath.

"All I know is the original owners use it as a deer lease."

"When is deer hunting season?"

Brantley grunted. "Now."

"Seriously?"

He nodded.

Atticus huffed. "Meaning, we might run into some hunters with guns?"

Brantley shrugged. That was the price of admission, he figured.

"When we came through earlier, I noticed fast food containers in the trash cans by the road."

"Which means someone's stayin' there. They might be waitin' for us."

It was possible. Especially since Archer and Reese had picked up another tail. He didn't know who they were dealing with. If they had half a brain, someone would stick by their hidey hole to keep it safe. If they didn't … well, Brantley was hoping they didn't because he wanted to get a look at the place.

He kept up his quick pace for a few more yards, then slowed, shifting to the west so they could come in from behind. He was going on the original real estate listing, which boasted several hunting cabins and a main residence on the property. It had been on the market for seven hundred eighty-one days, so there was no telling what condition it would be in. If the bent and rusted *For Sale* sign by the road was anything to go by, there was a chance it was falling in on itself.

Holding up a fist, Brantley stopped. Atticus followed suit, moving up beside him. Brantley pulled a pair of binoculars from one of the pockets in his pants. He used them to scan the area, looking for signs of life. He expected to see armed guards pacing back and forth. There were none.

Shit.

"What's wrong?" Atticus asked, his voice low.

Brantley passed the binoculars to him.

"No guards," Atticus said a moment later. "Looks empty."

Yeah, it did. Which meant one of two things: he was wrong and Kylie had never been here, or he was right but Kylie was no longer here. Either way, it wasn't what he was hoping to find.

Only one way to find out.

Taking the binoculars back, Brantley shoved them in his pocket, then removed his gun from the holster.

"Stay close until I tell you," he instructed Atticus before moving forward.

Atticus remained on his six, his weapon at the ready. Brantley kept his eye out for movement, but the only signs of life were a couple of squirrels chasing each other through the large oak tree in the front yard. And that pretty much told him there was no one outside.

The main house—or what he assumed was the main house—was nestled in between several oak trees, their branches stretched out, shielding the wraparound porch from the midday sun. The house appeared in decent condition. It could use a good spray-down to get the mold off the siding, but the roof wasn't sagging, and the porch wasn't leaning.

He heard no sounds as they moved closer. Still, they kept low, silent. Brantley used hand signals to direct Atticus to go to the front of the house while he moved to the back.

By the time he reached the porch, he knew for sure no one was there. The windows were open, and he could see through to the front. The few pieces of furniture inside were turned over, and cobwebs were growing from the ceiling.

"Son of a bitch," he muttered as he went inside.

They cleared each room as they went. Brantley started with the kitchen, moved to the living room, and then to the bathroom, leaving the two bedrooms to Atticus. By the time Brantley was walking back to the kitchen, he felt the full weight of disappointment. Nothing. Absolutely nothing.

"Hey, boss. You should come see this."

Securing his weapon, he walked toward the sound of Atticus's voice. He found him at the end of the hall in the larger of the two bedrooms.

"It looks like someone's been here," Atticus said.

Yeah. And whoever it was hadn't been there willingly. Not if the cuffs and chains were any indication. There was a wooden chair in the corner, a pair of cuffs dangling from the front two legs. On the floor was a twin-size mattress with a dingy yellow sheet. He wasn't sure whether yellow was the original color or if it had turned that way over time. Beside the mattress was a chain bolted to the floor with a cuff on one end. Probably used to keep their captive in place while they slept.

Atticus moved around the room, keeping to the outer edge while Brantley stood at the door, attempting to imagine Kylie chained up in this room. Surely, not. And damn sure not for nearly two fucking years.

"There's blood, boss." Atticus pointed. "Not a lot, but we might get DNA."

Well, the kid kept right on surprising him.

Brantley pulled out his phone and dialed Reese.

"Yeah?" he answered, sounding breathless.

"We're in the house. No one here."

"That's good to know."

"What are y'all doin'?"

"Archer's showin' off his Nascar skills."

"You haven't shaken the tail yet?"

"Not yet. On purpose."

"Well, when you do, meet us in town. We should be back that way in half an hour or so."

"Will do."

Brantley ended the call, then reached into another pocket, retrieving an evidence bag, a Q-tip, and a small vial he kept on him for this purpose.

"And Reese makes fun of you for wearin' those pants," Atticus said, grinning. "You got food in those pockets, too?"

"Maybe. Why? You hungry?"

Atticus shook his head, chuckling, then took the plastic bag when Brantley passed it over.

"Get a sample of the blood. I'm gonna check out the perimeter, make sure we haven't missed somethin'."

PRETENDING TO BE SURPRISED BY SOMEONE'S PRESENCE wasn't nearly as easy as it appeared on television. Not for Becs, anyway. Especially since seeing Allison brought back memories of the short time they'd worked together. She remembered the woman being bossy and bitchy. Then again, she also remembered that she hadn't been all that friendly to Allison either. Allison had rubbed her the wrong way from the beginning, and Becs hadn't been her best self.

None of that mattered now, of course. Allison was on their most-wanted list, and talking to her was crucial to this investigation. Becs had to put her personal feelings aside and do the job.

She left the table, intending to stroll right up to Allison, smile, and feign surprise at seeing her after so long. She made it to the table, but then kept right on going. Straight for the restroom.

"Chicken," she muttered as she pushed open the bathroom door. "Chicken, chicken, chicken."

Huffing her disappointment, Becs stared at herself in the slanted mirror over the sink.

"Definitely not investigator material if you can't even *talk* to someone."

She turned on the water, thrust her hands under the stream.

"You can do this," she told her reflection. "Go out there, walk up to her, and say *something.*"

She pressed the button on the soap dispenser and let the foam fill her hand.

"It's just a conversation. Not like you have to arrest the woman or anything. Evan can do that part." She rolled her eyes. "Or whatever."

Scrubbing her hands together, she continued to stare at her reflection. When she knew she couldn't stall any longer, she rinsed her hands and grabbed a paper towel.

"The second time has to be easier," she said as she walked out of the bathroom.

It wasn't. She walked right past Allison, wiping her sweaty palms on her jeans, her gaze locked on Evan, who was still sitting at their table.

"I can't do it," she told him, her hands trembling.

Rather than sit, she stood there like an idiot, not sure what to do next. Apparently, he wasn't having the same issue because he reached for her arm, pulling her toward him until she was forced to sit beside him in the booth.

"Relax," he whispered near her ear.

Oh, yeah. Sure. Like she could relax with his warm breath fanning her ear. It was bad enough she'd failed at being a super stealthy spy, but now she was going to turn into a puddle of goo beside him.

"We've got time," he said, his voice low, his fingertip soft as he moved her hair back.

She felt that barely-there touch throughout her entire body. It made the hair on her arms stand tall and her nipples pull taut in her bra.

This is not happening.

"She's not paying any attention to us," Evan said softly, and she swore she felt his lips brush her earlobe.

"But she knows we're here," Becs argued, hating that her voice was trembling. "I worked with her, Evan. And I wasn't exactly nice. I'm sure she remembers me well."

"That was a long time ago."

Not *that* long. Not to her, anyway.

"We just have to pretend we don't remember *her*."

"And how do you propose we do that?" Turning slightly to look at him, Becs's breath caught in her throat when she realized how close he was.

Evan's finger curled beneath her chin, and a second later, his lips were on hers. Before she could react the way a normal, cautious woman would, Becs found herself leaning in, her tongue sliding out to meet his. The kiss heated her from the inside out, the same way it had the first time her mouth mated with Evan's. It was intensely sweet and devastatingly familiar.

It took effort, but she managed to pull back without shrieking. She told herself she needed to maintain her cover because of Allison, which was the only reason she didn't smack him for that.

Okay, that was a lie. She didn't smack him because she could see he was just as dazed and confused as she was. The gleam in his eyes was brighter as he stared at her.

"I'm sorry," he whispered, his lips barely moving.

"Me, too," she said, meaning it. She was sorry for so many things, but most of all, she was sorry that Evan couldn't give her what she needed. If only she could sacrifice her happiness for a moment of delirium, then she could slake the lust, and they could move on, avoiding instances like this. But no, Becs had sacrificed far too much of herself for other people. She was doing things differently now.

Shoring up her nerves, she managed to get to her feet. She smoothed her hand down her shirt and turned, intending to talk to Allison, only to realize the woman was no longer sitting at the table. Her gaze snapped to the door when the bells sounded, and she saw her walking outside.

"She's leavin'," she told Evan before racing after her. As soon as she stepped outside, she called Allison by name.

The woman turned, clearly surprised.

"Hey!" Becs tried to sound as though she was a long-lost friend, thrilled to see her. "How are you?"

Allison's eyebrows angled downward as she stared back.

"It's me, Gladys," she said without thinking. "Gladys Overwith."

Allison's frown deepened.

When Becs was close enough, she dropped the facade. "That was a joke. I'm not sure if you remember me. Rebecca. I go by Becs. We worked on the task force together."

Allison shook her head. "I think you've got me confused with someone else."

"I'm pretty sure I don't. You're Allison Bogart, an FBI agent working for Martin Calloway."

There was a minuscule shift of the muscles over her left eyebrow that gave her away, but Allison attempted to play dumb. "I don't know who that is."

"But I'm sure you know Brantley Walker and Reese Tavoularis."

Allison's eyes shifted to something over Becs's shoulder. "I'm sorry. I've got to go."

Watching as Allison turned to walk away, Becs saw everything they'd worked for go right down the drain.

"No, wait," she said, grabbing Allison's wrist so she couldn't leave. "We need to talk."

"Let me go," Allison hissed, jerking out of her grip. "You've got me confused with someone else."

Becs was preparing her argument when Allison turned on her heel and raced off.

At that moment, Evan appeared at her side, watching as the woman they'd been looking for darted between cars. A moment later, she backed out of a parking space in a black, four-door sedan that looked like something the FBI would drive.

"Did you talk to her?"

"She kept sayin' I'd confused her with someone else." She looked at Evan. "That *is* her, right?"

"Yeah. That's her."

Becs pursed her lips, staring after the car as it left the parking lot.

"What is it?" Evan asked.

She looked at him. "I guess I was expecting someone a little less ... scared."

"Scared?"

Becs nodded. "Yeah. I'd go so far as to say that woman was terrified."

"Of what?"

"That's the sixty-four-thousand-dollar question."

Evan chuckled. "You are far too young to remember that show."

Smiling for the first time since he kissed her, Becs looked up at Evan. "You're right. I am. But are you?"

"Old man jokes. Nice."

She thought so.

CHAPTER TWENTY-SIX

TRAVIS HAD SPENT THE DAY AT THE resort, doing his best to focus. It hadn't been easy when the only thing he wanted to do was call Brantley to find out what his cousin had found. If anything. At the same time, he was intent on ensuring his brothers didn't find reason to question him. It wasn't easy because they were fairly astute, usually catching on to any shift in his mood.

Somehow he managed to make it through the day without calling Brantley and without raising eyebrows. The urge to make that call was still there, growing more persistent by the minute, but he was determined to let it go. He was fighting the hope that was building, refusing to believe that Kylie could be alive. It wasn't possible. No matter how much he wished it were.

Now, as he made his way up the stairs, he noticed Kate's light shining under the door.

He stopped, rapping his knuckle on the wood once before opening it. "Shouldn't you be asleep?"

She was sitting up in her bed, a pillow behind her and a book resting on her raised knees.

Kate glanced over and smiled. "I'm not tired yet."

Jerking his chin in the direction of the book, he said, "What is that?"

She turned the book so he could see the cover. "Mommy used to read this to me."

His chest tightened as it did whenever he heard pain in his children's voices.

"I remember." He walked over to the bed, sat on the edge by her legs. "You miss her, I know."

Kate met his gaze. He expected to see pain in her light brown eyes, but it wasn't there.

"What's on your mind?" he asked, curious.

She looked away. "Nothin'."

Travis patted her knee. "Talk to me, kid. Or I'll tickle you."

Kate jerked her knee away, giggling. "Don't you dare."

"I will," he warned, grinning.

"I'm thinkin' about Mommy."

"What about her?"

There was a glimmer of reservation in her eyes before she finally said, "Mommy came to me in a dream."

He understood that all too well because Kylie came to him in his dreams, too. Often.

"She was kinda there," Kate explained. "Kinda not."

"How so?"

Kate shrugged.

"Did you see her?"

"No." She shook her head. "But I could hear her. She sounded far away."

"Was it a good dream?"

She nodded. "She told me everything's gonna be okay."

"Mommy was always right," he told his daughter.

"Is," Kate corrected. "Mommy *is* always right."

Not sure what to say to that, Travis patted her knee again. "You should really get some sleep, kiddo. You've got school tomorrow."

Kate nodded, then set the book on the nightstand before fluffing the pillow and flopping down on it, before turning on her side, facing away from him.

"I love you."

"I love you, too, rugrat." He stood, turned off the bedside lamp, then leaned over and kissed her cheek. "I'll see you in the mornin'."

He made it to the door before Kate called him.

"Hmm?"

"Do you think Mommy could come back?"

Stopping at the door, Travis peered back at her. She had turned to look his way. The light from the hallway cast a glow of yellow over her face. She looked so much like Kylie, it made his chest ache.

"Why would you ask that?"

She shrugged again. "I don't know."

Something stirred in his chest. It was warm and surprisingly … comforting.

"Goodnight, honey."

"Night, Daddy-O." She yawned and rolled over. "I'll tell Mommy we aren't givin' up. She told me we shouldn't."

Travis closed her door, keeping his hand on the knob for several seconds. When he finally released it, that something he felt a moment ago shifted inside him. For the first time in one year, eight months, and twenty-four days, he *felt* something. He wasn't sure what it was, but he couldn't seem to fight it. It flowed through him, a powerful surge of … was that relief?

He made his way down the hall to his and Gage's bedroom, the same bedroom they'd once shared with Kylie. At first, Travis hadn't been able to sleep in there. It had been too painful. Then Gage had convinced him to try. Despite his pain, he'd given in and found that he felt closer to her there, even with her gone.

Closing the door, he looked around, took it all in. Gage had pulled down the blankets on the bed, but he wasn't in it. Travis could hear water running in the bathroom, figured he was in there brushing his teeth.

Staring at the bed, he swore he could see Kylie lying on it, stretched out beautifully the way she used to. So fucking beautiful, it hurt to look at her sometimes. He would give anything to get that back, to get *her* back.

Hope swelled and pulsed in his chest. The feeling was invigorating.

The door to the bathroom opened, and Gage stepped out. "You get Kate to put down the book?"

Rather than answer, Travis turned to look at his husband, admiring him. He was wearing shorts, as he always did when they slept. Having kids who would make their way to the bedroom for various reasons changed things. Gone were the days when they could sleep naked.

Gage stepped closer, worry creasing his brow. "What's wrong?"

"Nothin'." And for the first time in one year, eight months, and twenty-four days, he actually meant it. Nothing was wrong. Nothing at all. Because those holes that had been left with Kylie's absence, those cracks and fissures that had formed, were healing. Not because he was moving on from her. That would never happen. She owned a piece of his soul. Always would.

Gage moved closer. "Travis? You're scarin' me."

He reached for Gage, gripping the back of his neck and pulling him closer. Rather than tell him what he was thinking, Travis leaned in and kissed him. Hard. Demanding. He didn't hold back, couldn't. For the first time in so fucking long, he was riding the high that he got from hope.

"Travis…" Gage moaned, his hands insistent, eager.

He swore he could feel his blood pumping in his veins, his heart beating. He felt alive and powerful after months of endless darkness.

Travis made no effort to be gentle or to take his time. He stripped his clothes off, not waiting for Gage to assist.

"Lose the shorts," he instructed.

"What's goin' on?" Gage asked, still watching him, although he did shove his shorts down.

He grabbed Gage's wrist and pulled him closer to the bed. "Turn around."

It was apparent he wanted to ask more questions, but Gage did as Travis insisted, facing away from him. He put his arms around Gage, flattening his palms on his chest and pulling him back. He kissed his neck, soaking up the warmth of his body.

"Travis…" Gage moaned when he nipped him, then smoothed the sting with his tongue.

He plucked Gage's nipple with one hand while the other slid down his abdomen, inching lower until he could wrap his fingers around Gage's iron-hard dick.

"Oh, fuck," Gage hissed, his hips thrusting as he tried to fuck Travis's fist.

Travis sucked on his neck, not caring that he might leave a mark. He was supercharged, every cell in his body coming to life.

He growled softly, stroking Gage's cock firmly. "I need to be inside you."

Gage groaned.

Travis jerked open the nightstand drawer, grabbed the lubricant. Before Gage could ask anything more, he put his hand in the middle of Gage's back and pushed him down, his chest on the mattress.

He wasn't sure what had come over him, where this surge of life-infusing hope had come from, but he was past the point of questioning it.

"T<small>RAV</small>—" H<small>IS WORDS WERE CUT OFF WHEN</small> Travis's lubed fingers found his hole, pushing inside.

Gage wasn't sure what had come over his husband, but there was something different. He wasn't the same man who had gone through the motions of the day. Something had been triggered inside him, and for the first time in what felt like decades, he was seeing a spark of the man he'd once known.

"Spread your legs wider," Travis growled.

Gage shifted his feet, spreading his legs while his upper body remained pressed to the mattress.

"Better," Travis crooned, his fingers sinking in deeper, tormenting him with pleasure. "I used to fuck you like this. Remember?"

"Yes," he hissed, rocking back against the fingers fucking him.

"Kylie would watch, playing with herself."

Gage gasped. That was the first time Travis had mentioned Kylie in any way that wasn't soaked in sadness.

"I swear I can see her, Gage," he growled from behind him. "Watching me fuck you."

Closing his eyes tightly, Gage let the mental image form. He didn't have difficulty retrieving those memories. He thought about Kylie often. He was unable to let go of her, unwilling to forget all that they'd shared. While Travis had blocked it out, Gage had drowned himself in thoughts of her.

"Then she would move," Travis said, his fingers disappearing, replaced by the thick head of his dick. "She would position herself so you could eat her pussy while I fucked you."

Gage groaned, the hairs on his arms standing on end as pleasure annihilated him.

"I would fuck you hard"—Travis slammed his hips forward—"so you could spear her pussy with your tongue."

He swore he could almost taste her.

"Fuck, Gage," Travis growled, his words reverberating through him. "You feel so fuckin' good."

Gage fisted the blankets, providing resistance to Travis's punishing thrusts. It was all he could do, accepting the penetration, losing himself to the pleasure.

"Goddamn, that's good." Travis tapped Gage's right thigh. "Put your knee on the bed."

Travis paused long enough for Gage to maneuver, putting his knee on the bed. Then Travis was driving into him again.

"Oh … fuck … yes," Gage moaned. "Trav … fuck … just like that."

Their combined grunts and groans echoed through the space as Travis fucked him the way he used to. Like he owned him. He had no idea what had come over the man, but he didn't care. This was what he needed. To have Travis back, even if only for a few minutes.

It wasn't long before Travis had maneuvered him onto the bed, flattening him completely.

"Gage … baby … you ready for me to come?"

He couldn't form words, so he growled his approval.

"Fuck. It feels too good. Don't wanna stop," Travis grunted, pausing once again, this time pulling Gage's hips back.

He rocked up onto his knees, moving with Travis, not wanting him to stop either. He relished the way Travis's fingertips dug into his hips as he held him firmly in place, plowing him from behind.

Balancing himself on one forearm, Gage reached down, stroked his cock in time to Travis's thrusts.

"Oh, yeah. That's it. I want you to come."

Gage gritted his teeth, holding off for as long as he could. When Travis's grip became nearly painful, he knew his husband was close. He held on for several more thrusts before he let go with a guttural cry.

"Fuck," Travis roared, slamming into him one final time, his cock erupting, pulsing deep inside him.

When it was over, he was shocked once more when Travis fell on top of him, blanketing him the way he had long ago. Sex with Travis had been good, but it hadn't been quite like this in a long damn time.

Gage lay there, catching his breath while Travis shifted, his arms banding around him. They remained like that for long minutes, the sweat cooling on their skin.

"What was that?" he asked, hesitant to ask because he didn't want this to end.

Travis kissed his shoulder. "Hope, baby. That was hope."

He wanted to ask Travis what that meant, but he kept the question to himself. He didn't want to shatter the moment, not sure when or if they would ever get it back again.

Rather than question it, Gage decided to simply breathe.

CHAPTER TWENTY-SEVEN

When Archer received a text message from Atticus, asking him if he wanted to grab a beer at Moonshiners, he hadn't been able to refuse. It had been one of those days. The kind that consisted of excitement and intrigue but ended in disappointment. Their trip to Johnson City had revealed a few things, though not enough to do them any good. It was obvious they were headed in the right direction, but it seemed they might've gotten there too late.

Rather than sit in his room at the B and B, Archer figured sharing a beer with his new partner was a far more appealing way to spend his evening, so here he was, occupying a booth near the wall, waiting for Atticus to arrive.

He busied himself by checking his email on his phone, resisting the urge to look at his text messages. He knew Spencer hadn't texted or called, but that didn't stop his stupid, hopeful heart from wanting to look. You know, just in case. Somehow he managed, skimming emails, not really seeing much of anything.

"Hey, man. Sorry I'm late."

Looking up, Archer smiled. "No worries." Based on Atticus's wet hair, it was apparent he'd taken a shower.

"Let me grab a beer. You want another?"

Archer looked at the bottle, noticing for the first time it was almost empty.

"Uh, yeah. Sure. And grab a coupla shots while you're at it."

Atticus flashed a mischievous smile. "I like the way your brain works, Halligan."

Archer wasn't sure getting shit-faced was a good idea for either of them, but it seemed better than sitting there, wallowing in the disappointment.

An hour and a half later, they were well on their way to drunk. Okay. Amend that. There was a good chance Atticus was already there. Based on the way he was sitting, with his elbows resting on the table, it was possible he was doing it to keep himself propped upright.

"I'm not kiddin'," Atticus slurred. "He likes to watch."

"Sounds kinky."

"It is." Atticus took a swig of his beer. "Or it was. He's moved on."

"What do you mean moved on?"

Atticus shrugged. "He's keepin' his distance. Off doin' other things."

"I'm sure it's all in your head."

"No. It's his M.O. In the thick of it one minute, then off and ready for the next adventure. I don't know why I thought he'd be different with me."

"And Slade?"

"No idea. If I breathe wrong, he thinks I'm cheatin'." Atticus sighed. "I know you don't wanna hear about this. It's sad and pathetic."

Archer snorted. "It is not. It's your life. You're my partner. I'll gladly listen if you need to vent."

"What about you? You need to vent?"

He shrugged. "Maybe."

"All right, spill. Who's the lucky guy in your life?"

"There isn't one."

"I find that hard to believe."

"There was someone," he admitted. "But it didn't work out."

"Anyone I know?"

Archer stared at Atticus for a moment, considered holding back. It didn't seem fair, though, since Atticus wasn't having a problem opening up to him.

"Spencer Elliott."

Atticus leaned forward, a slow smile forming. "No shit? Slade's brother."

"You know him?"

"Met him once. Here, actually. He tried to get me to go home with him."

Archer tried not to let that bother him.

"I didn't, but I don't think he cared one way or the other."

Sounded like Spencer.

"You two hook up?"

"No. Went out a coupla times. It lasted all of a minute."

Grinning, Atticus flopped back. "What happened?"

"Nothing." Archer reached for his beer. "Absolutely nothing."

Atticus didn't say anything, but Archer got the feeling the man was studying him. He wanted to ask what he was thinking, but decided he didn't really want to know. Atticus had been in town for a while now; there were likely plenty of stories he'd heard about Spencer. Based on what Archer knew, they would be fabricated, but that didn't stop the rumor mill from grinding.

"I'm sorry it didn't work out for you, man. Spencer seems like a nice guy."

He was. But Spencer also seemed to be his own worst enemy. Archer wasn't sure there'd ever been a chance for them to begin with.

"You boys need anything?" the waitress asked, removing the empty glasses and bottles from the table.

"Two more shots, two more beers," Atticus said. "Put 'em on my tab."

"Will do."

When she was out of earshot, Atticus looked at him and grinned. "I'm startin' to think serious relationships aren't in the stars for me."

"Yeah?"

Atticus spun the beer he was still nursing. "This is the first one for me. Probably the last."

"Oh, I wouldn't rule it out yet. How old are you?"

"Twenty-five."

"Still young. You've got plenty of time."

Atticus stared at him, those green eyes catching the light and glittering with what Archer could only guess was mischief.

"You're speakin' from experience, huh? Because what? You're old and wizened?"

Archer huffed a laugh. "Somethin' like that. I'll be thirty next year. Old age isn't far off."

Atticus's grin widened. "I'm thinkin' you've got a few good years left."

"You think?" Archer teased.

The waitress appeared, setting down the shots and the beers.

"Thanks," he told her, earning a smile in return.

"Anytime, handsome."

223

When she walked off, Atticus leaned forward, lowered his voice. "That happen to you a lot?"

"What?"

"Chics hittin' on you?"

"From time to time."

"Whatever." Atticus laughed. "I think God made you gay to protect you from the ladies."

Archer grinned, staring back at Atticus. He wasn't sure he'd been this relaxed in … well, quite some time. He used to hang out with Simon and Paige, get drinks at the bar, chat for a while, but they rarely asked him about his personal life. Simon did it out of respect, although Archer would consider them good friends. And Paige … well, Paige was too busy talking about herself to really care about other people. He didn't fault her for it. It was just the way she was programmed.

"Riddle me this, Batman," Atticus said, chuckling. "If Spencer called you up right now and invited you over, would you go?"

"Sure," he said, although he realized he wouldn't leave Atticus to go to Spencer's. But that wasn't what Atticus was asking. "Yeah. I'd go."

Atticus took a long pull on his beer, and Archer pretended there was a gleam of disappointment in Atticus's pretty green eyes.

"What about you?" he asked because the silence was getting weird. "If Slade or Carson texted right now and told you to get home ASAP, would you go?"

"After I finished my beer … sure. I would."

They stared at each other for a moment, the silence settling in again. Archer ignored whatever was going on down south, reminding himself that Atticus was in a relationship. With two people.

Atticus lifted his shot glass, holding it up. Archer reached for his, did the same.

"To new possibilities," Atticus said.

They tapped glasses before downing the drink. Archer couldn't keep from staring at Atticus, wondering what would've happened if Atticus had been single when they met. For whatever reason, he felt a connection with the man. One he was eager to explore. Not necessarily in a sexual manner.

Big ol' liar, that annoying inner voice said.

Fine. Would he pass up a chance to fuck the man? If the tequila had any say in the matter, then no, he wouldn't pass it up. And though he didn't think the attraction was one-sided, he had to remember that Atticus James was off limits for a long list of reasons, the least of which being that he was his partner.

Plus, Archer was likely projecting since Spencer had shunned him. Rejection was a bitch, and Archer had experienced his fair share, despite what Atticus thought.

As he sat there, he ignored the persistent tequila-riddled thoughts and made a silent vow to keep this thing with Atticus professional and friendly. Nothing more.

"I should probably get home," Atticus said, looking up at him. "I'm sure Slade's gonna have a few things to say about me havin' a few drinks with my partner."

"Well, just tell him we were talkin' about the case."

"Wouldn't matter. I could record our meeting, play it back to prove it was innocent, and he'd still find a way to accuse me of cheating. Someone really did a number on him, and I'm not sure he'll ever get over it."

"He will." Archer stared at his beer. "Give him time."

"Time's the one thing I've got in spades." He grinned. "Patience, on the other hand…"

Archer knew the feeling all too well.

SITTING AT HIS DESK, REESE LOOKED UP when he heard Brantley's heavy footsteps.

The man appeared in the doorway, looking tired and sexy as hell. "You about ready for bed?"

Reese leaned back in his chair, stretched. "What time is it?"

"Time for you to get naked."

Chuckling, Reese glanced at the clock. It was after midnight, which meant he'd worked about three hours longer than he intended. For good reason, of course. He'd been going over photos of the house Brantley and Atticus had visited earlier. Rather than go there himself, he'd remained with Archer, leading their tails on a wild goose chase for the better part of an hour.

Not that it mattered. The house had been empty. If Kylie had been there, she was long gone now.

"What's on your mind, Tavoularis?"

Shaking off the thoughts, Reese got to his feet. "Nothin'."

"Don't lie to me."

"I'm not," he said sincerely, moving closer to Brantley. When his husband remained in the doorway, Reese walked up to him, put his hands on his hips. "I'd rather put it away for the night and think about it tomorrow."

"You sure?"

He nodded.

Brantley's big hand curled around the back of Reese's neck, urging him closer. "I can think of a few ways to distract you."

"I'm bankin' on it."

When Brantley's mouth settled on his, Reese leaned into the kiss, relaxing for the first time in hours. He sensed Brantley's disappointment in the day, and since he mirrored it, a distraction was exactly what they both needed.

As usual, Brantley became the aggressor, his hands firm as he turned Reese so that his back was to the wall. His mouth was urgent, yet sweet, his tongue insistent as it explored.

Reese had never been with anyone who could own him the way Brantley did. Then again, Reese hadn't realized it was exactly what he needed to be happy. To have someone who wouldn't hide their hunger, their need.

He thought back to what Archer had said earlier: *I happen to believe we're pre-programmed for a deep, emotional connection rather than sexual orientation.*

Reese had never thought about it that way, but as soon as Archer said it, the words resonated with him. It was true. Something inside him had connected with Brantley on an emotional level, and it had bloomed from there. The physical attraction had been scary at first, but nothing had ever felt as right before. Now, Reese couldn't imagine wanting anyone as much as he wanted Brantley.

Brantley's mouth traveled down his jaw to his neck. Reese tilted his head, giving him better access, letting the sensations wash over him.

"I want you naked," Brantley groaned, nipping at his collarbone. "Let me get you naked, baby."

Fueled by Brantley's need, Reese slid his hands beneath Brantley's shirt, soaking up the heat of him, feeling the strength in his hard body.

With frenzied hands, they started stripping away clothing, dropping it to the floor as Brantley maneuvered them into his office. Reese knew where he was going, knew what his intentions were, and he wasn't about to put up a fight. Not tonight.

No, tonight, he wanted to give himself over to this man, to revel in the pleasure that generated when they were together.

Brantley's mouth was wicked hot as he trailed his lips down Reese's chest, his stomach. It was all Reese could do to remain standing when Brantley went to his knees, working to free Reese's cock from his jeans.

"Jeezus," Reese hissed, palming Brantley's head when he enveloped his dick in the heated cavern of his mouth. "Fuck."

He helped Brantley remove his jeans as best he could while enduring the intensity of that blistering hot mouth on his cock. It wasn't easy, but he figured that was his husband's plan. Nothing with Brantley was ever easy, but damn if it wasn't worth it.

Once Reese was stripped of his clothes, he helped Brantley get rid of his while returning the favor: fingers fondling, mouth wandering, palms gliding over smooth, hot skin.

When they were both naked, Reese found himself on his back, Brantley's big, hard body lying over him. Skin to skin, mouth to mouth. The kiss was fiercely brutal and intensely gentle, all at the same time. It caused his brain to swim as lust bubbled in his bloodstream, making his skin prickle.

"Please," he whispered, wanting to feel more of Brantley. All of him.

"Anything, baby," Brantley moaned, shifting and manhandling Reese into position.

Hooking one foot over the back of the couch and planting the other on the floor, Reese made room for Brantley between his legs. Using his saliva as a lubricant, Brantley stroked himself. Then his husband shifted, aligning their bodies before slowly pushing inside him.

Reese hissed as pain-soaked pleasure assaulted him.

"Relax, baby."

He did, rocking his hips to change the angle, allowing him to take more of Brantley. Reese grabbed Brantley's ass, jerking him forward.

"Oh, fuck, yeah. Take me, Reese. Let me in."

Then the world stopped spinning as Brantley's mouth fused to his once more. Their tongues danced as Brantley fucked him, sliding in slowly, retreating. They remained like that for long minutes, the original discomfort morphing into exquisite ecstasy.

"You were made for me, Reese," Brantley mumbled against his mouth. "Just for me."

He believed that because nothing in his life had ever felt as perfect as this. As though every piece had clicked into place when Brantley Walker came into his life.

"Hold onto me," Brantley instructed.

Reese slid his hands up Brantley's back, holding him as Brantley began fucking him. Harder, deeper, faster. The couch groaned beneath their weight, but their cries of pleasure drowned out the sound as they chased that euphoria-driven release.

"Wait, Reese," Brantley said through gritted teeth. "I want you to come in my mouth."

Reese shook his head. "Can't. Wait."

He was close. Too close.

"Yes, you can. Oh, fuck … Reese!"

Brantley slammed his hips forward, his cock pulsing inside him. Reese fought the overwhelming need that surged into him. He gritted his teeth, the need overwhelming him.

"Your turn," Brantley said, moving off him.

A second later, Reese's cock was buried in Brantley's throat, and he was coming with a cry so violent, he wondered if he would even have a voice left.

Oddly, he didn't care.

CHAPTER TWENTY-EIGHT

Tuesday, October 4, 2022

CARSON HESITATED AT SLADE'S FRONT DOOR.

For some people, it was the middle of the night. For him, it was just after four, which meant the start of his day.

Granted, he was usually not attempting to sneak into other people's houses before dawn. He wasn't looking to get shot or arrested, so he tended to steer clear of such situations.

In his defense, this was all Atticus's fault. He seemed convinced that Carson was drifting and Slade was self-destructing. And fine, perhaps that was the case. Carson would admit he wasn't putting forth much effort to make this work. Slade made it difficult because it was clear he didn't trust him. And since Atticus was determined that this was an all-or-nothing relationship, Carson found his heart wasn't in it as much as he initially thought.

So, yeah, Atticus had a right to be skeptical about where this was going. He didn't blame the guy for wanting to keep it casual. That wasn't Carson's intention initially, but Slade also hadn't been anything more than a fantasy that played out in his head when he was with Atticus. When they introduced the flesh-and-blood man, it just wasn't playing out the way Carson had envisioned.

But as Atticus pointed out, they were supposed to be moving forward, so this was Carson's attempt at doing that. His last-ditch effort, perhaps.

He checked the front knob, noticed that it was unlocked.

To go in or not to go in? That was the question.

Fuck it. He was going in.

NICOLE EDWARDS

Turning the knob slowly, he pushed open the door and stepped inside the house. There was no security alarm to halt his progress, no dog looking to protect its territory. No, here in small-town, small-crime Coyote Ridge, most people slept with their doors unlocked and their windows open.

Probably not the sanest thing to do, but it worked in Carson's favor right now, so he wasn't complaining.

Slade's house wasn't much different than his own as far as layout. There was no fancy entryway, no foyer to hang your coat. There was a single closet behind the door, and the rest of the space was the living room, which was currently dark. Not even a lamp was left on in the corner.

To the left was the kitchen, which appeared to be dark from where he was standing, but that didn't stop him from being quiet when he closed the door behind him. Straight back was a single hallway that led to the primary bedroom, which Slade occupied. To the right, another hallway, this one leading to the second bath and two additional bedrooms. At one point, there'd been a total of four bedrooms, but Slade had knocked down walls and combined two smaller rooms to make a large one to accommodate his workout space.

Carson glanced in the kitchen, confirming no one was in there, before heading for the hallway. He didn't stop until he reached Slade's bedroom door. It was closed, as usual. He was the only person Carson knew who closed the door, even though he lived alone. Of course, he now had a roommate, but still.

He told himself he wouldn't care if he opened that door to find Atticus sleeping in Slade's bed. Why would he? This was what he wanted, right? To fulfill his voyeuristic dreams.

Funny how a couple of weeks ago, that probably would've been the case. Now? Not so much since somewhere along the way, Carson's heart had started disconnecting from what he thought of as his happily ever after.

Then again, this was what always happened. He lost interest quickly, and usually it was of no fault of the men he was with.

230

But that was a problem for another day. Right now, he had a single goal in mind, so he pretended it didn't matter. Deep down, it did. Not because he was jealous that Slade was with Atticus or vice versa. No, his jealousy stemmed from his being left out. He didn't want to be left out. He wanted to be as much a part of this as the two of them, but the reality was, he couldn't be since they lived under the same roof, and he didn't.

Which was the very reason he was there now. Creating a space where he could belong, even if for only a small portion of the day. Because if he couldn't get that much out of the relationship, he wasn't sure why he would even bother.

Taking a deep breath, he opened the door.

The room was pitch black, giving him no clue as to how many bodies were in that bed. He was committed one way or the other, so he closed the door and walked over to the bed. Since he hadn't bothered to get dressed, it took only a moment to slip off his pajama pants and slide under the blankets.

The sheets were cool, telling him Slade was the only one in here. The relief that came stole his breath and made his heart thump a little harder.

He pulled the blankets up and scooted toward the center until he was spooning behind Slade.

"I'm surprised you decided to join me," Slade mumbled, his voice thick with sleep.

Carson didn't respond; not sure he wanted to ruin the illusion. There was no doubt Slade thought he was Atticus, and the wound that acknowledgment created was deep and painful.

He slipped his arm over Slade, pulling him back until his body heat seeped into him. Unable to resist, Carson pressed his nose to the back of Slade's neck and inhaled his musky scent. The man smelled good. He always smelled good.

When Slade pushed back against him, Carson kissed his neck, trailing his lips lower, gliding over his shoulder. His skin was smooth and warm, and his taste ignited the lust Carson had always had for this man.

As much as he wanted to roll Slade over and slide into the heat of his body, he couldn't. Not until Slade realized he wasn't Atticus. And the only way to do that was to wake him up fully before he molested the man.

Carson relaxed once more, tightening his hold, hugging Slade from behind. He liked this. The familiarity. He'd missed this since their breakup. It was rare for Carson to become familiar with anyone because his relationships were generally short-term and at arm's length. For a reason. When he tried to get serious, things never worked out.

He'd been slightly disappointed when Atticus had taken everything off the menu except for sex. He understood it, even agreed with it. But he'd been hoping for more. Hoping he could *want* more. Sex was the easy part. Too easy, sometimes. Carson had thought there might be a future for him and Atticus, him and Slade. After his last conversation with Atticus, the illusion was fading, which was probably why he was there, in Slade's bed. Attempting to see if there was anything left to salvage.

Slade's hand covered his, their fingers linking before Slade pressed Carson's palm to his chest.

"Why're you here, Carson?"

So he does know who's in his bed.

"Because I miss you," he admitted.

"You mean you're horny?"

Leave it to Slade not to believe him.

Carson attempted to pull his hand back, but Slade tightened his grip. Asshole. That had been his plan all along. Not to show affection or intimacy by holding his hand, but to keep him from pulling away when he shot one of his all-too-familiar barbs.

Two could play that game.

"I said it right the first time," Carson whispered, pressing his lips to Slade's shoulder. He bit back the other words that threatened to spill—more explanations, more apologies—because Slade wouldn't hear them, no matter how loud he was or how many times he repeated himself. Slade was far too determined to cling to the past, to continue punishing Carson for all his misdeeds.

"What's the catch?"

"No catch," he said, feeling relief when Slade's grip loosened, but he continued to hold his hand. "I wanted to see you, so here I am."

"At five o'clock in the morning."

Technically, it was almost 4:30 a.m., but Carson didn't correct him. Instead, he said, "I wanted to see you before you went to work."

"See me? Or were you hopin' to find Atticus in my bed?"

Carson heard the doubt in Slade's tone, but that didn't explain why Slade was still holding his hand, keeping him close. Every now and then, his thumb would brush over his, gently, reverently.

"Will you just give me this, please?" Carson pleaded, not wanting to fight with him.

"Let me guess, you thought Atticus was in here, and you needed to know for sure? Or better yet, you already fucked Atticus, and he told you to give me sloppy seconds."

"Goddammit, Slade." Carson jerked away, flopping onto his back. "Why the fuck can't you just let the past go?"

"Why can't you just be honest with me?" Slade retorted. "We both know who you really want and that you're willin' to take the consolation prize—me—when he's not available."

Carson sighed. He didn't bother telling him that Atticus was likely asleep in his bedroom, and he could've gone there instead. It wouldn't matter what he said or did. It wasn't like Slade would believe him.

He was starting to think the man would never be capable of forgiving him.

ATTICUS ROLLED OVER TO LOOK AT THE clock.

His alarm was set for six because he needed to run an errand before he went to HQ, and now that he had a case to work, his priorities took precedence over sleep.

4:37 a.m.

What the fuck?

Frowning, he rolled back over, intending to utilize the time he still had. He barely got the blanket pulled up when he heard a gruff shout from the other room. It was followed by a slamming door.

Throwing the blanket off, he got to his feet. He considered grabbing his gun but opted to leave it. One day, that would be a bad idea, but he recognized the voice, so he knew that all-too-familiar tantrum wasn't coming from a stranger in the house.

Atticus opened his bedroom door and stepped out into the hallway, nearly colliding with a very pissed-off Slade.

"Where were you?"

Atticus frowned. "What?"

"Carson's in my bed. I know he's not here for me."

Oh, brother. Not this bullshit again.

"I was asleep. Until your rude ass woke me up."

Slade pulled back as though he'd been slapped. "Was your door locked?"

"You know it wasn't," he countered.

Slade frowned. "Bullshit. Why else would he come to my room?"

Atticus spun away from him, heading back to his bedroom. He wasn't in the mood for their bullshit right now. He had an hour left to sleep, and he intended to do it. What those two did was their business. Not his.

"Where are you goin'?"

"Where does it look like I'm goin'?" he muttered before closing the door.

This time, he locked it.

SLADE TRIED THE KNOB ON ATTICUS'S DOOR, intending to follow him into the room.

Locked.

"Sonuvabitch."

Fine. Two could play that game.

He spun on his heel and headed back for his bedroom. When he saw that Carson was still in his bed, he did his best not to look at the man. Definitely not at his bare chest or those rippling abs now on display since he'd turned on the bedside lamp.

"I'm goin' to work," he told Carson, tearing his gaze away.

"No, you're not."

"Yes, I am," he lied. Since he was currently working with Luca, there really wasn't anything for him to do at HQ, but Carson didn't need to know that.

"Slade. Come here."

He swallowed hard, hating the way his chest felt tight with hope. It always did that whenever Carson gave him any attention whatsoever. That was part of the reason he wasn't willing to give in to this. Yeah, he'd pretended that night when Atticus made Carson come over. Pretended to forgive the past, pretended it didn't matter. That was the night hope started to bloom again. The night Carson had accomplished the goal of confusing Slade with his sweet words and well-placed apologies.

But those only lasted for a minute before they got back to basics. Sex. The real reason they'd been so good together.

Sex was the easy part. He had never denied his attraction to Carson. Not ever. And having Atticus there, watching, had only made it hotter. Not to mention, Slade had gotten really good at having an audience. After all, that was what Carson's role in their previous relationship had been.

Oh, wait. It hadn't been a relationship because Carson wasn't interested in something real, something permanent. At least not with him.

And neither was Atticus, as he had so kindly informed him after their last encounter.

I think we should do more of this.

Yeah?

Definitely. Let's just keep it casual from here on out. Just fucking. You good with that?

Fearing he would sound like a love-struck moron if he insisted on more, Slade had said, *I guess I'll have to be.*

And now everything was falling apart.

"Come here," Carson repeated.

Slade looked at him. "Why're you here?"

Carson's jaw tensed as he took a deep breath and let it out slowly. "I told you. I missed you."

"You didn't come over to see Atticus?"

Carson shook his head.

"Why not?"

A huff of amusement came from Carson. "Can't it be enough that I wanted to see you?"

No, it couldn't because Slade didn't believe him. He wasn't sure he ever would.

"Why?"

"Goddammit, Slade. Come here."

Swallowing hard, Slade caved to the demand. He walked around to his side and dropped down on the bed, kicking the blankets away.

He knew he was being petty and stupid about this, but he'd already made an ass of himself by accusing Carson of really wanting Atticus instead of him. The best he could do now was apologize, but he'd been doing too much of that lately. To the point he wasn't sure he even meant it. If he did, why the fuck would he continue the pattern?

"I know you still don't trust me," Carson said, his voice low as he rolled to his side and propped his head on his hand. "But that's okay."

"No, it's not."

"It is." Carson placed his hand on Slade's chest. "We had somethin', Slade, and I'm the one who fucked it up. Now we have the chance to have somethin' again, and you're scared."

"I'm not—" He cut himself off. He saw no reason to lie. He *was* scared. Petrified, really. He knew it would take very little for him to get in deep with Carson again. He'd loved the man in a way he'd never loved anyone else. And unlike his feelings for Atticus, which were new and potentially based on lust rather than something more permanent, what he'd felt for Carson had been real.

His thoughts drifted to yesterday when he'd spent time with Luca and Honor, but then he shook them off as fast as he could, not wanting to dwell on it. Certainly not now.

Maybe he'd only imagined what he felt for Carson. It was possible. Right?

"That's why I'm here." Carson dragged his finger over Slade's chest. "Not to seduce you. I just wanted to spend a few minutes with you before the day got started."

Slade turned his head, met Carson's stare. "No bullshit?"

Carson shook his head. "None. I told you before, I'm not takin' this for granted again."

He had said that. And Slade wanted to believe him.

The only problem was, he didn't. Not even a little.

Carson's voice lowered. "It's gonna take time for me to prove it. I get that. But if this is what you want, I need you to stop fightin' me on it."

What if he didn't want it anymore? What then?

Slade swallowed past the knot that formed in his throat. "Or what? I mean, would you prefer to just be with Atticus?"

Something flashed in Carson's eyes. Something that looked a lot like pain.

"I'm sorry."

Carson exhaled heavily. "I don't think you are. I think you can't help but speak the truth."

Slade breathed in deep, let it out slowly. He was primed to argue, but it was difficult to argue with the truth.

"Maybe this isn't the right thing for us," Carson whispered.

And therein lies the problem.

Two days ago, Slade would've disagreed, thrown himself at Carson's mercy, and pleaded with him to give him a chance. But over the course of the past two days, something had changed. Something significant. Slade wasn't even sure he could admit to what it was. Not even to himself. Not yet.

Before Carson could get up, Slade grabbed his arm and pulled him back. "Wait."

Carson relaxed, and Slade rolled to his side, moving closer.

"Tell me the truth."

"Anything."

Slade scanned his face, but he wasn't sure what he was looking for. "Do you really see this goin' anywhere?"

Carson's expression didn't change; his eyes remained fixed on him. Because of that, Slade saw the truth in them. The same truth he'd seen so long ago, back when they'd been together. Carson had already disconnected. He was there, not because he wanted to salvage what they had, but because he wanted to know whether there was anything left.

Odd how Slade felt the same way.

"I don't think this is gonna work, Carson."

Carson tucked his hands under his head and stared up at the ceiling. "I think you're right."

"I thought I could—" He stopped talking when he realized Carson had agreed with him. "What?"

"You're right."

Slade frowned. "What about Atticus?"

Carson turned his head to look at him. "I don't know. I haven't talked to him."

"I think he's fuckin' Archer."

Slade felt the weight of Carson's stare when he looked at him. "He's not."

"How do you know?"

"Because Atticus is far too honest to cheat."

"*Pfft*. Honest? Why the hell would you think that?"

"Come on, Slade. Atticus is honest to a fault. I'm not sure the guy knows how to lie."

Slade seriously doubted that. Everyone lied. At least everyone he'd ever met did. And he was always the one being lied to, though he couldn't understand why.

"Well, he spends an awful lot of time with him," Slade groused.

"Aren't they partners?"

"Supposedly." Slade knew he sounded petty, but he couldn't help it. He didn't want to admit he might've been wrong, that he could be the one who had imploded their entire relationship with his insecurity.

"Deep down, you know Atticus isn't the sort who'd hurt anyone."

Maybe.

Still, acknowledging it wasn't going to make him feel better.

CHAPTER TWENTY-NINE

ATTICUS'S ALARM WENT OFF AT FIVE THIRTY. He was already awake, having slept in fits and starts since Slade had interrupted a damn good dream. Not that he remembered what the dream was about, but he knew it had been good. But like every good dream he had, it usually faded without him being able to remember.

With too much to do, he hopped out of bed and headed for the shower. Rather than make a mental priority list of the things he needed to focus on when he got to HQ, Atticus found himself thinking about Slade. About the way the man had come into his room, geared up for a fight in the middle of the damn night.

Would it always be like that? If they somehow managed to get past whatever obstacle was in their way at the moment, would Slade always doubt their sincerity? Was it even possible to have a relationship if that were the case?

Atticus didn't know the answer to any of those questions. He also didn't know what he was supposed to do next. Although he was angry at Slade for constantly thinking the worst of him, he wasn't sure he wanted to give it all up. Sure, he said casual was the best path for them, and he meant it. For the moment. But that didn't mean they couldn't look toward the future at some point. Once Slade had time to realize no one was out to get him.

Was there even a future for them?

Shutting off the water, Atticus grabbed the towel from the bar and rubbed it over his hair, removing the excess water before using it to dry off his body. When he was done, he secured it around his waist and moved to the sink. He wiped the mirror with his hand so he could see his reflection. He probably needed to shave, but he was skipping that step this morning. However, brushing his teeth was a must.

He took care of that, gargled some mouthwash for good measure, then ran a comb through his hair and styled it with his fingers before sauntering out of the bathroom. He was walking into his bedroom when he heard footsteps behind him.

"You went on a fuckin' date with Archer last night?"

Atticus came up short by the pure fury in Slade's tone. He slowly pivoted to face the man, noticing that his expression matched his harsh tone.

"What?"

"I just got a call that you and Archer were on a date. At Moonshiners."

"A call? From who?"

"It doesn't fuckin' matter. You were on a date," he accused.

Atticus took a deep breath. "It wasn't a date."

"The fuck it wasn't."

Taking a step forward, Atticus raised a hand to halt the tirade before it started. "I swear to—"

"Shut up," Slade snapped. "Just shut up, Atticus. Carson might think you're above lying, but I don't."

Okay, he'd tried being nice, but Slade was pushing. Atticus didn't want to fight, but he would if it meant defending his actions. "What are you talkin' about?"

Slade stared at him, his eyes flashing fury. "You're really gonna tell me you weren't at Moonshiners with Archer? Because I've got proof."

Atticus had to step back to keep from getting smacked with Slade's phone when the man thrust it his way. On the screen was a picture of him laughing while Archer sat across from him, a big grin on his face.

Someone had taken a picture of them? Who? And why?

"It wasn't a fuckin' date, Slade. When I got home last night, I wasn't tired, so I invited Archer to get a drink. To talk."

"Oh, yeah. I'm sure you talked. Sounds to me like y'all got all chummy while you were busy buyin' his drinks."

"Is that what you're pissed about? Because I bought his drinks?" Atticus huffed a sigh and spun around. "Fuck, Slade. Get over yourself."

Atticus went for the bag he'd left sitting on the dresser and grabbed the last pair of clean jeans he had in there. He grabbed underwear and socks, then proceeded to get dressed while Slade seethed behind him.

"You're not even gonna try to explain it?" Slade asked when Atticus was buttoning his jeans.

"You won't listen to me even if I do."

"Try me."

"There's nothin' to explain. We went to Moonshiners, had a couple of beers, a couple of shots, and we talked."

"You invited him. And you paid for his drinks. That's a date."

"Not when the guy's your partner." Atticus glared at Slade. "Are you tellin' me, Evan never bought you a drink?"

"That's different!" Slade spat.

"Why? Because Evan's straight? For fuck's sake, Slade. That's ignorant."

He huffed again, then walked into the closet and grabbed a shirt, pulled it on. When he came back, Slade was still standing in the doorway, his face red with anger.

"I want you out."

"I'm headin' that way."

"No. I don't mean for today."

Atticus stopped moving.

"I want you out of my house."

Well, that made the answer to all those questions pretty damn simple. No, there was no future for him and Slade.

Pivoting on his heel, Atticus returned to the closet and grabbed the rest of his clothes. Since he'd packed most everything for the trip to Dallas already and had yet to unpack, there wasn't much to get. He stuffed it all into the bag, then sat on the bed to put on his socks and boots.

"You're not even gonna apologize, huh?" Slade asked, still standing in the doorway.

Atticus glanced at him over his shoulder. "For what? I haven't done anything wrong."

"You would say that."

With another sigh, Atticus got to his feet, grabbed the bag, and headed for the door. Slade stepped out of the way, allowing him to get by. He made a quick pitstop in the bathroom to grab the few things he had in there, then hefted the bag onto his shoulder.

"Oh, and Atticus…"

When he reached the front door, he considered looking back but decided not to.

"Carson said he's done with this, too."

Yeah. That sounded about right. Then again, this had been doomed from the start, but he'd been too hopeful to see the truth.

COFFEE.

For whatever reason, Brantley needed it this morning. Lots of it. Maybe an IV of caffeine would help because the run hadn't managed to shed the fatigue.

"That's your third cup."

With his cup halfway to his mouth, Brantley paused, looked at Reese. "Are you the coffee police this mornin'?"

Reese grinned. "Maybe I should be. What's up?"

Brantley shrugged as he walked around the kitchen island and plopped down on one of the stools. He set his mug down, stared into the black liquid.

"I wanted to find her," he said softly, realizing he wasn't so much tired as he was disappointed. "Yesterday. At that house. I wanted her to be there."

"Don't give up yet."

It was difficult not to when everywhere they turned, they came up empty. They were being steered in various directions without a real path or destination, and he wasn't sure which way was up anymore. It was like a real-life shell game. Or one of those fun houses with smoke and mirrors. Everything was an illusion created to confuse and disorient.

Giving up felt like the only option.

"I think we—"

A knock on the back door interrupted Reese. Brantley turned to see Archer standing on the back deck.

"It's unlocked."

The glass door slid open, and the big man sauntered in. His gaze caught on Tesha when she got up from her bed, and as soon as he noticed her, Archer's face lit up like a kid in a candy store.

Yeah, they needed to get this guy a dog.

"What's up?" Brantley asked Archer as he squatted down to pet Tesha.

"Wanted to give y'all an update. I compiled the notes from the team last night."

"When did you have time to do that? Rumor is you were at Moonshiners gettin' shit-faced," Brantley teased.

He smiled, standing tall. "I'll admit, I was feelin' no pain, but I know when to stop."

Brantley reached for his coffee cup. "What information can't wait until we get to the barn?"

"Ignore him," Reese said. "He's grumpy this mornin'. You want some coffee? I'm makin' omelets."

As though cued, Archer's stomach rumbled, causing Tesha's ears to perk up and Brantley to laugh.

"Well, I guess that's settled then." Brantley pointed at the stool beside him.

"I'm not sure you heard," Archer began as he pulled out the stool, "but Becs and Evan ran into Allison Bogart yesterday. Here in town."

No, they hadn't heard that. "What did she have to say?"

"Nothing. She high-tailed it."

"Sounds about right." Smoke and mirrors, just as he'd said.

"Did you get the DNA results back yet?" Archer glanced between him and Reese.

Reese answered with a shake of his head. "Z said it'd take twenty-four hours."

"At best," Brantley tacked on.

"He's disappointed," Reese told Archer.

"Of course you are." Archer glanced over at him. "You're lookin' for a family member. One you thought you lost. There's not a tremendous amount of hope yet, but there's somethin', so it's only logical that it would get to you. We're gonna keep pushin' until we know for sure."

Although he didn't want the pep talk, Brantley appreciated it all the same. Archer was right. There was still plenty left to do. More than enough rocks to look under.

Hell, yesterday morning, he thought they were deluding themselves, thinking Kylie was alive. Based on what they'd uncovered in a short amount of time, Brantley couldn't help but think she was. She was alive, and Martin Calloway was keeping her locked away. Whether for punishment because of what happened to Juliet Prince, or because he was merely a sick SOB who got off on hurting people. Either way, the bastard was going down for this.

"I assume you and Atticus have an action plan," he said, sipping his coffee.

"Thanks," Archer told Reese when he passed over a mug. "We do."

"Good. You can—" This time the ringing of his cell phone interrupted, causing Brantley to look at the device sitting on the counter. "It's JJ."

He answered the call, putting it on speaker.

"Mornin'," he greeted.

"We're comin' home!" JJ squealed.

"When?"

"Today." Her voice was trembling, he assumed from excitement. "Our babies get to go home!"

"That's fantastic, JJ," Reese told her, standing at the island as he stared down at the phone.

Brantley was almost positive those were tears he saw in Reese's eyes. And fine, maybe he had a bit of moisture building up in his, too. He was thrilled for JJ and Baz, grateful that Noah and Naomi were well enough to come home so soon.

"If there's anything you need before or after, just let us know," Brantley told her.

"We're good. Baz went home to get the car seats. The doctor said around noon, so we're checkin' out of the hotel and we'll wait at the hospital."

"That's fantastic."

"I know, right?" JJ sighed. "Is there anything I can do for the case until then?"

Brantley looked at Archer. He was in charge.

"We've got it covered, JJ. You focus on those little ones. But I promise to keep you updated."

"You're a good man, Archer Halligan," she said with a smile in her voice. "Did you know he sent me an email update with everything that happened yesterday?"

Assuming she was talking to him, Brantley said, "I did not."

"Yep. Told me about the shenanigans with the tails and the blood you found at the house. Did you get the results yet?"

"Twenty-four hours," he and Reese said at the same time.

"Well, I'm keepin' my fingers crossed." Her voice took on a dream quality when she added, "My babies are comin' home."

"Let us know when we can stop by and see them. We'll wait for an invite so we don't interrupt your time with them."

"Soon," she said. "I promise." She took a deep breath. "Okay. That's all for now. I'll talk to y'all later."

"Later, JJ." He tapped the *end call* button on the screen.

"She sounds happy," Archer acknowledged.

"Oh, yeah. This is a huge relief after all they've been through."

"Well, let's try to ride this wave of good luck." Archer glanced between them. "And figure out where Kylie is so she can come home, too."

Yeah. What he said.

CHAPTER THIRTY

JJ WAS BESIDE HERSELF WITH JOY. So much so, she wasn't sure how her body could contain it all.

She was in the passenger seat while Baz was driving, their two little ones secured in their car seats in the middle row. If she'd had the option, JJ would've been nestled back there with them, but the size of the car seats wouldn't allow it, so here she was.

"I can't promise I'll get anything done ever again," she told Baz, peeking over the tops of the seats to see her sweet angels. "All I want to do is hold them."

"I'm sure you'll find a way," he said, reaching over and patting her hand. "And if you don't, that's okay, too."

"No, it's not." She chuckled. "There's a lot to do."

"There probably isn't. Remember, my mom and dad have been by here since the babies were born."

Yes, they had. She knew because Jules was keeping her updated, ensuring she was aware of everything she did, seeking permission even when it wasn't necessary. According to Baz's mother, everything was set up and ready for when Noah and Naomi came home. Their little clothes had been washed, their bottles cleaned and prepared for use, diapers purchased, blankets and sheets fresh and clean. Since they hadn't had the official baby shower, Jules and Wes had purchased the big things they would need, then promised the shower would be underway within days of their arrival at home.

JJ wasn't too worried about the shower. It wasn't necessary. Seeing everyone was about the most important thing that would come from it, as far as she was concerned. And whatever they needed, she had no doubt they would get.

"We'll have to figure out their schedule," she mused as Baz turned onto their street. "I hope it'll be synced."

She had read stories about twins whose schedules were opposite, making the parents crazy. Not that JJ thought she would go crazy. At least she hoped not. Then again, based on those very stories, she had learned sleep deprivation was a real thing.

Good news was, she had gone to bed early last night in hopes of the babies coming home today. And now, no matter how many hours she was able to sneak in, she would sleep better because she would be in her own bed, in her own house, with Baz and her babies nearby.

Baz pulled into the driveway and stopped the SUV, putting it in *park*.

"You ready to do this?" she asked, grinning.

"I'm ready."

Taking a deep breath, she fought the urge to jump out of the car, trying to keep her cool. Her excitement was palpable. She couldn't wait to sit on the sofa with her babies in her arms, not having to pass them off to a nurse who would spend more time with them than she would.

"You get the suitcase," he told her. "I'll get the car seats."

She wasn't going to argue since she could roll the suitcase and, as she'd learned a little while ago, a car seat with a baby in it wasn't all that light.

JJ hurried to drag the suitcase out of the back. When she came around the car, she found Baz walking toward the house, a car seat with a baby dangling from each hand.

How did he do that? He lifted them like they were made of feathers.

Smiling, she hurried after them.

Baz had the door unlocked and open before she got up the porch steps. He opened the door, then waited for her to go in first.

JJ ignored her debilitating fear of walking into a house without knowing it had been cleared. That was a new thing she'd developed after some of the trauma of the past year. The last thing she wanted was for her babies to know their mommy was a fraidy cat. She had to be strong for them.

Somehow, she managed to step inside.

"Put them over here," she said, gesturing toward the sofa. "I'll get them out."

Baz smiled at her, setting the car seats on the coffee table. "While you do that, I'm just gonna walk through, make sure my parents have cleaned it all up."

Some of the tension eased in her chest. Not only because Baz was going to check the house, but because he was doing it for her without calling her crazy. At times, she felt a little crazy, but she also knew deep down that it was warranted. For now.

He took the suitcase with him, so JJ sat on the couch, staring at her sleeping angels. They looked so comfortable, secured in the seats. She hated to move them, so she didn't, choosing to relax into the cushions and watch them sleep.

Never in her life did she think she would find so much joy in doing absolutely nothing, but this … this was perhaps the most complete she'd ever felt.

"My parents took care of everything," Baz noted when he came back out. "You want something to drink?"

JJ was still smiling as she shook her head. "I'm pretty sure nothing will ever compare to this feeling."

Baz came over, peeked at the babies. "What feeling is that?"

"This happiness." She felt her chest warm. "I can't think of anything that could make me any happier than bein' home with them." She looked over at him, grinned. "And you."

"I can think of one thing that would make *me* happier."

Surprised that he could possibly say that, JJ pursed her lips. "Seriously?"

He nodded, then right before her eyes, Baz eased down on one knee.

She sat up quickly. "What are you doing?"

Baz's turquoise blue eyes blazed with what she had come to realize was pure, absolute love. She knew because she'd never seen it until him.

"Jessica Nicole James—"

JJ shook her head. "What are you doing?" she repeated, her heart beating triple time.

"You've changed my entire existence from the first day I met you."

She continued to shake her head, although her heart was swelling in her chest.

"And you're right, there's not much that could be better than this moment. All four of us home, safe, healthy."

Her head changed direction when she nodded her agreement.

"There is one thing that could make this moment absolutely perfect."

"What's that?" The words came out creaky and weak.

"If you'll agree to marry me," he said, his voice thick with emotion. "Will you marry me, JJ?"

That was a question she'd longed to hear. At the same time, she'd never felt the need to rush it. Not with Baz.

But now that he'd asked…

Her nod was fast, her smile even faster. "Of course I will. Yes."

JJ threw her arms around him before he could get the ring on her finger. She wanted to hold onto him for a minute. He was the one thing in her life that she knew she could depend on, the one person who would be there to hold her together when she needed it. They'd been through a lot together, and while she hoped they didn't have as many speed bumps in the future, she wanted him to be by her side for all ups and downs, highs and lows.

"I love you," she whispered in his ear.

"I love you, too."

She pulled back to look at him. "You know if I change my last name to Buchanan, no one can call me JJ anymore. It won't make sense."

He laughed as he slid the ring on her finger. "I'm sure we'll figure it out."

JJ stared at the diamond that glittered on her finger. It was exactly what she would've picked out for herself. Not too big, not too small. The marquise-cut diamond was bold, the glitter intense. Both somehow suited her personality.

She looked up, met his gaze. "Do we have to have a big wedding?"

"Do you want a big wedding?"

She shrugged. As much as she'd loved helping to plan Brantley and Reese's wedding, JJ wasn't sure she wanted all the hoopla.

"Maybe something small, intimate. Family and close friends, only."

Baz cupped her face. "Whatever you want. I'll be there because you'll be there."

She smiled, then leaned in to kiss him.

And she realized, she'd been wrong earlier. It was possible to be happier than she'd been a few minutes ago. But nothing could ever surpass this. She was sure of it.

The day flew by before Atticus even realized it had.

The entire team was diligently working on following leads and tracing patterns in an effort to determine whether Kylie Walker was alive. Brantley and Reese had spent hours in Johnson City with nothing to show for their efforts. While they were driving around, Evan and Becs took another trip to the motel to talk to Decker and Meredith. Unfortunately, they didn't get anything more from them than they already had. But not for lack of trying. According to Evan, Decker was agitated and definitely hiding something.

Charlie'd had the most success. She had shifted her focus from Allison Bogart to Juliet Prince, confirming that Juliet was in fact Martin Calloway's daughter. According to her update, they had undergone a private adoption, and it did not look like the Arondas had ever told Juliet that she wasn't their biological child. There was no trace of her ever attempting to have the records unsealed. Charlie was also able to determine that Martin was the one who selected the parents, which meant he was well aware of where Juliet was at all times. And more than likely, he had something on the Arondas that he could use to blackmail them if he needed to.

At least that seemed to be his *modus operandi*.

Not that the adoption confirmation had done anything to help them find Kylie, but it did point toward a possible motive and might help them determine Calloway's intentions.

As for the DNA results from the blood they found in the house— which could clear up one enormous question—they hadn't yet heard from the lab. According to Brantley, they would get something by the end of the day. He hoped.

Atticus glanced at his watch. It was after six, so he had to wonder what Sniper 1 Security considered the end of the day. Most of the team had gone home, taking their laptops so they could be available if needed. He knew the team, knew they were likely logging back on as soon as they had their personal lives situated for the evening. Like Atticus, most of them spent just as much time online at home as they did in the office.

He heard the distinctive beep of a passcode being entered outside the door, so he looked up. A second later, Archer walked in.

"Hey. I figured you'd be at home by now," Archer said as he walked toward him.

I might be if I had a home.

"Just wanted to finish up a few things." Atticus leaned back. "What brought you back?"

"Same. Figured I could do some research while it was quiet."

It was definitely quiet.

Archer pulled out his chair to sit. "I meant to ask earlier, have you heard anything on the case Luca and Slade are workin' on? Do you think they might be back in the office tomorrow?"

"I haven't, no," he said.

"Thought maybe Slade would give you an update."

"We're kinda at odds right now," he muttered. "Apparently, buyin' your partner drinks equates to a night of cheating."

Archer went still beside him. "Oh, shit. Man, I'm sorry. I hope you cleared it up for him."

Atticus snorted. "Clear as mud."

"If it'll help, I'll be happy to tell him we were just talking."

Looking up, Atticus sighed. "It doesn't matter anymore. Slade kicked me out of the house."

"Shit." Archer turned toward him. "What about ... sorry, I forgot the other guy's name."

"Carson?"

"Yeah. What about him? Y'all working it out?"

"No," he said, although he wasn't sure of anything when it came to Carson. According to Slade, that was over, too. And since he hadn't heard from Carson all day—not even a response to the text message he'd sent a few hours ago—he was inclined to believe Slade.

What bothered Atticus the most about the whole situation was the fact that he honestly didn't care that it had burned to the ground. He knew he should feel *something*. Anger, sadness, confusion. Something other than resignation and a strong desire to move on with his life. The end of a relationship shouldn't be like that, should it?

"If there's anything I can do…"

"Yeah. Thanks. I'm over it. Movin' on."

Archer nodded and turned back to his computer. Atticus did the same, wanting to keep busy so his thoughts wouldn't stray to unimportant shit.

"You have a place to stay?" Archer asked after a few minutes.

"I was gonna find a motel nearby."

"What about the B and B? They've got a few rooms right now. According to Bristol, there's a lull until the end of the month."

"Yeah. Maybe." Atticus honestly didn't care where he slept. A bed was a bed as far as he was concerned. Hell, the couch only a few feet away would suffice for a few nights. Provided Brantley and Reese didn't get wind of his wandering ways. They had originally insisted that he put down roots rather than remain a nomad who spent his nights in motels. And, unlike his joking with JJ, his savings account was growing by leaps and bounds. Which meant he had no excuses.

Thankfully, Archer didn't push the matter, which allowed Atticus to focus on putting together a final update for the day. He had read what Archer sent out last night and wanted to expand on that to keep the team apprised while they worked this case.

"Were you able to find out anything about Terry Berry?" Atticus asked Archer. "And seriously? Who names their kid that?"

"Would you believe it if I said Mary Berry?"

Atticus stared at him, stunned. "Nuh-uh."

"His parents are Mary and Terry Berry, Senior."

"No shit."

Archer chuckled. "No shit. As for Junior, he's an ex-sheriff's deputy out of Blanco County. From what I can tell, he joined Censorious in the late nineties while he was still on the force. When he retired, he sought a higher role in the organization."

"Or maybe that higher role was the reason he retired," Atticus pondered.

"Good point. Possibly. Anyway, he's now second in command under Calloway. He owns about two hundred acres in Blanco, which is roughly fifteen miles south of Johnson City."

"And Johnson City is in Blanco County?"

"It is. Which may be why Calloway is out that way."

"Berry would know the area, having worked for the sheriff's department."

"More than likely."

Atticus pulled up a map to get a better feel for the area. He studied it for a few minutes, noting the route they'd taken to get to the house where Brantley believed Kylie had been kept.

"Do you think it's a coincidence that Rocky Road goes from 290 in Johnson City down to 281 in Blanco?" Shaking his head, Atticus grinned. "Rocky Road. It just keeps gettin' better."

Archer rolled his chair over to look at his screen. Atticus dragged his finger along the route he was referring to.

"What if they moved her that direction?" Atticus asked. "They realized their hidey hole was compromised, so they packed her up and moved her."

When Atticus looked up, he realized his face was inches from Archer's. His breath caught in his lungs, but he blamed it on surprise. He hadn't realized the guy was that close.

Or that he smelled that good.

Fuck.

"We should call Brantley," Atticus suggested, pushing his chair back and launching to his feet.

Archer returned to his desk. "Why don't we take a drive down there? Brantley and Reese were driving all day. We can head down, see what we can see—which likely won't be much at night—then we can call them if it's something worth looking into."

"Okay," he heard himself say, forcing his heart rate to slow.

"You good to drive? Or you want me to?"

"I'll drive." That was the only way he'd be able to resist looking at the man.

Just old habits that haven't died, he told himself as he headed for the door. *You're not attracted to Archer. You just think he's the easiest way to move on from Slade and Carson.*

Yeah. That was all it was. And no one liked a rebound, least of all a work partner.

And seriously. He'd have to be insane to even consider someone like Archer Halligan. The guy was ... he was ... *fuck.*

He was hot.

And smart.

And kind.

And generous.

And the guy fucking loved dogs.

Okay. There. Maybe that could be one for the con column. Atticus didn't like dogs. Only Tesha, but she didn't count. And maybe some of the nicer ones at Camp K-9. But that was all.

"You ready?"

Atticus jumped, surprised.

"Relax," Archer said, gripping Atticus's shoulder in a friendly manner. "It's all good."

Is it though? Atticus thought as he watched Archer walk toward the door.

IT TOOK THEM NEARLY TWO HOURS TO get to Blanco thanks to late evening traffic, but they made it. The trip had been... Well, *awkward* would be a good word for it.

Archer wasn't sure what he'd done to put Atticus on edge, but the man had spent the majority of the drive turning up the radio each time Archer attempted to make conversation. It didn't matter how many times he turned it back down, Atticus continued to inch it higher and higher until talking became impossible. Which was clearly his plan.

So he'd spent that time staring out the window, admiring what was known as the Texas Hill Country. It was definitely more interesting than the flat land that could be seen between Dallas and Austin. Hills and valleys, creeks and rivers made up the landscape. And when it got too dark to admire anything, Archer had stared straight ahead, attempting to come up with something to say that might put Atticus at ease.

Unfortunately, he kept coming up empty.

Finally, they passed a sign that told them their destination was only a few miles up the road.

"What's your plan when we get there?" he asked, figuring it was an innocuous enough question.

Atticus didn't look at him. "I have no idea."

Alrighty then.

"I need to stop for gas," Atticus said a few minutes later as they were nearing a Shell station.

"I'm gonna grab a drink. Want anything?" Archer offered.

"Dr. Pepper."

While Atticus pumped gas, Archer went into the small food mart, which was attached to an even smaller Mexican food restaurant. As was often the case, he felt people watching him as he perused the aisles of snacks and junk. He knew the clerk was sizing him up because that was what people tended to do when a man his size walked through the door. Immediately, they assumed they would need to defend themselves against him.

For the record, that rarely happened. And only when someone attacked him first.

He offered a hint of a smile as he made his way to the drink cooler at the back. He grabbed a Dr. Pepper for Atticus and one for himself. He tried to waste time, figuring Atticus appreciated the alone time. When he felt like he was starting to look like a stalker, he paid for the drinks and walked outside.

Atticus was already in the truck, waiting.

Whose idea was this again?

"You good?" Archer asked as he climbed into the truck, passing a Dr. Pepper over.

Atticus took it and dropped it into the cup holder before putting the truck in gear.

Okay then.

A few minutes down the road, Atticus pulled over abruptly, coming to a stop in the parking lot of a small shopping center that was closed for the night. He threw the truck in park and sat there, hands gripping the steering wheel.

"I'm sorry," Atticus said, though it sounded like he was gargling broken glass.

"For what?"

"Bein' a dick."

Archer chuckled. "I didn't notice."

"And no, I'm not good," he said through gritted teeth.

"Look, I get it. Breakups aren't easy. I'm doing my best to give you space."

Atticus's head turned slowly, his eyes coming to rest on Archer's face. "It has nothin' to do with the breakup."

"Oh." Archer frowned. "Somethin' else wrong?"

"Yes."

His eyebrows lifted, a silent signal to Atticus that he could continue without being verbally prompted.

"You," Atticus blurted.

"Me?" Archer was really confused. "What the hell did I do?"

"Nothing."

He stared, not understanding. "I did nothing? Meaning I'm not carryin' my weight or...?"

"No, of course you are." Atticus's grip on the steering wheel tightened as he turned his attention forward, staring out the window.

"I don't mean to be obtuse, but I'm lost here, Atticus."

"It's not you. It's me."

Archer couldn't help it, he barked a mirthless laugh. "That didn't help clear it up at all."

"You're my partner."

"That seems to be the case, yes."

"And I just got out of a very fucked-up relationship."

"So I've heard."

"And you're *in* a relationship."

"I'm not, but not for lack of trying," he admitted. They'd talked about Spencer last night, but Archer hadn't shared with him the details of their previous encounter. Since Archer hadn't heard from the man in over a week, he figured it was likely a subject not worth broaching.

Atticus's knuckles turned white as he continued to grip the steering wheel.

Feeling bad for the man, Archer reached over and grabbed his wrist, attempting to peel his hand away.

As soon as he touched him, Atticus turned, his eyes wide.

The next thing Archer knew, Atticus was kissing him. His lips were on his, his fingers twined in Archer's hair. The kiss was hot enough to spark a brush fire on the side of the road. Without thinking about what he was doing or the repercussions of it, he kissed Atticus back, taking control because it was his nature to do so. As soon as he cupped the back of Atticus's head, his tongue urgently exploring, the man moaned, causing Archer's dick to swell.

He couldn't remember the last time a kiss had been quite this … God, he didn't even know how to explain it. It seemed to go on forever, but at the same time, Archer wasn't sure it would be enough. It took everything in him to keep his hands in place, to not let them wander. He had an overwhelming urge to feel Atticus's skin against his palms. He wanted to touch every inch of him with his hands and his mouth.

It was pure insanity, but he couldn't stop it. The train had already derailed and was heading for a fiery crash.

"Archer," Atticus moaned, his hand tightening on the back of his neck. "Fuck."

Somehow, he managed to pull back enough to catch his breath. He didn't release Atticus. Wasn't ready to. Whether that was because he didn't want to cop to the insanity of what they'd done or because he feared Atticus would tell him it was a mistake, he wasn't sure.

They remained like that, their foreheads pressed together.

"That was…" Atticus sighed. "I don't know what that was."

Archer didn't either. Nor did he feel like filling in the blanks.

"We can't do this," Atticus finally said, his grip on Archer's neck loosening. "It's stupid. I'm clearly not thinkin' straight."

Ouch. That one hurt.

Archer managed to sit back, turning so that he was staring straight ahead. He was still catching his breath, his body hard as steel.

"I didn't mean it like that."

Nodding, Archer kept his thoughts to himself.

"I meant I just broke up with someone. They call this the rebound, right?"

Oh, great. That made him feel even worse.

What the fuck was wrong with him? How the hell did he keep getting caught up in these men who didn't actually want him, but rather something from him? Spencer had wanted him to take his virginity, and now Atticus was using him to get over his breakup with Slade and the other guy.

"It's cool," he lied. "We should probably drive before we attract the local cops. Trust me when I tell you, you don't want to deal with getting pulled over while I'm in the truck. It's not usually pretty."

Thankfully, Atticus didn't argue. He put the truck in gear and pulled out onto the road. He drove south until Archer instructed him to turn west on 7th Street. It would take them to Terry Berry's place.

Five minutes later, once they'd passed some athletic fields and several older houses, Atticus pulled off the road again. This time he turned off the truck and killed the lights.

"We're not there yet," he told him.

Atticus unbuckled his seat belt and lifted the steering wheel before shifting in his seat.

Archer didn't want to look at him, but he did anyway. "What?"

"I'm gonna say somethin' and you're gonna listen, okay?"

"Sure." He tried to play it casual. "What's up?"

"Slade and I have been on the outs for a little while, but I honestly thought there was a chance to fix it. He clearly didn't. And I haven't even talked to Carson, so I don't know where that stands. Since he hasn't made an effort to talk to me, I have to think Slade wasn't lyin' when he told me it was over with him, too."

Archer wasn't sure what to say to that, so he remained quiet.

"I should probably feel somethin'. Anger or disappointment. Hell, maybe even hurt."

Those seemed like logical responses to a breakup, sure.

"But I don't."

He wasn't expecting that.

"I jumped into that situation with both feet because there were two men interested in me. I thought it might work. At the very least, I thought we'd have fun. We did. At first. But ever since I got back from training, things have been goin' downhill. Slade's jealous, and Carson's constantly disappearing. I knew it wasn't workin' out, but like I said, I thought maybe we could figure somethin' out."

Archer stared at him, waiting for more.

"I'm not upset that Slade kicked me out or that Carson doesn't seem to give a shit one way or the other. I should be. But I know myself. Before them, I'd never been in a relationship. Not one. Maybe that's the problem. Maybe I fucked up because I'm not sure how it all works."

"I doubt that's the case. Sometimes it's just not in the cards." Archer knew that firsthand.

"Slade accused me of cheating, and his insecurities kept getting in the way. I never did. Never even thought about it. I thought we were havin' fun, but obviously I was wrong."

Archer had to look away. He couldn't take the intensity of those green eyes. He'd been intrigued by this man since the beginning, but he had to believe it was because he was excited about the prospect of a partner. He'd never had one. Not like this. And he seemed to mesh with Atticus. They worked well together. And yeah, he was easy on the eyes, which was a bonus.

"Archer?"

"Hmm?"

"Look at me, please."

He did, noticing the way Atticus's gaze shifted to his mouth. His dick twitched and swelled as the memory of that kiss flooded his gray matter.

"I want you to kiss me again."

Archer's breath lodged in his throat.

"But I know if that happens, we're both gonna question what we're doin'."

He was probably right.

No, he was definitely right.

"And that's not fair to either of us."

"Okay."

Atticus's eyes lifted, locking with his. "We're partners. We have to agree that anything else is … off limits."

Archer nodded because he knew that was what Atticus expected.

"So we're good?"

Another nod was all he could manage.

"Good." Atticus exhaled and sat back in his seat. He repositioned the steering wheel, then put his seatbelt on. "Let's recon the area, see what we're dealin' with."

"Yes. Let's do that."

Maybe then, Archer could stop coming up with ideas on how to get Atticus to kiss him again.

CHAPTER THIRTY-ONE

Wednesday, October 5, 2022

"THAT'S YOUR PHONE," BRANTLEY MUTTERED, HIS VOICE gravel-laced and irritated.

Reese stirred, his brain coming online as he heard the phone ring. It rang again and was accompanied by an elbow jab from Brantley.

Fumbling for the offensive device, he grabbed it from the nightstand and answered with a garbled, "Yeah?"

"Reese?"

"Yeah." He didn't recognize the female voice.

"I need to talk to you."

"Who is this?"

"Allison Bogart."

That kicked his brain into overdrive. His eyes opened. Thankfully it was dark in the room.

"We've been lookin' for you," he told her. "We have some questions."

"I know. I have some for you, too." Her words were rushed. "Can we meet?"

"Of course. When?"

"Two hours?"

"Okay. Where?"

"The diner. I'll meet you there. I have to go."

Before he could say anything more, the call ended.

"Who was that?" Brantley asked, sounding curious.

"Allison."

"What did she want?"

"To talk. Said she'd meet us at the diner in a coupla hours." Reese stared at his phone. "It was weird. She sounded scared."

"Well, I would be, too, if I were workin' for Martin Calloway."

"No, more like … like she was out of breath from runnin'." At least that was how it sounded to him. Then again, perhaps he'd projected it because she'd woken him up.

"Since it's almost oh-five-hundred, maybe she *is* runnin'," Brantley said as he got up. "Because that's what we need to be doin'."

Reese followed behind Brantley, getting up, taking care of morning business, then getting dressed. By the time he was tying his shoes, Brantley was on the front porch with Tesha, stretching.

"I'm ready," he told Brantley when he joined them.

"Good. Let's—" His sentence cut off when his cell phone rang.

Reese took Tesha's leash while Brantley answered. "Yeah?"

He couldn't hear what was said on the other end, but he could tell it was a man. Deep voice. Calm.

"Sure. We'll be at the diner in a couple of hours. Want to meet up then?" Another brief pause before Brantley said, "All right. See you there." Brantley ended the call and shoved his phone in his pocket. "Looks like it's gonna be a party. Travis wants to talk."

"You realize we're gonna have to tell him what we know, right?"

"Yep. Probably what we should've done already."

Great.

It was going to be one of those days, he could feel it.

Almost two hours exactly from the time Allison called him, Reese was sitting at a table with Brantley. Tesha was tucked up underneath by their feet, where she preferred to be. They were sipping coffee, holding off on the order until Allison and Travis arrived.

"I'm wonderin' what questions she could possibly have for us," Brantley said, spinning the napkin-wrapped silverware.

Reese had given him the high level of the call initially, but then ran it through almost verbatim when Brantley kept questioning him.

"I have no idea, but I'll take it because we've definitely got questions for her," Reese said, reaching over to still the spinning silverware.

Brantley looked up, grinned. "Am I gettin' on your nerves?"

"Little bit."

"Then let me order. Travis wouldn't expect us to wait."

"I'm not worried about Travis." Reese glanced at his watch. "Ten minutes. If Allison's not here by then, you can order."

"I'm gonna hold you to it."

While they waited, Reese checked his phone, skimming text messages and emails. He found the update from Atticus that came in shortly after midnight.

"Atticus and Archer drove down to Blanco last night," he told Brantley.

"For what?"

"To check out the property for Terry Berry, one of the top-level Censorious members."

"Terry Berry? Did his parents hate him?"

Reese ignored the question as he continued to read. "The email said they checked it out but couldn't get eyes on the house because it's situated too far back." He looked up. "Atticus said it's fifteen minutes from the house we checked out. On the same road."

Brantley frowned. "That can't be a coincidence, can it?"

Reese wouldn't think so, but with this case, anything was possible.

"Who're you textin'?" Reese asked when Brantley pulled out his phone.

"Atticus."

"Don't you want to order first?"

"You order for me."

When the waitress returned, Reese did exactly that, ordering Brantley's usual heart attack on a plate and some egg whites with a side of fruit for himself. He knew better than to push a healthier option on Brantley when they went out. The man wasn't above making a scene.

"Hey, man," Brantley greeted when his phone rang a couple of minutes later. "Where are you?"

Reese couldn't hear the response on the other end, but he continued to watch Brantley.

"We're at the diner," he said after a lengthy pause. "You and Archer have breakfast yet?" *Short pause.* "Good. Meet us here. We'll talk."

"I guess it's a good thing we got a table," Reese said when Brantley hung up.

The bells over the door chimed. Reese peered back over his shoulder at the same time Brantley said, "But I'm not sure it's gonna be big enough."

Definitely gonna be one of those days.

Travis walked into the diner, his gaze scanning the room.

"I'm meetin' someone," he told the waitress. "Can I get some coffee?"

She flashed a smile. "Sure thing."

While she went to do that, Travis made his way past the tables currently filled with people looking to fill their bellies before the day started. It wasn't until he reached Brantley and Reese's table that the nostril-filling aroma of pancakes and syrup actually smelled *good*.

How long had it been since that was the case? Since he'd enjoyed food rather than putting it in his mouth because his body required it?

At least one year, eight months, and twenty-six days.

"Mornin'," Brantley greeted when he approached.

"Mornin'. You expectin' someone else?"

"A few someones," Brantley answered. But we'll figure it out when they get here. Have a seat."

Travis pulled out the chair in time to see Reese's dog's head pop up. She stared up at him, clearly not sure what to think.

"I promise I won't step on you," he told her as he sat, positioning his feet around her.

"Where's Gage?"

"At home with the kids. And yes, he knows where I'm at." Travis looked up when the waitress stopped at the edge of the table. She set down a mug and poured coffee into it. "Thanks."

"Sure thing. Want somethin' to eat?"

"Pancakes," he told her.

He could sense Brantley's surprise, but he ignored it.

"Anything with 'em?"

"No."

He could feel his cousin's eyes on him, knew Brantley was likely wondering what the hell was wrong with him.

"Stop lookin' at me like that," he muttered before taking a sip of his coffee.

"Pancakes? Really?"

"Shut up."

"Who are you and what have you done with my cousin?"

Travis discreetly flipped Brantley off. "Shut the fuck up."

"He said it with a smile," Brantley mock-whispered to Reese. "Did you see that? A. Real. Smile."

Doing his best not to get irritated, Travis glanced between them. He could tell Reese had something on his mind, so he stared at him, figuring it was the fastest way to get the guy to spill.

It worked.

"We don't have confirmation on anything yet, but we did find a house that looked to be where Calloway was holdin' someone. We have no idea who it was, or why they were there."

He processed the words at a much slower rate than Reese spoke them.

"The place was cleared out," Brantley added. "But we did find some blood. Not a lot, but enough to get a sample. Z's havin' the lab run it. Hopefully it's enough to get DNA."

Travis's chest felt as though it was filled with air. His stomach flip-flopped, and he was positive his hearing cut out for a moment. It was very similar to when Brantley told him they thought Kylie was alive. He hadn't believed it at the time, but now he did. He couldn't explain why, knew it was irrational on so many levels. Yet, he couldn't deny it either.

And this information only added to his hope.

"You okay?" Reese asked.

Travis nodded. "Tell me what you need me to do."

Brantley frowned. "What're you talkin' about?"

"You're lookin' for my wife, aren't ya? You think she's alive."

Brantley didn't respond, simply stared.

"Tell me what I can do to help."

Brantley looked at Reese. "Am I hallucinatin'? I mean, I'm hungry, so it's possible, right?"

Travis resisted the urge to punch his cousin in the mouth. If it weren't for the fact he felt like he was alive for the first time in nearly two years, he would have.

But he had decided last night that it was time to take a page from his daughter's book. If Kate could believe without even knowing there was a possibility her mother was alive, then so the fuck could he.

AFTER TAKING A QUICK SHOWER AND GETTING dressed, Atticus sent Archer a text, asking if he was ready.

Last night, after they'd gotten back to Coyote Ridge, Atticus had intended to drop Archer off at the B and B and then head back to HQ to grab a few hours of sleep on the couch. Before he could do that, Archer convinced him to get a room, so that was what he'd done. And surprisingly, despite only falling unconscious for a few hours, he felt better than he had in a while.

He grabbed his wallet and keys, then headed out of the room, remembering to lock it because apparently that wasn't an automatic thing like it was in a hotel. When he reached the bottom of the stairs, the aroma of freshly baked muffins assaulted him, making his stomach rumble.

"Good morning," Bailey greeted. "Hungry?"

"If I said no, I'd be lyin'. But I've got a breakfast meeting with my boss. Smells delicious though."

It was a bit weird to be staying in a stranger's house. Even if that house was designed for people to stay in and the woman offering breakfast was simply doing her job.

"I can confirm it is," Archer said, walking toward him with what looked to be a blueberry muffin in his hand.

"We're havin' breakfast at the diner," he told him.

"This is just an appetizer." Archer flashed a smile at Bailey. "See you later this evening."

"Y'all have fun," she called after them.

"How is it you can look like *that* and always be eating?"

"Good genes." Archer grinned. "And CrossFit. Did you know there's a training center here? I mean, it's in someone's old barn, but it's possibly the nicest facility I've been to."

"I don't even know what CrossFit is," he admitted.

"I'll take you sometime. They'll kick your ass, but you'll love every second of it."

Atticus continued around to the driver's side, wondering if Archer's good mood could be attributed to that muffin. The guy seemed extra chipper today.

"Did Brantley say what he wanted to talk about?" Archer asked when they were both in the truck.

"No. And I didn't ask."

"Well, I guess we'll find out in roughly two minutes."

That was about how long it took to drive to the diner. It took just as much time to find a parking place because it was packed, the lot filled with trucks, many of them carting trailers behind them.

"Ranch hands get breakfast early," Archer said as they were walking to the restaurant doors. "It clears out closer to nine."

Atticus laughed. "I take it you spend a lot of time here?"

"I like the food."

Smiling, Atticus opened the door and walked inside, Archer right behind him. He wanted to pat himself on the back for managing to pretend he wasn't still thinking about that kiss, or the conversation they'd had afterward. His only reprieve from his wandering thoughts had been sleep, and *only* because he was exhausted. Now, in the light of day, he was going to abide by the rule that partners are off limits.

"Did you know Travis was gonna be here?" Archer asked as they started toward the table.

He shook his head and kept a smile on his face, praying that Travis's presence wasn't going to add unnecessary stress to the morning.

They made their way to the table, greetings being tossed around as they approached. Before their asses hit the seats, Brantley was signaling the waitress over.

"Give 'em a second," Reese told Brantley. "Maybe they need to look at the menu."

"You need to look at the menu?" Brantley asked, glancing between them.

"Nope," Archer said with a grin.

"I'm sure I can wing it," Atticus replied.

And that was just what he did when the waitress finished taking Archer's order.

"If there's anything left when you're done makin' that, I'll take exactly half of what he's gettin'," Atticus told her.

"Just give him the same," Brantley told her. "He can take the leftovers to go."

"Done," she said with a smile before walking off.

He could feel Travis watching the interaction while he ate pancakes.

As soon as she was gone, Brantley's expression went stern, his gaze sliding between him and Archer. "What did you find last night?"

A man who could kiss like a god.

He managed not to say that aloud, choosing instead to go with, "The house is set back from the road, but we were able to see people moving around."

"What house?" Travis asked, wiping his mouth.

"He's up to speed," Brantley added.

"Terry Berry. He's—"

"Martin Calloway's right hand," Travis filled in. "I've done my homework."

Brantley ignored Travis, asking, "Security?"

Archer nodded. "Looked to be. We stayed out there for a couple of hours. From what we could tell, they make a pass every forty-five minutes."

"One guard each time," Atticus added.

"I think it's safe to say they're worried about somethin'," Brantley mused, his attention on Reese.

"We thought we'd go back during the day, do some recon of the area, see if we can get a better vantage point," Archer told him.

Brantley looked defeated. "It might be our only option."

"Did you have somethin' else in mind?" Atticus asked.

Reese was the one who answered. "We thought we were meetin' Allison Bogart."

"Why would you think that?" Travis asked.

"She called. Said she needed to talk. Acted like it was urgent."

"Where are you meetin' her?"

Brantley waved a hand. "Supposed to be here. I don't think she's comin'."

"She didn't give an exact time," Reese clarified. "She said two hours. We're at least half an hour past that at this point."

"Did you try callin' her?" Travis asked.

"The number she called from came up blocked. I tried the number we have for her, but the phone's off."

"Maybe she had to stop for gas," Atticus said, trying to be positive.

Reese didn't look hopeful. "Yeah. Maybe."

"Any word on the DNA results?" Archer asked.

"Haven't heard yet," Brantley answered, leaning back when the waitress offered more coffee.

"I'll give Z a call when we're finished here."

Atticus was as anxious as everyone else to get the results back. The blood they'd found in that house belonged to someone. And while he hoped there wasn't a reason for Kylie Walker to be bleeding, he did hope the results would give them the answer they wanted. Knowing for sure one way or the other would help determine their next steps.

Obviously, if she were alive, the main objective was to find her and bring her home. If she wasn't, they needed to drill down and find a way to dismantle Censorious once and for all.

"Has Evan been able to get any more out of Meredith?" Brantley asked after the waitress delivered their food.

"No. And I'm not sure they will, either," Atticus explained. "He's convinced they're hidin' something."

"I'm sure she is," Travis muttered. "I don't even know why she bothered to show up."

Archer held up a finger as though signaling he needed a moment while he finished chewing, then said, "I know this might sound harsh, but have you considered using Meredith as bait to draw Calloway out?"

Brantley looked at Reese, then at Travis. Atticus could tell that some silent communication was taking place.

"We've got a large enough team," Archer continued. "We can keep her safe if we can control the environment."

"It's not a terrible idea," Atticus said, not sure why everyone had clammed up all of a sudden.

"It's also not necessary yet," Reese stated.

Based on Brantley's expression, he'd already had this conversation with Reese and got the same answer.

But Atticus had to agree with Reese. They had leads to follow. Putting a woman's life in unnecessary danger was a last-ditch effort. They weren't quite there yet. And if they were lucky, they wouldn't need to take drastic measures.

CHAPTER THIRTY-TWO

WHEN TRAVIS LEFT THE DINER, SOME OF the tension eased up, but not all of it. Brantley wasn't sure what to make of his cousin's behavior. Part of him didn't want to question it because there was a sense of relief that came with Travis's more laid-back demeanor. On the other hand, he didn't want Travis to bank everything on them finding Kylie.

Oh, it was true, Brantley'd started thinking that she was alive, too, so he couldn't fault Travis. But that didn't mean it was true.

"Did you tell Travis about the doctor and the funeral home?" Archer inquired after the waitress topped off their coffee.

"That we talked to them, yes," Brantley answered.

Atticus frowned. "But not that the casket is empty?"

"I kinda left that part out," he admitted.

"Probably best," Archer said. "He might head to the cemetery and start diggin' otherwise."

Brantley could almost envision his cousin out there wielding a shovel and a stern expression.

"You plannin' on tellin' him?" Atticus asked, still eating.

"Let's see what the day brings first." Brantley took another sip of his coffee, then pushed it away. "We've got one more stop before we head back to HQ." He looked at Reese. "You ready?"

Reese nodded, signaling the waitress over. It took a few minutes to take care of the payment, but once they did, they headed out to the truck, leaving Atticus and Archer to finish their meal.

"Where are we goin'?" Reese asked as he opened the back passenger door for Tesha.

"JJ's."

"It's kinda early, don't you think?"

"She's an early riser."

"With babies, that might not be the case anymore."

Brantley grinned. "It is."

"Tell me you gave her a heads up and you don't plan to just drop in."

"I'm not an idiot. I texted her *and* Baz to get the okay."

"And they both answered?"

Brantley glanced over at his husband. "Do you not trust me?"

"Not when it comes to followin' the rules."

He had to laugh at that because it was true. Brantley tended to straddle the line a lot of the time.

"That's why you love me, though."

Reese grinned. "It's one of the reasons."

He couldn't resist grabbing Reese's hand and linking their fingers as he drove to JJ's house. The day hadn't started off quite the way he would've preferred, but the fact that Reese was with him made it bearable. Hell, Reese's presence made everything bearable.

A few minutes later, they were pulling up in front of JJ's house, parking on the street. Brantley got out and waited for Reese and Tesha before heading up the narrow walkway to the porch.

He half expected to find JJ bleary-eyed and in her pajamas. After all, that was what happened when you had kids, right? You stopped worrying about your appearance because sleep became the only thing you could focus on?

"Mornin'," JJ greeted when she opened the door.

Definitely not bleary-eyed. Or wearing pajamas. Although she was wearing fluffy slippers, she had on jeans and a T-shirt, her hair pulled back, her face clean of makeup. She looked refreshed and far too chipper for that hour, especially for a new mom with twins.

"Mornin'," Reese replied.

"Come in. Noah and Naomi are napping," she said as she moved deeper into the house.

"Napping?" Brantley chuckled. "Isn't that pretty much *all* they do?"

JJ grinned. "They were awake for almost a whole hour."

"A whole hour?" he echoed. "And they get a nap for that?"

She giggled, leading the way to the kitchen. "Oh, hush it."

"You seem extra chipper this mornin'," Brantley told her.

"Oh, well, you know," she said, making a show of scratching her nose.

"Is that…?" Reese reached for her hand. "Holy shit. He did it? He finally asked."

Brantley frowned, glancing between them. "Asked what?"

Reese took JJ's hand and held it out in front of him.

Staring at the diamond on her finger, Brantley pretended not to notice. "What? What am I lookin' at?"

JJ laughed, then smacked him with her right hand. "Stop it."

Brantley grabbed her and pulled her in for a hug. "Congratulations."

She hugged him back. "Thank you."

"Where is the lucky guy, anyway?" he asked when he released her.

"In the shower. He said he wanted to go into work for a little while."

Brantley took a seat at the small island. "Why would he wanna do that?"

"Coffee?" JJ offered.

"Please."

"He wants to pitch in."

"He can do that from here," Reese told her, nodding when she offered him coffee.

"He's worried y'all don't have enough people."

"We've got bodies to fill the seats," Brantley told her. "But no one can come close to replacing either one of you. That doesn't mean we can't get things done."

"Did the new hires start?"

"Yep," Reese answered. "Darius has 'em loggin' Martin Calloway's movements for the past two years."

"Well, I did some research last night," she said, leaning against the counter with her coffee cup in hand. "I've been tryin' to figure out where the five-hundred k came from that Calloway paid Dr. Weaver."

"Any luck?"

"Censorious," she said. "It wasn't too hard to find."

"Find anything else while you were diggin' around?" *Anything that'll lead us to Kylie?*

"Oh, you know, just a few million sitting in offshore accounts. It's hidden behind shell companies, but it all comes back to Censorious."

"I wonder if the members know about that money?" Reese mused.

"You think Calloway's hidin' it?" Brantley asked.

JJ set her coffee cup down. "From what I can tell, no one else has access to those funds."

"What about personal accounts?" Reese asked.

"I was able to trace some transactions on what looks to be his main account." She reached for her cell phone. "I found it interesting that his wife doesn't have access to their money."

That was interesting. But not surprising.

"A couple of things caught my attention when I was scanning the account."

Brantley watched as her eyes glittered with excitement.

"I seriously doubt it's a coincidence, but he rented a private plane to take him from Dallas to Port Isabel."

The hair on Brantley's neck stood on end. "When?"

"March second," she said.

He knew she didn't mean March 2nd of this year.

"And?"

"And he stayed for twenty-four hours. Long enough to identify Juliet's body."

Brantley looked down into his mug. He remembered the phone call he'd received from Max Adorite, advising him to take his team to Starbucks so they'd have an alibi for her death. Oh, the mob boss had given him the option of taking Juliet into custody before the nice gentleman in the late-model Ford truck took care of business. Choosing to get coffee had been an easy decision, and Brantley hadn't lost a moment of sleep over it.

"He also identified the body of a Mexican national who was found dead in his truck."

Lifting his head, Brantley stared at JJ. "Shit."

She studied him. "I take it that doesn't surprise you?"

"He knows Max had her killed."

JJ frowned. "Max?"

Brantley shook his head. "He's known all along."

"And that means, what?" she prompted.

"It means he blames Max for his daughter's death."

"But that can't be the reason he took Kylie," JJ said firmly. "He'd already paid Dr. Weaver and relocated her before then."

"It's not why he *took* her, but it could be why he *kept* her."

"To draw Max out?" Reese asked.

"Why would Max care?" JJ questioned.

"He wouldn't. But he probably knows about Max's relationship with Travis."

JJ picked up her coffee cup. "I didn't realize they had a relationship."

"Friendship," Brantley corrected. "Or business acquaintances. Whatever they are."

JJ frowned. "But what does that get him? It's not like Max is gonna walk into the FBI headquarters and surrender because Calloway kidnapped his *business acquaintance's* wife."

She wasn't wrong.

"I haven't figured that part out yet." And God knows he'd spent enough time thinking about it.

"We know that Martin Calloway went to Port Isabel to visit Juliet." JJ pondered. "The ticket was purchased before her death, so did he go down there to help her? Was he plannin' to get her out of the country?"

"Did Juliet know he was her father?" Reese inquired. "I thought we determined she didn't know."

"I don't think she did," JJ told him. "But that doesn't mean he can't pretend to be her white knight. He's an FBI agent. Maybe he gave her some story about how she helped with a case, and he wanted to return the favor."

Brantley wasn't sure what Calloway might've told Juliet. Or if he even talked to her at all. They hadn't uncovered anything that proved Juliet knew who he was.

"You said he identified the body of the man who killed her?" Reese asked.

"I find it hard to believe that guy would've stuck around." Shaking his head, Brantley added, "Probably crossed over into Mexico as soon as it was over."

JJ nodded. "It's possible Calloway tracked him down in Mexico, killed him, then dragged his ass back to Port Isabel. Like a big fuck you to Max."

"Anything's possible." Brantley got to his feet. "But none of it tells me where Kylie is now. We know she's not in that grave."

"I take it you haven't heard back on the DNA yet?"

"Not yet," Reese answered.

Brantley looked at him.

Reese nodded. "I'll give Z a call."

"I saw Atticus's notes about the property they visited last night," JJ told him. "Sounds like it's worth a visit. Maybe get a drone overhead, see what's goin' on in there."

A drone. Brantley hadn't considered that, but he liked the idea.

"We're gonna find her," she said softly.

Brantley met her gaze, held it. "If he suspects we're gettin' close, he might not have any reason to keep her."

JJ's dark eyebrows dipped low. "He has a plan for her. I don't know what that is, but I know that much."

That was what Brantley was worried about.

JJ TOOK A SIP OF COFFEE, THEN set the mug down. She studied her best friend. As usual, she wasn't able to get a good read on Brantley. She knew he was thinking about Kylie. Likely about how he would bring her home, or maybe even what the odds were that she was still alive.

It was difficult to think that she could be after all this time. Not quite two years, but pretty damn close. What *were* the odds of her being alive? Slim to none? Especially if Martin Calloway had kidnapped her. Had he gotten her the medical attention she needed? Based on the records JJ had hacked into, Kylie's injuries had been extensive. So much so, it was a wonder she had survived at all.

Those were all questions she'd been trying to answer. The whole team had.

Her attention shifted to the doorway when Baz appeared. She smiled, unable to help herself.

"Hey," Baz greeted Brantley. "Something wrong?"

"We were just talkin'," she explained. "Reese went to call Z."

"No word on the DNA, huh?"

"Not yet." JJ was crossing her fingers that they would get something. She didn't know how that worked, but she'd watched enough television to know they wouldn't be able to get anything if the sample was degraded. Since they didn't know how long ago someone had been kept in that room, it was anyone's guess.

"Any chance you could ping Allison Bogart's cell phone?" Brantley asked, glancing between her and Baz. "She called Reese this mornin'. Said she needed to talk. We were gonna meet her at the diner, but she never showed."

"She called you?" JJ walked into the living room to get her laptop from the coffee table.

"Reese," Brantley told her. "A little before five."

"From what number?"

"He said it was blocked."

"A burner, then. I have no way of trackin' that one, but I can try the one we have for her. If it's on," she said, setting the computer on the kitchen island. "Last time I tried to ping it, it was off."

As she was logging in, Reese walked into the kitchen. All eyes shot to him.

He shook his head. "Z's gonna call the lab."

That wasn't the news she was hoping for, but it sounded about right. The team had uncovered quite a bit of information in the past few days, but not enough to locate Kylie or to confirm Calloway's whereabouts. For some reason, JJ didn't think they were together. Martin Calloway seemed too smart to be holed up with a woman he technically kidnapped. *If* that was what happened.

Hell, there was a good chance Kylie was in witness protection and off living her life. Maybe she had amnesia and didn't know who she was. She could be in Idaho picking potatoes or something. They did that there, right?

JJ focused on the task at hand, keying in the information to get Allison's phone to give her a location.

"It's off," she said, disappointment swamping her. She chewed on her bottom lip for a second, then began typing. "Let me just run a couple more things. You said the call came in a little before five, right?"

Brantley nodded. "Yeah. She called Reese."

It didn't always work, but JJ tried backtracing the incoming call from Reese's cell phone. It wouldn't provide a number, but it could give a... "That's weird."

Baz looked at the computer over her shoulder. "Is that the house where they found the blood?"

"Yeah."

"Allison was there?" Brantley asked.

"Looks like it."

Something blipped on the screen.

Baz leaned in. "Was that...?"

"Her phone?" JJ nodded. "It's on."

"Where is it?"

"At that house. No, wait. It's movin'."

With Baz looking over her shoulder, they watched as the dot on the screen moved.

"She must be in a car because it's movin' too fast for her to be on foot." JJ looked at Brantley and Reese. "Maybe she got a late start on the day."

"It disappeared," Baz noted.

JJ glanced down at the screen again. The dot was gone.

"Damn it," she muttered.

A soft sound came from the monitor on the counter. Her head snapped up, and a smile replaced her disappointment. "Someone doesn't wanna take a nap."

"You want me to—"

She cut Baz off mid-sentence, putting a hand on his chest and gently urging him back. "I got it."

His amused chuckle was all she heard as she hurried toward the twins' bedroom. She went in quietly, not sure whether they were both awake or only one.

"Hey, little man," she whispered, peering down into the crib at her beautiful angel. "You're supposed to be nappin'."

He sniffled in preparation for a cry, but she picked him up and gently cradled him against her shoulder. She'd learned that he liked to be upright while Naomi preferred to be nestled in her arms.

"How about a diaper change?" she told him, carrying him over to the changing table. "I'm bettin' money that your sister'll be awake by the time I'm done."

That was how it seemed to work. She wasn't quite a pro at the diaper change, but she was getting there. She'd cut her time in half yesterday when she realized that their patience ran quite thin when they were hungry.

"Let's go see Daddy, then I'll come back and get your sister changed."

As though she'd been doing it her entire life, JJ cradled Noah against her shoulder, using one hand to secure him while she grabbed the dirty diaper with the other.

In the kitchen, she found Baz working on her computer. When he heard her, he looked up, and she immediately saw the love on his face.

"Where's Brantley and Reese?" she asked, noticing the abandoned coffee cups on the counter.

"Said they'd swing by this afternoon if they can get away. Didn't want to get in the way."

"More like Uncle Brantley's scared to hold a baby," she told Noah as she passed him to Baz. "But that's okay. I'll make sure he gets plenty of practice, just you wait and see."

CHAPTER THIRTY-THREE

"Mornin', Boss."

"Good morning."

"Hey."

Reese followed Brantley and Tesha inside the barn, Brantley rattling off polite responses to those who were greeting them.

After leaving JJ's, Reese's mind had been running nonstop in an attempt to figure out how to find Kylie. Ever since that brief conversation with Allison, he was filled with a sense of urgency. Something in her tone had triggered it, and it wasn't lessening as the day progressed.

His conversation with his brother hadn't gone the way he'd hoped. Rather than telling him that they'd identified someone based on the DNA, Z had informed him they were having difficulty with the sample they'd provided. He claimed he had someone doing another test to see if they could get any identifying markers, but that could take time.

They didn't have time.

He couldn't help but put himself in Kylie's shoes, trying to imagine what the past two years had been like for her. He had some experience with being held against his will, confined with only his basic needs being met. He hoped like hell that wasn't what Kylie was going through.

And yes, he'd taken a page from Brantley's book and was now jumping on the Kylie-is-alive bandwagon with both feet. He knew it was premature, but he couldn't help himself. And definitely not after seeing Travis that morning. The man had done a complete turnaround from the last time he'd seen him. It was possible he actually smiled a time or two over breakfast.

How could Reese not believe?

He only hoped they weren't in for a huge disappointment. Losing her once had been painful. Twice would be … unthinkable.

"What's everyone workin' on?" Brantley asked.

Reese looked from one face to the next. Evan, Becs, Atticus, Archer, Jay, Charlie, Holly, Elana, and Darius. They were all there, all sitting at their desks, laptops in front of them. He couldn't remember the last time he'd come in there, and they'd all been diligently working. Usually, at least two people were making casual small talk.

Not today.

It was as though they knew the clock was running out.

Was it? That was the question Reese couldn't answer. If Kylie was alive and Martin Calloway was keeping her somewhere, what were his plans for her? He had a reason, clearly. Was he looking to punish Max or Travis for Juliet's death? Or was there something bigger at play?

"JJ was able to get me into the traffic cameras in Blanco," Holly answered. "It's a long shot, but I thought I could see what's goin' on down there. I mean, I doubt Kylie's walkin' around, but you never know."

Based on the chains and cuffs they'd found in that house, Reese had a pretty good idea how she was spending her time, and it wasn't window shopping in a small town.

"I'm working with Austin Trexler on getting a drone for the area," Charlie announced.

"I'm getting more info on the list of Censorious members that Simon put together," Jay said.

"How many so far?" Reese inquired.

"Ninety-three." Jay sighed. "And that's just the big dogs. We haven't even gotten to the soldiers yet."

Reese had a feeling that list was going to get much, much longer.

"I'm tracing Meredith's steps after she left Coyote Ridge," Becs stated. "We think she's hidin' something, but we don't know what. Thought maybe this would help."

"It won't," Brantley told her. "I appreciate the effort, but Meredith's actions are the least of my worries. I think she's simply a pawn in this game. She might've been important to Calloway at one time, but I don't think that's the case anymore."

Becs turned to face him. "Is there somethin' you'd like me to focus on?"

"Allison Bogart," he answered.

"I've got some information compiled," Charlie told Becs.

"I'm mostly interested in her recent activity," Brantley added. "Where has she been for the past six months?"

"We've got some details," Charlie said.

"Get more. Dig deeper."

"I can definitely do that," Becs said, her expression reflecting the same trepidation Reese was feeling.

Evan cleared his throat. "I'm gonna focus on—"

His words were cut off when Reese's cell phone rang. He wasn't sure why the entire room went silent, but it did. He pulled the phone from his pocket and glanced at the screen. When he looked up, he noticed Brantley watching him intently.

"It's Z," he said because it seemed they were all waiting for him. He tapped the screen and put the phone to his ear. "Hey."

"Well, I've got news."

Reese couldn't tell by his brother's tone whether that news was good or bad. "And?"

"The lab was able to make an identification."

Grinding his teeth was all Reese could do to keep from demanding his brother get on with it.

"The blood you found belongs to Kylie Walker."

Reese's breath lodged in his throat, his gaze snapping to Brantley's. He nodded.

"Were they able to determine how old the sample was?" he asked Z.

"The only thing they could tell me was that it was less than a year old. They couldn't pinpoint more than that. It does confirm your theory that her death was faked."

Yes. Yes, it did.

"Thanks, Z. I need to…" Reese wasn't sure what he needed to do. At the moment, breathing seemed to be his main focus.

"Go tell her husbands. They'll want to know," Z said. "I'll call you later."

"Yeah." Reese ended the call and shoved the phone in his pocket.

He glanced at the members of his team, noticing the hope that sparkled in nearly every pair of eyes staring back at him.

"They confirmed the blood belongs to Kylie. It's less than a year old."

"She's alive?" Holly asked, her voice thick with emotion.

"We don't know that for sure," Brantley interjected. "We do know she didn't die when we thought she did. And we'll continue to work under the assumption she's alive. Which means right now, our one and only objective is to find her. Once we do that, we can worry about Martin Calloway and Censorious. We'll take them down, I assure you. But they go on the back burner. Everyone's focus is on findin' Kylie."

"Understood," Atticus said. "We'll work on gettin' that drone, then we'll get boots on the ground in Blanco and Johnson City."

Brantley nodded. "Good. In the meantime, Reese and I are gonna give Travis and Gage the news."

Reese wasn't sure that was a great idea. At least not until they had confirmation that she was still alive. But he understood Brantley's reasoning. Travis and Gage deserved to have all the information they had.

"Come on, Tesha," Reese said. "Let's go for a ride."

She was at the door waiting for them when Reese made his way across the room. He felt as though he was walking through a dream. He had a destination, even if the path to get there was fuzzy and distorted.

"You good?" Brantley whispered as he pushed the door open.

Reese nodded. He wasn't sure that was true, but it was all he could offer.

ARCHER SAT AT HIS DESK, STARING AT his computer screen.

He was antsy, restless. The thought of sitting behind a desk while a woman was being kept prisoner out there … somewhere… It didn't matter that he didn't know where to look. He only knew that sitting there wasn't getting him the answers he wanted.

"You good?" Atticus asked from beside him.

As he'd done all morning, Archer avoided looking at his partner. Every time he did, he thought about that kiss. The one that had rocked him to the soles of his boots. He knew there was nothing he could do about it, but that didn't stop his brain from hitting replay on that memory every few minutes.

"Jesus," he grumbled, shoving to his feet. "I need some air."

While everyone else worked to find Kylie, Archer headed outside. He pushed through the door and out into the humid morning. The chill had since dissipated, replaced by warming temperatures and an annoying stickiness to the air.

Still, it was better than sitting in the barn, listening to Atticus breathe.

When he heard footsteps on dry leaves, he turned in time to see Slade walking from the parking area.

"Hey," he greeted, attempting to be polite.

Slade grunted, ignoring him.

"Well, that went well," Archer muttered when Slade disappeared into the barn.

Rather than follow his instincts and go back to the barn to see what had brought Slade in, Archer paced. It wasn't his business. Didn't matter if Slade was there to work or if he'd come to talk to Atticus. It didn't matter.

Because temptation was too great, Archer resisted the pull to go back in by heading toward the parking lot. The farther he got, the better off he would be. He took that to heart, following the path of the driveway to the road. When he reached the road, he turned around, came back. He had no idea how many times he'd repeated the back and forth when he stepped aside so Slade's truck could pass.

Only it didn't.

"You better treat him right," Slade said, his tone rife with warning.

Archer met his gaze. "What?"

"You heard me. He's a good guy."

Feeling defensive, Archer said, "Tell me somethin' I don't know."

"I'm not here to fight with you." Slade looked at the road. "I just came by to get somethin'. I know you two have a thing."

"A thing?" Archer fisted his hands at his sides. "He's my partner."

"Yeah. That's what he says, too. Don't worry. You're not the first partners here to hook up. Fucking isn't a crime."

"You're delusional, you know that?"

"No. You're in denial. But don't worry. I have no plans to get in your way."

Archer opened his mouth, but then closed it. This was pointless. Slade wasn't going to believe anything he had to say because the man was already convinced the world was out to get him. He was too blind to see a good thing when he had it, so it was his own fucking fault that he'd lost Atticus.

"Treat him right," Slade called as he drove off.

Shaking his head, Archer started back down the driveway. As he was reaching the house, he looked up to see Atticus watching him, his green eyes intent, boring a hole right through him.

"What did he say to you?"

"Nothin' important." It was the truth.

He turned on his heel, gearing up to make a trek in the other direction. Before he could, Atticus grabbed his arm.

"Stop, dammit."

He did, but he didn't look at Atticus. He couldn't.

"I'm sorry if he said somethin' to piss you off."

Archer pulled his arm from Atticus's grip. "He didn't."

"No? Then why're you stompin' around out here?"

There was so much accusation in Atticus's tone, Archer couldn't help but respond to it. He turned, this time staring down at Atticus, pinning him in place with a stern glare.

"You wanna know what my problem is?"

Atticus frowned, but he didn't step back even as Archer moved closer. "Yeah. Enlighten me."

"You are," he said, his voice low.

He took another step forward, and this time Atticus stepped back. Archer took another and another until they were hidden from view of the barn.

"I'm your problem? Why?"

"Because you fucking kissed me," he said in a harsh whisper. "You fucking kissed me, Atticus, and it's all I can fucking think about."

He'd never been one to use curse words to punctuate his sentences, but it seemed he was more upset than he'd thought.

Sighing heavily, he looked up, relaxing his neck, forcing himself to calm down. "Sorry. That was uncalled for."

"Look at me," Atticus insisted.

He kept his head tipped back. "I can't."

"Archer."

Jesus. He should not like the way Atticus said his name. He shouldn't.

"Please."

And fuck if he didn't like that, too.

When he was able to stop grinding his teeth, he brought his head to level and looked at Atticus again.

"I can't stop thinkin' about it either," Atticus said, his green eyes glittering. "But we can't."

Archer wanted to argue, but he had no defense. Atticus was right. As partners, they owed it to one another to refrain.

"I can't help myself," he admitted. "I fantasize about…" Archer let the sentence hang, knowing it was wrong to go down that road.

"What?" Atticus whispered, his eyes imploring.

"It doesn't matter," he huffed.

Atticus grabbed his shirt, pulled him closer. "Tell me."

Archer held his stare, leaning in until Atticus was pinned between him and the house. God, this was so fucking wrong, but he couldn't stop it.

"I fantasize about stripping you, then running my tongue over every inch of your body."

Atticus shuddered.

"But I'm not lookin' for a one-and-done deal, Atticus. And you've already said partners are off limits."

Atticus nodded. "I did say that."

"And you meant it."

Atticus's throat worked as he swallowed hard. Archer expected him to agree, but he didn't. When he didn't say anything at all, Archer forced himself to move back, to eliminate the temptation.

He started back down the driveway, needing to put distance between them so he could focus on the case. They had definitive proof that Kylie Walker's death had been staged. Now it was a matter of determining whether she was still alive. And if she was, finding her and bringing her home.

Until that happened, he had no business fantasizing about anything. Least of all his fucking partner.

CHAPTER THIRTY-FOUR

"WE HAVE A TAIL," BRANTLEY TOLD REESE as they headed toward Alluring Indulgence Resort.

He'd called his cousin to let him know he needed to talk, and Travis had directed them to meet at the resort.

Reese leaned forward, using the passenger side mirror to get a view of the vehicle.

"Black sedan," Brantley said. "Government plates."

"The FBI?" Reese asked.

"Looks like it."

"I can't see the driver. Is it a woman?"

"Not unless she's got a buzz cut." Which he figured was possible, but based on the size, he was pretty sure the driver was male.

"Not Allison, then?"

"Definitely not a tiny blonde, no. And I'm pretty sure it's not Calloway, either. Younger."

Whoever it was didn't appear to be trying to conceal themselves. They remained behind them until they reached the resort's parking lot. When Brantley pulled up to the valet station, the sedan kept driving.

"Well, I guess they don't want to talk." Brantley looked at Reese. "Let's get this done so we can head down south and see what we can find."

"Good morning, Mr. Walker," the valet greeted as though Brantley made a habit of coming to the resort. Since he was positive he hadn't seen the guy before, he had to assume whoever was manning their cameras had shared his name with the staff.

And yeah, it was still as awkward as it had been the last time he was there.

They made it into the lobby and over to the concierge desk after being greeted by two more employees, both using their names.

"That really is weird," Brantley whispered to Reese.

"Good morning, Mr. Walker. I've been told to send you back when you get here. Mr. Walker is waiting for you."

He had to smile because that just sounded ridiculous. "Thanks."

They started toward the hallway that would lead to the offices when the door opened and the man who'd been following them walked in. He was wearing jeans and boots, a white button-down shirt with the sleeves rolled up.

The guy looked vaguely familiar, but Brantley wasn't sure why.

"Sir, you'll need to check in at the desk," the doorman instructed, doing his best to steer the guy in the right direction.

"I don't need to check in," the man said. "I need to talk to *him*."

When the guy pointed his way, Brantley stopped and turned. "Do I know you?"

The man approached, and it was then that Brantley noticed he hadn't shaved and his eyes were bloodshot. Either he was getting over a late night where he'd tied one on, or he was having a bad day. Whatever it was, the guy was not getting enough sleep.

"Kieran Elliott," the man said, his eyes scanning the room.

Brantley frowned. "Slade's brother?"

Continuing to look around, he nodded, then met Brantley's gaze. "I need your help."

"With?"

Kieran's brown eyes, filled with determination and a hint of panic, settled on his face. "My partner's missing. I need your help findin' her."

Shaking his head, Brantley said, "I'm sorry. My team can't take on another case, we're—"

"Her name's Allison Bogart."

Brantley's spine went ramrod straight, and he felt Reese do the same beside him.

"I talked to Allison this mornin'," Reese told Kieran. "She called me."

Kieran's eyes widened. "When?"

"Just before five."

"Shit."

"What makes you think she's missin'?" Brantley asked, curious.

"We have a system. We check in every two hours, give or take ten minutes. I haven't heard from her since last night." Kieran looked at Reese. "What did she say to you?"

"That she needed to talk. We were supposed to meet at the diner around seven. She didn't show."

Kieran's jaw bunched, a clear sign that news wasn't what he'd hoped to hear.

"Do you work for the FBI, too?"

A quick nod was all Kieran offered as he stared around the space as though that might get him answers.

Someone cleared their throat behind him, causing Brantley to turn. Travis and Gage were walking their way, looking as formidable as ever.

"What's goin' on?" Travis asked, glancing between the three of them.

Brantley was wondering that, too. "That's the million-dollar question."

When their FBI friend turned around, Travis took a step closer. "Kieran?"

Watching the man, Brantley noticed something pass on his face, an unnamed emotion.

Gage stood beside Travis, taking in the newcomer. "You two know each other?"

"He's my cousin," Travis announced. "What're you doin' here?"

Gage pointed at Brantley. "Your cousin, too?"

Brantley shook his head. "Lorrie's side."

"Ah."

Kieran swallowed hard, his gaze shifting, as though he couldn't maintain eye contact with Travis.

"Y'all've probably met," Travis said, "but it's been a while. Kieran, this is my husband, Gage. Gage, Kieran Elliott."

Again, Kieran did his best not to make eye contact, which made Brantley suspicious.

"Why are you here?" Travis repeated, pinning Kieran with a questioning expression.

"He says his partner's missing," Reese said, clearly unnerved by the silence.

"Partner?"

"FBI," Reese explained. "He works with Allison Bogart."

"How long've you two worked together?" Brantley asked.

"Six months," Kieran said, seeming to find the toe of his boot fascinating.

"Doing what?"

His gaze lifted, coming to rest on Brantley's face. "An undercover assignment."

Jesus, it was like pulling teeth. "Focused on?"

Kieran swallowed again, his Adam's apple bobbing. "Censorious."

Brantley's shoulders tensed. "Meaning what? That you've infiltrated the group?'

He nodded. "Allison was already workin' with them. I was handpicked to go in, pretend to be interested in their work."

Brantley did not like the direction this was going. "You do know Allison's in Calloway's pocket, right?"

Kieran grimaced. "Not by choice, I assure you."

Putting his hands on his hips, he squared off with Kieran. "And your role?"

"Ultimately, I'm responsible for gettin' her out, but…"

"But what?"

When Kieran didn't respond, Brantley's frustration level reached its tipping point. He took a step closer. "What aren't you tellin' us, Kieran?"

Kieran's brown eyes widened, and there was something in them … something that looked a lot like … fear.

If it weren't for the fact that Brantley was desperate for answers, he would've felt sorry for Kieran. Whatever it was that the man was holding back was clearly difficult for him.

Unfortunately, Brantley had surpassed his capacity for empathy.

Travis stood there, waiting for his cousin to share whatever was bothering him. It was urgent based on the man's expression. And likely personal if Kieran's avoidance of eye contact was anything to go by. Not that they were close or anything, but Kieran was family, so he thought that meant something.

Taking a step forward, he decided to get this show on the road. "Look. I'm sure Brantley'll help you look for your partner, but right now—"

"I know where Kylie is," Kieran blurted.

A roaring sound erupted between his ears as he stared at the man, wondering if he'd heard him correctly.

"Where?" Reese insisted, stepping forward, inserting himself between Travis and Kieran.

"I can't tell you. Not until you agree to help me."

The roaring intensified, as did the fury that propelled him forward. Before he knew he was doing it, Travis had shoved Reese out of the way and had Kieran by the shirt, jerking him forward.

"Tell me," he seethed. "Where the fuck is she?"

Kieran's eyes were wide, but he didn't back down. He shook his head. "Not until—"

Travis released his grip on Kieran's shirt, causing him to stumble back. He lunged, then threw a punch that glanced off the man's jaw. He threw another and another, and he would've continued if it weren't for Brantley and Gage pulling him off of him.

"Let me go," Travis insisted, lurching forward, not finished beating on the man.

"Travis, stop," Gage said firmly, speaking right in his ear. "This isn't helping."

Maybe not, but it made him feel better.

"I'll take you to her," Kieran spat, wiping the blood from his lip. "Goddammit, Travis."

Travis was vibrating. Every cell in his body was hyped and alert.

Kieran's gaze swung to Brantley. "But I need your help."

"We'll help you," Reese stated, the lone source of reason in the sea of chaos. "We will. But if you know where Kylie is…"

"Is she alive?" Gage asked, his voice trembling.

Kieran looked at him, a wealth of sympathy flooding his face. "Yes. And she's safe. For now."

Brantley shoved forward. "Was that a threat?"

"No! Jesus Christ." Kieran's expression turned hard. "I got Kylie out of there. Allison and I are the reason she's alive right now."

Travis growled. "You won't be for long if you don't fuckin' tell me where she is."

Kieran looked around, as though realizing for the first time that there were other people. "I can't tell you. It's not safe for her. But I can take you." He looked at Brantley. "Just promise me, you'll help me find Allison after."

"Yes. Of course. After," he hissed. "Now where the fuck is she?"

"You can follow me," Kieran told him.

Travis shook his head. "Bullshit. You'll ride with me and Gage. You navigate. I'll drive."

"Fine."

"We'll follow," Brantley stated, gesturing toward the door.

Travis led the way.

CHAPTER THIRTY-FIVE

ATTICUS WAS SITTING AT HIS DESK, DOING his level best not to look at the door, waiting for Archer to return, when his cell phone rang.

"Yeah, boss," he said, answering immediately.

"We're headin' to Johnson City. I need you and Archer to get down that way now. I don't know exactly where we're goin', so you'll have to track my GPS. Reese'll keep you updated as best he can."

Because of the urgency in Brantley's voice, Atticus was already on his feet, heading for the door. "Sure thing. Somethin' wrong?"

"We don't know yet. We've got a guy claimin' he's Allison Bogart's partner. He says he knows where Kylie is."

"No shit?" Atticus put some extra pep in his step. "We're on our way."

"Thanks, Atticus."

He wasn't sure what Brantley was thanking him for, but that was the least of his worries as he made a beeline for his truck.

"Archer!" he shouted at his partner, who was nearing the house on whatever weird ritual he was in the middle of. "We've gotta go. Now."

Less than a minute later, Archer was in the passenger seat as Atticus sped down the driveway.

"Can you send Becs a text? Let her know what's goin' on?"

"Might be helpful if you let *me* know what's goin' on."

Atticus glanced over briefly, then returned his attention to the road.

"Brantley called. A guy claimin' to be Allison's partner says he knows where Kylie is."

"No shit?"

Atticus smiled because that was the same thing he'd said when Brantley had delivered the news.

"He happen to say where Allison was?"

"No." That was probably the last thing he cared about if the man had claimed to know where Kylie was.

They spent the next hour and fifteen minutes with the radio on and very little conversation. Atticus wasn't sure what to say, so he was grateful for the reprieve. Based on how quiet he was, he figured Archer felt the same.

Unfortunately, the lack of conversation made it easy for Atticus to replay Archer's words over and over again in his mind.

I fantasize about stripping you, then running my tongue over every inch of your body. But I'm not lookin' for a one-and-done deal, Atticus. And you've already said partners are off limits.

I did say that.

And you meant it.

Yes, he had meant it. But that was before Archer made that declaration. Now he wanted nothing more than to give in to this ridiculous attraction simply so he could lose himself in someone. Someone who might actually want more than to dominate and control, or to observe him in the throes with another man.

It was wrong to want that. More than wrong, probably. They were partners, and Atticus knew that relationships could screw that shit up.

Well, he didn't actually *know* that. He didn't have firsthand experience with it. But he did have experience working with someone he was involved with, and that hadn't been easy. And it likely wouldn't be easy going forward. Slade would probably make sure of that.

Desperate to get his mind on other things, he glanced Archer's direction. "Can you pull up Brantley's GPS? He didn't give me an exact location."

While his partner did that, Atticus prepared to turn into the town proper.

"Wait," Archer pointed straight ahead. "Don't turn. They're farther north. And they're still movin', so it looks like we caught up to them."

Atticus remained on the highway, noticing that it changed names. The area felt more rural than before, with more houses, more land. The homes appeared older, situated in small neighborhoods made up of two or three streets. When they neared a large church, Archer instructed him to slow down.

"You're gonna turn left right up here," he said. "It's not a major intersection, so give me a sec."

Atticus slowed as much as he could without impeding traffic.

"Okay. Here."

Following the direction of Archer's pointing finger, he put on his blinker and moved to the center turn lane, waiting for a pause in traffic before turning left onto a narrow asphalt road. It was barely wide enough for two vehicles to pass at the same time, so he figured it was a good thing no one was coming toward him.

When they reached an intersection with a 7-Eleven, Archer directed him to keep going straight, so he did. The farther they drove, the worse the road became. It was washed out on both sides, and what was left had potholes and large dips that made for a rough ride. There were houses, some mobile homes, and a couple of fields full of old junk cars.

Trusting that Archer would tell him where to go, Atticus continued to drive, moving as quickly as he dared.

"This road ends up here, you're gonna turn left."

Sure enough, the road ended—kinda—at a giant tree, but there were no stop signs, no street signs, just a yellow arrow pointing to the left.

Atticus went left, following the narrow road lined with mesquite trees and powerlines.

"Is that a river?" he asked, looking past Archer at the flow of water running parallel to the street they were on.

"Yep. Pedernales. And from what I can tell, they're right up here."

"Are they stopped?"

"Doesn't look like it. The dot keeps moving. Faster than if they were on foot, but slower than you."

Atticus slowed, continuing straight until he saw Brantley's truck and a black Cadillac Escalade.

"That's them," he told Archer so he could put his phone away.

As though they'd been waiting for Atticus to catch up, the two vehicles went a little farther and then pulled over to the right.

Looked as though they'd made it.

BRANTLEY STOPPED BEHIND TRAVIS'S SUV AT THE same time he noticed Atticus's truck pulling up behind him.

"Looks like he's openin' the gate," Reese said as they watched Kieran push open a rusted metal bar that blocked the narrow gravel path.

"Call Atticus. I have no idea what we're walkin' into, but I want him and Archer to be ready."

"You don't think this is a trap, do you?"

"I don't know what to think."

Brantley focused on the vehicle in front of him while Reese relayed what little details they had to Atticus and Archer.

"Yeah," Reese said. "Kieran claims he's got Kylie. I assume she's here. We don't know what's up ahead, though, so keep your eyes open."

Brantley pulled forward when Travis did. They bumped along the driveway that wound deeper into the dry grass and spindly mesquite trees.

He had no idea what he expected to find, but it certainly wasn't a quaint little blue house with hardwood siding and a massive stone patio that appeared to circle the house. Based on the entry, he'd figured the house would be falling in on itself.

Definitely not the case.

"It backs to the river," Reese noted when they slowed to a stop.

Before he could put the truck in *Park*, Travis and Gage were out of the SUV.

"Please, let her be okay," Brantley muttered, getting out of the truck, prepared to follow.

"SHE'S HERE."

"If you're lyin' to me, Kieran…" Travis figured his cousin could fill in the blanks. As it was, he wanted to beat the man bloody. According to him, he'd known Kylie was alive for a few months now, but Kieran didn't bother to fucking tell him? Didn't think it was necessary to share that information? To give his children a chance to stop grieving?

Travis's heart was beating like a bass drum in his chest. The roaring in his ears could've been the river, but he had a feeling it was his blood rushing through his veins. The farther they'd gone, the more anxious he'd gotten.

He had no idea whether Kieran was fucking with them, although he couldn't figure out why he would. He was family. Sure, he worked for the FBI, and yeah, he had kidnapped Kylie, but not the way Travis had initially thought. Or so Kieran had tried to explain. If the man was to be believed, he and Allison had actually kidnapped Kylie from her kidnappers. At least that was what he claimed.

According to the tale his cousin had weaved on the drive down, Kieran had been sent in to infiltrate Censorious and get Allison out. It was a deep-cover, off-the-books operation that only a couple of people knew about because the FBI was investigating one of their own: Martin Calloway.

That was when he learned that Kylie was being held hostage. Unable to do anything that would blow his cover, Kieran had managed to position himself so that he could keep an eye on Kylie, ensure she was safe. Then, when Kieran learned that Martin was going to dispose of Kylie because he no longer had any use for her, he made the decision to get her out of there. His partner, Allison, had insisted on helping, although crossing Martin Calloway was a likely death sentence. They had bided their time, waiting until the last second in an effort not to tip off Calloway. They'd managed to get her out safely, but then had no choice but to hide her to keep her that way.

"There are biometric locks," Kieran informed him as they approached the front door. "I installed them, as well as a high-tech security system, two days ago. At Kylie's insistence."

The thought of his wife living down here, settling in as though this was her new home, did not sit well with him.

Kieran unlocked the front door, then stepped inside to key in the code for the security system.

Travis looked at Gage, preparing himself for the worst.

"Kylie?" Kieran called out. "It's me. You in here?"

Silence.

Travis frowned at his cousin. Was he fucking with them? "Where the fuck else would she be?"

"During the day, she likes to sit down by the river," he said, clearly sensing Travis's fury.

"Outside? What's the point in all the security?" he demanded.

"Where is she?" Gage insisted, rounding on Kieran.

"I swear to you, she's here."

Swallowing hard, Travis glanced back to see Brantley, Reese, the dog, Atticus, and Archer walking through the door. Brantley tipped his head in the direction of the hallway. The four of them were armed, weapons out, as they began moving through the space.

"Clear," Atticus called from the kitchen.

"Clear," Archer called from somewhere off to the left.

"Clear here, too," Reese said, returning with Tesha leashed and walking beside him.

"The alarm was set," Gage said harshly. "She'd have to be inside."

"There's a bypass on the door in the bedroom," Kieran explained. "She has a hard time bein' confined to the house."

Travis headed to the back door, unlocked it, and stepped outside. The back patio was covered with leaves that had fallen from the trees. There was a stone path that led from the house to the river, also hidden by falling leaves.

He stared out, looking for her, but didn't see her. He fought the urge to clutch his chest. The pain was intense, the fear. He'd gotten his hopes up and—

"There she is," Gage whispered, grabbing his arm. "Fuck. There she is."

Travis followed the direction Gage was pointing, and he was lucky his knees didn't give out.

"Oh, Jesus, Travis." Gage's voice broke. "It's her."

"Kylie," he rasped, the word drifting softly into the air. He cleared his throat, then shouted her name.

Her head turned, and he saw the surprise register. Her cornflower blue eyes widened, and then there were tears. Hers. His. Gage's.

Travis headed for her at a run, Gage at his side. He didn't stop until he was standing in front of her, praying to God this wasn't a dream, that his eyes weren't playing tricks on him, or he wasn't in some drug-induced hallucination.

"Travis," she whispered, tears streaming down her beautiful face. "Gage. You're here."

When she ran into his arms, Travis caught her, holding tight as Gage moved in behind her. They stood like that, the three of them sobbing as the world righted itself on its axis after one year, eight months, and twenty-six days.

CHAPTER THIRTY-SIX

REESE DIDN'T BOTHER TO HIDE HIS TEARS. He couldn't if he'd wanted to. Seeing the three of them like that...

"You have a lot of questions to answer," Brantley told Kieran. "A fuckin' lot."

"I know." Kieran's brown eyes were wide. "And I will. I'll tell you everything you wanna know, but I need your help first. I have to find Allison."

"What makes you think she didn't go back to Calloway?" Archer asked.

While they had stood by the house, watching Travis and Gage approach Kylie, Kieran had given them a quick rundown of how they'd gotten to this point. His story was that he'd taken Kylie when he learned that Calloway had no intention of giving her back to her family. He claimed he told her they had to lie low until the heat died down so that Calloway didn't come after her family, and she agreed.

That was only a few days ago.

Reese had to admit, it sounded plausible. He knew Kylie. Knew she would do whatever was necessary to protect her family. Even if it meant not being able to see them.

"Because she wouldn't," Kieran replied. "Last I talked to her, she was goin' to fill you"—he looked at Reese—"in on what was going on. She said y'all could be trusted."

"Nice to know someone thought so," Brantley grumbled.

"Look. I thought it was best for everyone at the time. I thought we could take down Calloway first."

Brantley gripped Kieran's shoulder roughly, pointing with his other hand. "You see that. That's your fuckin' family right there. You kept her from them."

"I know."

Kieran sounded genuinely apologetic. At least to Reese. He wasn't sure Brantley could see through his anger at being deceived. It would take time for them to figure out everything that happened. Until then, they had to do what they could to help Kieran.

"We're gonna find her," Reese promised him. "Where would they hole up? The rest of Calloway's people."

"They were keepin' her in a house—"

Brantley looked at him. "The one on Rocky Road?"

Kieran nodded.

"They cleared out. Where would they go from there?"

"The main compound is in Blanco. It belongs to a former sheriff's deputy."

"Terry Berry," Atticus supplied.

"Yeah."

Reese addressed Atticus and Archer. "You two need to go back to the compound. Keep an eye on things. If you see anything off, let us know."

Atticus nodded. "Will do."

"On your way there, call Evan, fill him in on what's goin' on," Reese continued, speaking to Atticus. "Tell him to route everyone's focus to finding Allison. He can reach out to JJ. She was helpin' us this mornin'."

Without wasting another second, Atticus and Archer took off out the front door.

"I want to clean this place out," Brantley stated, looking directly at Reese. "Anything and everything that could tie back to Kylie needs to be removed. We'll take it back to HQ. Figure out what to do with it later."

"She doesn't have much," Kieran told them. "She insisted she wouldn't be here long."

"How much danger will her family be in?" Brantley asked, his full attention on Kieran.

"Martin Calloway's unstable. And he's obsessed with Max Adorite. He believes that Travis and his family are his way of infiltrating the Adorites."

Reese didn't understand why anyone would make that correlation. "Why?"

"Because he knows Max killed his daughter on Travis's orders."

Reese looked at Brantley. He saw surprise on his husband's face, which offered a modicum of relief. He was fully aware of the phone call Brantley had received while they'd been down in Port Isabel. Knew Max had given them a choice, and Brantley had taken option A—get somewhere that would provide them with an alibi while his man took care of Juliet. But he hadn't been aware that Travis had played a part in it.

Putting himself in Travis's shoes, Reese understood. Mostly. He couldn't fathom ordering the death of anyone, but if someone had taken Brantley from him…

No, Reese couldn't say what he would be willing to do to avenge his husband's death. And he prayed to God he would never find out.

SHE COULDN'T BELIEVE THEY WERE THERE.

Kylie didn't move, not wanting to risk waking up if this were a dream because her husbands were there. She could feel their warmth, hear their breaths. It was surreal and a relief.

The nightmare was finally over.

One year, eight months, and twenty-six days.

That was how long it had been since she'd seen her husbands.

That was how long it had been since she'd held her babies.

That was how long it had been since that crazy bitch hit her with her car, and her world was upended because some crazy bastard had a hard-on for justice. At least that was what she'd gathered during her time in captivity. And she'd thought Juliet Prince was psychotic. She had nothing on her biological father. Martin Calloway was a monster.

For most of that time, she'd been confined, kept as a prisoner, refused everything except for her most basic needs. Then Kieran came along and promised to save her from it all, but asked that she give him time. She'd tried arguing with him, insisting that he could do what he needed to do without her. For the first time since she'd been taken, she'd seen actual sympathy in the eyes of one of her captors. He'd promised he would get her home, but insisted this was the only way to protect her family.

Kylie hadn't needed to hear more than that. The mere thought of her babies being in danger was enough to get her to comply. But the moment her captors attempted to kill her, Kieran had come rushing to the rescue, fending them off and getting her to safety.

"You ready to go home?" Travis asked, his big arms still wrapped firmly around her.

She nodded, not sure her voice would work if she tried to talk.

When he released her, Kylie managed to remain upright. Her knees felt like Jell-O, so she took a second to compose herself. When Travis pulled her against his side and Gage took her hand, she was able to breathe a little easier. They walked like that toward the house, and that was the moment she took her first deep, cleansing breath since the nightmare started all those months ago.

She prayed like hell that it was really over.

NEARLY FOUR HOURS LATER, BRANTLEY WALKED INTO the house, feeling slightly off-kilter.

How was it possible that everything could change in the blink of an eye? One minute, Kylie Walker was dead, her death mourned by many. The next, she was standing there, breathing.

"You okay?" Reese asked, placing a hand on his arm.

Brantley nodded. "I will be."

"Let me get Tesha her dinner, then we'll talk."

He wasn't sure what there was to talk about. They'd spent the drive back on their phones, making calls, letting people know what happened. The team was aware thanks to Atticus and Archer sharing the details. His family now knew and would likely be doing whatever they could to get Kylie acclimated to her life again.

He wondered how that would be. Brantley remembered the day he'd come home after being discharged from the hospital. Having spent most of his adult life in the military, he'd been set free to do whatever he wanted. It hadn't been easy. Then again, he'd never had his choices taken from him. Kylie hadn't had a say in what happened to her. Would she jump right back in as though she was never gone?

He watched Reese. Not for the first time, he wondered about his husband's transition back into his normal life after being held captive. Reese rarely shared details of that time in his life, and Brantley chose not to push him. He knew all too well why people compartmentalized the bad shit, and the thought of forcing Reese to relive it wasn't something he looked forward to. But there was a good chance Reese knew exactly what Kylie was going through.

Those were questions that would have to be answered later. Right now, he wanted to clear it all out for a little while.

Brantley continued to watch Reese in the kitchen, doing the same thing he did every night. Seeing him like that, doing something so mundane, filled him with a sense of peace. At one time, he'd been floundering, not sure which way was up, then Reese Tavoularis walked into his life, and that all changed. Yeah, maybe there were some speed bumps and an influx of chaos from time to time, but there was still peace beneath it all.

Unable to help himself, he walked up behind Reese and put his arms around him.

Reese relaxed against him.

"I love you," Brantley whispered.

"I love you, too."

For the moment, that was enough.

CHAPTER THIRTY-SEVEN

SITTING ON THE COUCH WITH NOAH CRADLED in her arms, JJ found herself smiling. It was almost midnight, but she didn't care. Time blended at this point since the babies had yet to get on a regular schedule. But they were working on that.

"Today has been a good day, little man," she told her son. "Kylie's home."

He wouldn't know what that meant, nor would he remember this day the way that she would. It was the day that a family had been reunited after so much pain, so much loss.

A beep sounded to her right, so she glanced over at her laptop, which was perched on the arm of the couch. A red, flashing dot appeared, signaling a location.

"Hmm." Shifting, JJ reached over, tapped a few buttons to get more information. "You're on the move again, aren't you, Allison?"

"Are you talkin' to yourself in here?" Baz asked as he strolled into the room.

JJ peered up at him, smiled. "Is Naomi asleep?"

He nodded. "For now, anyway."

If they were lucky, she would sleep for a couple of hours.

"Why don't I take him?" Baz offered. "I'll get him settled, and you take care of that."

She didn't want to let Noah go, but he was already dozing.

After passing the sleeping baby to his dad, JJ began typing, gathering as much information as she could about Allison Bogart's location.

"Shit," she muttered. "This can't be good."

Grabbing her phone, JJ was about to dial Brantley's number, but paused, remembering that he'd put Atticus and Archer in charge of this particular mission. While she wasn't currently in the office as an active member of the team, she was still a member of the team. It was only right to do things according to protocol.

She dialed Atticus's number.

"Hey, JJ. What's up?"

"I just got a ping on Allison's cell phone. Where are you at?"

"Sittin' in my truck, waitin' to see if these fuckers will come out of their hidey hole."

JJ laughed, wondering whether Atticus knew how much he sounded like Brantley just then.

"Is there somethin' else we should be doin'?" Atticus asked.

"Hold on. Let me pull up your GPS, so I can see how close you are."

A few keystrokes later, two more red beacons popped up on the screen, one belonging to Atticus, the other to Archer.

"Is Archer with you?"

"I'm here," Archer said, his voice coming in clear.

"Hey," she greeted, still smiling.

"Hey, girl. What's up?"

That got another laugh bubbling in her chest, and she realized how much she missed the team already. She wasn't ready to go back to work yet because that would mean leaving her babies, but she did miss them.

"Y'all are about two miles from Allison's phone," she told them. "I can send you the coordinates, but it won't matter until it stops movin'."

"She's on the move?" Atticus asked.

"Yeah. I don't think she's in a vehicle because she's not gettin' far."

"Shoot those coordinates to Archer's phone," Atticus instructed. "We'll head that way. Maybe we can get to her before she disappears again."

"Again?" JJ asked, even as she sent the information to Archer's phone.

"Becs and Evan ran into her at the diner. Tried to talk to her, but she pretended she didn't know them."

"I remember seein' that in the notes."

"Then she called Reese to meet, but never showed."

And now her partner was looking for her. What in the hell was this woman up to?

"SHOULD WE CALL BRANTLEY AND REESE?"

Atticus kept his attention on the road, relying on Archer to give him directions. "No. You saw them back at that house. Let them process. If we can't get to her, we'll call them."

"Roger that. You're gonna make a right up here. Half a mile or so."

He continued to drive. The farther they went, the less populated the area became, and that was saying something considering these small towns had far more trees than people. There were no more streetlights, only his headlights stretching out in front of them to break up the darkness.

"Take a right at the next street," Archer instructed.

Slowing so he didn't miss the turn, Atticus watched for the reflective sign.

"JJ says she's moving again," Archer noted. "But she still doesn't think she's in a car."

"So what? She's at a house? Maybe walkin' around?"

"Could be."

"How far away are we?"

"A mile or less."

Atticus slowed, not wanting to come up on her too quickly. Considering how dark it was out this way, there was a good chance he might run over her if she was out for an evening stroll. Then again, he could hear coyotes off in the distance. Probably not the safest place to get your exercise if you were a night owl.

"Pull over here," Archer said. "And shut off the lights."

The truck bumped along as he left the road, coming to a stop in the grass. Atticus shut off the lights, pitching them into darkness; the only lights were those in the cab of the truck. He turned off the engine to cut those, too. Then they were left with Archer's cell phone screen.

Archer spoke softly in the darkness. "I show we're almost on top of her."

Since his eyes hadn't quite adjusted, he couldn't see much past the hood of his truck. The thought of getting out and wandering through the woods, risking a run-in with a snake or some other creature that lurked out there at night, did not fill him with joy.

But it had to be done.

Unbuckling his seatbelt, Atticus reached into the back seat, retrieving two flashlights. He passed one to Archer.

"You come prepared, huh?"

"I try. Come on. Let's see what she's up to out here."

Rather than be reckless and invite a rattlesnake bite, they kept to the road. Atticus led the way, with Archer right behind him, guiding him with his voice.

"If she's out here," Archer whispered, "she's gonna be here."

He couldn't see shit, so Atticus stopped. "Here, where?"

The next thing he knew, Archer's big hand curled around his wrist, lifting his arm out in front of him.

"About twenty yards that way."

Atticus kept his breathing under control, ignoring how good Archer's touch felt.

"Do we head that way?" he asked, keeping his voice low.

"I'd say we have to."

Just as he was about to turn on the flashlight, headlight beams lit up the darkness to their right.

"Hold that thought," Archer said, grabbing Atticus and moving them into a cluster of trees.

They crouched there, hiding behind a couple of skinny trees until the car moved past. There was no way whoever was driving wouldn't see his truck, but there was nothing Atticus could do about that now.

"Is that her?" Atticus asked when they were shrouded in darkness again.

Archer's phone screen lit up. A second later, he said, "No."

"Really? So what? They left her out here to—Fuck."

Realization dawned, causing him to stand up and move back to the road. He turned on the flashlight and scanned the area with the beam.

"Which direction?" he asked as they walked slowly.

"Keep going straight."

Atticus moved slowly.

He had a bad feeling about this. A really bad feeling.

ARCHER DIRECTED ATTICUS A FEW MORE FEET, then grabbed his shoulder to stop him. He saw her before Atticus did, the body discarded in a heap, her clothes ripped and torn from her body, legs bruised and mangled, arms askew.

But that wasn't the worst of what they'd done to Allison Bogart.

A moment later, his partner muttered, "Son of a bitch."

Yeah.

"They fuckin' killed her."

Yep. And based on the gaping wound on her throat and the blood oozing from it, there was no need to check for a pulse.

Atticus's voice was weak when he rasped, "What the hell?"

Because he had no intention of being caught by the police, Archer grabbed Atticus's wrist and dragged him back toward the road. He didn't need the light because his working memory was actively guiding him.

"Call Brantley," Archer told Atticus when they reached the truck.

When Atticus didn't respond, he turned to see him standing there, eyes wide.

Archer didn't need to be a doctor to know that Atticus was going into shock.

"Was that your first dead body?" he asked, stepping closer.

Atticus nodded.

Yep. Definitely in shock.

Archer took Atticus's hand and steered him around to the passenger side, urged him into the truck, then made his way back around. He got behind the wheel and started the engine. He shifted into *Reverse* and used his taillights to guide him the short distance to the road they'd turned off of.

Once they were headed toward town, he grabbed his phone, doing his best to keep from driving into a ditch while he pulled up Brantley's number.

"Yeah?" Brantley answered, his voice echoing in the truck.

"We've got a problem."

"What's that?"

"We found Allison Bogart."

"Good. Where?"

"Not good," he corrected. "She's dead."

"Son of a bitch. Where are you?"

"On the backroads where we lost the tails the other day. We followed JJ's coordinates to a field, found Allison's body. Now, we're heading to Johnson City."

"You touch her?"

"No." No one had needed to. Whoever had killed her had done so by slashing her throat. It had been a gruesome scene. Enough that Archer knew there was no surviving it.

"Okay. Get to town. We'll head that way. I'll call Kieran so he can bring in the authorities. They might want to talk to you."

"I'm pretty sure we crossed paths with whoever did the evil deed. Silver Honda Accord," he told his boss, then rattled off the license plate number he'd noted when it passed. "It's the same one that was tailin' us."

"Good work. Sit tight."

"Will do."

Archer set his phone in the cupholder when the call disconnected. He glanced over at Atticus, noticed the man was staring straight ahead, hands clasped tightly in his lap.

Shock could be a bitch.

Fifteen minutes later, Archer was walking out of the small convenience store with two Dr. Peppers. He made his way to the side of the building where he'd parked to keep them off the security cameras. Turned out, it wasn't necessary because he'd noted the store didn't have any.

He caught sight of Atticus still staring straight ahead, so he went over to the passenger side and opened the door. He reached across him and unbuckled his seat belt.

"Here." He unscrewed the lid on one of the Dr. Peppers, then held it out to him. "Drink this. Then get out and walk around for a minute or two."

Atticus took the bottle, lifted it to his mouth. He drank. As he did, some of the color returned to his face.

Archer remained where he was, standing beside Atticus, the door open wide. "That was horrific," he said. "And let me tell you, it never gets easier to see."

"They…" Atticus shook his head, not finishing the sentence.

Archer didn't need him to. He knew what the man was referring to. As though slashing her throat wasn't enough, they had cut out Allison's tongue, likely as a warning to whoever was looking for her. According to Kieran, Allison had helped him get Kylie to a safe place when they learned Calloway had given the order to kill her. And because she had betrayed him, Calloway had probably ordered Allison's death, too.

"Do you think he did it?" Atticus asked.

"Who? Calloway?" Archer shook his head. "I doubt he gets his hands dirty." The bastard had too much to lose. "But he instructed her killer to do it."

Atticus took a deep breath and exhaled heavily, his Dr. Pepper still in his hand. Archer took it from him, then reached over him again and placed it in the cup holder.

"I'll never get over seein' her face."

"You will," he assured Atticus, placing his hand on his thigh. As soon as he did, he realized what he was doing, so he jerked it back. "Sorry."

"Don't be." Atticus looked at him, his green eyes glowing in the light from the dashboard.

Archer held his stare, unable to look away. He wanted to kiss this man so badly. Hell, he would settle for putting his arms around him and holding him. But that wasn't the deal they'd made. As his partner, Atticus was off limits, and Archer had agreed to abide by the rules.

Forcing himself to look away first, Archer took a step back. "Brantley'll be here soon. I figure the police might want to talk to us. If they don't, we'll head back."

"Yeah." Atticus exhaled heavily. "I didn't realize you got the license plate."

"It's a thing I do without realizing it," he admitted.

"What do you mean?"

"I just see details."

"Like a photographic memory?"

"I don't know, maybe. I just notice things and I remember them. For a while, at least. Not indefinitely."

"If I asked you about that license plate number next week, would you have remembered it?"

"Probably not."

"Interesting."

"How so?"

Atticus shrugged. "I just find it cool, that's all."

Archer grinned. At least he'd gotten Atticus's mind off what he'd seen in that field.

Atticus turned to get out of the truck. "I think I need to walk around for a minute."

Moving out of his way, Archer took the other Dr. Pepper from where he'd set it on the truck's bed rail. He opened it and took a long drink, watching as Atticus walked a few yards away and then back.

It really sucked that he was such a stickler for rules because the urge to grab Atticus and kiss him was damn near too powerful to resist.

But resist he did.

NEARLY THREE HOURS LATER, BRANTLEY STOOD AT the road, watching as investigators blocked off the area as a crime scene. Because Allison Bogart worked for the FBI, they'd come in and taken over. Probably for the best, since he wasn't sure that some of the local cops weren't on Calloway's payroll.

"What happens next?" Reese asked Kieran, who was remaining back, looking as though someone had ripped his guts out.

Kieran shrugged. "I've been benched until they can investigate."

Seemed redundant to him, but Brantley figured that was par for the course when it came to the government.

Kieran slowly turned, facing Brantley. "I want to find this fucker."

"You just said you were benched."

"But you're not."

Brantley watched him, not sure how much he wanted to reveal to a man who'd kept a pertinent detail from his own fucking family. The fact that Kieran had been protecting Kylie didn't matter when he could've easily told her family that she was alive, and they could've stepped up to help her. Instead, he'd taken it upon himself to decide what was best for everyone.

"Look, I get you don't agree with what I did. But it's done. I thought it was the best thing. You don't know him, Brantley." Kieran thrust a hand in the direction of the body. "He's capable of worse than that."

Brantley figured as much. Martin Calloway was working his own agenda. He wasn't above using anyone and everyone to get what he wanted. The problem was, they didn't know what he wanted. Censorious's manifesto was one thing. But this … killing an FBI agent so heinously after blackmailing her and her family for years … it seemed like overkill.

No pun intended.

He could feel Reese watching him, knew his husband wondered what the plan was. Brantley wasn't sure yet. He intended to take down Censorious, but after seeing this, he knew he had to protect his team. He would not leave them vulnerable to this. That would require them to refocus their efforts. No more going off half-cocked.

"You can help," he told Kieran. "As a consultant to my team."

It was evident by the gleam in Kieran's eyes that he wasn't keen on the idea. It was also clear that he didn't have many other options.

"Fine." Kieran nodded curtly. "I'll help in any way that I can."

"Good." Brantley glanced at Reese, then back to Kieran. "I'm gonna give my team a couple of days to relax before we go balls to the wall. Monday mornin', meet at my house. Our headquarters is in the barn."

"I'll be there."

Brantley watched as Kieran made his way over to one of the FBI agents.

Reese stepped up beside him. "You really think it's a good idea to bring him on?"

"I do. He knows what goes on within the organization. That's the part we're missin'."

"True."

"With his help, we'll find out what Martin Calloway's endgame is. Once we figure that out, we'll dismantle his house brick by brick until we destroy it once and for all."

CHAPTER THIRTY-EIGHT

Sunday, October 9, 2022

BRANTLEY STOOD ON HIS UNCLE'S FRONT PORCH, beer in hand, watching as a dozen or so kids chased each other through the front yard.

When Travis had called him and insisted that he come to Sunday dinner at Curtis and Lorrie's, he hadn't been able to refuse. Then again, half the town hadn't refused either because they were there, celebrating Kylie's homecoming.

Granted, it wasn't all rainbows and roses. It was obvious that Kylie was doing her best to acclimate. It had to be difficult after being gone for so long, held captive, not knowing what the next day would bring. And the same went for the family who had mourned her death and spent nearly two years trying to make peace with it.

He'd watched the kids, wondering how they were adapting. Kate seemed to be dealing with it better than the rest, but she wasn't leaving her mother's side. Kade and Avery appeared hesitant, but hopeful, maybe? The same didn't appear to be the case for Haden and Maddox, who had been two and one, respectively, when their mother disappeared from their lives. They were far more interested in laughing and playing with their cousins.

It would take time, but the family dynamic was strong. Brantley knew they could overcome just about anything.

He continued to check on Kylie, watching her from a distance. There were moments when she looked lost, almost sad. Others, when he could practically feel the relief coming from her. He hoped to learn what happened to her, but that was a story for another day.

A hard hand smacked him on the shoulder. "How's married life treatin' ya?"

Turning, Brantley grinned at his cousin Kaleb. "Can't complain. You?"

Kaleb's gaze sought out his wife, who was sitting in a lawn chair beside Kylie. "Marryin' that girl was the best thing I ever did. She gave me all those heathens." He nodded in the direction of the kids chasing each other around the Halloween decorations that were being put up.

"And you've got your hands full, huh?"

"More than. But it's worth it." Kaleb's expression turned serious. "I wanted to thank you."

"For?"

"For bringin' her home. Travis told us what you did. How you were determined to find out the truth."

"That's what we do for family, right?"

"You made this family whole again."

"I didn't do it alone. My team deserves the credit for this one."

"Yeah, well. They've got damn good leaders. Speakin' of… Where's your better half?"

"He got wrangled into helpin' with the decorations." Brantley turned to look out at the yard once again. "Who's responsible for all those damn skeletons?"

"That'd be Ethan's doing. He thought it would be funny to create a zombie army usin' skeletons. Every year, he adds to the collection."

There had to be at least thirty of them, some full-size, others miniature. Most of them had been modified so they were funny rather than scary. At the moment, Ethan was tying one—wearing a Dallas Cowboys jersey—to a post on the house, arranging it so that it looked like it was climbing.

The front door opened behind him. A second later, boots thudded on the wooden porch. A firm hand gripped his shoulder, causing him to look over.

"That's my cue to check on my wife," Kaleb said. "Talk to you later."

Brantley nodded before turning his attention to Travis.

"Thanks for comin'," the man said, stepping up to the railing beside him.

"Thanks for invitin' us. My parents still inside talkin' to your mom?"

"Oh, yeah. Iris and my mother are plannin' the next family reunion."

Brantley frowned. "Didn't we just have one of those?"

"Six years ago."

Damn. It had been that long? He hadn't been able to attend, but he'd gotten an earful from his mother. Apparently, his cousin Jared had done a damn fine job of putting it together.

"Well, as long as I'm not in charge, I'm sure I'll be there."

Travis rested his boot on the bottom porch rail. "I heard about Kieran's partner. What they did to her."

It was brutal and vicious. So much so, Brantley wanted to end those bastards simply so they couldn't do it again. And he wanted to make it painful.

"What happens next?" Travis asked, his voice low.

"We're goin' after them," he said simply. "I'm gonna get RT and Z to help. These people are ruthless, and while my team is brilliant, they haven't gone up against anything like this. I'm not takin' any chances."

"Let me know what I can do. I'll stay outta your way," he tacked on quickly. "But I can do what needs to be done. Just say the word."

"You need to focus on your family right now, Trav."

His gaze swung out to where Kylie was sitting. "Trust me, I am. It took my daughter remindin' me that we can't give up, can't stop hoping for somethin' better. That was when my hope returned. And then my wife did."

They stood like that for a few minutes until Curtis came out to round everyone up for dessert. Travis took the lead, wrangling everyone toward the house. The kids barreled inside, leaving the adults trailing after them.

Brantley was standing back, watching the excitement, when Reese joined him.

"That's a lotta kids, huh?" Reese drawled.

"Oh, yeah. A lot."

"I don't know how they—" His words cut off as the sound of tires on gravel announced the arrival of someone else.

Brantley turned, watching the SUV pull down the driveway, inching slowly closer. Through the windshield, he saw two familiar faces.

"What are they doin' here?" Reese asked.

"No idea."

"Were they invited?"

Brantley shrugged. "Not that I know of. Go get Travis."

While Reese went in to get his cousin, Brantley started down the porch steps toward the driveway. He intercepted Meredith and Decker before they could get too close to the house.

"What are y'all doin' here?" he asked, keeping his voice smooth and even.

Meredith looked at Decker.

A commotion sounded behind him, causing him to look back. Travis, Gage, and Braydon had barreled out of the house and were walking toward them at a fast clip.

"You can't be here," Travis bellowed. "Not today."

"We aren't here to cause problems," Decker said. "I swear it."

"Then you need to go before my wife sees you."

The screen door on the side of the house slammed.

Too late.

Jessie and Kylie were coming toward them, their father, Joe, not far behind.

"Why are you here?" Braydon asked, sounding as though he was ready to strangle the woman.

Meredith was staring at her daughters, her eyes wide, chin trembling. It was clear she hadn't expected to see them.

"We need your help," Decker said, glaring at Brantley.

"With?"

Decker stepped forward, ignoring Meredith's tears as she continued to look at Jessie and Kylie.

"Cicily Rose," he said simply.

The name was familiar, but it took a second for Brantley to place it. That was the name on the back of the photograph Atticus had found in Decker's trailer.

"What about her?"

Meredith turned to look at him. "He's got her."

Brantley frowned. "Who's got her?"

Decker swallowed hard. "Martin Calloway."

Meredith moved closer to Decker. He took a step to the side, as though he didn't want her too close.

"Who is she?" Travis asked.

It seemed difficult for Decker to form words, but he took a deep breath and finally said. "She's my daughter—"

"*Our* daughter," Meredith corrected.

"—and that bastard took her."

"You have to find her," Meredith pleaded.

For the first time since Brantley met Decker Bromwell, he saw something other than arrogance or indifference. He saw absolute terror.

"How long has he had her?" Reese asked.

"A week and a half."

Brantley frowned. "And you're just tellin' us now?"

"He threatened to kill her if we didn't back off."

Confused, Brantley looked at Reese. This was the first they were hearing about it?

Reese shrugged, clearly out of the loop as well.

"Will you find her?" Meredith asked.

"Of course they will," Kylie said, stepping forward.

Brantley glanced over at her.

"That would make her their sister," Reese noted softly.

Yeah. It would.

"Please, Brantley," Kylie pleaded, the fear in her eyes real.

He nodded, then looked at Decker. "Yeah. We'll help."

Time to call in the team for another round of finders keepers.

Atticus lay on the bed, staring up at the ceiling. The room had grown dark with the setting sun, but he hadn't bothered to turn on a lamp. He didn't care. This was the extent of his plans for the evening. To lie there, wide awake, staring into the darkness.

As long as he kept his eyes open, he didn't see that mangled body in the field.

He'd spent the past few days trying to force that image from his brain, to no avail. He had worked, compiling notes and details on what happened. He had chilled, watching TV in the main room at the B and B. The only thing he hadn't done was sleep. When he tried, the nightmares came.

He had no idea how long it would take for him to stop seeing that, but he hoped it was soon. He was exhausted.

A thump sounded from the room next door. He knew that was Archer moving around. Every now and then, another thump would sound, but then it would be quiet.

More than once, he had considered going over there, knocking on the door, and asking Archer to replace that mental image with something else, something salacious. The only thing that kept him from doing so was the principle of the matter. He had told Archer that they couldn't act on the attraction. They were partners, and because of that, they couldn't cross that line.

Atticus wanted to cross that line. Hell, he wanted to decimate that line.

That wouldn't be fair to Archer.

But would it really be so wrong? Just one night. The two of them.

Before he knew what he was doing, Atticus was sitting up. Then he was standing. A few seconds later, he was opening the door and stepping out into the hall.

One night. It would curb the craving and eliminate that horrific image.

He pulled his door closed behind him, committed.

Taking a deep breath, Atticus squared his shoulders and turned. Before he could take a single step, he heard footsteps bounding up the stairs. A moment later, Spencer Elliott appeared, looking as cocky as ever.

"Hey, man," Spencer greeted with a grin. "I didn't realize you were stayin' here."

Atticus nodded. "Just for a little while."

"Well." Spencer flashed a grin, stopping in front of the door to Archer's room and knocking lightly. "Wish me luck."

Atticus didn't wish him anything, but he did slip back into his room and hunt for his headphones.

No way could he sit there in the dark and listen to Archer and Spencer. If he was subjected to that torture, he wasn't sure he would survive it.

Stay Tuned

I hope you've now forgiven me after leaving you hanging in *Missing Pieces*. As you can now tell, there was no way for me to tie up the story quickly. It's still ongoing, so I hope you're looking forward to more from Brantley, Reese, and the rest of the task force.

For those of you who want Kylie's full story, you should know I will be writing it. I can't write it within the Brantley Walker: Off the Books series because it isn't fair to the team, but I will be adding it to The Walkers of Coyote Ridge. I don't have an ETA at this time, but it is on the list of upcoming books.

Each book in this series is a full-length novel involving a new case and the continuation of the relationship between these two men. I promise not to keep you waiting long for each installment.

If you enjoyed Smoke and Mirrors, please consider leaving a review.

— ACKNOWLEDGMENTS —

While writing is a solitary task, it's not a completely solo project. Because of that, I'd like to thank those who've assisted in one way or another. As a side note, I received no compensation for these acknowledgments, so they are in no particular order.

Steven: Thank you for understanding that sometimes I can't get up from my desk because the characters are too loud. And thank you for tending to my bosses (Moscato and Hennessy) during those moments when I'm lost in the story!

Hennessy and Moscato (a.k.a. the high-maintenance golden retrievers who tell me what to do every day): Thank you for ensuring I get my exercise every day. And for making me get up from my desk at least once an hour.

Chancy: The feedback you provided for this book made me happier than I've ever been. You're always so candid, so I know that you will give me the truth. This time there was so much positive, I knew I'd done something right. Thank you for that.

Jenna: I made you cry. That made me happy. Thank you for that. LOL

You, the reader: Thank you for your patience and understanding. As soon as I finished writing Missing Pieces, I started writing this one. That was due to your feedback and your need for more. Thank you for that. Oh, and thank you for reading, for writing a review, and thank you for hopping on social media and telling your friends about the book. You're a badass like that.

You can find the Walker family tree on Nicole's website.

About Nicole Edwards

New York Times and *USA Today* bestselling author Nicole Edwards spends her days stringing words together to make complete sentences. Sometimes not. Her best friend is coffee, and she has a love/hate relationship with sarcasm. She's been accused of having a filthy imagination, which she admits is true.

Nicole lives in the suburbs of Austin, Texas. She proudly claims one husband, three grown children, and two bosses (better known as the dogs). When she isn't writing, watching football or hockey, or keeping her bosses happy, you can probably find her with a book in hand.

Before you go!

Now that you've read one of my books, I'd like to think we can consider ourselves friends. And since friends usually hang out, I want to let you know where you can find me.

NIC NEWS: If you haven't signed up for my newsletter and want notifications regarding preorders, new releases, giveaways, sales, etc., then you'll want to sign up. I promise not to spam your email, just get you the most important updates.

RAMBLINGS OF A WRITER BLOG: My blog is used for writer ramblings, which I am known to do from time to time.

NICOLE NATION: Visit my website to get exclusive content you won't find anywhere else, including sneak peeks, A Day in the Life character stories, exclusive giveaways, cards from Nicole, or join Nicole's review team.

NICOLE NATION ON FACEBOOK: Join my reader group to interact with other readers, ask me questions, play fun weekly games, celebrate during release week, and enter exclusive giveaways!

INSTAGRAM: Basically, Instagram is where I post pictures of my dogs, so if you want to see epic cuteness, you should follow me.

NAUGHTY & NICE SHOP: Not only does the shop have signed books, but there's fun merchandise, too—plenty of naughty and nice options to go around. Find the shop on my website.

WEBSITE:	www.NicoleEdwards.me
FACEBOOK:	/Author.Nicole.Edwards
INSTAGRAM:	/NicoleEdwardsAuthor
TIKTOK:	/@nicoleedwardsauthor
BOOKBUB:	/NicoleEdwardsAuthor
GOODREADS:	/nicole_edwards

By Nicole Edwards

Brantley Walker: Off The Books

All In

Without A Trace

Hide & Seek

Deadly Coincidence

Alibi

Secrets

Confessions

Bounty

Off Course

Chain Reaction

To Have and To Hold

Missing Pieces

Smoke and Mirrors

The Jamesons Of Coyote Ridge

Hot Chocolate Wishes

Rough & Dirty

Club Destiny

Conviction

Temptation

Addicted

Seduction

Infatuation

Captivated

Devotion

Perception

Entrusted

Adored

Distraction

Forevermore

AUSTIN ARROWS

Rush

Kaufman

DEAD HEAT RANCH

Boots Optional

Betting on Grace

Overnight Love

Jared (a crossover novel)

DEVIL'S BEND

Chasing Dreams

Vanishing Dreams

MISPLACED HALOS

Protected in Darkness

Salvation in Darkness

Bound in Darkness

OFFICE INTRIGUE

Office Intrigue

Intrigued Out of The Office

Their Rebellious Submissive

Their Famous Dominant

Their Ruthless Sadist

Their Naughty Student

Their Fairy Princess

Owned

PIER 70

Reckless

Fearless

Speechless

Harmless

Clueless

PRIMAL INSTINCTS

Chase (Volume 1-3)

Capture (Volume 4-6)

Claim (Volume 7-9)

HEROES & HAVOC

(Sniper 1 Security, Devil's Playground, Southern Boy Mafia)

Wait for Morning

Beautifully Brutal

Without Regret

Never Say Never

Beautifully Loyal

Without Restraint

Tomorrow's Too Late

NAUGHTY HOLIDAY EDITIONS

2015

2016

2021